ROWE IS A PARANORMAL STAR!" ~J.R. WARD

PRAISE FOR DARKNESS POSSESSED

"A story that will keep you on the edge of your seat, and characters you won't soon forget!" - Paige Tyler, *USA Today* Bestselling Author of the X-OPS Series

"*Darkness Possessed...*is an action-packed, adrenaline pumping paranormal romance that will keep you on the edge of your seat... Suspense, danger, evil, life threatening situations, magic, hunky Calydons, humor, fantasy, mystery, scorching sensuality, romance, and love – what more could you ask for in a story? Readers – take my advice – do not miss this dark, sexy tale!" ~*Romance Junkie*s

PRAISE FOR DARKNESS UNLEASHED

"Once more, award winning author Stephanie Rowe pens a winner with DARKNESS UNLEASHED, the seventh book in her amazing ORDER OF THE BLADE series...[an] action-packed, sensual story that will keep you perched on the edge of your seat, eagerly turning pages to discover the outcome...one of the best paranormal books I have read this year." ~*Dottie, Romancejunkies.com*

PRAISE FOR FOREVER IN DARKNESS

"Stephanie Rowe has done it again. The Order Of The Blade series is one of the best urban fantasy/paranormal series I have read. Ian's story held me riveted from page one. It is sure to delight all her fans. Keep them coming!" ~ *Alexx Mom Cat's Gateway Book Blog*

Praise for Darkness Awakened

"A fast-paced plot with strong characters, blazing sexual tension and sprinkled with witty banter, Darkness Awakened sucked me in and kept me hooked until the very last page." ~ *Literary Escapism*

"Rarely do I find a book that so captivates my attention, that makes me laugh out loud, and cry when things look bad. And the sex, wow! It took my breath away... The pace kept me on the edge of my seat, and turning the pages. I did not want to put this book down... [Darkness Awakened] is a must read." ~ D. Alexx Miller, Alexx Mom Cat's Gateway Book Blog

▨▨▨

Praise for Darkness Seduced

"[D]ark, edgy, sexy ... sizzles on the page...sex with soul shattering connections that leave the reader a little breathless!...Darkness Seduced delivers tight plot lines, well written, witty and lyrical - Rowe lays down some seriously dark and sexy tracks. There is no doubt that this series will have a cult following. " ~ *Guilty Indulgence Book Club*

"I was absolutely enthralled by this book...heart stopping action fueled by dangerous passions and hunky, primal men...If you're looking for a book that will grab hold of you and not let go until it has been totally devoured, look no further than Darkness Seduced."~*When Pen Met Paper Reviews*

▨▨▨

Praise for Darkness Surrendered

"Book three of the Order of the Blades series is...superbly original and excellent, yet the passion, struggle and the depth of emotion that Ana and Elijah face is so brutal, yet is also pretty awe inspiring. I was swept away by Stephanie's depth of character detail and emotion. I absolutely loved the roller-coaster that Stephanie, Ana and Elijah took me on." ~ *Becky Johnson, Bex 'n' Books!*

"Darkness Surrendered drew me so deeply into the story that I felt

Ana and Elijah's emotions as if they were my own…they completely engulfed me in their story…Ingenious plot turns and edge of your seat suspense…make Darkness Surrendered one of the best novels I have read in years." ~*Tamara Hoffa, Sizzling Hot Book Reviews*

༺❂༻

PRAISE FOR ICE

"*Ice*, by Stephanie Rowe, is a thrill ride!" ~ Lisa Jackson, #1 *New York Times* bestselling author

"Passion explodes even in the face of spiraling danger as Rowe offers a chilling thrill-ride through a vivid--and unforgiving--Alaskan wilderness." ~ Cheyenne McCray, *New York Times* bestselling author

"*Ice* delivers pulse-pounding chills and hot romance as it races toward its exciting climax!" ~ JoAnn Ross, *New York Times* bestselling author

"Stephanie Rowe explodes onto the romantic suspense scene with this edgy, sexy and gripping thriller. From the very first page, the suspense is chilling, and there's enough sizzling passion between the two main characters to melt the thickest arctic ice. Get ready for a tense and dangerous adventure." ~ *Fresh Fiction*

"Stephanie Rowe makes her entry into Romantic Suspense, and what an awesome entry! From the very first pages to the end, heart-stopping danger and passion grab the heart. ... sends shivers down the spine... magnificent... mind-chilling suspense... riveting... A wonderful romance through and through!" ~ *Merrimon Book Reviews*

"[a] thrilling entry into romantic suspense... Rowe comes through with crackling tension as the killer closes in." ~ *Publisher's Weekly*

༺❂༻

PRAISE FOR CHILL

"*Chill* is a riveting story of danger, betrayal, intrigue and the healing powers of love… *Chill* has everything a reader needs – death, threats, thefts, attraction and hot, sweet romance." ~ Jeanne Stone Hunter, *My Book Addiction Reviews*

"Once again Rowe has delivered a story with adrenalin-inducing action, suspense and a dark edged hero that will melt your heart and send a chill down your spine." ~ Sharon Stogner, *Love Romance Passion*

"*Chill* packs page turning suspense with tremendous emotional impact. Buy a box of Kleenex before you read *Chill*, because you will definitely need it! …*Chill* had a wonderfully complicated plot, full of twist and turns. " ~ Tamara Hoffa, *Sizzling Hot Book Reviews*

PRAISE FOR NO KNIGHT NEEDED

"*No Knight Needed* is m-a-g-i-c-a-l! Hands down, it is one of the best romances I have read. I can't wait till it comes out and I can tell the world about it." ~*Sharon Stogner, Love Romance Passion*

"*No Knight Needed* is contemporary romance at its best….There was not a moment that I wasn't completely engrossed in the novel, the story, the characters. I very audibly cheered for them and did not shed just one tear, nope, rather bucket fulls. My heart at times broke for them. The narrative and dialogue surrounding these 'tender' moments in particular were so beautifully crafted, poetic even; it was this that had me blubbering. And of course on the flip side of the heart-wrenching events, was the amazing, witty humour.…If it's not obvious by now, then just to be clear, I love this book! I would most definitely and happily reread, which is an absolute first for me in this genre." ~*Becky Johnson, Bex 'N' Books*

"*No Knight Needed* is an amazing story of love and life…I literally laughed out loud, cried and cheered.… *No Knight Needed* is a must read and must re-read." ~*Jeanne Stone-Hunter, My Book Addiction Reviews*

Darkness Possessed
ISBN 10: 1940968038
ISBN 13: 9781940968032
Copyright © 2014 by Stephanie Rowe.

Cover design ©2014 by Peter Davis. Cover design, book layout, and epub creation by Peter Davis. Cover photos courtesy of iStockphoto.com.

ACKNOWLEDGEMENTS

Special thanks to my beta readers, who always work incredibly hard under tight deadlines to get my books read. I appreciate so much your willingness to tell me when something doesn't work! I treasure your help, and I couldn't do this without you. Hugs to you all!

There are so many to thank by name, more than I could count, but here are those who I want to called out specially for all they did to help me with this book: Alencia Bates, Kayla Bartley, Jean Bowden, Shell Bryce, Kelley Curry, Denise Fluhr, Sandi Foss, Valerie Glass, Christina Hernandez, Heidi Hoffman, Jeanne Hunter, Rebecca Johnson, Dottie Jones, Janet Juengling-Snell, Deb Julienne, Bridget Koan, Felicia Low, Phyllis Marshall, D. Alexx Miller, Jodi Moore, Judi Pflughoeft, Carol Pretorius, Kasey Richardson, Karen Roma, Caryn Santee, Summer Steelman, Nicole Telhiard, Regina Thomas, and Linda Watson.

And lastly, thank you to Pete Davis at Los Zombios for another fantastic cover, and for all his hard work on the technical side to make this book come to life, and for the most amazing website. Mom, you're the best. It means so much that you believe in me. I love you. Special thanks also to my amazing, beautiful, special daughter, who I love more than words could ever express. You are my world, sweet girl, in all ways. And of course, to my awesome dog, who endured such hardship sleeping next to me in his big armchair while I worked, just so that I would have company. What a dog!

▨▨▨▨

DEDICATION

For Jeanne Hunter, a dear friend and awesome woman. Good luck on your journey! !

DARKNESS

POSSESSED

THE ORDER OF THE BLADE

CHAPTER 1

Rhiannon Diaz perched silently on the top of the eight-foot wrought-iron fence. She was utterly still, a barely visible shadow on the fence that wound around the lush grounds of a nouveau riche mansion on the outskirts of Boston. Despite the heavy clouds and lack of moon, the night gleamed brightly from the flood of light pouring from every window. She took a deep breath, her fingers loosely gripping the metal for balance, as she quickly and instinctively surveyed the property, analyzing it for traps, dangers, and the best way to access it. Her feet were bare, and her toes curled around the narrow bar, as if it were one of the trees of her childhood.

This time, however, she was not holding a bow, with a quiver of lethal arrows slung over her back, and she was not exactly the wiry, fly-through-the-air, irreverent lightweight she had once been. This time, she was in skin-tight black leather pants that had enough elastic to contain the evidence of too many late-night chocolate binges. Her dark gray, long-sleeved top went all the way to the tips of her fingers, except for a small slit for her thumb.

Around her throat glittered the amulet that had saved her life five years ago. She'd contemplated having it surgically attached to her neck to make sure it never, *ever* came off, but in the end, she'd concluded that just getting a titanium chain was the slightly less insane solution. Of course, each time she woke up after another nightmare, she was ready to call the nearest plastic surgeon and get it done. So far, she'd restrained herself, which gave her hope that maybe, just maybe, there was a well-adjusted stable person buried deep inside her damaged psyche somewhere.

She shifted her weight, trying to wiggle the numbness out of her toes after being in a crouched position for so long. Hard to believe she had once been a predator who could wait many hours for the right moment to strike. But at least she was way better at war-paint makeup now than she had been as a kid, so that was one win for the "getting older" camp. Her face was painted with dark, glittery makeup that she knew made her dark eyes look even more dangerous and mysterious than they already did. Her thick black hair was pulled back in a viciously tight bun, completely obscuring all sense of femininity.

She had to admit, she loved tying her hair up like that. Men liked long hair, and there was a certain macabre pleasure in twisting it up so tightly that no male would ever get to admire it, touch it, or otherwise get a chance to bask in it. It was hers, and hers alone. And yes, she was well aware that part of the reason she tied it up was so that no man could grab her by the hair and yank her around. A little pathetic, but true. Some lessons could never be unlearned, even after five years of safety. Better to be safe than dragged through the dirt by her hair, right?

Rhiannon ran her fingers over the dagger perched at her hip, smiling faintly at the memory of her tenth birthday when her mother had presented it to her, officially granting Rhiannon warrior status in the tribe. The blade was ten inches long, and rubies glittered in its golden handle. A faint pink glow emanated from it, and she knew it was ready. She was ready.

It was time to be the woman she hadn't been for a long, long time.

She tested her balance on the top of the fence as she studied the second floor balcony, where her target was waiting, oblivious that she was coming after him. The built-in pool glittered with blue light, and the glass sides made it easy for her to look through the water. Floating like the king of his world was the man she had come to see.

No, not see. *Hunt.*

Silently, moving with the innate grace that had never abandoned her despite living in civilization for the last five years,

Rhiannon leapt gracefully off the top of the fence, landing on the soft, perfectly manicured grass without a sound. She could feel the humming of the sensors for the burglar alarm, but they didn't notice her.

She raced across the lawn, her senses on alert, but nothing in this loud, bright, overly saturated neighborhood was sensitive enough to notice a shadow drifting across their world. Exhilaration rushed through her as she skirted undetected across the yard, a feeling of power she hadn't experienced in so long. Moving even more swiftly now, she reached the house and deftly ascended the brick exterior, her fingers and toes easily finding the miniscule openings that she needed. As she broke the plane of the second floor balcony, she paused just long enough to verify that her target was still there.

Philip Wellfleet's eyes were closed, and his head was resting against the edge of the pool. Thick muscles rippled across his shoulders and down his arms, and his stomach was chiseled even at rest. He was far more masculine than any man she'd seen since she'd left the jungle. His hands were relaxed, drifting in the crystal clear water, but on his knuckles were scratches and bruises, the ones she had known she would see after meeting his wife earlier in the day. He exuded strength and danger. And more than that, he practically bled arrogance, the kind of man who felt he owned everyone in his life.

No wonder his wife was terrified of him.

Rhiannon thought back to the well-dressed woman who had slunk so furtively into the shelter earlier that day, a scarf hiding the bruises on her face. A woman who could afford a lawyer, but was too terrified to act. She'd been counseled about her options, as was every woman who came in the door, but that wasn't enough for Rhiannon. Sometimes, a woman needed more, the kind of help that was never allowed, not in this world that Rhiannon was trying so hard to fit into.

She'd long ago stopped caring about anyone or anything. She'd failed her mother's edict that it was her duty to use her powers to protect others. All she cared about was survival. One day at a time. That was all she could focus on. But the pain and vulnerability in that woman's eyes today had awoken something in Rhiannon, something dark and primal that she couldn't suppress. It had cracked open a fissure in her shields, awakening old wounds and scars that she tried so hard to keep crushed inside her.

And so she'd come, and it felt so damn good to be here.

Philip reached for his glass of champagne without even opening his eyes. *No more,* she whispered. *No more victims.*

Rhiannon moved suddenly, pulling herself up over the railing. Philip sat up with surprising speed, and by the time Rhiannon had landed on the marble beside his head, he had a gun pointing at her heart, a smug look on his face.

Rhiannon froze, her heart suddenly hammering in fear. Holy cow. How had she not realized that he was awake and tracking her approach? With sudden trepidation, she became all too aware that a few extra pounds were not all that separated her from the predator she'd once been. She'd lost her edge, that mental intuition that always knew when danger was present. Fear gripped her heart. If she couldn't even out-maneuver this human, what about the real enemy? José Vasquez, the man she'd fled five years ago. An immortal warrior who had bested her even when she was in her prime? Oh, *God.* Instinctively, she looked over her shoulder, suddenly terrified that the man from her nightmares would be standing behind her, laughing smugly that she hadn't even heard him coming.

Nothing was behind her except a sliding glass door to a bedroom suite, and a potted palm wafting in the gentle breeze. José wasn't there. But she couldn't shed the sudden chill slithering down her spine, like invisible fingers stroking her as a prelude to a sudden attack.

"Well, hello, there," Philip said, jerking her attention back to him. He grinned, his steel gray eyes sliding over her body with a heated appraisal that made nausea turn in her stomach. "I don't know who you are," he said, "but you're mine now."

You're mine now. The hated words ripped through the terror consuming her, jerking her out of her stupor. "I am not!" She lunged for him, moving faster than he could begin to conceive. His eyes widened in shock as she tore the gun out of his hand and leapt into the water. In one swift move, she straddled him and lodged her dagger against his throat.

Neither of them moved as the sound of the gun

clanking against the patio below drifted up to them. The water in the designer pool sloshed over the edges, spilling across the tile. She could feel the warmth of the water through her leather pants, like a hot caress against her skin. "Let's just get one thing completely clear between us," she said, her voice low with threat. "I belong to no one."

She could feel the muscles in his sides against her calves, and she had to fight not to pull away from the sensation of a man's body against hers. *Really, Rhiannon?* After five years, she still couldn't bear the inadvertent touch of a naked man? He was her prisoner, not an assailant. Dammit. She was not going to wimp out here! Gritting her teeth and summoning her resolve, she shoved aside her fear. Instead, she narrowed her eyes and let him see her intention. She was not the victim. Not anymore.

But he didn't shrink in fear. He just grinned with the cocky arrogance of a man who had no clue exactly how powerful a woman could be. "You're here to kill me? I don't think so."

His dismissiveness of her strength made her hesitate, then anger rushed through her, fury at herself for letting his comment affect her self-confidence, even if it was only for a split second. Yes, against some she was impotent, but not against this worthless man. "It doesn't matter what you think," she snarled, unable to keep old emotions from embittering her voice. "It only matters what I think. And quite frankly, I think that I can kill you pretty easily." Which was true. He was a human, after all. See? Start small. Kick some human butt. Develop the self-confidence to tackle immortal fire-wielding warrior. A fine plan, she was pretty sure.

Not taking her gaze off him, she raised her left hand toward the lawn and asked for help. There was a low rumble as if the earth itself was stretching, and then a wind blew across the balcony. His eyes flicked to the left, and then widened.

She couldn't keep the grin of pure delight off her face as the lawn came to life. How good did it feel to connect with the plants again? It had been so long! The grass was undulating, blowing violently in the wind. The trees were bucking under the onslaught, and even the bushes were screaming with fury. With a loud roar, the vines that were decorating his patio tore from their trellises and raced up the same path that she'd climbed only moments before.

Philip screamed as the plants erupted over his balcony and swept themselves around him in a violent assault, trapping him.

With a loud hissing, they began to pull him down into the churning water.

"Stop it! Jesus! Let me go!" Philip was fighting violently, shouting for help, but she knew any assistance he summoned would come too late.

With pleased satisfaction, she watched him sliding down into the water. Reality faded, and for a moment, she no longer saw the pompous, close-shaven face of a hedge fund trader. She saw only the dark and gritty face of the man who had claimed her so long ago. It was José who was being dragged to his death beneath the water. As she watched, something hardened inside her. Her soul went numb, and she became the cold, hard warrior she had been trained to be, the one she'd had to call upon to survive her years in captivity.

Some part of her, the part of her that used to be humane, twisted and turned in resistance, rebelling against the fact that she was about to kill a man in cold blood. But empathy was so far gone from her that she felt nothing as she watched his chin sink into the water. "You beat your wife," she said softly. "You're the bad guy."

His eyes widened. "Is that what this is about? Jesus. I'll never touch her again, I swear. I love her! I will never touch her again!"

She closed her eyes at his screamed promise. His terror of impending death scraped across her bones. She felt his desperation, and she knew that this man who had lived his life never feeling fear, was terrified. He had heard her. He would live in terror of her forever, and that terror would deliver change. It had worked. She had to stop.

But she didn't want to stop. She wanted to destroy him, like how she'd wanted to destroy the man who she hadn't been able to kill. The man who had kept her captive and—

No. She couldn't think about that. Her past was over. This man was all that mattered.

She gazed down at him as his mouth and nose slipped

below the surface of the water, his eyes begging for the mercy he'd never shown his own wife. She narrowed her eyes, a bitter hardness clenching around her heart as she watched him suffering...scared...trapped...his own wants and needs meaningless...feeling every emotion that he'd made his own wife suffer for so long.

"How does it feel?" she whispered, crouching lower, so her face was next to his, her chin brushing the surface of the water. "How does it feel to have no control over your body or your wants? To be at the mercy of someone who doesn't care one bit about you? *How does it feel?*"

His eyes widened, and she saw in them something else, a fear of who she was as a person, a realization that he was at the mercy of someone so messed up that there was no chance for humanity ever to prevail.

It was how she had felt for so long, how she had looked at the man who had done the same thing to her. Dammit. She wasn't José. *She wasn't like that.*

She had to stop.

With an agonizing effort, she wrenched her hand down and released the plants. They fell silent at once, and the vines went limp around him, floating harmlessly in the pool, as if they were an artistic element designed to create a magical atmosphere.

He jerked upright, sitting up so his face was out of the water, sucking in oxygen with such desperation that she felt her own lungs burn with the ache she remembered too well. Red lines streaked his body, marks from where the vines had gripped him so tightly. "Who the fuck are you?"

She lowered herself further into her crouch, taking over his personal space, the dagger still against his throat. Her feet were still on either side of his hips, which brought her crotch just above his naked pelvis in an intimate position that made her want to leap up and run away. But she had to make sure his wife was safe. She had to make sure he understood.

"I protect women," she said in a low voice, letting him see the deadly intention in her eyes, just as she used to do back when she was a kid, and she'd been protecting her jungle. "I know when they need me, and I will come. You don't get two chances. Never hurt her again. Not with your hands. Not with your voice. Not with your actions." God, there were so many ways for a man to hurt a woman, especially his wife or any woman that was bound to him in that way. "Do you understand? Give her a large bank account with her own money so that she can leave whenever she wants. Give her the freedom to make her choice." That was the only thing that mattered. *Freedom to make her choice.* That was the gift she could give his wife.

Philip nodded. "Okay. I swear I'll do it."

Rhiannon leaned even closer to him. She caught a whiff of his aftershave, and something clenched in her belly when she realized that he smelled good. Dear God. How could she think a man smelled appealing? Fear struck her hard as she realized she was still vulnerable, that a man could still get to her. If this man, with whom she had no connection, who was complete scum, could make her notice his aftershave, then what about—?

No. No. *No.* José was dead. *Dead.* He wasn't coming for her. It was over. *Over.* But her breath became shallow, and she had to fight to keep herself from running...because she could never be certain that her ex-husband was actually dead.

Her hand started to shake from fear she couldn't suppress, and she knew she had to leave before she fell apart. She felt her connection to the plants fizzle away, and they retreated back to their places of rest as if she'd never called them. She knew she wouldn't be able to call them again, not with the panic and fear hammering through her.

"Don't make me come back. Because I will." Somehow she managed to keep her voice steady, despite the panic starting to grip her, despite her growing terror that she was in danger, that she couldn't keep herself safe anymore, that José was hunting her and would find her.

No! She couldn't think like that! She had to make Philip think she was still the woman who had almost murdered him with a snap of her fingers, and not let him see that she was nothing more than a pathetic, damaged woman who knew how to do nothing but run and hide anymore.

"I won't." He nodded, and his gaze flickered nervously to the vines creeping back across the lawn to where they belonged. A few leaves floated in the water, brushing up against his knee. "What are you?"

She realized he'd changed his question. No longer was he asking "who" she was, but rather, "what" she was, as if she were some freak who wasn't even a person. As if she wasn't even a woman anymore, as if her years with José had somehow robbed her of all that made her who she was. She shook her head, startled by the tears suddenly burning the back of her eyes. "I hunt bad men, and I *will* be back." Then, before she could fall apart, she tore herself away from him. She vaulted over the railing, landed on the patio two floors below, and sprinted across the yard.

She scaled the fence, dropped onto the sidewalk beyond, and then ran through the shadows and into the night.

She tried. She really tried. She thought of ice cream. She sang her favorite song. She pictured the adorable face of a Labrador puppy with its floppy ears. She even envisioned unleashing a contingent of mutant ninjas onto the jungle to track down José while she sat on a tropical beach enjoying a sunny, perfect alibi. In desperation, she even tried to remember what it felt like to put on a pair of pants that used to be too small, but now fit. She thought of everything good she could possibly manufacture, but in the end, nothing worked.

She didn't even make it two blocks before the tears won.

CHAPTER 2

The air was oppressive and blazing hot, as if a thick sludge of humidity was crushing the earth. The moisture clung to Zach Roderick's flesh, suffocating him. Tall trees stretched endlessly up toward the sky, their bare trunks a stark contrast from their plush canopies. Streaks of sunlight filtered through the branches, like dust-filled beams fighting to survive the darkness of the jungle floor.

Relentless, almost violent buzzing pounded at his head, and huge, black insects circled around him, hunting him. Wild calls of tropical birds and grunts of hidden animals echoed around him, nearly concealing the rasping sound of a massive snake sliding through the branches. Zach could smell the oppressive stench of a river, but the foliage was so dense he could see no more than a few yards in any direction. It was a place of wildness and untamed danger. Even the ground was so thick and moist, Zach felt like it could suck him right into the earth in one ruthless move. The weapons branded on his arms burned and vibrated, ready for him to call them out and use them to protect against the danger he could sense in the air.

He clenched his fists, unwilling to arm himself with his three-pronged sai until he knew it was time to fight. Too many brutal lessons had stripped him of his desire to strike a lethal blow unless he had no other option. Unfortunately, in his line of work, he didn't get his first choice very often. As a member of the Order of the Blade, an elite group of Calydon warriors tasked with the mission to protect innocents from Calydons who had gone rogue, his job required him to cut down men who had once been sane, some of whom had once been his friend or teammate. Sometimes, he'd even been responsible for killing the women who had driven them to such insanity.

He hated it all, but he saw no other alternative for what he needed to accomplish.

Right now, he wasn't on duty to hunt rogue Calydons. His only job was to find a way to save the life of his teammate, Thano Savakis, and that's why he was here in this jungle, swatting at bugs and prostrating himself to a team of Calydons he knew he couldn't trust.

Moments ago, his team had been in a wooded forest in southern Washington, fighting for their lives against deadly beasts outside the entrance to the nether-realm, the doomed, deadly realm that bred creatures worse than demons. They'd been fighting side-by-side with a group of unknown Order members, led by Rohan, a powerful warrior Zach knew from many centuries ago, a Calydon he didn't trust for one minute. Rohan had not appeared to recognize him, but Zach didn't believe it, which had made him even more suspicious of the situation.

Shit had gone down, and Thano had gone rogue, descending into the maddening hell that stalked every Calydon at every moment. It was a hell from which there was no recovery, to which the only answer was to slaughter the male before he could kill too many others. No rogue had ever reclaimed sanity in a thousand years. To go rogue meant the complete destruction of one's humanity, and the utter, irreversible capitulation of one's soul to pure, merciless evil.

And yet, Rohan and his crew had claimed they could save Thano. Zach and his team had allowed them to take action—which had resulted in Rohan's crew almost killing Thano. He was alive now, but unconscious, trapped in the thrall of the magic that Rohan and his team had used against him. Even unconscious, he was still consumed by the deadly insanity that stripped him of all humanity, the curse of going rogue.

Rohan had said they would take Thano to heal him, and Zach had followed when they'd begun to vanish into thin air. There was no chance he was leaving Thano's life in the hands of the man who had betrayed his own leader so many centuries ago.

And now, it appeared that Rohan had taken them to a tropical jungle, one that Zach had never been to, and he wasn't liking it one damn bit. With his instincts screaming in warning, Zach moved closer to the massive black stallion on which his unconscious teammate was strapped. He readied himself in a protective stance as Apollo and Thano finished materializing, shimmering as they completed the transformation from incorporeal to living flesh. Their grounding was barely complete when four other Calydon warriors appeared out of thin air.

A split second later, as if he'd delayed his appearance to arrive last, the leader of this other Order materialized. Rohan shimmered into flesh, his hooded cloak obscuring his face, while the dark brands of swords almost glowed on his skin. He was taller and broader than the others on his team, pulsating with energy that seemed to ripple outward from him and coat the atmosphere with magic...the kind of magic that would slither into a man's bedroll while he was sleeping and strangle the life from his soul without ever awakening him.

The five Order members dominated the clearing with their bulk and strength, and Zach's weapons burned even more fiercely in his arms. Usually, one against five were odds that didn't make him blink an eye, but these warriors were Order, like him, which meant they were as powerful as he was. He couldn't afford to fight them, not with Thano's life at stake, and not when he was stranded in some remote jungle, a world where Zach had no foothold, no teammates to back him up, and no idea what was going on.

Zach studied Rohan, the mysterious warrior whose face was hidden behind his hood, just as it had been so many centuries ago when Zach had known him briefly. He'd thought Rohan was long dead, and he'd figured the world was a better place for that fact.

But he was alive, and as ominous as he'd ever been. "Where are we?" he asked.

Rohan turned his head toward him, his face nothing but a black shadow beneath the hood. "We're in a jungle."

Zach didn't bother to look up at the thick canopy of trees dripping with moss and vines. "I can see that. Where are we?" He repeated the question, unwilling to let the other warrior duck his interrogation. "South America?"

Rohan shook his head in refusal, shutting down Zach's request for information. "We need to make camp before dark. Fortify our defenses." He nodded at his team, who silently disappeared into the woods, ostensibly to set up camp.

Rohan began to move toward Thano, but Zach stepped in his path to block him. "No one touches Thano except me."

Rohan snarled, and a blue light crackled from his fingertips.

"Don't even think about it." Zach immediately called out his weapons. With a crack and a flash of black light, the sai that were branded onto his forearms leapt into reality, exploding into his hand. He pointed the blade at Rohan's throat, and the older Calydon went still.

"Put it away," Rohan commanded.

"What the fuck did you do to Dante?" The question burst out before Zach had even realized he was thinking it, but the moment he asked it, he knew he wanted an answer about what had gone down between Rohan and the leader of Zach's Order, Dante Sinclair.

Many centuries ago, Zach, Rohan, and Dante had been a team. Led by Dante, they had resurrected the Order of the Blade, reassembling the only force in existence strong enough to slay Calydons who had succumbed to the demon blood that ran hot in their veins, men who had once been good, and now were destined to destroy all that was worthy and deserving in their lives. Back then, Zach had left the team briefly for personal reasons, because he'd met—

The image of the raven-haired woman he'd loved flashed into his mind. Grief and anger flooded him so violently that he didn't have time to block it, and his knees almost buckled at the assault of emotions, at the anguish and guilt that was as raw as the day that it had all happened. He gripped his sai, fighting desperately to regain control of his thoughts, to shove aside the visceral self-loathing and terror that flooded his body, and the sense of failure that had almost destroyed him completely.

Blood trickled from his palm, and he fought to loosen his grip on the sai as he refocused on the warrior standing before him, the man who'd been Dante's sworn backup when Zach had left. And yet, when Zach had reunited with Dante years later, his master was alone. Rohan had vanished, Dante's woman was missing, and his mentor had barely been alive. Dante had been as fucked up as Zach, and they'd pulled each other out of the abyss that was consuming them.

Zach had told Dante about what had happened to him when they'd been apart, yet Dante had never spoken of what had happened with Rohan and his own woman, but whatever it was had changed him forever. Never again had Dante spoken of the woman who had been his soul mate. Never again had Rohan's name so much as crossed his lips. The Calydon who had once been Dante's best friend had disappeared completely, and Zach knew that something unforgivable had gone down between the two warriors.

And now, he wanted the answers that Dante had refused to give him. "What happened with Dante?" he asked again.

Rohan didn't respond. A dark menace filled the air, but Zach didn't back down.

Finally, Rohan answered. "I didn't think you recognized me." There was a hint of surprise in Rohan's voice. "It was long ago."

"I was twenty-seven years old, not an infant." When Rohan hadn't acknowledged that he recognized Zach when they'd first encountered each other outside the nether-realm, Zach's instincts had fired up at the deception. He'd played along, trying to assess what Rohan's agenda was.

But now that Thano's life hung in the balance, Zach was done with playing games. He wanted results, and he wanted them now.

"Leave it alone, boy."

Boy. Back then, Zach had thought he was a man. He'd thought he had already suffered enough to learn what he needed to know. He'd been wrong. Fucking *wrong.* But he was a man now, a warrior with an agenda stronger even than Rohan's, whatever that might be.

Rohan shifted slightly, and Zach followed him with his sai, keeping the prongs tight against the warrior's flesh. Warnings were vibrating in Zach's body, and he felt Apollo, Thano's horse, at rigid attention behind him, ready to do whatever was necessary to protect his master. "What happened with Dante?" he demanded for a third time.

Rohan shook his head. "It's in the past."

"The past is always inextricably linked to the present," Zach snapped. "What the fuck is going on? Where have you been for a thousand years? What did you do to Thano? And how the hell are you going to save his life?"

Rohan smiled.

Zach didn't know how he knew that Rohan had smiled when he couldn't see his face, but he did. He could feel it in his mind, a stoic veneer stretched thin, devoid of any humor or good will. "I'm not going to save his life," Rohan said simply.

Zach's fingers closed more tightly around the handle of his sai. "You *will* save him. You don't get to take down an Order member and walk away."

"I'm not going to save him," Rohan said softly. "Because I can't."

A low growl began to build inside Zach's chest. "You said—"

"I can't save him, but you can."

Zach stared at him, trying to grasp the unexpected twist in the conversation. He knew Rohan never wasted words. He meant what he said. "What?"

"That's why I brought you here." Rohan slid one index finger along the blade of Zach's sai, taunting the younger warrior, as if to say that he knew Zach would never strike. "To save him. I can't do it. I need you, and that special talent of yours."

Foreboding began sliding down Zach's spine. "You didn't bring me here. It was my idea."

One eyebrow quirked up, but again, it was a move Zach sensed rather than saw. "Was it?"

Zach stared at him, quickly replaying the events that had wound up with them here. He and Thano had been assisting another Order member, Ryland Samuels, on a quest that had sent them into the nether-realm. When they'd shown up at the entrance, Rohan had been waiting for them with his own team. He'd given no sign of recognizing Zach, and they'd attacked the three Order members when they'd tried to pass.

Zach had assumed they had been guarding the entrance

to the nether-realm. What if they hadn't? What if they'd been waiting for them? But how would they have known—

Shit. With grim realization, he recalled Rohan's gift: the ability to see certain aspects of the future. Swearing under his breath, he looked at the man who he had once admired, and once almost murdered. "You knew I was going there, didn't you? You weren't guarding the entrance. You were waiting for me to show up, so you could trap me." Son of a bitch. Rohan didn't give a shit about Thano. He'd used Thano to get Zach to come with him. Now, he was going to use Thano to force Zach to do something for him, something that Zach suspected he would never do otherwise.

One nod was all he got in response.

But the acknowledgment that he was correct was enough.

Too late, Zach realized that he'd been played, and Thano's life was now at stake.

CHAPTER 3

"What did you do?" The unexpected voice was like a shot, leaping out of the shadows at her.

Rhiannon froze, her fingers going still over the computer keys as her gaze snapped to the far side of the darkened office. Standing in the doorway of the overcrowded backroom of their counseling center was Jordyn Leahy, the director of the women's shelter Rhiannon had started working for six months earlier as an admin. Jordyn couldn't be more than a couple years older than Rhiannon, but she carried an air about her that made Rhiannon think she'd lived many more years than she looked. Maybe it was the business suits and pristine bun she always wore, the steady set to her jaw, or the dull brown frames of her reading glasses. Or maybe it was just the way she tended to observe silently before reacting to any situation.

Right now, however, she was wearing jeans and a pink tee shirt, with her blond hair up in a ponytail. She wasn't wearing glasses, and her eyes were big and blue, making her look like she was about twelve years old. She looked young, and Rhiannon realized she had no lines of age on her face. So, she was actually a woman who was young, but had a lifetime of experience behind her.

Like Rhiannon.

Despite her fresh-faced appearance, Jordyn's gaze was penetrating and unyielding, a startling departure from the warm, nurturing persona she used with the battered women who snuck in their front door. "Well?" she prompted. "It's after midnight, and you're skulking around our offices. What's going on?"

"Um..." Instinctively glancing at the open window and calculating how fast she could make it to that exit if the need arose, Rhiannon cleared her throat. Her pulse thundering, she casually leaned back in the folding chair, trying to give the impression that she had nothing to hide. She didn't want Jordyn on alert. If Jordyn thought Rhiannon wasn't going to bolt, it would take a split second longer for her to react if she fled. Those precious milliseconds delaying Jordyn's reaction could be the difference between Rhiannon getting away, and being trapped.

It was so late that she hadn't expected anyone else to be in the office. She hadn't wanted to go home tonight. She was still too shaken up by her reaction to the man in the pool, both the fact that she'd responded to him as a woman, and the fact that he'd gotten a jump on her with his gun. She felt vulnerable, and that scared her. Although she'd wanted desperately to retreat to the apartment that had become her sanctuary, going there had seemed like a poor choice, because if someone wanted to find her, home is where they would look. Instead, she'd come to the office, but it had taken only a few minutes before she'd begun to feel a creepy sensation down her spine as if someone was watching her.

Had it been Jordyn, before she'd presented herself? Or was someone else lurking in the shadows, waiting for the right moment? If there wasn't a threat right now, there would be soon.

There was no safe place now. She'd blown it.

Glancing again at the window, half-expecting to see an untamed warrior standing there, ready to grab her, she managed a nonchalant shrug in response to Jordyn's question. "What are you talking about?" She tried to keep her voice as calm as possible.

Jordyn's blue eyes were glittering with interest. "Do you remember that woman who came in earlier today? The one with the expensive suit?"

Rhiannon swallowed at the reference to the woman she'd been avenging tonight on that second floor balcony. "Sorry, I wasn't really paying attention." She swiveled the chair restlessly, unable to sit still. What did Jordyn know?

Jordyn slowly strolled into the makeshift office and

eased into the folding chair in front of Rhiannon's desk. "Do you like plants? Like vines? Do you have an affinity for vines, Rhiannon?"

Rhiannon went still, trying to keep her face expressionless. How on earth did Jordyn know what had happened? The fear that had been circling restlessly in her mind all evening suddenly congealed in her stomach. If word got out, she might be found. Dammit. For five years she'd never tapped into her powers. She had played it straight, hiding who she was, knowing it was her only chance to survive. One night, one mistake, and the safe crevices she'd managed to crawl into had been exposed.

"Vines?" she echoed blankly, keeping her voice neutral. "What do you mean?" Even as she spoke, she eased her finger to the delete key. Flashing on the screen was her personnel file, the only remaining information on the computer that related to her. Once she deleted it, all evidence that she'd ever existed here would be gone. How many times had she erased her footprints in the last five years? She didn't want to be erased anymore...but she wanted to be found even less.

"I mean," Jordyn said evenly, "that the police got a 911 call from that woman's house tonight. She had put me on the notification list in case her husband became abusive, so I showed up, thinking she was being attacked. But the police got a very strange story from her husband."

Rhiannon swallowed as a frisson of fear shivered down her back. Had he really told someone the truth? Why would he have risked it? Everyone would deem him insane. Women like her didn't exist. Yes, sure, most humans accepted that Calydons existed, but that was about it as far as supernatural beliefs went, other than the standard woo woo about vampires and werewolves. Certainly no one would believe that someone like her existed, someone who could manipulate vegetation and the earth itself. He would never have told anyone that vines attacked him...would he? "Really?" She kept her voice neutral. "What was the story?"

Jordyn waved her hand dismissively. "It was all very unusual. He was babbling about a witch who showed up with a ruby dagger. Weirdly, he said that she was able to make the plants in his yard attack him. He had red lines all over his body, which he said were from the vines wrapping around him like ropes and dragging him underwater." She was watching Rhiannon with a steady gaze.

Rhiannon forced herself to meet Jordyn's stare, taking comfort in Jordyn's dismissive wave. "Doing drugs, was he?"

"That was the general consensus, until…"

She didn't want to ask, but she knew she had to know. "Until what?"

"Until we watched the security video."

Oh, shit. Rhiannon felt her stomach drop. She hadn't even thought of that.

Jordyn leaned forward. "I think," she said softly, "you may not want to wear that amulet in public for a little while."

Rhiannon's hand instinctively went to the glittering jewel strapped around her neck. Without it, she would probably not be alive, and if she were alive, she would wish she were dead.

"Your makeup was very dramatic and obscured your identity quite well, but the amulet was very visible on the security video. Every last detail of it." Jordyn raised her brows. "I always thought it was quite striking, so I noticed it right away." She winked. "Of course, not everyone has my incredible powers of observation, so it's possible you could staple it to your forehead and march into the police station, and no one would notice. Then again, it's possible that maybe I'm not the only one with an eye for unusual, ancient artifacts worn around a woman's neck. We don't really know, do we?"

Rhiannon felt the blood drain from her face as she instinctively covered the necklace in a gesture that was meaningless now. She tried to come up with some sort of plausible explanation for the moving vines, but the fear hammering at her obliterated all strategic thought. She'd been compromised, *truly compromised.* She'd been caught on video, and the police would be sharing the information with other agencies to try to identify her. It would not take long until José's minions found her, and if José were still alive…

No. She couldn't let him find her. *She couldn't go back.*

Jordyn leaned back in her chair, apparently oblivious to Rhiannon's rising panic. "The police have named the mysterious woman Poison Ivy. She's considered dangerous. They're looking for her. They're investigating everyone his wife knows. Poison Ivy interests them. A sexy woman who is armed and dangerous, willing to attack one of the wealthiest men in the entire city, who appears to have a magical connection to plants, is going to be headlining all the police scanners tonight." She rolled her eyes in apparent disgust. "Such a typical male thought process, isn't it? They see one sexy woman with the power to knock them on their butts, and they drop everything to find her, even though you didn't actually hurt anyone. Heaven forbid they go after the idiots running around with shotguns and drugs, right?"

Rhiannon stared at her boss. "You're not mad?"

"Mad?" Jordyn chuckled as she pulled out her hair elastic and redid her ponytail. It was a little crooked, which actually made her look even prettier and more approachable. "The only thing I might be a little mad about is that you didn't actually hurt him, but I suppose he probably begged and screamed for mercy, right?"

Rhiannon nodded slowly, still trying to figure out exactly what Jordyn's response to this was. "He did get a little desperate," she admitted.

"Fantastic." Jordyn grinned, looking decidedly more cheerful than when she'd first walked in. "I love making bullies scared. Nice work, Rhee." She raised her brows, a thoughtful look suddenly on her face. "By the way, you looked really good in that outfit. Why do you hide that body under those baggy jeans and sweaters?"

That was much too long of a story, too long to tell when she needed to be out of the city within minutes, or risk being found. Rhiannon shook her head, still keeping her hand covering the amulet. "I need to leave." But where would she go? This was the first place she'd found to settle in five years.

"No, you most certainly do not need to leave," Jordyn snapped. "What kind of remark is that?"

Rhiannon stared at her, startled by the vehemence of her boss. "What?"

Jordyn was studying her intensely, keen intelligence glittering in her brilliant eyes. "I hate that man," Jordyn said calmly. "He's evil. His wife has no chance to defend herself against him, even though she has money. His power is too strong, and his reach is too far. There are a lot of men like him in the city. *Lots* of men who need a visit from a woman who makes them understand fear for the first time in their lives."

The unspoken message hung in the silence between them: Jordyn wanted Rhiannon to engage in a repeat of what had happened tonight.

She realized that Jordyn wasn't asking who she was, or how she controlled the plants, or where she was from. Either she didn't care, or she knew so much more than she was letting on. Alarm trickled down Rhiannon's spine, like frigid ice water oozing into each vertebra like the fingers of death. "I can't do it."

Jordyn gave her a grim smile. "You have to do it. Again, and again, and again. As long as it takes until I have no more clients who walk in the door. You can help, so it's your duty."

"No." Rhiannon sat up, rebelling against the same words that her mother had tried so hard to drum into her. Words she'd lived by until they had destroyed her. Duty had almost taken her life, and her soul was nothing more than a dried-out shadow of what she had once been. She lived minute-by-minute now, always on edge, always on the run. All because she had tried to do her *duty.* "You don't understand. I can't do it. I can't stay now." She looked down at the computer and jammed her finger onto the delete button. A message box came up asking if she was certain she wanted to delete the personnel file. *Yes.* One more click, and then she was gone.

Her throat tightened unexpectedly at the sudden surge of loss, but she resolutely pushed back from the computer. She had no time to grieve the loss of a life or an identity. It had to be this way. When she disappeared tonight, there would be no evidence that she had ever existed, or ever even set foot in this city.

Except for the security videos. Dammit. What was she going to do about those? "Did the police keep the videos?" She stood up and strode across the room for her jacket, focusing on her exit strategy instead of throwing herself across the desk and bawling that she never wanted to leave.

Jordyn leaned back in her chair, watching her gather her belongings. "Of course they did."

For a split second, Rhiannon considered trying to break

into the police station to get them, but quickly dismissed it. She would have no idea where to look, and it would waste valuable time. She knew she had no choice but to simply disappear. It was the only way to ensure she stayed alive…and free. She shrugged her jacket on, and picked up the small duffel bag that contained her leather outfit from earlier in the evening. "I have to leave town tonight. I can't come back—"

"It's you," Jordyn said suddenly. "I can't believe I didn't realize it."

Rhiannon went still, then looked at her boss. "What's me?" She had a feeling Jordyn wasn't talking about Poison Ivy. Jordyn had already come to a definitive conclusion about that one, and Rhiannon had been too shocked to figure out how to deny it quickly enough. So what was she talking about now?

"You're one of us. You're running from someone. You're hiding from a man. Who on earth could hurt *you*, a woman who can summon the very earth to help her? Who could make *you* afraid?" Jordyn's voice was gentle now, so full of understanding that the tears suddenly burned in Rhiannon's eyes for the second time that night.

Rhiannon's hand instinctively went to her hip, where she used to keep her dagger. Right now, it was back in the bag, because walking around with a ruby dagger attached to her hip wasn't exactly citified. She hated that she couldn't wear it all the time in the city. She felt naked and vulnerable without it. "He's dead." She hoped. She thought. She prayed. "But his friends aren't."

The significance of her words was like thick tension dropped into the night. Chills trickled down her skin as she articulated the fear that had been haunting her for five years. The fear that the monsters José had been cultivating would come after her and find her, demanding payment for what she had done to their leader. And if somehow, someway, José had survived, and *he* was personally hunting her... Oh, *God*.

A dark, desperate side of her knew that he probably wasn't dead. If she'd killed him, she would have felt it all the way to her soul. She'd felt nothing…which was a very, very bad sign.

She had wrenched herself free from his grasp once, but she was no fool to think she could get away from him again.

She'd gotten lucky, and she could never go back to that hell. She was done fighting. All that was left was hiding.

Jordyn sighed, suddenly looking ten years older again. "What can I do to help you?"

Oh, if only it were that easy. Rhiannon shook her head. "No one can help me. It's so much more than you can understand. Than anyone in this world can understand."

Jordyn cocked her eyebrow. "In this world? Where are you from?"

Rhiannon didn't answer. It was too much to explain that she hadn't meant another planet. Just a life experience that was so different from this one that it was like an entirely different world. And she wanted to give no shred of information that could be used to expose her.

After all her years of experience, Jordyn would understand that sometimes secrets were a woman's only defense. Jordyn nodded once, but then surprised Rhiannon with her next statement. "I can make the videos disappear," she said. "What if I did that? Could you stay? Could you help?"

For a split second, Rhiannon was tempted. But then she shook her head. "If I did it, every time I helped, I could get caught on video again."

Jordyn smiled, and this time, it was a smile that bred hope into Rhiannon's heart, because it was a smart, strategic smile of a female born to be a warrior. "Planning is everything, Rhee. I'm very, very good at strategy, and I really hate men who hurt women. We can work around things like video cameras."

Rhiannon stared at her, and sudden yearning coursed through her. It had been so long since she'd had a friend, a woman she could count on. She'd been ripped from her life fifteen years ago when she was barely sixteen years old. She'd spent ten years at José's mercy, barely surviving a hell that had almost destroyed her. The five years she'd been on the run ever since had been both a gift of freedom, and a constant living terror that at any minute, she would be found.

But Jordyn gave her hope. For a moment, she was filled with a burning desire to say yes to her, to team up with this admirable woman and help others. But even as she thought it, the familiar shield closed around her heart, shutting out the humanity and emotions that had been her downfall. Silently, she shook her head as she reached for her purse. "I'm not that woman anymore, Jordyn. I'm sorry."

She turned to walk toward the door, but Jordyn's voice stopped her. "I think you could be, Rhee."

Rhiannon looked down at her hands, and she saw the scars on her fingers. "No," she said softly. "I can't."

Then, without so much as a backward glance, she walked out of the first place that had felt safe since the day she'd walked away from her tribe to hunt the man who had become her captor, her lover, and her destruction.

CHAPTER 4

Zach lowered his sai from Rohan's throat, his muscles taut with readiness. He would not stay with Rohan and the others. He would not subject Thano or himself to this kind of manipulation. But now was not the time to try to disappear. Rohan was ready. He'd never let them go. Not right now. Not when he so clearly had a plan for Zach. He would have to bide his time before disappearing with Thano and Apollo. "What do you want from me?" His tone made it clear that Rohan wasn't going to get it.

"Come." Rohan turned away, striding across the clearing to a particularly thick cluster of trees. The shadows surrounding it were unnaturally dark and impenetrable, even for a rainforest. It was early evening, and shadows were stretching, but darkness held that one section in its ruthless grasp.

Zach looked over his shoulder at Apollo. "Be ready to take him away from here," he said quietly. "Don't let anyone take him off you." He felt asinine talking to the horse, but Thano always acted as if the horse could understand. Right now, the equine was his only ally.

To his surprise, the stallion met his gaze, the dark brown eyes wise with intelligence. The horse nodded once, ever so slightly, and turned away. He began to crop the low vegetation, but as he did, he carefully, subtly began to inch his way to the far side of the clearing, preparing his exit.

Damn. The horse had gotten it.

Zach nodded at the animal, then turned to follow

Rohan. He kept his sai out and ready, as much against Rohan as in preparation for whatever it was that held the darkness in such tight thrall.

His long black cloak swishing behind him, Rohan strode briskly across the clearing. His body was as muscular as it had been all those centuries ago, but there was a leanness to him now. It was as if his flesh melted away and left only muscle and aggression behind. He moved with the grace of a wildcat, his strength rippling beneath the surface. His legs were clad in the black fur of the dreisen tiger, a mythical beast known for its great bravery and loyalty. Had he killed one? They were revered and honored beasts according to legend. Terrible luck came to those who dared to take the life of one of those creatures.

He recalled that Rohan had been wearing the same fur when he'd known him all those centuries ago, but back then Zach hadn't understood the significance of it. Now he did.

Rohan didn't even look back as he stepped into the shadows, instantly enfolded by the darkness. Zach didn't think that he'd dematerialized, but rather that he'd simply entered an area so dark that no light could penetrate.

Zach slowed as he reached the dome of blackness. He hesitated, rapidly assessing his options. They could make a break now. No one was around to stop them. But if he left, what would happen to Thano? What if this was the only way to save him?

He couldn't let Thano down. He had to find out. Rohan might be a treacherous bastard, but he had powers far beyond anyone Zach had ever met. He glanced over his shoulder to see Apollo watching him intently, his master still strapped securely across his back. "You're in charge," he said to the horse. "If I don't come back, get Thano back home." He had no idea where home was in relation to where they were, but he had a feeling the horse probably did.

Apollo stomped his front hoof once in acknowledgment, his black face bobbing in a nod.

Wondering if he was going insane thinking the horse was supporting his battle strategy, Zach turned back toward the woods. He paused for a split second, reaching out with his preternatural senses. But he could hear nothing but absolute silence, see nothing but impenetrable blackness, and smell nothing but the dampness of the jungle around them.

There was no way to know what he was about to encounter, and he had no backup.

He gripped his sai, wishing he had access to the one weapon that had been able to defeat Rohan, the one weapon that made him more than the other warriors. Fire had once been his weapon of choice, a destructive force that could take down almost any threat.

But it was no longer his to call. Even the little connection he'd been hanging onto seemed to have disappeared over the last few days, leaving him with nothing but his sai. Most Calydons would have no problem being left with the steel weapons that had chosen them. Not so with Zach. He'd always relied on his fire, and the sai felt like an imposter in his hands.

But that was all he had, so he was going to make it work for him.

Steeling himself to do whatever was going to be necessary, he strode into the blackness after the man who'd betrayed the Order so long ago.

The moment he stepped over the border, Zach felt like a thousand pounds of pressure was bearing down on him. He could barely lift his leg to take another step, and the weight around his chest was so strong he could barely suck in a breath. And it was pitch black. Utter and complete blackness.

Swearing, Zach flicked his finger, trying to call up a flame to give him light. Any flame. He didn't even need a fucking fireball. Just a damned spark.

But there was nothing. Not even a spark of the raging inferno that used to explode off him if he so much as sneezed. Now? Not a damn thing.

Shit.

This wasn't good.

There was a crack and a flash of black light, and then a blue light suddenly flared ahead. Zach squinted his eyes against the sudden brightness. He could see the glowing outline of Rohan, standing ahead. He'd called out his sword and was holding it by his side. The blade was glowing blue, lighting up their space.

Quickly, Zach looked around, taking inventory of

where they were. It was immediately apparent that they were still in the forest. He could see the tree trunks, the bushes, and the canopy of trees above. But everything was cast in an eerie blue glow from Rohan's sword. It was as if the rest of the forest could not penetrate the bubble they were in.

As his eyes adjusted, he noticed that Rohan appeared to be standing next to a man. Zach eased forward, and he tensed when he saw it was a Calydon. The warrior was strung up, dangling from a tree, his feet several yards above the forest floor. His arms were chained above his head, and thick manacles encircled his ankles. His head was drooping down as if he were unconscious, but his muscles were taut, as if he were ready to launch an attack at any moment. Then Zach noticed something that made his gut clench.

He had no hands. They had been cut off at the wrist.

"What the hell is this?" He raised his sai again, moving into a ready position. "What did you do to him?"

"He's one of mine." Rohan was still standing beside him, his sword hanging loosely in his right hand.

Disgust was a sour burn in the back of his mouth. "This is how you treat your team?"

"This is how I try to save their lives."

The chained warrior moved suddenly, lunging toward Rohan with speed Zach had never seen before. The prisoner attacked Rohan, trying to take him down with his bare feet. Rohan raised his sword, for a few brief moments, a vicious battle ensued between a warrior's feet and Rohan's sword. The warrior's hands and arms were not accessible, because he had *no fucking hands to hold his weapon with,* so it was his feet that he attacked with, unleashing incredible precision and force.

Zach stood ready to defend himself if the fight came his way, but he didn't interfere. He didn't care who won. All that mattered to him was that these two crazy bastards stayed in this darkened bubble, and didn't go back out to where Thano lay defenseless and unconscious. But hell, he could barely comprehend the speed, strength, and sheer violence of the battle between Rohan and his prisoner. Impressive as hell, but at the same time...Zach's fingers tightened involuntarily around his sai. Could he protect Thano from them on his own, armed only with a sai? He gritted his jaw, refusing to truthfully answer his own question.

The skirmish took less than a minute, and then the warrior was unconscious again, courtesy of a devastating blow to the head by Rohan with the flat of his sword, an impact which sent sparks of blue electricity crackling violently through the other warrior's body. His scream of anguish ripped through the night before he collapsed again, his body swinging rhythmically from the chains as he descended into oblivion once more.

"Explain." Zach kept his sai up as Rohan lowered his weapon. What kind of leader treated his team like that? "What the hell's going on?"

"This is Trevor Swan," Rohan said. "He went rogue twenty-three days ago."

Zach glanced again at the poor bastard strung up without his fucking hands. "You did this to him because he met his *sheva?*" The curse of the Calydon was to go rogue upon meeting and bonding with his *sheva*, the soul mate he was destined for. After completing the bonding stages, he was destined to go rogue and destroy all that mattered to both of them. The only way to stop him was for her to kill him. Once he was dead, she would be so overwhelmed with anguish over the fact she had killed her mate, that she would take her own life. It was a bitter, hellish way to go, especially for Calydons, who were driven by strong passion and desire...which was why Zach had taken precautions long ago to make sure he never ended up with a *sheva*.

With the recent possible exceptions of a few Order members, there was no happy ending once a Calydon had met his mate. The only way to stop the curse was for either the *sheva* or the Calydon to be killed. The Order killed the Calydons to protect the innocent, except when the Order was involved, in which case it was the *sheva* who was cut down...until recently the Order had started letting their *shevas* live. Now, things were all fucked up, and Thano was paying the price.

Zach ground his jaw as guilt attacked him. If only he had adhered to the ancient tradition that he and Dante had started of killing *shevas* to save the lives of the Order members, Thano would be sitting around, cracking jokes, and being an irreverent ass, instead of being strapped down on his horse like a crazed monster.

Zach could still remember that moment when Ryland had finally found the woman he'd been hunting, that moment when electricity had flooded the air. He'd *known* there was something going on with her. He should have taken her out right then, but no, he'd become complacent, accepting the modern way of thinking, forgetting the true danger of the *sheva*. And now Thano was going to die because of it.

"No," Rohan said, "there was no *sheva* for Trevor. He was on a mission for me, and he went rogue. I haven't been able to bring him back."

"Really?" That caught Zach's attention for a moment. It was rare for a Calydon to go rogue on his own. Not unheard of, but rare. Not that it excused Rohan's treatment of him. "So you strung him up and cut off his hands? Because that certainly seems like the kind of thing a good leader would do."

"His hands are not cut off," Rohan snapped. "They have been rendered useless. It was the only choice I had to keep him from trying to kill us, and forcing me to make the choice I don't want to make." The steely edge of Rohan's voice made Zach snarl. His voice was cold, showing no compassion or regret for what he had done to the man who worked for him. The bastard was like pure ice.

And what did he mean, Trevor's hands weren't cut off? Zach narrowed his eyes, moving closer to the imprisoned warrior. As he neared, he saw a black outline where his hands should be. Another step and he could finally see that his hands were actually still attached to his wrists. They were encased in black webbing that seemed to undulate as it crawled over his flesh. He'd never seen anything like it before. "What the hell is that?"

"He can't call out his weapon if he can't hold it," Rohan said. "But in a few days, the webbing will become a part of him. It will consume his hands and begin to move down his body. Eventually, it will overtake him completely. At that time, I will either have to let him die, or free him to become a rogue that I will be forced to kill."

Zach swore under his breath, his skin crawling at the

fate of the warrior before him. "Is that what you plan to do with Thano? Because there's no way I'll let you do it."

"Thano is sufficiently unconscious. As long as he stays that way, I will not have to act." Anger suddenly seemed to course through Rohan, and the already heavy air thickened. "This is not how it should be, Zachary. Our warriors should not be held hostage by an ancient demon curse to go rogue. These are good men, honorable soldiers who do not deserve this fate."

Zach didn't buy into the outrage. He knew Rohan was a man who would slaughter an innocent to further his own agenda. No one and nothing was allowed to stand in the way of Rohan's mission, which had once been to protect the earth realm from the demon beasts that snuck out of the nether-realm to prey upon the innocent. Who knew what his mission was now, but it certainly wasn't about the wellbeing of the poor bastard who was strung up. Rohan was a man without mercy, every single time.

"Even if Thano wakes up and attacks everyone," Zach said quietly, venom lacing his voice, "if you so much as breathe on him, I will hunt you down and destroy you and everything that matters to you. And you know I can do it."

Rohan didn't know that the weapon Zach had bested him with so long ago was no longer accessible to him, and Zach wasn't about to tell him that the kid who had once held back an epic volcano of fire by erecting a fire wall could no longer even toast a damned marshmallow on his palm.

The cloaked warrior went still, perhaps remembering the time Zach had brought him to his knees so long ago with an array of well-placed fireballs. "I will do whatever is necessary to protect my team," Rohan said. "Your Thano will not be permitted to harm anyone."

Zach walked up to him, striding evenly across the clearing until he was standing in front of the unconscious warrior that Rohan claimed to be protecting. "What the fuck are you playing at here, Rohan? You bring me in here to show me one of your own warriors who has gone rogue. You can't heal him. All you can do is string him up like a monster, and yet you brought Thano here under the pretense that you could save him from being rogue. You lie. You can't save him, can you?"

"No. I can't save Trevor from his rogue state." Rohan's

voice was bitter, so bitter that it was almost convincing. *Almost.* "You, however, can save him."

"Me?" Zach snorted in disgust. "You've got some balls if you think that I'm going to help your man when my teammate is almost dead out there. You lost the chance for my loyalty a long time ago." He snarled at Rohan. "I'm leaving, and don't bother trying to stop me. We both know you can't."

Again, a total lie, but Rohan didn't know that.

"No. You will not leave without helping Trevor."

"I'm here for Thano," Zach snapped. "Nothing else." Inadvertently sliding one last regretful look over the chained up warrior, wishing he was at liberty to help the poor bastard, Zach turned on his heel and strode back across the blue-lit area toward the place he'd entered. A part of him felt like he was betraying his own kind by not helping Rohan's warrior, but at the same time, he'd taken an oath to the Order of the Blade, and to Thano. Nothing trumped that oath. *Nothing.*

Rohan's voice stopped him. "The same thing will save Thano and Trevor." The words were heavy with meaning and intent. "If you save Trevor, you will also save your man."

Zach stopped in his tracks, inches from the edge of the darkness.

Son of a bitch.

Now he got it. Now he got it all.

Rohan needed his help to save his teammate. Any good leader knew that his value was only as strong as the men who worked beneath him. Nothing was more important to Rohan than his mission, so he would be relentless to protect his team, which meant he would be relentless in forcing Zach to help him.

Resentment coiled inside him, and he fisted his sai as he turned back. He opened his mouth to tell Rohan to go to hell, then his gaze flicked involuntary back to the dangling Trevor. He looked almost dead now, limp, like he was a meat carcass that had been strung up for carving. Was that Thano's fate, too? The handful of Calydons Zach knew who had come back from the edge of going rogue had been brought back by the women they loved, reclaimed by sanity before they had truly gone rogue.

Thano was completely rogue, and he had no woman to save him. There was no out for him. No way home.

What if Rohan was right? What if he could save Thano? If Rohan really believed this task would save Trevor from the hell of being rogue, and Zach sensed that Rohan did, then he wasn't lying when he said it would save Thano as well.

Zach ground his jaw, looking over his shoulder toward where he'd left Thano and Apollo. He couldn't see them, but he knew they were there, waiting for him to work a miracle and save the day.

He knew then that he had no choice. If Rohan believed Zach could save Thano and Trevor, then there was a very real possibility he might be able to do it. Zach couldn't walk away from even an infinitesimal chance of saving his teammate. Swearing, he lowered his sai and faced the man he'd never thought he would trust again. "Okay then. Tell me what you want me to do."

Rohan smiled, a smug smile that settled in Zach's mind like a thorn. "You have chosen well, apprentice. We have much to prepare, and then we will talk."

"Apprentice?" Zach narrowed his eyes as he shored up his mental shields. This was one warrior he wasn't going to let into his head. "I was never Dante's apprentice, and I sure as hell am no one's apprentice now. Give me the details. That's all I want from you."

"No. You were not Dante's apprentice," Rohan agreed. "You are mine, and you always have been."

CHAPTER 5

Her street seemed darker than it had been the last time she walked down it.

Rhiannon realized it had been a mistake to stay at the office until after midnight. She, a girl who had once thrived in the darkness, now couldn't help but look over her shoulder as she hurried down the sidewalk. She froze suddenly when she thought she saw something move in the shadowy doorway across the street. She stared at it, her heart pounding, waiting to see if anything moved.

Nothing did.

She started walking again, then whipped around, and looked at the doorway again, trying to catch someone who might have moved when she'd stopped looking. Again, she thought she saw a whisper of movement, like the slipping of a wraith into a crevice, but then there was nothing. She swallowed, her mouth suddenly dry.

It was faintly windy, and a crumpled paper towel tumbled down the street, bouncing around as if invisible fingers were flicking it along. A newspaper flapped against the street post, trapped by the metal base. A hissing sound caught her attention, and she looked up just as something black streaked past, above her head. A bird? A bat? Or something that didn't belong in the city?

Her skin prickled in fear, and she looked back at the doorway. Nothing moved this time. Nothing at all. Just a shadow —

Something moved to her left, and she spun around, searching the tiny fenced yards of the brownstones that flanked her street. A squirrel sprang out of the bushes and bolted across the street, moving fast, too fast. Since when did squirrels come out at night?

No. She needed to chill. There was nothing out in the street tonight. It had been only five hours since her appearance on the balcony. Not enough time for word to get out. Not enough time for anyone to find her. She was being ridiculous, letting old fears rule her.

God, she'd forgotten what it felt like to feel so jittery. She hated that José still had that kind of power over her, even though she was thousands of miles away and he was dead. But even as she thought it, a flicker of worry settled in her gut. Was he dead? Truly? He had to be.

But she didn't know for sure.

She forced herself to turn away and start walking down the street again, trying to stay calm. But she couldn't keep herself from walking quickly, and she couldn't keep herself from looking into every shadow, and jumping each time one seemed to move. The clouds were heavy across the moon, making the shadows drift and dance. Once, she had loved the shadows. They had provided cover for her. Now all she could think was that they provided cover for something else. For someone else. For the nightmare that had never left her.

As she hurried down the quiet street, she slipped her hand into her bag and wrapped her fingers around the hilt of her dagger. She couldn't exactly run around holding it ready in the streets of Boston, but she would be prepared if she needed it.

She covered the last two blocks to her house at a run. Each time she looked back, shadows moved. Trash whipped past her, driven by the wind. A soda can banged against her ankle, making her jump. Even as she chastised herself that her fear was groundless, she vaulted up the six stairs to her building in one leap, no longer calm enough to hide the athleticism that an ordinary human should never have.

She jammed her key into the lock on the front door and slipped inside. The light in the entryway was out, casting an eerie dark glow around the foyer. She swallowed, knowing that in the six months she'd been here, no light had ever been out. She'd chosen to live in this building because the man in charge of maintenance lived on site, and he was fanatical about keeping it up.

And now the light was out.

Her heart pounding, she raced up the stairs to her third floor apartment. More lights were out in the hallway, and the stairs creaked under her feet. Had they always made so much noise? She'd never noticed it.

No lights shined under the doors of her neighbors. They were all asleep. She felt completely alone, even in this building full of people. She reached her apartment door and slipped her key inside the lock. She turned it but when she went to grasp the doorknob, the metal was cold. It felt as cold as if it had been outside in a cold Boston winter, not inside in a stuffy old brownstone.

She jumped, even as she forced herself to smile. Because it was not cold that came with her nightmares. It was heat. A cold doorknob should make her feel better, not worse. But right now everything felt off, and everything that wasn't as it should be felt dangerous.

She hurried into her studio apartment, and all the lights were blazing, as they always were. Every closet door was open, every cabinet was open, and she could see under her bed even from the front door. There wasn't a place that anyone could hide that she wouldn't see them from the entrance to her apartment, giving her time to flee. No one was hiding in her home.

Satisfied that her apartment, at least, was still safe, she kicked the door shut behind her and threw the six locks closed. She dropped her bag on the floor by the front door and sprinted across the studio. Ten minutes, she told herself. She would give herself ten minutes to gather all she could and then be out the door.

But as she grabbed the duffel bag from under her bed and began to shove her meager belongings into it, a sense of sadness settled in her heart. She didn't want to leave this time. She'd felt like it had been long enough that it would be safe to stay here. She realized that she'd actually let herself believe that she wouldn't have to run again. She had begun to think of it as her home. A home that was safe, where she could sleep soundly and not be terrified of what she would find had been done to her when she woke up. A place where she could eat when she wanted to, sleep when she wanted to, choose who touched her, and who she touched. A place where she belonged.

All that was gone, all because she'd lost her cool and gone after a bastard tonight. It was her fault. She'd been stupid.

Seven minutes later, she was packed. She was just grabbing her car keys when she heard something rattle against her window. She whirled around, facing the glass panes as she whipped her dagger out. After a long, terrifying moment with her pulse pounding in her ears, she realized rain was battering against the glass, a gentle pitter-patter that reminded her of home.

This time real homesickness filled her, a longing for the world that she truly belonged to, the world she could never go back to.

Rhiannon paused for a moment, then sheathed the knife and walked over to the window. She grabbed the sash and threw it open. The damp air washed across her, and she closed her eyes, inhaling it deeply into her lungs. There would never be anything as beautiful as the feeling of being in the rain, and breathing in the air saturated with dampness. It eased into every cell of her body, and she felt herself relax. As long as it was raining, she felt like everything would be okay.

She rested her palms on the windowsill and leaned out. She had long ago removed the screen so that she could feel the outdoors just like this. She closed her eyes and let the rain splash across her face. The rivulets ran down her cheeks like the tears she had long ago stopped shedding...until tonight.

Laughter drifted across the night toward her, and she opened her eyes. Rounding the corner of the next building was a young couple. The man was tall but lean, and he had his arm around the shoulders of the woman with him. Her hair was plastered to her head from the rain, and both their clothes were completely soaked through. Neither of them was wearing a coat, and it was apparent they had been caught unprepared by the sudden deluge.

But the woman was looking up at the man, her lips

parted in joyous laughter as he gazed down at her. He wiped the rain off her cheek and then bent his head. The kiss was so innocent and so happy that Rhiannon felt it slice through the shields on her heart. The raindrops on her cheeks mixed with tears as she rested her chin on her palms and watched the couple kiss.

There was something so magical about the joy they were sharing. It was obvious that the woman was happy, and that she trusted the man whose arms were wrapped so intimately around her. She was kissing him because she wanted to with all of her heart, and the way his hands were resting on her hips was a sweet statement of the trust and connection between them. He wasn't trying to dominate her. She wasn't afraid of him. As the girl's arms slid around his neck, a sad envy settled in Rhiannon's heart. What would it be like to be excited for a man's kiss? What would it be like for a man to hold her gently? What would it be like to have the ability to choose who to give herself to? To kiss without fear?

The couple broke the kiss, and the woman was staring up at him with an almost radiant smile on her face. The man took her hand and tangled their fingers together. Together they began to walk again, taking their time as they splashed through the puddles and let the downpour saturate them—

A hand closed around Rhiannon's throat and yanked her back into the room. She gasped for air as she grabbed the muscular forearm, trying to pry it off as she was slammed backward against a hot, muscular body. "José knew you weren't dead," a low voice snarled.

Dear God. She knew that voice. José's deputy, Raoul, one of the twisted bastards who had tormented her for so long. Terror ripped through her. *He'd found her.* "No!" she screamed her protest as she twisted violently, tearing herself out of his grasp. She leapt for the window, but he caught her bun and jerked her back. Pain tore through her scalp as he dragged her across the floor, ripping her tight bun out of its carefully coiffed prison.

Writhing against his grip, she grabbed her hair, trying to protect herself from the pain as she fought to get free. Frantic, she stretched out her hand, reaching for the potted ferns near her window. *Help me!* A wind began to rattle through the room, and the ferns began to grow—

"Fuck that!" Raoul hurled her onto the wooden floor, and immediately jerked her hands behind her back. She felt the cold rush of metal against the backs of her hands, and knew that he was going to put on gloves that would block her power. Fear tore through her and she screamed, fighting desperately to get him off her. But as always, he was so much stronger than she was, his weight easily keeping her crushed against the ground, pushing the air right out of her lungs.

Her finger slid inside the glove and she screamed, twisting desperately to try to get free. She couldn't even focus enough to concentrate on calling the ferns. They sat there in their pots, yards from her, doing nothing but drifting in the breeze from her open window. Her knife was sheathed, out of reach. She had nothing to protect herself. Nothing.

Panic assaulted her, sheer, raw panic, as she felt the all-too-familiar restraints taking away her freedom. With a shout of fury, she bucked her hips, shoving him off her so she could scramble out from under him. She fell on her face as she tried to stand up, and the one glove that had been partially on her hand slipped off.

She lunged for the plants by the window, and her jaw slammed into the pot as she fell. A fern brushed her cheek, and she commanded its response, praying that being so close to it would give her enough power to control it. "Now!" she commanded, just as Raoul grabbed her shoulder and dragged her away from it.

The ferns didn't respond. Her fear was too deep, paralyzing her and cutting her off from the very source of her power. The plants just sat there, useless, as Raoul jerked her back. She slammed her knee into his crotch, and he roared with pain as he grabbed his balls. She tore herself out of his grasp and raced for the front door. It flew open just as she neared it, and in burst another one of José's men. She skidded to a stop, scrambling backwards as he lunged for her. His meaty fingers locked around her wrist and yanked her forward—

A loud crack exploded through the night, and suddenly the man holding her fell to the ground with a loud crash.

"Really? You still think I can't help you?"

Rhiannon looked up sharply to see Jordyn standing in the doorway, a handgun in her right hand. Her boss was standing with her feet spread, her jaw tense. She looked far more than the manager of a shelter for battered women. She looked like a warrior, the kind of woman Rhiannon had grown up around. Warmth flooded her, and for the second time that night, she felt like this woman could be her friend. Behind her, she could hear Raoul's moans of pain as he writhed on the floor. "Thank you." Her hands were shaking, and she could barely breathe.

"So? You going to stay now?" Jordyn casually walked over to Raoul and pointed the gun at his heart as he started to stand. She pulled the trigger, and he dropped to the floor, blood from his body pooling on the floor. Her move was utterly cool, without remorse, as if she'd taken down many men in her life.

"I wish I could stay, Jordyn, I really do. But this isn't over." Rhiannon picked up her bag, and looked down at her assailants. There was a bright red stain on each of their chests, but she knew it wouldn't last for long. "They'll heal that in less than a minute. I have to go."

Jordyn's eyes widened as she glanced at the man on the floor. "A minute? I hit them both in the heart. They should be whining about the injury for at least a half hour. It's not like they're rogue."

"It takes a lot more than that to hurt that kind of Calydon." Rhiannon hurried past Jordyn and started to run down the stairs.

Jordyn followed her, moving as quickly as Rhiannon. "Why do you have Calydons hunting you? I thought they usually hunted other Calydons. Rogues."

"Generally, yes. But these are different." She reached the front door and yanked it open, hurrying out into the rainy night. "These hunt me."

"Why?" Jordyn followed her to the street where Rhiannon tried to flag down a cab. It sped by her, not even slowing down.

Rhiannon shook her head as she tried to wave down another cab that breezed by her. Dear God, she had to get out of there now. She heard a crash in her apartment, and looked up sharply. Shadows were moving and she knew the men would be after her in seconds. "Jordyn. I don't have time to talk. José is alive. He's going to come find me. There's nowhere to hide. I have nowhere left to go that's safe."

Jordyn glanced up at the apartment, and her eyes narrowed. Not with fear, with focus.

"What are you going to do?"

God, she didn't want to say it. She didn't want it to be real. But there was no other choice. José was alive. And now he would know that she was alive. There was only one option.

"Rhiannon?"

There was another crash from upstairs, and then she heard footsteps pounding down the stairs of her building. "Oh, God. I have to go!" She started to run. She knew she could never outrun them, but there was no other option.

"Wait!"

She spun around toward Jordyn. "What?"

Her boss held up a set of car keys. "Want a ride?" She clicked the button, and the car right next to Rhiannon beeped. It was a Porsche, built for speed.

She didn't even bother to answer. She just lunged for the passenger door and yanked it open. By the time she had shut the door, Jordyn was already in the seat beside her, jamming the keys into the ignition.

As the engine roared to life, the two Calydons burst out the door to her apartment building. They spotted the Porsche immediately, and lunged toward it. Jordyn calmly shifted into drive and jammed the accelerator. The little car exploded forward, leaping out into the deserted street.

Rhiannon twisted around in her seat, watching as the two Calydons broke into a sprint, chasing after them. "They're coming."

"Is one of them a runner?"

Rhiannon glanced at her boss. "A runner?"

"A Calydon whose gift is speed," Jordyn said calmly, with the knowledge of a woman who had seen it all. "That's the only kind who could catch us in this pretty baby."

Rhiannon twisted around, and saw with relief that their two pursuers were fading into the night. "No, it doesn't look like it." She leaned back against the seat and watched her boss, a woman who shot men, drove a Porsche, knew about Calydon traits, and wasn't fazed by having an employee who could control plants. "Who are you, Jordyn? How do you know so much about Calydons? You didn't even blink an eye about what I can do. What are you?"

Her boss looked over at her, and her face was grim. "I'm half of what I used to be," she said quietly.

"Which is what?"

Jordyn shook her head. "Half of what I used to be," she repeated. She looked at Rhiannon. "I am a *sheva,*" she said quietly. "I killed my soul mate to try to save our daughter. I was too late. They're both dead, and now I try to save women from the bad men they love."

Tears filled Rhiannon's eyes, springing free before she could stop them. "I'm so sorry," she whispered. She knew that pain. She knew that pain so well. "Your soul mate went rogue?" She glanced at Jordyn's forearms, but she was no longer carrying the brands of her mate. Was that because he was dead? Would death really free a woman forever from her soul mate?

Jordyn nodded. "Yes indeedy. It was a grand old time." She didn't bother to hide the pain in her voice.

Rhiannon looked away, fighting against memories that would haunt her forever. "At least he had the excuse of being rogue," she said softly. "At least he was insane when he hurt you and your daughter."

Jordyn managed a grim smile. "He was a good man before he went rogue," she said quietly. "I loved him, before he tried to kill me and murdered all our friends and family. It's hard to remember the good man, sometimes." She looked over at Rhiannon. "I have never been as scared as I was the night he went rogue. No woman should ever have to be afraid of the man she loves. Ever."

Rhiannon understood then. She understood it all. When a Calydon bonded with his mate, he was destined to go rogue and destroy everything that mattered to either of them. Fate commanded that the *sheva* kill him to stop him, and then kill herself in despair over his death. For Jordyn to have killed a rogue Calydon meant she had powers and inner strength that an ordinary woman didn't have. For her to have been strong enough not to kill herself after she took the life of her soul mate was almost unheard of. "How did you do it? Not kill yourself?" She needed to know, because that was a fear that lurked over her all the time. What if she killed José, and then wanted to die?

In her heart, that possibility had haunted her for the last five years, the knowledge that if she'd really managed to kill José when she'd escaped, then she should have been so devastated that she would have had to kill herself. She'd been fine, which she'd feared indicated that José was still alive, and now, her fears had proven true.

Jordyn managed a small smile. "I did. I killed myself eight times. But I had a friend who worked with me to bring me back from the dead. He had skills, and I'm somewhat immortal in my own right. After eight times, my grief had finally abated enough for me to handle steak knives without trying to shove them into my chest." She shrugged. "I was lucky. Most *shevas* don't get that chance to live again once they succumb to the *sheva* destiny."

A cold chill settled in Rhiannon's bones. She knew she wouldn't have the luxury of being revived repeatedly until she finally got over her grief. "So that's why you opened the shelter. To help women who are tied down to the wrong men."

Jordyn nodded. "It's what I do. I'll do it until the day I die." She took a deep breath and smiled at Rhiannon. "Where to, sweetheart? What do you think? I can take you to my place. It's a fortress."

"No. A fortress isn't enough against Calydons like that. You know that." A fortress wouldn't be enough against an ordinary Calydon, the kind that Jordyn had killed, and José was even more of a threat. He was so much more dangerous and powerful than any of the others. More than anyone could stop. And yet, she had to find a way to do it.

Jordyn hesitated, and then nodded a silent assent. "What are you going to do?"

"I need to go to the airport."

"All right. That sounds like a good plan." Jordyn gunned her engine. "Where are you going?"

Rhiannon bit her lip. She wanted to say she was running

away. She wanted to say she was going to go deep underground and hide again. But she knew it was impossible. Not with José alive. He would find her.

She shuddered, suddenly feeling cold. José was really alive? Restlessly, she ran her hands over her forearms, over the tattoos that hid the marks that branded her as his *sheva*. She knew she had no choice. Dear God, was she really going back? She was. She knew she was. It was her only chance at surviving. "South America," she said quietly. "Home." No. Not home. No longer home. "Hell."

Jordyn glanced at her. "Why go there? You think you'll be safe?"

"No. It's the most dangerous place I could go." Rhiannon met the gaze of the one woman who might actually understand what she had to do. "But that's where he is. I have to find him, and kill him before he gets me."

Jordyn frowned. "He's going to kill you?"

"No. It's worse than that. I could handle it if that was all he wanted to do." She bit her lip against the fear hammering at her. She fought off the memories, knowing that if she let herself remember what it had been like, the fear would paralyze her, and she would never be able to go back. "He has to die, Jordyn. It's the only way."

Jordyn stared at her, and for a split second, Rhiannon thought she was going to condemn her. What kind of woman boldly stated she was going to track down the man she was bound to forever and kill him in cold blood?

But Jordyn didn't condemn her. Instead, she shocked Rhiannon into silence when she said, "Give me forty-eight hours to get coverage at the shelter, and I'll go with you."

Rhiannon's throat tightened up even as she shook her head. "I can't," she said. "I have to leave now or he'll find me. I can't risk your life anyway. If you die, who will help all the women here? This is my battle."

Jordyn sighed. "How did I know you would say that?" As she spoke, she reached into her wallet that was sitting on the console between them and pulled out a credit card. She held it out to Rhiannon as the little car hurtled down the highway. "Credit cards leave a paper trail that's too easy to track. Use mine to book your ticket, and to buy supplies once you get down there."

Rhiannon shook her head, touched by the offer, but knowing she couldn't take it. "I can't take your money."

Jordyn continued to hold it out. "You have to," she said quietly. "Your only chance is surprise. You'll never win if he knows you're coming, will you? If you use your own credit card, he'll know, won't he? He'll track you."

Rhiannon bit her lip, then nodded. "Yes. Yes, to everything you just said." They both knew the truth. She might not win no matter what she tried. But surprise would at least give her a chance.

Silently, she held out her hand, and Jordyn put the credit card in it. "I'll pay you back," she said.

"I don't need money," Jordyn said as she took the exit for the airport. "I just want you to stay alive. Got it? I'll accept nothing less from you."

Rhiannon managed a smile. "You're a little bossy, you know that?"

"Of course I am. That's what makes me so charming." Jordyn winked at her, and Rhiannon smiled for real.

A brief oasis before she descended into hell.

CHAPTER 6

You are mine.

Rohan's words kept haunting Zach, seeping into his focus as he prepared his end of the campsite for himself, Thano, and the horse. What had he meant when he'd said Zach was his apprentice? It made no sense, but he'd spoken the words with a conviction that had brought ice to his bones.

Rohan had meant it, and Zach didn't like it. He didn't like anything about this situation.

Zach slanted a look to his left, watching as the remaining members of Rohan's team finished the trench they'd quickly dug around their campsite. They'd diverted a nearby river so that it flowed around them like a moat. Inside the circumference of the moat they'd set ten-foot torches into the earth around their campsite, spacing them at five-foot intervals. Rohan had told Zach to light them, but Zach had ignored him. He figured being rude and dismissive was better than coming clean that he didn't have fire anymore.

Night was falling fast, and in another few minutes, it would be pitch black. The torches and moat had made the campsite small, but Zach had brought Apollo inside the circle anyway. He still hadn't unstrapped Thano from the horse, and he wasn't going to, not until he was convinced it was safe.

Which would most likely be never.

He spread out the two bedrolls that one of Rohan's team had offered him, and he checked the water level in the bucket he'd dragged over for Apollo. Something about the tension level of Rohan's team, and the urgency with which they'd erected those torches had made him pretty sure he didn't want the horse wandering even those few yards past the torches to the nearby stream.

They'd even set up torches around the black pit of hell that Trevor was inside, and those were less than a foot apart, as if they had added extra protection for the warrior who wouldn't be able to defend himself.

Zach could smell the food cooking over the campfire, but he didn't join them, deciding to wait until he was beckoned. Rohan had refused to give any more details about the mission, and Zach wasn't going to prostitute himself by asking.

Instead, he walked over to Apollo, who was contently eating the plants that Zach had brought in for him. He ran his hand over the horse's soft nose as he checked the straps holding Thano to the saddle. There were red marks on Thano's wrists, and Zach grimaced, knowing he had to get the younger warrior into a better position before too long. Yeah, he was immortal like the rest of them, but he wasn't going to leave him strung up like Trevor. "Soon, Thano. Just hang in there a little longer."

"Zachary." Rohan's command was like a sharp crack through the night. "It is time."

"The guy's a pig," Zach said in a low voice to his teammate. "When you're better, let's kick the shit out of him together, okay?" He patted Thano roughly on the shoulder and began to turn away.

Then, curiosity prevailed, and he thumbed back one of Thano's eyelids. Even in his unconscious state, his eyes were glowing red. The red of rogue. Shit. The kid was in trouble. "I swear to you, I will fix this."

He jerked his chin at Apollo, who stomped his hoof, then he turned and walked toward the other warriors.

As he strode toward them, he took a moment to assess them more carefully.

All but one of the warriors were seated in a semicircle around the campfire, sitting directly on the ground. Rohan's team had arrived with five warriors, but two others had joined them, sliding into camp while they'd been setting up, apparently waiting to meet up with them.

Zach had paid attention, and knew their names now. Eric Hunter, the tallest except for Rohan, was irreverent and bold, reminding him of Thano, only with an edge. Maddox Crowley, who walked with a slight limp, suggesting an injury that even a Calydon couldn't heal. James Wolfe, who had slipped back his hood once just far enough for Zach to see that he had piercing blue eyes that were like icicles. Zane Hart, who looked like a reject from Hell's Angels, with his black leather and studded ears. Axel Knight, whose arms were the palest of flesh, almost like a ghost barely holding onto physical form. Ethan Lagat, apparently the youngest one, and the only one he'd ever heard laugh, was standing behind the group facing outwards, as if he were watching the forest.

Zach recognized Ethan's ready stance and knew that he'd been assigned first watch. What threat could possibly be so great that six of the most dangerous warriors alive needed to assign someone guard duty even when everyone else was still awake and ready?

All six of the warriors still had the hoods of their cloaks up, which cast their faces into dark shadow. In the darkness, their black cloaks made them almost impossible to discern. They were like six shadows on which the reflection of the flames were dancing. Zach couldn't tell the difference between any of them, except for Rohan.

Rohan stood a good six inches taller than the others. Even in a seated position, his shoulders were well above his team's, and considerably broader. Given that the other six warriors were all heavily muscled, it was quite a statement. The loose sleeves of their cloaks reached all the way to their wrists, hiding the brands that marked them as Calydons. During the battle with them outside the entrance to the nether-realm, all of them had called out swords. It was unusual to see warriors all carrying the same weapon. In the Order of the Blade, all of the warriors had different ones to call.

Why did these men all have the same one? And why were they all identical to Rohan's?

Zach felt the brands on his own arms burn in anticipation as he neared the campfire. He didn't like being unable to see the faces of the others. A warrior could tell a great deal from the facial expressions and body language of his enemy, which was probably why they wore the cloaks.

He was kind of impressed with the effect of the cloaks, actually. It was good stuff. Annoying, from his perspective, but good.

He crouched beside the fire and took a wooden bowl and spoon from one of the others. It was filled with a stew of some sort that appeared to have assorted vegetables and some kind of meat. He was surprised to hear his stomach rumble, and he realized that he was hungry. It smelled good.

Silently, he began to eat, spooning the hearty meal into his mouth. He ate fast, unwilling to eat leisurely when he didn't know what would happen in the next minute or five. "What's with the torches?"

No one responded, and he couldn't feel their energy. He realized that he still had his mental shields up from when he blocked Rohan earlier. Calydons were highly skilled at connecting telepathically with other Calydons when in close range. He wasn't interested in getting up close and personal with them, but at the same time, he realized those moments when he had felt Rohan smile in his mind had actually helped understand the situation.

Reluctantly, he eased down his mental shields and opened his mind to theirs. At first, he felt nothing. Then he began to probe, reaching out mentally to connect with them.

The first thing he felt was fear.

Fear? From these seasoned warriors? He went still, raising his head to look at the ring of torches around them. "What's out there?" he asked, with renewed urgency. His weapons were almost straining at his flesh, reacting to the threat and preparing to defend him.

It was Rohan who answered. "We are not welcome in this jungle."

"I'm beginning to sense that. Did you piss off the folks handing out the party invitations or something?"

Rohan leaned forward and raised his head to look directly at him. Zach could feel his gaze burning into him. "There are creatures in these woods. Dangers that are unique to this habitat. Calydons, but not like us."

"No, not like 'us.' Don't lump me with you guys. I'm not one of you." He injected a challenge into his voice, daring Rohan to make another bold claim about Zach being his apprentice.

But he didn't. He simply said, "You and I are different, yes, but not different from each other the way we differ from the Calydons in this jungle. These are dangerous, even to us."

Despite his distrust of Rohan, Zach felt his intrigue beginning to grow. There weren't many creatures who were dangerous to Calydons. "Dangerous how?"

Another faint smile from Rohan. "They are empowered by their leader, a young Calydon named José Vasquez. He is molding a new kind of Calydon, a kind far more powerful and more dangerous than any we have seen before. He drives them mad until they go rogue, and then he brings them back to sanity. But they still have the powers from when they were rogue."

Zach tapped his spoon on the rim of his bowl as he contemplated this information. "When Calydons go rogue, they're almost impossible to kill." That was why the Order of the Blade had been formed, because no ordinary Calydons could ever defeat a rogue. They were so driven with rage and anger that they could not be stopped, sort of like what meth did to humans. The only disadvantage the rogues had was that they were insane, which gave the Order the benefit of intelligence and strategic thinking when trying to defeat them. The idea of a rogue Calydon who was *also* in possession of his mental faculties…it was almost unthinkable to contemplate how unstoppable that warrior would be.

Rohan nodded. "They are not good men."

And there it was. The issue. Power always had the potential to corrupt, and power in the hands of an amoral lunatic was dangerous indeed. He whistled softly, beginning to understand the level of threat they were dealing with here. "What's their plan?" But even as he asked it, he grimaced. His job here was not to take on a bunch of enhanced bad guys terrorizing some South American jungle. His mission was Thano. "How does that relate to Thano?" he amended, changing the focus of his inquiry.

Rohan leaned forward. "José is in possession of a staff that he uses to bring his warriors back from the state of being rogue. You must retrieve that staff."

Retrieve the staff. That was such a concrete solution to saving Thano: a staff that brought warriors back from the rogue state. Hope leapt through him, the first hope he'd felt since Thano had gone rogue. Was there really a way to save him? All he had to do was find José's staff and use it on Thano? A part of him wanted to jump up and head out after José right then and end this thing, but he was too experienced for that. So, instead, he took a mouthful of the stew while he considered this new information. A simple statement, that was obviously very deceptive. "Why can't you get it? Why do you need me?"

"Because you have fire."

Zach went still at the words. "Fire?" he repeated softly.

"Fire. It's the only way." Rohan gestured at the torches that surrounded him. "These torches will keep us safe tonight, but they aren't enough to get the staff. You are the only way, Zachary."

Zach closed his eyes as defeat tried to overtake him. Thano's survival depended on him being able to use fire? Son of a bitch. He hadn't been able to summon fire for a battle for more than six hundred years. His fire had been fading for a long time, and over the last day or two, the final vestiges of it had deserted him. "Why is fire needed?" His voice was soft, hoping that Rohan's answer would give him another option.

"Because he's a fire god."

Rohan's reply was so unexpected, that all Zach could do was stare at him. "A fire god? What are you talking about?"

Rohan served himself some more stew. "Are you not familiar with the ancient Greek and Roman myths? Zeus, Apollo, Artemis, and all the others?"

"Well, yeah, of course I am. But those are myths. Stories of fantasy and imagination."

"Yes," Rohan acknowledged. "Many of the stories are the product of human invention. However, most of it is grounded in some level of fact. Very powerful beings that control the fundamental aspects of life exist. Call them gods if you wish, for want of a better term. They don't bother with the earth realm much these days, but sometimes they show up here. When they do, it's generally not a good thing for any of us. Most of the gods have no moral compass whatsoever."

Zach ran his hand over his jaw, scraping his knuckles against the rough stubble. A god? The kind that could create a tsunami simply by sneezing? Shit. What was he getting into? "If you're correct that we're dealing with a fire god, why would the torches stop him? What if he just sticks them in his armpits and uses them as a nice little self-massage tool?"

"The fire wouldn't stop him," Rohan agreed. "But it seems to appease his minions when they hunt. They never bother us if we have fire." He nodded at the moat. "That's just in case one of them changes his mind. It won't stop them, but it might give us a fraction of a second longer to react and defend ourselves."

"So why do you think I can make a difference?"

"José controls fire. He bends it to his whim. He can use it as a weapon in any way he chooses. He's impossible to get close to. He would incinerate us all within a millisecond." Rohan shrugged. "You might survive."

Zach swore under his breath. In the old days, yeah, sure. He would've been all over chasing down some arrogant fire god who could save his teammate. But now? He glanced over at the torches around him and surreptitiously flicked his index finger toward one of them and commanded the flame to rise.

It stayed exactly as it was.

It had been only days ago that he'd been able to feed a campfire. Now he couldn't even do that. "Is he always on fire? Or does he have to turn it on?"

Rohan shrugged. "I don't know. Everyone I've sent to go after him has died. All I find is their burned-out carcass." His voice grew hard. "He has killed three of my warriors. It ends now."

"You sacrificed three of your warriors to save one?" Zach's gaze slid thoughtfully toward the dark shadows that concealed Trevor. What was so special about Trevor that it was worth the sacrifice of so many warriors to save him?

"How many of my warriors would you sacrifice to save Thano?" Rohan challenged.

"None. I wouldn't ask any of them to sacrifice themselves. I would do it myself." Zach was disgusted that Rohan had sat back in his little protective campfire while he sent his team to their death. "What kind of a leader are you? Sending others to die instead of handling it yourself?"

Rohan stared at him, and a dark, angry loathing seemed to wrap itself around Zach. "You will leave in the morning. I'll give you all the information I have about the location of his lair. You will leave Thano here in our safekeeping while you seek that which will save him."

"No. Thano goes with me." There was no chance he was leaving Thano behind with Rohan.

But Rohan shook his head. "This is battle, Zachary. You would really bring an unconscious teammate into battle with you? How will you protect him and save yourself at the same time? Have you really lost so much of the knowledge that Dante imparted to you?"

Anger roiled through Zach and he lunged to his feet. "What do you know about Dante? You betrayed him. Don't ever mention him. You lost the right to speak his name."

Rohan didn't move, but tension suddenly seemed to echo through his body. "Sit, apprentice. Anger never serves. I would have thought you'd learned that by now. If you want to save Thano, you have one choice, and you know it."

There was a nicker of alarm from Apollo. Zach spun around to see the horse staring intently into the woods past the flames. His ears were pricked, his nostrils were flared, and his tail was swishing violently. His muscles were quivering and taut, as if he were ready to bolt at any second.

Instantly, all the other warriors were on their feet. There was a crack and a flash of black light, and then they were all armed. The warriors all fanned out so they were facing the woods at intervals. Zach moved beside the horse so he could keep Thano at his back. He reached out with his preternatural senses, searching for information his eyes could not glean from the impenetrable darkness.

A thick, heavy veil of malevolence drifted through his mind and coated his flesh. Apollo shifted restlessly, and Zach held up his hand for silence. The horse went still but he didn't take his gaze off the woods.

Then Zach saw a small orange glow on the other side

of the moat. It appeared and disappeared so quickly, he almost doubted whether he'd seen it. Except he knew fire, and he knew what he'd seen. It had been a flame about three inches tall hovering in midair. Either it had been in the hand of a warrior he couldn't see, or someone had projected it into midair.

No one react. Rohan sent his command telepathically. *Let them pass, but be ready.*

Zach's muscles were taut, ready to attack. But he had no idea what was out there or how many of them. It would be foolish to initiate contact when he didn't know what he was facing. So he stood there, beside his fallen teammate, waiting.

He saw another flame flare and disappear. And then another. They were all over the woods, like fireflies on steroids. Son of a bitch. How many were out there? A thousand? Or was it only one, a gifted creator who could generate many different flames? How in the hell was he supposed to take that on when he didn't have any fire talent anymore?

The night became dark again, but no one relaxed. Not yet.

A sudden movement from his right caught his attention. He spun around just as Thano opened his eyes. They were red. Bright, deadly red. "Thano?" He kept his voice low, only loud enough to carry the short distance to his teammate. "You with me?"

But even as he asked the question, he saw Thano's hand flex. There was a sudden, violent burst of hatred, and Thano's muscles bunched to tear himself free. With one quick move, Zach slammed his sai against the side of Thano's head. But it didn't knock him out. Instead, Thano turned to look directly at him. Zach had a split second to realize that the situation had just turned deadly, and then Thano unleashed a scream of murderous rage. The straps binding him broke as he launched himself off Apollo at Zach. There was a flash of black light as his halberd appeared in his hand. He thrust the pronged spear at Zach's throat, still screaming.

"Back off," Zach shouted as he parried Thano's blow to the side. But as he did so, Thano struck with his second halberd, plunging it deep into Zach's shoulder. Gasping in pain, Zach saw Thano winding up for a deadly blow with his other spear, and he knew he had no choice. "I'm sorry," he said as he raised his sai and thrust it straight into Thano's chest.

Thano dropped to the earth, twisting violently as he struggled to pull the sai out of his body.

Zach crouched beside him and grabbed his shoulders. "Thano," he said urgently. "Come back to me! You're stronger than this crap! Come on, man—" He gasped as Thano jammed his weapon into Zach's stomach.

Rohan suddenly appeared beside him, his sword flashing with blue light. He slammed the flat of the blade against Thano's head, just as he had with Trevor. Thano screamed in agony and electricity sparked through his body, torqueing him ruthlessly. But even as he writhed in pain, he fought to thrust his halberd into Rohan, trying to kill him with his last breath.

"Hold him down!" Rohan shouted.

Zach threw his body over Thano's torso, using his weight to pin him to the ground. Then he grunted as two other warriors leapt on top of him. Their combined weight was barely enough to keep Thano on the ground, and Zach dug his boots into the earth, trying to hold him down as Rohan tried to grab his hands. Zach realized he was going to bind Thano's hands as he'd done to Trevor. "No," he shouted, trying to shoulder Rohan away. "Don't do it!"

"It's his only chance," Rohan yelled back. "Otherwise we have to kill him. You know that!"

"Don't—" Zach grunted as Thano bucked him off, and he flew across the campsite. "Shit!" He leapt to his feet just as Apollo stepped across Thano, two feet on either side of his master. Oh, shit. The horse was going to keep them from getting to him—

Then, to his surprise, the horse dropped to the ground, using his entire body weight to pin Thano beneath him. Thano grunted, and Zach saw him dig his boots into the ground to push off. For a split second, he was too shocked to react. Thano's legs had stopped functioning months ago after he'd been abducted by a black magic wizard, and yet he was flexing his muscles and moving them—

Shit! Thano was mobile! Zach leapt to his feet and launched himself across the campsite. He grabbed Thano's legs as the other three warriors did the same. The four of them fought to hold on as Rohan went for his hands.

Zach watched in agony as Rohan wove that same black webbing around Thano's hands. Within seconds, his hands were no longer visible, trapped in the hell that would doom him. Thano's halberds fell to the ground beside him, useless appendages that he could no longer use to hurt them or to protect himself. Once secure, Rohan reared back and hit Thano's head with such a blow that Zach felt the earth tremble beneath him.

It was only then that his friend finally went still.

For a moment, none of them moved. All the warriors were still breathing heavily from the effort it had taken to subdue Thano. When sane, Thano was incredibly strong, as strong as all the other Order members. But rogue? He had strength far beyond any of them.

It was Apollo who moved first. The massive stallion lurched to his feet and carefully stepped across his master. Then he turned and brushed his nose over Thano's cheek, blowing softly against his skin. Then he turned his head and focused his massive brown eyes on Zach.

Zach knew what the horse was asking.

With a low groan, he rolled off Thano's legs, grimacing at the deep wounds in his shoulder and stomach from Thano's attack. He would have to spend the next few hours in a healing sleep to recover from them. His own teammate, the one Order member who was a genuinely nice guy, had tried to murder him.

Only if Thano's mind was well and truly compromised would he ever have done that. There was none of Thano left. Just the madman.

Zach propped himself onto his elbow and looked at the face of the youngest Order member. His dark hair was caked in blood and dirt. His face was drawn and peaked, making him look centuries older than the thirty-five years he was. He thought of all the times Thano had pulled the Order from the brink of implosion with a timely wisecrack or some irreverent speech that cut through all the crap that they lived with. Of all the members of the Order, Thano was the good guy.

He had to live.

And if José's staff gave him the chance for the impossible, to recover from a certain fate from which there was no exit...

There was no longer a choice to be made. Fire or no fire, he was going after José's staff.

Zach looked over at the horse and nodded once. Apollo raised his upper lip and then snorted his approval. Zach smiled grimly, then felt Rohan watching him.

He looked up at the older warrior, expecting to feel that same smug smile in his mind. But he didn't. All he felt was regret and a pain so deep that it was almost unbearable. Then the pain was gone, and he knew Rohan had shielded his emotions again.

"We will keep Thano safe while you heal," Rohan said quietly. "When you wake, we will prep you, and then you will go."

This time, Zach didn't argue. The choice was obvious. There was no other way.

He put his hand on Thano's leg to keep him close, then surrendered to the healing sleep of the Calydons, hoping, for the thousandth time, that his healing sleep would heal the one thing about him that was truly broken: his fire.

Because he was going to need it.

CHAPTER 7

The jungle smelled rich with the dampness of fertile soil. The trees were alive with the chatter of birds and the rustle of animals. Rhiannon closed her eyes and breathed deeply as she let the power of her birthplace roll over her and seep into her body. The freshness of the air seemed to cleanse her of all the grime and pollution that had accumulated during her years of living in civilization. She could almost feel her cells coming back to life and embracing the deep nourishment of the land she was meant to live in.

She went down on one knee and crumbled some dirt between her fingers, watching the rich, brown loam fall back to the earth from which it had come. To her surprise, she felt her throat tighten, and tears burned in her eyes. She hadn't realized how much she'd missed being home. It had been two days since she had left Boston. After much hard traveling, she'd almost reached the region that had once given her life...and then betrayed her.

A sudden sound broke through her focus and she went utterly still, listening intently. Another sound, quiet yet heavy, came from her right, and she recognized it instantly as the footstep of a creature that was too big to be a human, but could easily be a heavily armed Calydon. Without taking time to stand, she pivoted on her knee as she swept an arrow out of her quiver and pulled her crossbow off her shoulder. In less than a millisecond, she nocked an arrow and pointed it at the cluster of bushes from which the sound had come.

She knew she was in the open more than she wanted to be, but relocating into the trees would attract more attention than staying completely still. Her mottled brown and green cargo pants and jacket would help her blend into her surroundings. Even her crossbow still retained the colors of the jungle that had once been her home.

There was silence. No movement followed the steps that she had heard, which made her tension rise even further. Whatever it was had become aware of her, and it was waiting for her to move in the same way she was anticipating its next step.

Penetrating silence prevailed, each trying to outwait the other. The muscles in her arms began to tremble, and she realized how out of shape she was. There had been a time when she had been able to hold her bow at the ready for hours, outwaiting even the most patient of enemies. Now, it had been less than a minute and already her arms were shaking. Her hamstring was cramping from the uncomfortable position she'd frozen in. A trickle of sweat was dripping down her brow, and she knew it wouldn't be long before it went into her eye. It wasn't even hot compared to what the jungle often was, but she could feel the steam rising off her body, curling her hair, and dampening her clothes.

With grim trepidation, she realized she had gone soft. She was in no condition to take on José and think she could walk away. She'd lost to him even when she'd been fit and in her prime. Now? She couldn't even hold an arrow ready for more than a minute. Her pulse began to hammer in her throat, and she willed it to quiet, knowing that José would be able to hear her heart pounding if he was the one in the bushes.

Please don't let it be José. She wasn't ready to face him yet. If she met him now, she would have no chance. A cold fear gripped her, and her fingers tightened involuntarily around the arrow, even as she fought to stay relaxed. Physical tension would throw off her aim. She had to stay loose.

Then she caught a scent, drifting to her over the complex smells of the jungle. It was the scent of a man. Not José. A stranger. He smelled of sweat, adrenaline, and something else. A deeper scent that seemed to reach inside her and unfurl in her belly. She instantly recognized her response as attraction.

Desire. Lust. Dear God, *she wanted this man.* Fear gripped her with sudden cruelty, freezing her muscles and obliterating all thought from her mind except for a raw terror that screamed at her to run. *Run. Run!*

Her instincts knew she had to stay utterly still, but the fear of her attraction to a man was so deep that she could not make herself stay. Attraction was a trap. Desire could be twisted to hurt her. Lust was a cruel lie. Wanting a man was doom, torture, and a hell she'd never survive.

Instead of staying still and hidden as she should have, panic forced her to act. She leapt to her feet, spun around, and ran blindly through the forest, her boots thudding noisily on the ground. Branches tripped her, and plants seemed to spring up out of the earth to grab her ankles. She couldn't even focus enough to ask them to help her instead of hurting her. Her mind was a swirling miasma of terror and memories, screaming at her to run and escape while she still had the chance.

"Hey!" The man shouted at her, his deep voice booming through the jungle.

The rich bass of his voice plunged through her flesh and ignited a fire inside her, a relentless infusion of need and longing that made her want to turn and charge right toward him instead of away from him. "Oh, God, no. Not again." Tears streamed down her cheeks as she sprinted through the jungle, not even paying attention to where she was going. She couldn't remember the layout exactly. Her mind was fragmented with fear and terror, just as it had been so long ago when she had run for her life through these very woods. She stumbled over a root and tumbled to the earth, barely getting her hands out in time to cushion her fall. Her crossbow jammed into her jawbone and she gasped as the pain shot through her.

She hadn't even finished falling when she was already back up on her feet, stumbling as she tried to keep going. Trees loomed above her on all sides, but the branches were too high for her to reach, and she couldn't focus enough to ask the trees to help her. Everything she had as a weapon was gone, disintegrated by the fear ripping through her.

Then she realized there were heavy footsteps thundering after her, getting closer and closer. He was chasing her! She put on another burst of speed, her breath burning her lungs as she fought for air. Her legs were trembling, shaking with exhaustion as she asked her body to do things it hadn't done in so long.

She frantically tried to focus enough to take in her surroundings and understand where she was. She couldn't keep this up. She had to find a way out. She had to—

A hand closed on her shoulder, and fingers dug into her flesh, pulling her to a stop.

With his touch, all conscious thought fled from her mind. She grabbed the dagger from where it sat on her hip and spun around, striking as she turned. Her blade hit flesh, plunging deep inside thick muscle before she'd even finished her turn to see who was after her.

The dark brands on his forearms told her all she needed to know. It was a Calydon, and her dagger was in his heart. She spun the rest of the way around, facing him as he fell.

"Shit!" The warrior's dark eyes widened in surprise as he stumbled and went down to his knees.

Rhiannon ripped her dagger out of his chest and went still, bracing her legs in a ready position as she held the dagger ready. She knew she had to keep moving, but she couldn't run anymore. Not yet. She needed time to recover. She had nothing left. Her breath heaved in her chest as she desperately tried to get air.

She saw the blood pouring from his chest, and realized she'd struck a clean blow into the heart. Instinct had shown her where to find a heart on a Calydon, taking into account his height when she'd made her blind strike. Maybe she wasn't a total loss. Maybe she still had some of her old skills. Maybe she still had a chance to survive.

She took another deep breath, trying to recover from her run. She knew the respite from his injury wouldn't last long, but the heart had been a good place to hit.

He looked up at her as he pressed his palm to the wound on his chest. "Why the hell did you do that?" His voice had the same effect on her as before. It eased through her body like a warm, seductive caress of pure temptation. And now that she could see what he looked like, it was even stronger.

His eyes were dark brown, flecked with bits of gold. His

stare was intense, sinking deep into her very soul as he gazed at her. She felt herself flush under his stare, her body pulsing in response to the heat of his attention. For a moment, the world seemed to freeze, and she was caught in his spell, in his raw masculinity and strength. His cheekbones were sculpted, giving him a regal appearance, despite the heavy growth of whiskers. His disheveled dark hair gave him an aura of danger and lethalness that should have terrified her...but she found herself riveted by him instead.

His shoulders were broad, but not as broad as José's. Unlike José and his men, who wore camouflage pants, lean boots, and sported bare chests as if impersonating some ancient warrior, this Calydon was wearing the garb of civilization. His blue jeans were dirty and torn. His black T-shirt was loose and ragged. He was wearing hiking boots, but they appeared to be heavily insulated as if they were meant for trekking through snow and ice instead of the brutal heat of the jungle. He didn't look like he belonged to this jungle or to José, but the twin dark brands on his forearms told her all she needed to know.

He was a Calydon, and that meant he was a threat, no matter how intense her reaction to him was. In fact, he was even more dangerous *because* of the way she wanted to fall under his spell. Men knew how to take advantage of a woman's attraction to them. They preyed upon it, twisting it to their advantage. She knew better than to want a man, but her fingers actually twitched with the need to lay her hand over his wound and take away his pain, to feel his flesh beneath her palm, to move closer and lose herself in the incredible strength and power of his being.

"Yeah..." he said softly, his gaze locked onto hers, as if he were having the same intense reaction to her that she was having to him. "Who are you?" he asked. "What's your name?"

"Who am I?" The question jerked her back to the present, to the very real danger he presented. If he'd been sent to find her, his quest would have to end now. Even as she thought it, resistance pulsed through her, and she realized she didn't want to kill him.

Grimly, she took a step back as she pulled another arrow out of her quiver. She set it in the bow and aimed it right between his eyes. "What do you want?"

She needed to know whether he had stumbled across her accidentally, or if José already knew she was here. Then, once she had her answers, she would do her best to kill the man kneeling before her.

She ignored the stab of regret at the notion of killing him. Sure, he smelled incredible and had eyes that had momentarily melted right through the fear of men that she kept wrapped so tightly around her. That didn't mean she was going to make the same mistake that had once almost killed her. Never would she trust the wrong man, or any man, again.

Never.

He would have to die. There was simply no other option.

* * *

She was a warrior.

Zach went still, startled by the sight of this slight woman taking aim at his head. His chest hurt like hell from her clean hit with the dagger, and he could feel weakness sapping the strength from his body as he lost blood he couldn't afford to lose. He was already down too many pints after all Thano had inflicted upon him, serious wounds he hadn't taken time to heal completely before heading out.

By the time he'd left, Thano had been strung up beside Trevor, like a couple of carcasses ready to be butchered, that insidious black webbing locked around his hands. Zach had grabbed several hard biscuits and headed out, moving with an urgency he'd never felt before. He'd left Apollo inside that black vortex in the woods standing guard over Thano. He knew the horse would protect Thano from whatever was outside those torches, but he was pretty damn certain the stallion would be no defense against Rohan if he decided to act, or against that webbing as it took over Thano's body.

How much time did he have? Not the five days that Trevor had. Rohan had pointed out that the webbing had already traveled half an inch from where it had begun. He said some poor bastards were more vulnerable to the webbing than others, and it was going to take over Thano fast. Rohan had guessed three days max before he had to take it off and fight Thano to the death or let him die...but it could be less.

After hearing that grim timetable, Zach had been on his way within five minutes. Irritatingly, he'd gotten lost as hell within three hours. Frustration and desperation mounting, he'd been in a cold sweat by the time he'd stumbled across this woman sifting through dirt like she owned the damned place.

And now, she had an arrow aimed very competently at his head, which wasn't exactly the kind of help he needed. He didn't move, assessing her quickly, trying to decide whether he needed to attack or whether he could talk her down. Even as he thought it, disquiet rumbled through him at the thought of attacking her.

He didn't waste time going all soft and fuzzy on women anymore, but this particular woman called to him in a way he hadn't allowed in a very long time, making him hesitate before classifying her as the enemy. Her dark hair was in a tight bun, but thick sections had snuck free, curling in damp tendrils around her neck. Her eyebrows were almost black, arched in a seductive curve that smoothed across her high forehead. She wore no makeup or jewelry, with the exception of a red amulet around her neck. Sweat dotted her neck, glistening beads that sparkled along the silver chain of her necklace. Her loose cargo pants hung low around her hips, not hiding the curves or athleticism of her body. Her shoulders were pulled back and her jaw was relaxed as she held her bow steady, the stance of a confident, prepared warrior.

But her eyes were what captivated him. Like her hair, they were raven black, but they were not the cool, reserved eyes of a warrior. They were turbulent pools of emotion. He could see fear in them, fear so intense that it prickled at his flesh. His sai burned in his arms, not to fight her, but to defend her, to cut down whatever it was that was haunting her so mercilessly.

That wasn't even the extent of his reaction to her. Beneath her fear roiled something else, something that affected him on a visceral level, a pulsing sensuality that seemed to call to him…

The realization hit him like an assault, a realization so devastating that his breath froze in his lungs, trapped by a paralyzing horror. *He wanted her.*

Jesus. He didn't do that anymore. *Never.* He knew it

wasn't a *sheva* reaction, because his runes were too strong. He was simply reacting to her as a woman, and *that* was not okay.

"Why are you after me?" This time, when she asked the question, she tightened her grip on her bow, readying to unleash the arrow into his skull.

There was no doubt she was absolutely ready to do her best to kill him, and damned if he didn't think that was hot as hell. Shit. What was he doing thinking like that? There was no damn way he was ever going down that road again with a woman. He was never tempted anymore. Ever. He had to stay focused. He shook his head once, trying to clear out the jumble of lust and desire fighting for acknowledgment. "I need directions."

For a moment, his statement hung out in the air, unacknowledged.

Finally, she spoke. "Directions?" Disbelief etched every syllable she spoke. "You're a Calydon warrior, armed and dangerous, in the middle of the jungle. You expect me to believe that you're breaking every male stereotype and asking for *directions?*"

He couldn't halt his flicker of amusement at her reply. "Yeah, well, I'm not a typical guy, I guess. I need to get somewhere in a hurry, I have no idea where the fuck I am, and I don't have time to hike to the nearest gas station and buy a map. So, yeah, directions." He couldn't keep his gaze from flickering over her body again, but this time, he noted the well-worn boots that were laced halfway up her calves, the perfect fit of cargo pants that had seen many wearings, and the lean muscles of her arms. "And you look like you know your way around here. I don't suppose you hire out as a guide?" Even as he asked the question, something started to hum inside him, anticipation at the idea of being isolated in the jungle with her and having her on his team. Or maybe it was just that he was so impressed with his idea of hiring a guide who knew what she was doing, and fired up that she might give him a chance to find the fire god before Thano passed the point of no return.

She didn't lower the bow, and her eyes narrowed. "Where are you going?" she asked sharply. It was a challenge, not an inquiry.

"Have you heard of a Calydon named José Vasquez?

Some sort of fire god?" Zach didn't miss the flash of absolute terror across her face, and he saw her shoulders convulse with sudden tension.

That was all the warning he got before she unleashed the arrow at his head. Swearing, he dove to the right. The arrow skimmed the side of his head, cleaving a small furrow in his flesh. By the time he was on his feet, there was already another arrow in her bow and she was pulling back the string.

"Hey!" he shouted as he called out his sai with a crack and a flash of black light. "I'm not here to hurt you!"

Not even hesitating, she released the arrow again. This time, he managed to get behind a tree. Somehow, she had anticipated his move and the arrow seemed to follow him as if it were tracking directly to his heart. It went straight through the trunk of the tree and out the other side. He leapt back as the tip of it emerged out of the wood. It came to a stop with more than eighteen inches of it protruding from the backside of the tree, the tip less than a millimeter from his throat.

Damn. She was good. He liked that. All the better to have on his team.

Adrenaline pounded through him as he dove silently to the right, sliding behind a bush as he readied his sai. But when he came up, she was gone.

He went still, searching with his preternatural senses, trying to find her. There was silence, too much silence. The birds had gone quiet. The animals had stopped moving. Even the wind seemed to have stilled. His skin prickled in awareness and he went down on one knee, poised to attack as he searched the woods around him for the cause of the forest's reaction.

There was a heavy weight in the air, the same malevolence that he'd felt the night before around the campfire. He knew without a doubt that the evil wasn't coming from the woman. She had fought him out of fear and desperation, not out of evil. Something else had joined them in these woods.

Something that might have been hunting her.

The thought that this evil had grabbed her made something inside him clench, a gut wrenching tension that actually hurt. His instinct was to leap to his feet and race after her, even though he had no idea which way she'd gone. Instead, he eased up, keeping his mind utterly quiet as he reached out in all directions, searching for the sound, the scent, or the movement that would tell him what he needed to know.

For a moment, he sensed nothing but the void that the jungle had become. And still he didn't move. He was too seasoned to react prematurely, and he knew that whatever it was still had to be close by. It would have to move eventually, and then he'd track it.

After what felt like an eternity of agonizing wait, but was probably less than five seconds, he heard a faint grunt of pain from his right. It was a masculine grunt, the sound of a man. Zach was on the move within a millisecond, sprinting almost silently through the forest as he hurtled toward his prey.

CHAPTER 8

Rhiannon gasped as she was grabbed from behind. This time, it wasn't simply a hand on her shoulder. This time, she was torn ruthlessly off her feet and jerked backward. She fought for balance as she fell, and then saw who had grabbed her. One of José's Calydons. *Luther.*

Fear leapt through her, but she didn't freeze this time, unlike when she'd been attacked in her apartment and been momentarily paralyzed with terror. She felt different in these woods, and old instincts rose fast. She slammed her palm into his throat with as much force as she could summon, even as her other hand went to her hip for her dagger. He let out a grunt of pain as her fingers closed over the hilt of her weapon. She whipped it free and drove it upward—

He slammed his fist down on the back of her hand, knocking the dagger from her grasp. She lunged for it as it fell toward the earth, but he jerked her back and threw her over his shoulder. She gasped as she landed on his muscular shoulder, his rock-hard body knocking the breath out of her.

For a moment, all she could do was hang onto him as she fought for air. Her hand was numb where he'd hit it, her fingers throbbing uselessly.

That one moment of her recovery was all he needed. His arms locked around her like steel cords, and he broke into a run, sprinting through the jungle, taking her toward José. "Stop, Luther," she shouted. "Let me go!"

He didn't even slow, and he didn't loosen his grip. Of

course he wouldn't. Luther was as ruthless as the rest of them, almost like an automaton following José's orders. There was no humanity in him. No mercy. "I'm not his," she screamed as she slammed her elbow into the base of his skull. It was the only place she could reach, and he stumbled. She hit him again, and then he grabbed her hair, jerking so hard to the side that her neck felt like it was going to snap in half.

A scream leaked from her throat, and she grabbed at her hair, trying to stop the pain. Tears pricked her eyes as she fought to stay conscious. And still, he pulled harder, each step he took twisting her body even more painfully. She knew she was going to pass out, or he was going to break her neck, whichever one came first. He wouldn't let go until he had her at his mercy.

Tears burned in her eyes, and she summoned self-discipline she hadn't had to call upon since she'd escaped from José the first time. Willing herself not to feel the pain, she let her hand drop from his, and forced her body to go completely limp. The pain was extraordinary, but she closed her eyes, willing her mind to that place she used to go when she didn't want to experience what was happening to her. For an excruciating moment, the pain became almost too much to bear, and then suddenly Luther relaxed his grip on her, apparently concluding that she'd passed out.

He waited another moment, as if to be certain she wasn't faking it, and then he let go of her hair entirely. Her head flopped back toward where it was supposed to be, mercifully taking the pressure off her neck. She forced herself to stay relaxed, and let her head bounce against his bare back. She felt his sweat against her cheek, and the scent of man seemed to rise all around her. The heat from his body burned through her clothes everywhere she touched him, and she wanted to throw up at the feel of a man's body against hers. Her instincts were screaming at her to fight, but she knew her only chance to escape was to be patient. She would have one opportunity, and he had to be completely unprepared for her to make a break for it.

As each step took them closer and closer to José, bile built in her throat. Somehow, she forced herself to stay limp, making her body as heavy as she could as he ran. With each step, she let her arms bounce further down his back, allowing her body to slide just a little lower, so subtly he would think it was nothing but gravity at work on an unconscious woman.

She felt his muscles relax even further as he turned his attention to where he was going, no longer worrying about restraining her. He leapt over a fallen tree trunk with ease, a brutal reminder of just how physically dominating José's warriors were. He landed easily, but that slight jarring was just enough to make her slide in his relaxed and slightly sweaty arms, giving her the extra two inches she needed. She moved instantly, slamming her hand between his legs. The camouflage pants he wore gave him no protection as she grabbed his balls and twisted violently, mercilessly attacking the only vulnerable spot on him.

He howled with pain and stumbled, pitching forward as he grabbed his crotch with both hands. Instantly, she ripped herself out of his arms. She landed hard on the ground, and then lunged to her feet—

"Bitch!" He grabbed her ankle and jerked hard, yanking her off balance.

She fell to the ground, and he was on her, his hands around her throat. She gasped, fighting for air as she clawed at his hands, but already, she could feel her mind starting to blacken as he cut off her oxygen. Fear ripped through her, terror at what would happen to her if he rendered her unconscious. She was more scared of being unconscious around José and his warriors than anything else, because the horrors that she had awoken to so many times were more than she could cope with, the stuff that had been haunting her nightmares for so long. Her survival instinct kicked in now, a frantic unthinking defense to save her own life. She kicked and punched violently, fighting him hard now, using every trick she knew to get away, but it was obvious she had no chance. She simply wasn't as strong as he was, and she was out of practice from so many years away from the jungle.

He grinned at her, those green eyes hard and cold as he watched her struggle, barely needing to expend any effort to hold her there as his fingers tightened around her throat. Black spots danced in front of her eyes, and she felt the weight of his body pressing into her, shoving her into the ground, trapping her. *No!* She screamed her protest in her mind, even as the forest began to spin. Dear God. How could she have been so stupid?

How could she have thought she could come back and win? She turned her head to the side, trying to find an opening in his grip to breathe, but he was applying too much pressure. Weakness pervaded her body, and her hands fell to her side as the oxygen deprivation rendered her useless.

Hopelessly, she met his gaze, and she knew that the life she had fled from before was nothing compared to what awaited her in punishment for the fact she tried to kill José and then had fled. She knew she couldn't endure it again, but even as she thought it, she knew she would have to. No matter how weak she became, José would never push her to the point that she died, because then all the fun would end.

Weakly, she grabbed Luther's wrist, trying one last time to escape, a useless gesture borne from the instinct to survive. But it was no use. She was his once again—

Just as her eyes started to close, she saw the flash of a slick, three-pointed steel weapon slam into Luther's chest. His eyes widened, and his hands grabbed at what looked like a giant fork lodged in his body. He released her with one hand to yank it free, but then another identical weapon slammed into the side of his head. He flew back, literally lifted off her and flung backwards by the force of the blow.

Rhiannon gasped, sucking air back into her lungs as she rolled onto her side, coughing and clutching her neck. She knew she should get up and run, and she tried to pull herself to her knees, but the world began to spin again. She had no choice but to bow her head, and close her eyes, digging her fingers into the earth as she fought not to collapse.

She heard footsteps racing toward her, and fear drove her muscles to react. She lurched forward, trying to stand up. She made it halfway up, and then fell, lurching forward—

Strong hands caught her, keeping her on her feet. She jerked her gaze up, and she found herself staring into the eyes of the Calydon she'd stabbed only moments before encountering Luther. She instinctively reached for her hip, but her dagger was gone. Oh, God—

He gripped her shoulders more tightly. "My name is Zach Roderick. I'm not going to hurt you." He jerked his head toward the Calydon sprawled on the ground behind her. "I'm not one of those pieces of shit," he said. "I'm not even from this damned jungle. I just need to save my friend and get the hell home." His gaze drifted down to her neck, and she knew there would be dark bruises forming. His mouth thinned, and his voice dropped about two octaves, a dangerous, lethal tone that sent shivers down her spine. "And apparently, I need to save you as well."

He didn't have a regional accent, none of the intonations of a man who had made this jungle his home, and his eyes... Now that she could see them up close, she could see that his eyes were alive with expression, not the merciless pits of violence she was used to. Then she stiffened. What was she thinking? He was a Calydon. Did she need to know more? "I don't need saving," she snapped as she pushed back from him, swaying slightly as she tried to find her balance. Her head was pounding, her muscles shaking violently, and her neck hurt terribly, but she was not going to lean on him, or anyone else.

"No?" He cocked an eyebrow and brushed the tip of his finger over her throat. His touch was light, almost gentle, and for a split second, she was too shocked to pull away. All she wanted to do was close her eyes and go utterly still, absorbing the feel of his hand on her throat. It almost felt as though he were taking away the pain, and soothing the damage. His touch felt *kind*. Tears suddenly burned in her eyes, emotion welling up from that place inside her that she worked so hard to keep locked tightly up.

She quickly pulled back, putting her hand over her neck as if that simple gesture would protect her from him. God, no, she couldn't make that mistake again. She couldn't trust a man, and never a Calydon. "No," she whispered. "Never touch me."

His forehead furrowed, and his eyes narrowed. "I won't hurt you."

She shook her head. "I need to go." She realized suddenly that she wasn't holding her crossbow either, and her quiver was no longer strapped over her back, which meant she was completely unarmed.

She whirled away from her rescuer, quickly scanning the woods around them. None of her weapons were there. "Oh, no," she whispered, panic starting to build as she began to retrace their steps. The branches were cracked and broken from their battle, and she hurried back along the path they'd left.

"Looking for this?"

She whirled around to see her rescuer holding up her cache. In his right hand were her dagger and her crossbow, and in his left was her quiver, the strap broken. She went still, horrified. He was taunting her with her weapons, knowing that she would never be able to take them away from him.

He shook his head in apparent amazement. "You really think I'm not going to give these to you?" He tossed them gently at her feet. First the dagger, which she lunged for and grabbed instantly. His expression was inscrutable as he lobbed the crossbow at her feet, followed by the quiver.

She retrieved them, scooting backwards into the cover of the trees while she armed herself. It wasn't until she had an arrow set in place that she finally took a breath.

Zach hadn't moved, and he hadn't tried to come after her. He just set his hands on his hips, watching her. "My friend is dying," he said quietly. "I need to save him. That's why I'm here. I'm not one of the bad guys."

Rhiannon heard the desperation in his words, and on some level, they resonated as true. He'd saved her from one of José's warriors and even given her back her weapons. No one working for José would have done either one of those things. But at the same time, she didn't understand who he was or what a Calydon was doing in this jungle if he wasn't connected to José.

But still, he had saved her when she couldn't save herself. She wasn't foolish enough not to understand how significant that was. There would be others after her. Many others. If she fled the rain forest, José would hunt her down. Maybe she would evade him, and maybe she wouldn't. But she would never be able to stop looking over her shoulder, unless she ended it now. The last ten minutes had made it abundantly clear that she couldn't do it by herself, but with Zach by her side, maybe she had a chance. "What do you want?"

Zach clasped his hands over his head, as if he were trying to give the impression that he was harmless...as if she would ever believe that. He studied her for a moment, as if he were contemplating how much truth to give her.

She waited for him to decide, carefully studying his features so she could learn them well enough to determine what he wasn't telling her. She'd learned to protect herself by watching the facial expressions of José and the others, and figuring out when they were lying and when she could believe them.

He finally met her gaze, his dark brown eyes were unabashedly honest. "I'm a member of the Order of the Blade," he said, pausing as if that was something she was supposed to know.

She shook her head and jerked her chin at him to continue. Somewhere in the back of her mind, the phrase sounded vaguely familiar, but she couldn't place it.

One eyebrow went up, as if he were surprised she didn't know. "The Order of the Blade was founded several thousand years ago to protect innocents from rogue Calydons. That's my sworn oath."

She stared at him, trying to comprehend what he was saying. "There are Calydons that *protect* people?" She remembered now hearing rumors about the Order, but she'd always dismissed them as stories started by fan girls who wanted a bad boy in their beds and had created this fantasy as a way to glorify them.

"Yeah, and we're good at it." He still hadn't looked away, openly inviting her to see the truth in his eyes. "Thano Savakis is on my team, and he went rogue."

She stiffened at the words and looked over her shoulder. A rogue? "Is he nearby?"

"He's unconscious. He's not coming after anyone right now."

There was an edge to his voice that drew her attention, and she looked at him again. This time, there was no mistaking the pain in his eyes. Guilt. Determination. *He cared*, she realized. He cared about this friend of his. Suddenly, her throat tightened, and she knew she was losing her mind, seeing emotions in the eyes of a Calydon just because she was so desperate for help. "So?" she challenged, her defensiveness making her voice harsher than she'd intended.

Zach didn't seem bothered. "Apparently, there's a hot shit fire god who has some sort of implement that can bring sanity back to a rogue. I want it. I need it. *Thano needs it.*"

She stared at him, his words sinking in. He was talking about José. He wanted José's staff. He wanted to track down José and steal from him, in order to save his own teammate that he so clearly cared about.

There was no doubt about his loyalty to Thano. It was etched in the lines on his face, and his words were heavy with urgency and desperation. He was a man who would fight to the death to save his teammate, which meant he would fight to the death to get to José. She knew he would. She could see it in his expression. "Do you know where this fire god is right now?" she asked. Fire god, though? She knew José could do a lot of stuff with fire, but he was a Calydon, not some all-powerful god. Rumors had turned him into more of a monster than he already was.

Zach's expression darkened with anger he didn't bother to hide. "The intel I got on him was crap. I'm on my own to find this piece of shit and save Thano." He surveyed her, taking in her outfit, but at the same time, she felt heat burning on her flesh as he studied her. She didn't like it when men studied her so intently anymore. She wanted them to not notice her.

But before she could warn him off, his gaze went back to her face. "You look like you know your way around this jungle. As I said earlier, I'll hire you to be my guide. I'll pay you well, and—" he studied her speculatively, his gaze settling on her bruised throat and the dangling strap of her broken quiver, which was still lying on the ground by her ankle. "I'll keep you alive and safe while you're working for me."

Hope leapt within her. Was this really possible? She was being handed an armed escort who would stay with her right until the very end? As soon as she asked the question, the fragile hope faded again. It was impossible. Coincidences like this didn't happen. How did she know he wasn't working for José, and figured it would be easier to deliver her if she happily agreed to follow him through the jungle? She couldn't trust him.

But then again, if he was telling the truth, she needed him. Desperately. She wasn't a fool. She'd had limitations before, and there were even more now.

Zach shifted restlessly. "I don't have a lot of time," he said, an edge of impatience cutting through his tone. "Yes or no?"

God, she wanted to say yes, but she was terrified of being wrong, of trusting the wrong man again. "Prove it."

He cocked an eyebrow. "Prove it? Which part?"

"That I can trust you."

"Prove that you can trust me?" He studied her for a long moment. "You're a warrior," he said thoughtfully. "Your instincts should tell you what you need to know."

Yes, they should. But she had long ago lost faith in them. Right now, when she looked at this man, all she could see was a hero who had saved her, and that made her want to fall down to her knees and cry in exhaustion, turning herself over to him. The urge was so great that it terrified her. She knew that she was so desperate for hope that she could very possibly see good where there wasn't any, just how a person dying of thirst in the desert would see a mirage. She shook her head wordlessly. "I can't," she said.

"Can't what?"

"Trust my instincts."

Understanding flared in his dark eyes, and for a moment he didn't move. Then he slowly walked over to her, and he went down on one knee just as she started to tense at his proximity. "My sister and her two children were murdered by a rogue Calydon," he said quietly, his gaze burning into hers. "On that day, as I stood over their broken bodies, the ones I had failed to protect, I made them a promise." His voice was hard, so steely that it almost broke with the tension. "I swore on their souls that I would spend the rest of my life fighting that battle and protecting innocents like them, to save the lives of all those to make up for the ones I didn't protect."

Her throat tightened at the deep anguish on his face, and instinctively, she reached out to touch him, wanting to take away his pain as he had hers. Her fingers brushed his hair, a soft, damp silkiness that felt so good that she jerked her hand back, horrified that she'd touched him on her own.

He didn't react outwardly, but his sharp eyes softened at her fearful reaction. "I swear on their souls that I'm telling the truth," he said softly, as if he could lessen her fear simply by gentling his voice. And weirdly, it worked. His voice was kind and soothing, and she felt it wrap around her like a warm embrace.

He held out his hand to hers, as if offering to show her that nothing bad would happen if she touched him. "I swear on my family's souls that I'm telling the truth about Thano, the fire god, and my promise to take you under my protection until this is over, if you'll help me find him."

She felt the depth of his promise in every cell of her body, and chills ran over her skin. She didn't know how this Calydon had become so humane, but he had. There was no doubt about his pain, and his commitment to avenge his family's murder. Silently, she nodded, too overcome with emotion to speak.

He raised his brows. "Is that a 'yes, oh wondrous Zach, it would be my great honor to escort a mighty warrior such as yourself into the hell that no one can survive?'"

A tiny, almost imperceptible laugh slipped free. "It's a 'yes, I'll be your guide,'" she said. "I don't know about the rest of it."

He grinned, his eyes lighting up. "You know the way to the fire god?"

The thought of heading toward José made her tense, and she realized suddenly that at some point she had lowered her bow to her side, forgetting to stay armed. Zach had made her forget her fear, even for a brief moment. For that, she might indeed call him wondrous. But for now... "Yes, I know the way. I'll take you." She held out her hand to stall him as he started to get up. "Say it again. Your promise that you'll protect me. Promise that you'll never, ever use force or mind control against me. Swear it on your sister's soul."

Something flashed in his eyes, something so dark and predatory that she took a step back. "Is that what's been done to you?" he asked in a voice so low she could barely hear it. "Is that why you're so scared?"

CHAPTER 9

Rhiannon stiffened at Zach's question, unsettled by how intense his gaze was, as if he could see right through her walls to the nightmares she tried so hard not to think about anymore. She lifted her chin, trying to make him see her as the warrior she once was, not the woman who was afraid to sleep at night. "Swear on your sister's soul," she repeated. "Swear that you'll never hurt me or try to control me."

This time, Zach didn't simply offer his hand and wait for her to accept, which, of course, she never would. This time, he took her hand himself, and before she could protest, he laid it over his heart, over the wound she'd caused that was already healing. He flattened her palm over his chest, and then placed his hand over hers, sandwiching her fingers between his hand and his heart.

Fear coiled in her belly, but at the same time, to her surprise, she didn't want to pull away. Something about the warmth of *his* body felt comforting and reassuring, instead of threatening and dangerous. So, instead of running, she eased down to her knees in front of him, not taking her gaze off him.

Face to face they knelt, and then Zach spoke. "What's your name?" he asked.

She could feel his words vibrating in his chest, as if they were a part of his body. "Rhiannon Diaz," she whispered.

He nodded. "Rhiannon Diaz," he repeated.

The sound of her name on his lips made her stomach tighten, but not in fear. It was something else, something that felt good and safe. Instinctively, her fingertips tightened against his chest, digging in ever so slightly, not to hurt him, but to hold onto him.

Zach squeezed her hand, as if welcoming her touch. "Rhiannon Diaz, I swear on the soul of my sister and her children that I will protect you. I also swear that I will never use force or mind control against you. *Ever.* You're under my protection, and you're free to stab me any time you feel unsafe."

She stared at him, and then another laugh escaped. "Stab you?"

He nodded. "If you get scared, or I trigger a memory for you and you need to strike out to feel safe, it's fine. I can heal. Just do it."

She smiled then, the first real smile she'd felt in so long. "Okay. I promise to stab you whenever I feel the need."

He grinned back at her, a beautiful, amazing smile that seemed to touch deep in her heart. "Well, then, let's go find a fire god, shall we?"

Her smile faded as the reality of their situation came crashing back down on her. "Yes." She dropped her hand from his chest, almost surprised when he allowed her the freedom to break the contact. She didn't understand him, and she knew it would be foolish to have too much faith in him, but it was tempting. "Let's go." She started to turn away to pick up her bow, which was on the ground beside the quiver, when he stopped her with a touch to her arm. She glanced back at him. "What?"

"Thank you for your help."

She smiled, and again, something softened around her heart. "No," she said. "I'm the one who needs to thank you."

He cocked an eyebrow. "Why is that?"

She grinned at him, suddenly feeling relief she hadn't felt in a very long time, enough relief that she almost felt giddy. "Because the fire god you're after is hunting me. That guy you just attacked? There will be a lot more of them. If you're going to keep me safe, which you promised to do on your family's souls, you're going to be a very, very busy man." She smiled at him, expecting him to look intimidated, or even a little shocked at what he'd just gotten into.

But he simply held out his hands. The two weapons he'd

thrown at Luther began to vibrate where they were still lodged in his prone body, as if Zach was calling them to return to his own flesh. They suddenly tore themselves free of Luther and hurtled through the air right back to his hands. They slammed into his palms with a thwack, then shimmered and disappeared as he sheathed them back into his body. His muscles were taut, his jaw hard, and his eyes focused as he carefully surveyed their surroundings for any enemy. "I'm ready," he said, his voice vibrating with power and focus. "Bring it on."

For a moment, she couldn't do anything but stare at him. He was huge, this warrior who had declared himself her protector. He was so chiseled he could have been a sculpture of male perfection, and he seemed to emanate such strength that she should be terrified. Was this formidable presence really on her side? Could she truly trust him? It was almost too much to conceive of. Men like this caused pain. Men like this were the ones she had been brought up to protect the jungle from. Men like Zach were the enemy.

But even as she thought it, something inside her shouted its denial, that he was different. That this time was different. That this time, she didn't have to be afraid. She didn't want to run from him. She wanted to touch him. Her hands burned to feel his skin beneath her palms again. She had never touched a man like that before, and no man had ever stood by to let her. It had always been different, terrible experiences that haunted her every night—

He looked over at her, and one eyebrow went up. "What is it?"

Heat flooded her cheeks, and she shook her head. "Nothing," she muttered. She grabbed her crossbow off the ground, slung it over her shoulder, and brushed by him, heading in the same direction Luther had been going.

She hadn't realized she'd been holding her breath until she relaxed at the sound of Zach's footsteps falling in behind hers. He was keeping close, keeping her safe…keeping his promise.

* * *

Eric Hunter had made his decision.

The only question that remained was when to execute

it.

He kinda figured now would be as good a time as any. Aligning himself with Rohan's crew was a dead end. He'd invested a hell of a lot of time in Rohan, but it was clear now that the warrior wasn't the leader that he'd been hoping he was. He'd spent a year with this crew, all based on one damned ritual by an old seer who had told him that he would find the answers he needed with Rohan. His brother had believed in the truth of the blue smoke, so Eric had sought it out to find him, and he'd listened to the advice. For twelve months, he'd followed Rohan into hells worse than death, and none of them had led to his missing twin brother.

Screw the smoke's advice. He was going to have to go somewhere else to find out what had happened to Tristan.

Eric leaned against a tree, casually watching Rohan and the others sparring with their swords, trying to hone their skills in case the big bad fire god and his team showed up. A thousand years of practice wasn't going to save their asses, but Eric was somewhat impressed that Rohan was willing to risk it to save his teammate.

The guy might be an ass, but Eric had to respect any leader willing to take a hit to save one of his soldiers. In another life, he might even like the guy. Or he might shoot him. It depended on his mood. Right now, he was in a kill first and bond later mood, so yeah, the friendship thing wasn't going to happen.

The early afternoon was heavy with humidity, and the bugs were fierce, except around him. He eyed the thick swarms of bugs around Rohan and the others, close enough to annoy them, but not distract them.

Yeah, it was time. Eric grinned. He always had fun doing this part. With a flick of his pinkie, the humming intensified, and the Calydons swore as the insects swarmed under their hoods.

Within seconds, the entire team was fighting a battle against one-inch bugs that were too quick and small to get with a sword, but who had teeth that could do serious damage. Whistling casually, Eric strode across the clearing, slung his duffel bag over his shoulder, and strode past the howling crew. People never took small assailants seriously. The first rule of engagement was to never underestimate the opponent, whether it was bugs, or a new teammate who had been lying to them since the day he'd joined them. "I'll get some plants to ward those off," he called out. "I'll be back in a sec."

There was a howl of outrage as someone got stung, and Eric chuckled again as he walked off, his boots thudding carelessly through the underbrush. He knew the guys would appreciate the good-bye once the welts were gone. It was a guy thing. No hugs. Just assault bugs. All was good.

He took a deep breath as he walked, his body relaxing as he left the crew behind. He stripped off the cloak and shoved it into his duffel, relieved to be free from that damned constriction. Jeans and a tee shirt. Yeah, that was the guy he liked to be. The year with Rohan and his team hadn't been a bad one, but he wasn't a follower kind of guy, and it hadn't been his cup of tea to run around being a minion to someone else. He liked doing his thing the way he wanted to, and he liked making his own calls.

And now he was solo again, and it felt good.

He chuckled as another howl of outrage echoed through the jungle, and then laughed aloud when someone yelled his name. Yeah, he'd figured it wouldn't take long for them to figure out it had been his farewell present. He was pretty sure they knew what a thoughtful guy he was—

A woman stepped out of the woods in front of him, with a bazooka aimed at his head. "Stop."

He stopped. Not because he was really worried about what a hand-held missile launcher would do to him, but because the sight was a little unexpected. It wasn't every day that a guy deep in a South American jungle ran into a petite blond woman in jeans, a hot pink tank top, a ponytail, hoop earrings, and hiking boots so new they were still shiny, who was aiming a massive weapon like she knew exactly how to handle it. He jerked his chin in greeting. "What's up?"

"What's your name?"

He contemplated how to answer. Usually, he made some shit up when strangers asked him that. It was never a good thing to hand out vital stats to people he didn't know. But this felt different. Maybe it was because of the long scar down her right biceps. Maybe it was because she just looked so damned small in the massive jungle. Or, maybe it was because he thought women with guns were hot. Or maybe, it was because he just liked her voice. He'd been with guys for the last year, doing some pretty nasty shit, and her voice just sounded *nice*. "Eric Hunter," he said decisively. "What's yours?"

She cocked her head. "Do you live here?"

"In the jungle?" He noticed that she'd completely ignored his question, but he was actually sort of riveted by her laser-like focus on what she wanted to know. He found her interesting.

She nodded.

"Nope." He held up his duffel bag. "I was having a sleepover with the guys, but I have other places I need to be. They aren't being any help at all, so I decided to ditch them. I was just heading out." He let his gaze run over her body again, and this time he noticed the perfectly manicured fingernails, the thin gold chain with the diamond pendant around her throat, and the artfully streaked highlights in her hair. "You're not local either, are you? What's your name? Why are you here?"

She narrowed her eyes and studied him for a long moment. "Do you have a *sheva*?"

"A *sheva*?" He realized that she'd seen the brands on his arms and assumed he was a Calydon. Shit. He'd worked a lot of magic to convince Rohan and the others he was a Calydon for the last year, but that *sheva* thing was one trait he was never going to pick up, no matter how badly he needed to convince anyone. He held up his hands and took a step back. "No, I'm not that kind of guy. I'm always on the move. I don't settle down like that."

A small smile tweaked the corner of her mouth, and she lowered the gun. "You're a commitment-phobe? Isn't that a little archaic?"

He had to admit, she was even prettier without the weapon aimed at him. "Just being honest. I like expectations to be up front. Name?" Yeah, she was cute, but he was losing control of the conversation, and he didn't like that.

She leaned the gun against her thigh. "My name is Jordyn Leahy. I'm here to find my friend."

"Jordyn Leahy." He rolled the name around on his

tongue, surprised by how right it felt, as if he'd heard it before. "Sounds familiar. Do I know you?" Yeah, there was pretty much no chance that he could possibly know her, but her name...shit... he felt like it was in the back of his head.

For a split second, panic leapt across her face, but it was gone almost before he could be sure he'd seen it. "God, I hope not," she said. "I don't like the Calydons I've known before. Listen, have you seen a woman in the jungle? She has dark hair, and wears a red amulet around her neck?"

He shook his head. "Where are you from?" Shit, he was sure he knew her.

"Boston." She looked past him, scanning the woods. "What about a Calydon named José? Have you run into him?"

"José?" He shrugged. "No. We haven't run into any Calydons except the crew I came with, though my boss is hunting for a Calydon named José as well. We haven't found him, which, from what I gather, is a good thing for our life expectancy. Based on rumors, I think he'd kick all our asses at the same time. Where did you live before Boston?"

She sighed and ducked into the bushes. He instinctively leapt forward, alarmed by the fact she might disappear on him. He jerked the branches back, and then barely got himself stopped before he plowed into her. She was bent over a massive backpack, stowing her gun on the side of it. Her jeans stretched across her incredibly nice ass, and he couldn't quite manage not to appreciate it before she turned around.

Her gaze narrowed. "Checking me out? Really? We're in the middle of the jungle, Eric. You're such a stereotype."

He grinned. "Maybe I just want you to think I'm a stereotype. Maybe I'm really this artistic soul who spends months at a time in seclusion on a mountaintop writing love poetry."

She raised her brows at him in a look of such disbelief that he almost felt chastised. "Some people think I'm funny," he grumbled.

"Some people aren't trying to find their friend before she gets murdered by her soul mate," Jordyn said as she grabbed the backpack and hoisted it over her shoulder. "I still can't believe I let her get on that plane alone," she muttered as she picked up a hunting knife as long as her arm. "I am going to be pissed if I got here too late to help her. If she's dead..." She bit her lip and shoved past him, barely even noticing him as she headed out through the forest.

Eric stared after her as she strode away, her blond ponytail swinging gently as she slapped at a bug, and then another. He flicked his finger, and the insects moved away from her, granting her passage. Swearing, he watched her go, replaying her words in his head. She was trying to track down a Calydon who was planning to kill her friend? Shit. A bazooka wasn't going to be much good against that, and he had a feeling she knew it.

She was going to get herself killed, wasn't she?

He ground his jaw and ran his hand through his hair. He couldn't go with her. He'd already wasted a year and gotten nowhere. He had to go back to where Tristan had last been seen and try tracking him again. Tristan wasn't going to live forever, and when he died, Eric would die as well, and once they were both dead, then who would live on to honor their family's name, whatever it really was?

She stopped suddenly, and then turned around to face him. "Louisiana."

He went still, his heart suddenly starting to hammer. "What?"

"Louisiana," she said. "That's where I'm from. A small town on the edge of the swamps called Parrish Creek. If I die, I want someone to know that." Then she turned and walked away.

For a split second, he was too shocked to move. *Parrish Creek.* Son of a bitch. Parrish Creek, Louisiana, population 956, was the last place Tristan had been seen alive. Shit. No wonder her name had sounded familiar. She had a connection to that place, and maybe even to Tristan.

He broke into a sprint, and caught up to her in less than a second. "I'm coming with you. You can't take on a Calydon by yourself. You need me."

Jordyn stopped so quickly that he took two steps past her before he caught himself. "What?"

"You need help. I'll help. I'll come." He was no fool. He knew Jordyn was on a mission to find her friend, and she'd have no time to stand around answering questions. So, he'd go with her and grill her on the way.

She stared at him. "Why?" Her hand tightened around the knife.

He swore and held up his hands. "I'm not going to attack you. I'm offering to protect you. That's a good thing. You could thank me."

"Really? You checked out my butt. You flirted with me. You're a self-proclaimed player when it comes to women. You're from a breed of warriors who are well known for their insatiable lust and their tendency to go rogue when things go bad. And now you're following me through an isolated jungle. On what planet would that make me feel safe and appreciative?" She pointed the knife at him. "Go away."

He wiped off the charming smile he'd just been preparing to use on her, deciding that might get him stabbed. "My brother is missing." He didn't usually grant women the truth, but he had a feeling the truth was the only way he was going to get to walk next to her without cutting off his own balls to prove he wasn't going to attack her. As much as he needed to find his brother, going eunuch was just too much, so he decided to settle for the truth instead. "I need to find him, and I think you can help. I'll help you with your friend, and you help me with my brother."

Her eyes narrowed, but not with disbelief. "Really. I can help you with your brother. That makes complete sense." Skepticism dripped from her voice, so yeah, they were making progress from utter disbelief.

"He was last seen in Parrish Creek. No one in that place will talk to me because I'm an outsider. I need information, and I need help navigating it." He studied her closely. "Your name sounds familiar, Jordyn Leahy. I know I've come across it while tracking my brother."

Wariness flickered across her features. "What's your brother's name?"

"Tristan Hunter."

The shock of recognition on her face was like a jolt right to his gut. "Tristan?" she whispered. "Tristan's your brother? And he's gone missing?"

Son of a bitch. This couldn't be real. He'd found someone who knew his brother in the deep jungle of South America? Shit. That damned seer with the blue smoke could have just mentioned

Jordyn's name and sent him to Boston instead of making him trek around with Rohan for the last year so that they'd meet in some forsaken jungle. Magic was just never thoughtful in that way. "You know Tristan?"

"Know him? He saved my life. Eight times." Her blue eyes bore into his. "What happened to him?"

"Eight times?" Jesus. He knew what Tristan could do, and he knew that Tristan never did it. She hadn't meant *that*, had she? "You mean, he defended you?"

Slowly, she shook her head. "If he's your brother, you know what I mean."

Son of a bitch. "He brought you back from the dead. He's not allowed to do that. He never does it."

"He did it for me." She met his gaze. "What happened to him, Eric?"

"That's what I'm trying to find out. And you're the first lead I've gotten." Well, not the first one. There was one more. He paused. "Do you believe in vampires?"

Jordyn's eyes widened, and her face paled. She stared at him for so long he began to feel stupid. He gritted his teeth, already regretting bringing it up. It wasn't as if he had proof. Just rumors circulating. "Nevermind—"

"Yes."

His gaze shot to hers. "You do?"

"When you grow up in the Louisiana bayou, you hear stories and see things that you wish you'd never seen, especially at night." She gripped the strap of her backpack so tightly her knuckles were white. "You think Tristan…" Her words trailed off as Eric shook his head.

"I don't know. I hope not. I just…" He shrugged. "I need to find him." He was still trying to grasp the notion that Tristan had resurrected this woman eight times. At what cost? Why had he done it? What did Jordyn mean to him? Was Jordyn Tristan's woman? The thought of it made something clench in his gut. Jesus. What the hell was going on? Whatever reason Tristan had had for saving Jordyn, it meant one thing for sure: Jordyn was important to him. Not just important. Critical. Life-and-death critical, or he never would have done it. And *eight times*. "I need your help. He needs your help."

Jordyn nodded once, her gaze steely. "Of course I'll help. I owe him." She looked over her shoulder into the woods, and he knew what she was thinking. How did she choose between her friend and Tristan? She looked back at him. "Rhiannon first," she said. "Tristan would agree."

He wanted to argue. After searching for a year, wondering how much longer the two brothers could stay alive when they were physically apart, he wanted to grab Jordyn and head straight to the bayou, but she was right.

Tristan would kick his ass if he showed up to rescue him without making sure that Jordyn's friend was safe first. Growling under his breath, he nodded. "Fine, but let's make it fast." Like, really, damn fast. How hard could it be to track down a girl and her ex in over a billion acres of rainforest? They'd be out by sunset.

He'd make sure of it.

CHAPTER 10

This was not how Zach had imagined tracking down the fire god and saving Thano. He'd envisioned something like charging into camp, decapitating José with his pinkie, racing home waving the staff victoriously over his head, saving Thano, and then spending the next five hours on the receiving end of Thano's good-humored barbs for taking so damn long to save him.

Instead, he was apparently pretending to be a statue, which, no matter how he tried to frame it, just didn't feel like progress.

He had not moved for almost fifty-seven minutes, and had not breathed for seventeen of them.

He'd just stood there, insects crawling down his neck, while Rhiannon lay on her back in the middle of the jungle, her arms and feet spread, her eyes closed, and her mouth parted slightly.

For the first ten minutes, he'd been completely distracted by the way her shirt stretched across her chest, accentuating her seriously tempting, rounded breasts. He hadn't been blind to the way her shirt rode up slightly, revealing an expanse of bare stomach above the waistband of her camouflage pants. And he sure as hell hadn't been able to keep himself from watching the beads of sweat trickling in rivulets down her chest and disappearing under her shirt.

He'd never thought of sweat as lucky before, but yeah, well, watching those droplets slide over her skin like that... Lucky was the word that came to mind. He was pretty sure that being jealous of sweat wasn't a sign that it was going to be a good day.

She bolted upright suddenly, and slammed her hands down on the dirt by her hips. "Seriously? How am I supposed to concentrate when you're making so much noise?"

He blinked. "What noise? I haven't breathed in an hour. You do realize that's pretty difficult to do, don't you? Not every guy could have delivered the way I did."

She glared at him. "I can hear your heart beating. It's kind of loud."

"My heart?" He stared at her. "You want me to stop my heart from beating?"

She brightened. "Can you do that?"

"No, I can't do that."

She groaned and flopped back on the ground, draping her arms over her face in an impressive display of aggravation. "I thought Calydons were great warriors. How come a warrior can't manage to be stealthy?"

He scowled. "I am stealthy. I just happen to be alive, which accounts for the heart-beating thing. You, however, might want to consider that you're a little oversensitive. I mean, you're fifteen yards away from me. If my heartbeat is really that distracting, then it might be a reflection of your inability to concentrate. And how are you hearing my heartbeat anyway? It's pretty damn quiet."

She sighed and sat up again, wrapping her arms around her bent knees. Her hair was starting to come out of its bun, and some of the strands were pretty long. He wondered how long it would be when it was down. It looked thick and soft. How soft?

"Okay," she said, interrupting his wandering thoughts. "You're right. It's not you." She sighed again, and looked so despondent, he couldn't help but feel a little inadequate that he couldn't stop his heart for her.

She tucked a stray tendril back into her bun. "The reason I can hear your heart is because I've trained myself to listen for heartbeats. It was the one thing that José didn't bother to hide from me. I could tell from his heart rate what mood he was in and what he was planning to do to me." She shrugged. "It was sort of this pathetic little victory to know his plans before he did them. Yay, me, right?"

He grinned at her cheerleader attempt. "Hey, small victories add up." Assuming he was now allowed to resume normal body functions and physical activities, he rolled his shoulders and scanned the woods around them, just to make sure no one had dropped in for a visit while he was playing frozen and obsessing over her stomach. "You want to tell me now what you were trying to do?" She'd been stubbornly uncommunicative when she'd dropped to the ground and ordered him to stand guard and make no sound an hour ago. Since she was the one who knew her way around, he'd gone along with it.

Five minutes into the silence, he'd decided he was much too amiable of a guy, but when he'd tried to break the silence, she'd shut him right down. Now, at least, she was talking. Always a bonus when it came to a woman.

She ran her fingers over a branch. "I used to be able to communicate with vegetation. I was trying to connect with the forest. The plants would be able to tell me where José was and everything that is going on in the jungle." She pressed a kiss to the leaf. "They don't talk to me anymore," she said quietly.

"Why not?" He ran his fingers over a nearby leaf, and felt only the damp coolness of the plant. It wasn't talking to him either, which wasn't exactly unexpected.

"Because I'm an emotional wreck, probably. It's a total drain on my resources to be on the edge of descending into a sobbing pile of mush on the ground all the time, you know?"

"You?" He shot a surprised look at her. "You seem like you totally have your shit together."

She laughed then, and tucked another stray strand of hair behind her ear, refusing to capitulate to its apparent desire to be unrestrained and free. "It's all a lie, Zach. I'm a mess." Her smile faded. "But we need help from the plants to deal with José. He's too much to deal with on our own."

"Nah." Zach walked over to her and held out his hand to pull her to her feet. "I've killed a lot of bad guys in my life. I'm really good at it."

She raised her brows. "He's not your average jerk."

"I'm not your average superhero-type. So, we'll fit." He wiggled his fingers at her to invite her to take his hand, but he couldn't help but think about the fact that Rohan had said the only way to defeat the fire god was with fire. Which he didn't have anymore.

Not that it mattered. Rohan was not a god. He didn't know everything. He had no idea what a fantastic warrior Zach had become. "Come on. If you're not going to merge brain cells with the plants, you might as well get vertical."

For a moment, she eyed his hand as if he had the plague. He was just about to pull it back and pretend he'd just been stretching, when she surprised him by reaching up and wrapping her hand around his.

The moment her palm slid against his, he felt electricity spark between them. Rhiannon sucked in her breath, and her eyes widened. "Wait!" She tightened her grip on his hand and grabbed a plant with the other. She scrunched her eyes shut, and whispered something under her breath.

He decided maybe he should stop breathing again.

He even tried to slow his heart down, but that wasn't going to work, not with her small hand gripping his so tightly. Every one of his senses was attuned to her. He could feel her pulse hammering in her wrist beneath his fingers. She smelled like fresh earth and nature. This close to her, he could see the little lines of tension around her mouth, and the soft curve of her lips. She was incredibly feminine and delicate, even with her cargo pants, hiking boots, and the dagger at her hip.

"Damn." She released his hand suddenly and opened her eyes. "When you first touched me, I felt something spark through me. For a split second, I heard the symphony of the jungle, sounds I haven't heard for so long." She eyed him curiously. "I thought you were the link, but then it went away."

"We could try touching again." He tried to keep his voice devoid of inflection. He really did, but he couldn't quite stop the leap of adrenaline at the idea of "touching" and "Rhiannon" in the same thought.

She backed up a step. "You looked at my breasts when you said that."

Shit. "Did I? Sorry. I didn't mean to." Jesus. What the hell was wrong with him? "I was just thinking that it would be good to get the jungle on our side. If there's a way to get the plants back in your head, that would be a good thing, right? That's all I meant." Yeah, right. That was all he meant. He thought she was hot as hell, and no amount of denying it was going to change that fact. And apparently, he was complete crap at hiding it. He grimly watched her back up another step, like a skittish fawn who had just noticed she was standing next to a hungry predator. The moment the analogy went through his mind, he realized that she was right.

That was exactly how she made him feel. Like a predator after a helpless fawn. Not that she was helpless with her dagger and bow, but there was something about her beneath the tough veneer that was vulnerable and broken. That's what he saw. That's what he was responding to. And that's what made him feel like a complete ass for wanting her.

He held up his hand to tell her to stop retreating. "Wait."

She eased to a stop. "What?"

He met her gaze. "I made you a promise back there, didn't I? That I wouldn't hurt you?"

She nodded.

"If I touch you sexually without your permission, that counts as assault in my book. So, yeah, I think you're sexy as hell, and I want to pull you into my arms and chase away all the shadows haunting you until there's nothing left in that mind of yours except me, but I'm not going to cross that line. It's not the way I am." He ground his jaw. "And honestly, Rhiannon, you're too damned tempting. I haven't wanted a woman this badly since my wife, and that's not a place I want to go again. I can't need a woman that badly again—" He cut himself off, too late, grimacing at what he'd revealed. His wife? Jesus.

She blinked. "Your wife? You're married?"

"Was. She's dead." Shit. He didn't want to talk about that. He couldn't talk about that. He picked up her crossbow. "Which way?"

He'd expected platitudes about his dead wife, but she didn't give him any. She just stood there looking at him, her face alive with a miasma of undecipherable emotions. "Was she your *sheva*?"

"No, she was not." He picked up her quiver. "I married her because I loved her." He held up his arm to show the runes on his flesh. "I use these to block the *sheva* bond, so there was nothing between us except us. No bonds. Just her. Which way do we go?"

She was *still* staring at him, her brow furrowed. "She married you of her own free will? Voluntarily? You didn't force her or anything?"

"Force her? Seriously? Why? Do I look like such an ogre that no woman could love me?" He was in a rank mood now. The conversation was leading to too many things he didn't think about anymore. "Yeah, Rhiannon, she loved me. She shouldn't have. And now she's dead. Any more questions?"

"One."

He glared at her. "Another question? Did you fail to notice that I don't want to talk about it?"

She nodded. "Of course I noticed. But I still have another question. Just one more."

Hell. The woman was relentless. Why the hell wasn't she like other people and backing off when he made it clear he didn't want to talk about it? Gritting his teeth, he turned to face her, giving her his worst scowl, daring her to ask it. "What's the question?"

She asked it. "Did you kill her?"

He stiffened at the question that hit so close to the truth that he actually felt a stab of pain in his chest. "What kind of question is that?" But even as he shot the retort at her, he saw the vulnerability in her eyes, and realized that it wasn't an accusation about who he was. It was driven by her own fears about what men were like. His anger faded instantly, and he shook his head. "No," he said quietly. "I didn't. I tried to save her." Tried, and failed. *Failed.*

Her shoulders relaxed, and her face softened as she touched his arm. It was a soft touch, barely a brush against his skin, but it was riveting. "I'm so sorry you lost her," she said quietly, finally giving him the words he'd expected when he'd first said it. But he knew they weren't simply platitudes. She meant them, and for that reason, her words felt different. More real. Comforting, even. "Thank you for telling me," she added.

Zach nodded briefly. "You needed to hear it."

"I know." She smiled, the first smile he'd seen that

reached her eyes, lighting them up from within.

She was so beautiful that for a moment, he forgot to breathe. It was like seeing the first burst of sunshine after a bitter winter storm—even more stunning because of all the darkness that had preceded it.

Grimly, he realized the truth. After not noticing a single female for over six hundred years, since his wife had died, he'd lost his touch in keeping women out of his line of sight. He'd noticed Rhiannon. No, not just noticed her. He had been sucked straight under her spell, just at a time when his teammate's life depended on him.

Her smile faded. "What's wrong?"

"You're distracting me."

Her eyebrows shot up. "You want me to stop my heart from beating?"

He blinked at her joke. "What?"

"Sorry. I couldn't help it. I thought it was funny." She grinned. "You made me feel better, apparently good enough to tease you, even."

He narrowed his eyes. "I made you feel better? Because my wife died?"

"No, not because she died, you big lug. Because you showed me that you have emotions, Zach, and that's a beautiful thing. It's been a long time since I've felt emotions like that, or seen them in someone else. I'd forgotten what it was like to feel."

Grimly, he shook his head. "Don't get too comfortable with emotions. I don't like them. You probably won't get any more from me."

"I think I probably will. They're a part of you." She smiled at him as she slung her mended quiver over her shoulder. "Okay, since we can't get help from the jungle, we're just going to go solo. We have one stop to make, and then we'll camp for the night. Then..." She met his gaze, her face becoming solemn. "We'll be at his lair by late morning."

Zach straightened up, redirecting his thoughts away from her as a woman and back to battle. "That's where he keeps his staff?"

There was a brief hesitation, and then she shook her head. "He always keeps it with him. We'll need to find him and kill him to get it from him." She turned away quickly and began walking through the jungle.

He didn't move, staring after her, replaying her words in his head. Her hesitation. The way her eyes had darted from his when she'd spoken. Son of a bitch. She'd just lied to him. Which part of her statement had been a lie? What was her game?

Swearing under his breath, he strode after her, the brands on his arms beginning to tingle, as they always did when danger was near. Was Rhiannon the danger he was sensing? Or was she leading him straight into a trap? Or were they being hunted?

He had a feeling he'd be finding out soon.

No problem.

He was ready.

As he followed her, he realized that he was really, really hoping that she wasn't the threat he was sensing.

Damn. He was starting to like her, wasn't he?

* * *

Was it really bad that the story about Zach's dead wife had put her in the best mood she'd felt in years? Did that mean she had turned into some heartless wench with no basis in humanity? Or maybe she was just some lust-driven harpy who thought it was great that the red-hot warrior following behind her was emotionally scarred and lovelorn, just needing a good woman to bring him back?

No, she knew that wasn't true.

Well, she did think he was quite beautiful, and that was such a rare occurrence for her that she wanted to leap for joy at the fact that she could admire him without being terrified of the fact he was a male. His grief had been real, and it had brought tears to her heart for the losses he had suffered, so she knew she wasn't heartless.

No, the reason his story had made her so cheerful was because the depth of his pain, and the mutual love between him and his wife had been so evident. The thought of a woman being with a man because she wanted to had felt like a lie her whole life...until that moment. Until she had seen love in that strong face of his. Until she had heard the love in his voice, love that had been genuine and not some mindless, terrifying connection driven by the *sheva* bond.

Zach had loved. Zach had been loved. It could really exist. *Not every man was bad. Not every union between a man and woman was destructive.*

It gave her hope. Hope that life could be more than what she'd been living. Hope that maybe there were things in life that healed instead of hurt. Zach was a Calydon, and yet he was different. He was a good man, and he was on her side. She realized she was whistling, and grinned.

"You liberate me," she said, as she glanced over her shoulder at her escort. Zach was only a yard behind her, staying as close as he had for the last hour. He was carrying one of his sai, and his head was turning in constant surveillance of their surroundings.

He caught her glance, and his gaze narrowed. "Do I?"

Wow. He sounded annoyed. Apparently, being lauded as a psychological inspiration wasn't on his list of feel-good activities. Okay...time for a subject change. "So, we're heading to a place where my tribe stores weapons. There should be a good supply there to help us." As she said it, a spark of excitement leapt through her. Yes, her tribe had abandoned her, but she was still so excited to reach their cache. What if someone she knew was there? What if she saw a friend? They were far from her tribe's home base, but it would still feel so good to connect with them. She'd hated them for years. She'd felt betrayed by being sent off to capture José, and then being left there for a decade, without anyone trying to rescue her.

But now that she was back, the thought of seeing her tribe was so exciting that suddenly, she didn't care anymore about the past. They were her family, her roots, and the most important thing in her life. Who was she kidding, that they could have rescued her? It would have been a suicide mission. It was so obvious now, but for years, she'd been so bitter that no one had come to save her, that they'd left her to such a horrible fate.

"Weapons?" He picked up his speed until he was walking next to her. "What weapons work against this guy? He's a Calydon, right? Talk to me about him. What do you know?"

His voice was clipped and intense, all business.

She shrugged. "Yes, he's a Calydon. His weapon is a scythe, but he doesn't fight with it much. He usually uses fire. He's an amazing warrior."

Zach shoved aside a branch blocking his path. "Tell me about the fire."

"He can generate flames. He can throw fireballs. He can ignite something a hundred yards away with just the flick of his finger," she said. An etching on a tree trunk caught her eye, and she stopped. Her heart leapt when she saw the double arrow carved into the tree. "Oh, my God," she whispered, placing her palm over the mark. "This is my tribe's mark. Someone was here." Tears suddenly filled her eyes for the loss of the family she'd once had. Why hadn't she seen any of them on her flight out of the jungle? God, she was so close to home, the home she'd left so many years ago.

She realized suddenly that Zach was studying her intensely. Embarrassed, she wiped the tears off her cheeks. She couldn't afford to be a weak female right now. She had to be the warrior she was trained to be, or José would defeat her, even with Zach on her side. "I'm allergic to this tree," she muttered. "It always makes my eyes water." She spun away, hurrying with renewed energy toward the cache. "Fire doesn't burn José," she said. "Sometimes he sets himself on fire and walks around, burning up anything he touches just for fun."

Zach didn't seem surprised by the information that José could set himself on fire. "Does water work on him?"

"A little won't do anything, but if you completely submerge him in a deep enough body of water that he can't burn off in time, yes, it'll shut him down." She noticed a well-worn path beneath her feet. It was so overgrown she hadn't noticed it before, but now she saw it. It was the trail of her people. She was on it! Excited now, she broke into a run, barely even noticing the branches slashing across her face.

Zach loped easily beside her, using his sai to cut them a path as they ran. "You don't happen to have an ocean with you, do you?"

She glanced over at him. "No. You?"

"Forgot it. So, we'll just have to fight him." He sounded

thoughtful, not overly concerned.

"We can't just fight him," she said. "We need the weapons in my tribe's cache—" They burst out of the trees into the clearing, and she gasped, falling to her knees in shock at the sight. "Oh, my God," she whispered.

She'd found her tribe. Every last one of them.

Or what was left of them.

CHAPTER 11

For a moment, Zach thought it was a festival of kites. More than a hundred white flags were hanging from branches high overhead, fluttering in the wind. On each flag were ancient symbols he didn't recognize, in different colors. Some had dozens of markings, most had several, and there were a couple that had only a single mark. On the ground in the center of the clearing, was a pile of white rocks, constructed into a pyramid with three red arrows jammed in the top of it, apparently straight through a rock.

Blue and yellow paint was streaked across the forest floor in frantic, random patterns, splattered across trees, and drifting on the surface of a small pond off to the left. Clearly, some sort of ritual or festival had gone on here. "What is it?"

Rhiannon didn't answer. She was on her knees, her fingers digging into the dirt as she stared up at the flags. He realized that there were tears streaming down her cheeks, and her face was white with shock.

His adrenaline kicked in, and he instantly called out his other sai in a crack and a flash of black light. "What is it?" This time, the question was different. This time, the question was tight and hard, laced with adrenaline. "What's wrong?"

"The banners," she whispered. "Each time one of our tribe dies, we hang a tapestry that details the events of her life. We honor her with a ritual that protects her soul in the afterlife. After we hang the banners, we use arrows to protect her soul. If she dies in battle, we bury her on site in honor of her sacrifice."

She stared up at the trees. "This isn't our burial ground," she whispered. "This is new. These are new graves."

A cold prickle began to slide down Zach's spine. "So, every flag represents a tribe member who died on this spot?"

"Yes." She stared up again at the flags. "So many," she whispered, her voice thick with tears she was fighting to hold back.

There was a sea of flags, but there were only three arrows. Someone hadn't been able to finish the rituals. He was willing to bet that the last survivors had been struck down as they tried to honor the fallen. "How many people were alive in your tribe the last time you saw them?"

"Just over a hundred," she whispered.

Together, they stared up at the fluttering white flags above them. Well over a hundred of them. No words needed to be said. They had all been here, and they were all gone. Given Rhiannon's skills, he was willing to bet she came from a tribe of highly skilled warriors, ones who were well versed in the jungle and its dangers. And yet, they had been utterly wiped out. "Who would hunt them like that?"

She looked over at him. "José," she said softly. "My tribe had been in this jungle for a thousand years. We were the protectors of the jungle from any enemy. When José came in, he was more than we could stop. So many died trying to defeat him that we retreated. He was wiping us out. There was a prophecy that one could stop him, that one girl would be his downfall." She held out her hand and pointed to a seven-pointed black star on her palm. "The tribe thought this mark meant it was supposed to be me. I was sent to stop him when I was sixteen. I failed. And now they're all dead." Her voice broke as she stared again at the banners, then she sucked in her breath as she stumbled to her feet. "Oh, my God."

"What?"

"That one's mine." She pointed to one with a few green symbols on it. "That's my life story. It stops when I was sixteen." She looked at him. "They must have thought I died right after I left the tribe. There's nothing after that." She shook her head. "No wonder they didn't come. They thought I was dead." She stumbled to her feet. "I have to finish the ritual. I need arrows.

I need to free them."

A prickle trickled down Zach's spine as she stepped forward into the clearing. "No!" He grabbed her arm and pulled her back.

"No!" She tried to twist out of his grasp. "Let me go!"

"Why is your banner here? You didn't die here. Wouldn't yours have been hung in your tribe's burial ground since they don't know where you died?"

She went still, staring at him. Then she spun around, searching the trees. He became aware of an eerie silence in the jungle. "There are no animals around us," he said quietly. "No insects. Everything has left this area."

Her hand went straight to her dagger, just as he would have expected from a warrior. "It's a trap," she said quietly. "For me. José knew I would go out there to finish the ritual."

"You think he didn't really kill everyone? That they aren't dead?"

"No, he definitely did." She shook her head. "Those are our banners. Someone in my tribe made them. I would bet that everyone did die here, and then José found mine and moved it here." She closed her eyes. "That means that he knows where our home is. Was." She looked at him, with heavy grief in her eyes. "If he found our home and was able to steal my banner, then there's nothing left of it. No one was left to defend it." She bit her lip, as if to contain emotions she didn't want to feel.

She looked up into the trees surrounding them, and he followed suit, searching for something out of place, like a sniper perched on a branch, a net ready to drop on them, or any other kind of trap.

He saw nothing out of the ordinary that was cause for alarm. "You see anything?"

She shook her head, still searching, just as he was. "He would want to trap me, not kill me," she said quietly. "He would want to detain me until he could get here."

He ground his jaw, trying to decide what to do. A part of him wanted to trigger the trap and get a sense of how powerful this fire god was. But he wasn't completely without a functioning brain. It was a fool's move to walk into a trap and have no idea what it would be. "We skip it. We go around."

"No." She pointed to the center of the clearing, just to the right of the pyramid of stones. "The weapons cache is in the ground out there. We need the weapons that are in there. Without them, we have no chance."

He shook his head. "No. Not worth it."

Rhiannon glared at him. "I understand that you have no clue how powerful José is, but I do. If you want to save Thano, then you better listen to me. We need those weapons, or else José is going to kick your ass, and you're going to die. And if you die, then Thano dies. So, stop being an overly macho jerk and listen to me. We need those weapons!"

Zach ground his jaw, but finally he inclined his head in agreement. "Fine. We'll get the weapons." He leveled his sai at her. "That was uncool to play the Thano card, though."

She used the tip of her index finger to point the sai away from her, almost managing to keep the smugness out of her smile. Almost. "Men are so easy to manipulate," she said. "All you guys want is to be the hero."

"On that one you're wrong." Zach eyed the clearing, trying to assess the best, most unpredictable way to access the cache. "Fuck heroes. I'm so done with that shit." He realized he hadn't kept the bitterness out of his voice when she shot him a surprised look. "A hero is a dumb shit who will betray those who count on him," he said, before she could ask. "Fuck heroes. Just fuck 'em. I tried to be a hero once, and my family died for it, so don't pull that card on me. Stay here. I'm going to get the damn weapons." Before she could protest, he gripped his sai and walked straight out into the clearing.

He made it almost all the way to the pyramid when all hell broke loose.

* * *

He heard it before he saw it.

An almost silent crackle and spark, barely audible. His skin prickled, and sudden heat plowed through his stomach, searing his flesh from the inside. It took a split second for him to register what he was feeling, because it had been so long since he'd felt it. *Fire from within.*

Then he felt a sudden pressure beneath his feet, as a

massive amount of energy surged through the earth. No, the fire wasn't from within. It was coming from below. The air suddenly became empty and barren, a complete void so dry that his lungs burned in protest. Jesus. There was no oxygen in the air. Holy crap. He knew what that meant. He used to make that happen. Fire was sucking oxygen out of the atmosphere. It had to be a massive fire to drain the air like that. *Massive.*

He was so shocked that for a split second, he couldn't move. It was as if he had been catapulted into the past, into a world that had once been his. It felt like his soul was lunging for what was coming for him. Every part of his body screamed for release, his need so strong that his cells felt like they were already on fire. *Yes—*

"I can't breathe," Rhiannon gasped from right behind him.

Her gasp jerked him from his stupor. "Fire's coming!" He spun around, scooped her up in his arms in one swift move, and bolted for the trees. The earth was searing hot, burning through the soles of his boots, and the air was utterly dead. The noise began to crescendo around him, a screaming, roaring fury as if they were already surrounded by flames.

But they weren't. Not yet. Where the fuck was the fire? He knew it was going to explode at any second, and it was going to rip the hell out of them. Rhiannon was gasping in his arms, her hands clutching her throat as she tried to suck oxygen out of the air that had been robbed by the fire.

And then he saw it.

Ahead of him, a faint golden light glowed beneath the earth, forming a ring all the way around the circumference of the clearing. Shit! The fire was coming up from beneath the earth! He put on a burst of speed and leapt into the air just as the flames exploded out of the ground, shooting straight up toward the sky in a fiery inferno. He tucked Rhiannon's head against his chest, using his body to shield her as the flames exploded past them. For a split second, they were trapped in the flames, surrounded on all sides, and then his momentum carried them through it.

He landed twenty feet past the flames, hitting the ground hard. Rhiannon spilled from his arms. She screamed, slamming her hands down on the flames licking away at her pants. He lunged for her, tackled her, and then threw himself on top of her, using his body to try to smother the fire.

The flames burned against his flesh, and it hurt like hell. Swearing, he wrapped himself around her, cradled her head, and rolled them both across the jungle floor, whipping them in a frenzied logroll across the earth. As he rolled, he tried to pull the flames into his own body and steal them from hers and from their clothes. It should have been easy and automatic to absorb the fire into his own body, but he couldn't do it. It was as if the flames were no longer a part of who he was. "Shit!" He whipped them into a faster roll, slamming them across roots and rocks until finally he could detect no more fire.

He rolled another few yards just to be sure, and then finally stopped. For a moment, neither of them moved. Rhiannon's arms were around him, her face was buried in his neck, and their legs were tangled together. He had one hand behind her head to protect it, and the other arm was locked around her waist.

They were both panting, and he could feel her chest heaving against his as she sucked in air. He lifted his head, and they looked at each other. Then, as one, they both turned to look toward the clearing.

The ring of flames reached at least two hundred feet into the sky. It was an impenetrable wall of fire, a prison from which she never would have escaped. The flames were orange, red, blue, and white. So hot, so fierce, so impressive. A flicker of envy went through him at the sheer magnificence of what José had created, but it was instantly chased away by the grim reality of what they were facing.

"No weapons for us," Rhiannon said. "We'll never get in there."

"No." Not only did they not have the cache of weapons she'd been so certain that they needed, but now Zach fully understood what they were up against. No weapons would defeat José, no weapons short of the fire that he commanded.

Even in his heyday, Zach wouldn't have been able to produce what José had created *without even being present*. Yeah, Zach had to admit he'd been pretty good. He'd been the kind of warrior who could erect a wall of fire strong enough to deflect a volcano, turn himself into a fireball, and use his fire to defeat Rohan. Not only had he been able to generate fire from within himself, but he'd been able to walk through a wall of fire for days and never so much as singe an eyebrow. Those skills weren't enough to defeat José, but at least he might have had a chance.

Over the last few centuries, he'd been aware that his fire capacity had been diminishing, but he hadn't really believed it was truly gone. He'd assumed it was just because he didn't want to use it, and that it was still there for him if he needed it, until the last few days when it had completely disappeared.

In that split second before the flames had erupted, he'd felt something inside him, something hot, something like the man he had once been. For that second, he'd had hope. He'd thought that facing death was going to bring it back to life.

But it hadn't.

Once he had been a fire warrior.

Now? He looked down at his arm, and saw that his flesh was blackened and disfigured, burned to a crisp from the fire.

Now, he was nothing more than a man who would burn.

They were in trouble.

Rhiannon moved in his arms. "José will see that fire," she said suddenly. "He'll be on his way here. We need to get out of here." She pulled out of his arms, and leapt to her feet. "We need to go."

He didn't argue.

She was right. They had to vacate, and fast.

Swearing, Zach broke into an easy run, keeping pace as Rhiannon ducked through the jungle, moving fast to get them away from where José would soon be. As they ran, a dark feeling settled on Zach. The man he needed was on his way to the fire right now, and what was he doing? Running away like a coward instead of facing him.

Except he wasn't a coward. He knew he wasn't. He was a warrior who knew when he'd been beaten, and he wasn't a fool. They could not defeat José. Not right now. To stay would be to fail, and he would not fail again.

But as he followed Rhiannon deeper into the jungle,

he felt an invisible noose begin to tighten around his neck, a familiar feeling he hadn't felt in centuries, not since the night he'd held his dead family in his arms and realized that there was no way to defeat the enemy.

Today it was a different enemy, but failure would have the same result: the death of someone he was supposed to protect. Something had to change, or Thano would die...and Rhiannon would become José's prisoner once again.

No. He could not allow that to happen.

But what the hell could they do against a force like that?

He knew what they needed. They needed his fire, and they needed it fast. The fact he couldn't so much as sneeze a spark?

Yeah, that was going to be a problem.

* * *

Jordyn didn't want to admit it. She really didn't. She prided herself on being independent, self-sufficient, and able to take on any challenge.

But there was no way to deny it. Faking it any longer was just not going to help her situation. With a sigh, she set down her backpack as Eric walked up to her. The man still looked fresh and spry after six hours of hiking, while she felt like her shoulders were going to break off and fall to the earth, forever decimated by the assault of the too heavy backpack.

"You find something?" Eric asked.

His deep voice rumbled through her with the same intensity that it had every time he'd spoken over the last six hours. She'd tried to ignore it. She'd tried to lie to herself. She'd tried to hum loudly to drown out his voice. She'd tried reminding herself that he was a flirt who was probably the world's worst boyfriend. Nothing had worked. The fact was simply that she thought he had the sexiest voice of any male she'd ever heard in her life. She just liked to hear him talk, and she'd been goading him on all day just to hear him respond.

"No." She plopped down on her backpack, giving up on asking her legs to hold her up any longer. "I'm lost."

"You are?" He looked around at the dense vegetation surrounding them. "That's odd. You seemed like the type who would be able to flawlessly navigate a billion acres of unfamiliar jungle without a map or a compass."

She eyed him. "I'm too tired, hungry, thirsty, and discouraged to deal with sarcasm."

"I'm not being sarcastic. I meant it." He settled his dark brown gaze on her. "You know you're impressive, don't you? You're sexy as hell, yeah, but you've got something else going on. If I were Rhiannon, I'd be damned glad to have you on my side."

She narrowed her eyes. "You're making fun of me." She waved her hand at the jungle. "I know that I screwed up. We're lost. I don't know where to find her. And I don't need you making me feel bad."

"Hey." Eric strode across the ground and crouched in front of her. He propped his forearms over his muscular thighs, which made his biceps flex. The man was solid muscle, and with his dark hair, dark eyes, and sculpted jaw, he was incredibly good looking. "Do I look like I have trouble attracting a woman's attention?"

Her cheeks flamed, and she jerked her gaze off his pecs, which were visible beneath his slightly-too tight gray tee shirt. "No," she said.

"Exactly. I could be a complete ass and still get pretty much any woman I want. So, why would I waste my breath complimenting you if I didn't mean it?" His eyes glittered. "I'll be honest with you, Jordyn. I'm not that poetry-writing guy I mentioned earlier. I have no tact. I have no use for pretty words. I say whatever's on my mind. Life is too short to play games, so I don't. If I say it, you can be assured I mean it."

Her heart fluttered at the raw intensity of his voice, and the depth of his stare. His gaze was boring into her, unflinching and unyielding. "So, you never lie? Is that what you're saying?"

He hesitated, then shook his head. "Nope. I'll totally lie if it serves my purposes. But that's different."

She blinked. "Different? How? You just said that you won't say it if you don't mean it, but then you said you'll lie if it serves your purposes. How do those work together?"

He looked at her as if she had two heads. "Because I like you. I wouldn't lie to *you*. I only lie to people who I don't trust. You're important to Tristan, you obviously care about him, and you're risking your life to save your friend. That's all I need to know about you. You're good. You don't get lies from me. Ever."

He said it like it was the most logical thing in the entire world, as if she were insane to think that there was even a remote possibility that she would get anything other than honesty and trust from him. It was his absolute conviction in the logic of his words that convinced her that he meant it. She could trust him. The realization sent relief cascading through her, and she even had an insane urge to smile. The man actually, truly thought that she was competent enough to traverse the jungle without a map or a compass and find Rhiannon without batting an eye? He did. And she liked it. "You're a little insane," she commented, finally breaking into a smile. "You do realize that, don't you?"

"Yeah, I do." He didn't move. He was still watching her, still crouching only less than a foot from her knees. He was so strong and physical, such an immense presence that he made the massive jungle seem cozy and intimate. "But as long as you get me, it's all good. You with me?"

She raised her eyebrows. "You mean, do I believe that every word you utter to me will be the absolute truth, and I can completely trust you, even though you're a total stranger and probably very dangerous to just about everyone you encounter?"

He nodded. "Yeah. Exactly. You with me?"

She grinned. "I think I must be as insane as you are, because yes, I think I'm with you."

"Awesome." He held out his hand. "Let's shake on it."

She regarded his hand warily. "Is this just an excuse to touch me?"

He broke into a grin then, a lecherous smile that seemed to light up his face. "Of course it is. I've been walking behind you all day, checking you out. I know you'd stab me if I made a grab for your ass, so I figured I'd start slow with a handshake and gradually lure you under my spell, until you beg me to rip off your clothes and make mad, passionate love until we're both too exhausted to do anything, except make love again." He nodded at his extended hand again, as if she might be too blind to see it hovering inches from her thigh. "So...shake on it?"

She knew he was trouble. She was well aware of the raw potency of his effect on her. She wasn't blind to the fact that he was determined to get her naked as soon as possible, despite the fact they were both in hot pursuit of people they cared about.

She was absolutely certain that touching him was the worst idea in the entire world, if for no other reason than because it was going to make him think that he had her right where he wanted her.

But she couldn't help it. The man was just too damned tempting. She wanted to shake his hand, and feel his fingers slide over her bare flesh. She wanted to feel the heat of his skin against hers. She wanted to let his strength wrap around her.

As much as she wanted all that, however, what she wanted even more was to never relinquish control to a man again. So instead, she leaned forward, so that her breasts were less than an inch from his fingertips. She held that position for a moment, watching his eyes darken and his jaw tighten as he fought not to look down and inspect her cleavage.

"Eric."

"Yeah?"

"The only one who will ever be begging for sex is you," she said.

For a moment, there was nothing but heated silence between them. Then a slow grin spread across his face. "I don't beg."

"I don't either."

His grin widened. "Then I guess we're never going to have sex."

"I guess not." The tension sizzling between them was electric. "So, we'll just have to go save Rhiannon and Tristan instead."

He didn't pull back. "We could do both. Fast sex. Save the day. More sex to celebrate the victory. We could fit it all in. An effective warrior knows that downtime is critical to keeping his...or her...edge."

"Then you'd have to beg, though." She held her breath, wondering if this arrogant, macho male would dare to drop his façade long enough to actually put her in charge. If he begged, what would she do? She'd be tempted. It had been so long since a man had ignited her interest like he did. He completely fascinated her.

He shrugged, a slow, sensual lifting of his right shoulder. "Would you be worth it?"

She bit her lip. "Probably not," she admitted. The man exuded sensuality as if he were made of it. There was no way she could deliver what he was used to, but it was pure, decadent fun to pretend.

His smile grew wider. "A challenge. I *like* it." He leaned forward until his mouth was almost touching hers. "One kiss, Jordyn. Just to see."

CHAPTER 12

She swallowed. "We need to find Rhiannon."

"I know we do." His lips were so close that they brushed against hers as he spoke. "I'm not actually going to have sex with you right now. Not until Rhiannon is safe. Not because I'm some moral guy, but because once I get my hands and mouth on your body, I'm not going to want to go anywhere else for at least a week. Maybe two. Fast sex would come later. I couldn't do a quickie right now, not with you. But I want a kiss. One kiss." She could feel his breath on her mouth. "I'm begging you, Jordyn. One lightning-fast, devastating kiss."

Her heart was hammering. "I don't kiss men anymore. I don't like men."

"Then that's convenient, because I'm not really a man."

She stared at him. "You mean, you're a Calydon?" She rolled her eyes. "Fine. I don't kiss Calydons. Men. Whatever. You fit both categories."

"Actually, I fit neither."

She nodded at the brands on his arms. "Then those are...what exactly?"

"Magic." He waved his hand over them, and they vanished, leaving behind unmarred flesh. "I lied to the guys I've been with for the last year." He moved his hand again, and they reappeared. "Nice, huh? Took me a while to get them right. I can even do the black light thing with my swords. It's good shit."

"Oh..." She looked at him with new interest. Not a Calydon? That made him infinitely more appealing. "So, not a

Calydon? And...not a man?" Instinctively, she looked down, and saw a large bulge in the front of his jeans. No, definitely a man. She looked back at his face. "What do you mean?"

"I mean..." His hand slid around to the back of her head, his fingers a sensual caress on the back of her neck. "I'm all male, but I'm so much more than what you think." Then, in a move so quick she had no time to resist, he pulled her against him and kissed her.

His mouth was hot. His tongue was decadent. His kiss was pure intoxication.

And she loved every single bit of it—

Cold metal suddenly pressed against her cheek. Her eyes snapped open, and she saw that they were surrounded by five hooded warriors holding swords. The tallest one had his sword tip against the back of Eric's head, and the others were all pointed at them...except for the one digging in to the side of her face.

She went still, her heart hammering when she saw the brands on the warriors' arms. *These* were Calydons. Holy crap. José? Had he snuck up on her while she was stupidly letting Eric seduce her? God, what an idiot she was!

"You left," the tallest one said.

"I did." Eric's hand tightened around the back of her neck, pulling her closer instead of releasing her. "If you don't remove that sword from this lovely woman's cheek, I will kill you all." His voice was pleasant, but edged with steel that made her body clench with absolute delight.

She couldn't deny it. She was a sucker for a man with a protective instinct.

The other warrior seemed to hear the same edge, because the sword was instantly pulled back from her face. With a rush of relief, she realized that this crew must have been the team that Eric had referenced, the ones he knew.

So, these guys weren't the enemy, and they weren't José. Relief rushed through her, and she started to pull back from Eric, embarrassed to be caught in a clinch with some man she didn't even know.

He shook his head and tightened his grip on her, as a slow, predatory smile curved his mouth. "Just so they know you're under my protection. This crew is so untamed that they need to know that."

"What are you talking about—?"

He kissed her again before she could finish the question. Not a quick kiss. A kiss just as decadent and thorough as the one before. Heat plunged through her, a mindless, searing heat that seemed to tear through every cell of her body. She was just sagging into his ridiculously strong frame when he broke the kiss.

He grinned at her. "That was fun. I like fun stuff like that."

She felt her cheeks heat up at his cheeky attitude. Dammit. She should have had more discipline than to succumb to his kisses. "Shut up." She finally managed to extricate herself from his grasp and turned to face the others.

The leader still had a sword pressed against the back of Eric's head, but since he wasn't concerned about it, she wasn't going to be either. She set her hands on her hips and surveyed the warriors. Five of them. All well-muscled, all wearing melodramatic black cloaks that hid their faces, all of them holding matching swords that made them look like some expensive striptease group. She had too much experience with Calydons not to be tired of their macho attitude. "It's old, guys. Really old. Just be normal."

Not a single one of them tossed back his hood.

Eric tossed his arm around her shoulder in a casual statement of possession, which she sidestepped quickly. He shot her an annoyed look, making her grin as she turned to the tall and silent crew surrounding her. "So, have any of you seen a woman with black hair wearing a red amulet? I'm looking for her."

The five warriors stared at her. Well, they appeared to be staring at her. It was difficult to tell with the hood-thing going on. Or maybe, they were just napping. Either way, no one was answering her.

Eric turned toward the leader. "I'm out, Rohan" he said. "I have somewhere else to be."

Rohan shook his head. "Not now. We need you."

"You always need me. I gotta go." He picked up his

duffel and swung it over his shoulder. "Let's go, sweetheart."

She ignored the endearment, and slung her backpack over her shoulder, staggering several feet when the weight of it landed on her beleaguered body. These guys weren't going to be any help, and if they weren't going to be useful, she did not want to be around them. She knew too much about Calydons to want to prolong her time with them.

"No." Rohan set his sword in front of Eric, blocking his path. "A warrior under my command is fighting for his life right now. No one leaves until he's safe."

Eric turned his head to look at him. "We can't do anything," he said quietly. "It's up to Zach. Taking down a fire god is outside our skill set, and you know it."

"No." Rohan stepped forward, his muscular thighs clad in some sort of black fur. "We have to try."

Jordyn cleared her throat. "Um, well, you guys have some stuff to work on, so I need to go." She began to back toward the jungle...then stopped when she realized she had no idea at all where to go to find Rhiannon. She still couldn't believe she'd lost Rhiannon's trail. She was usually so much better than that. "Does anyone know where a guy named José lives in these woods?"

Five heads turned toward her, and this time she was certain of it. "You know José? The fire god?" Rohan asked.

"Um..." His question had just a little too much edge to it to make her think it was casual. She glanced at Eric, wondering whether this was one of those truth times, or lie times. He shook his head slightly to indicate the latter. "No," she said. "No, I don't know a fire god."

Rohan laughed softly. "You're a poor liar. How do you know him?"

She bit her lip. "I want to play croquet with him."

Eric coughed.

Then she cocked her head at Rohan, suddenly thoughtful. "Why? Do *you* know him?"

Silence.

"Whoa." She turned around so she was facing him directly. "You do know him, don't you? Where is he?"

"He'll kill you," Rohan said.

A cold fear ripped through her belly. This was the man Rhiannon was going after? The one that Eric didn't think five Calydons could defeat? Oh, Lordy. "Then it's even more important that I find him," she said.

No one responded, but Eric was watching her with great interest.

Their macho silence infuriated her. "Dammit. I am so tired of Calydons." She dropped her bag and untied the bazooka from it. She turned and aimed at Rohan. "Tell me where to find him. My friend needs help."

Eric was grinning now.

"A gun won't hurt me," Rohan said.

"No, I know that. But the powdered demon bile in it will."

There was silence, and then all five of them burst out laughing. Apparently, they had no clue about the effect of powdered demon bile on Calydons. Too bad for them.

Eric, however, wasn't. He was looking decidedly interested. "You have powdered demon bile in there?"

"Yep. I got it in Parrish Creek. It's very expensive, but it works." She raised the gun and aimed it at Rohan. "Have you, by any chance, heard of the infamous Calydon Sir Walter Parker?"

Rohan went still. "The most powerful Calydon of the modern era. He destroyed a thousand square miles of outback before he was killed. He was unstoppable."

"Yes, he was." She smiled, absolutely refusing to let herself think of the night he'd died. "I was his *sheva,* and I'm the one who killed him. Powdered demon bile. It works. So put down your damn swords, because my friend's in danger, and I need to help her."

Rohan whistled softly. "That was you?"

"Yes, me."

"You're not dead. You should have killed yourself. That's what *shevas* do after they kill their rogue soul mates."

"I know. I'm not dead, and he is, so I have stuff to do." She kept her voice even, refusing to even contemplate all that she'd experienced since the first day she'd met Walter. "So, Rohan, do you want to help me, or do you want me to kill you? Your choice. I'm too tired to make any decisions."

"Can I see some?" Eric asked. "Do you have extra?"

"Of course. Why do you think my backpack is so heavy?"

Eric dove into her backpack and pulled out a silver canister. "This it?"

"Yes, but be careful." Yes, he wasn't a Calydon, but she didn't want him to spill it. She was saving it for José. She knew how much it had taken to bring down the man she loved, and the more she heard about José, the more she was beginning to worry that she didn't have enough. She glanced back at Rohan, and almost dropped the bazooka in surprise when she saw that he was down on one knee, as were all the others. "What are you doing?"

Eric went still beside her. "Holy shit," he muttered. "They're honoring you."

Rohan bowed his head, and the others followed suit. "Sir Walter was a great warrior," he said quietly. "It was his honor to be brought down by the woman he loved. You are welcome in my circle at any time."

Jordyn's throat tightened at his words. She knew that Walter had loved her, and she hated that their bond had destroyed everything they'd had. God, she *hated* that *sheva* bond. Slowly, she lowered the gun, her hands suddenly starting to shake. Eric carefully slipped it from her trembling hands, his brow furrowed. "I got it," he said quietly.

"I need to find my friend," she said. "That's all I need." She couldn't get Rhiannon's expression out of her mind, the look of fear when she'd said she was coming back to face José. She couldn't let Rhiannon go through what she'd experienced, especially since Rhiannon wouldn't have Tristan to help her through it. "If you can help me, please tell me."

Rohan didn't respond, and Eric put his hand on her shoulder. "I'm going with her," he said shortly. "If you know where this guy is, tell us."

"You will die if you go after him," Rohan said again.

Jordyn swallowed. She'd died before, and she didn't want to do it again, but she wouldn't let Rhiannon face him alone. "That's my choice, not yours."

Again, there was no response, and she became frustrated.

"Nevermind. I'll find a way." She turned around, startled when Eric handed over her backpack, as if he'd been simply waiting for her to turn around. He had already strapped her gun back in place.

"They won't help," he said simply. "They have issues."

She shrugged on the backpack, and her shoulders were screaming with pain almost immediately. Eric's eyebrows went up, and she turned away, refusing to let him see she was tired. "Let's go."

Eric fell in beside her as they headed past the group of Calydons, and into the darkening jungle—

"Wait."

She and Eric both turned at Rohan's command. "What?"

"Night is coming. You won't survive in the jungle at night. We would be honored to host you at our camp tonight."

She shook her head. "No, thank you—"

Eric touched her arm, and bent his head, so that only she could hear. "We should do it," he said quietly. "The jungle isn't safe at night, and I might be able to get a lead on José if we stay. Rohan knows more about him than he's telling us."

She looked up at him, unable to keep the worry off her face. "I don't trust Calydons anymore," she said. "I don't want to stay with them." She hated to admit it, but she had baggage with Calydons now. She'd seen how bad they could get when they turned rogue, and she still had nightmares of glowing red eyes hunting her.

"I know you don't. But to save Tristan and Rhiannon, it's our best option. I'll never leave your side, I swear."

She bit her lip and looked back at the hooded warriors. "They're creepy. I can't even see their faces."

"They're all skinny computer geeks. That's why they dress like that. No one would be scared of them otherwise."

She snorted. "They have awfully big muscles for skinny computer geeks."

"It's stage makeup. They're very talented at deception." Eric was so deadpan, that she couldn't help but laugh softly.

He was right. She wouldn't serve Rhiannon if she were dead, or spent the next twenty years of her life wandering through the jungle completely lost. "Okay."

He nodded. "Okay." He slipped his hand around her elbow, drawing her close to him. "We accept your invitation."

Rohan nodded, and as a single unit, all the warriors rose to their feet. "You will follow me."

Jordyn stiffened as the warriors flanked them, a tight group around them as they headed into the forest. Eric kept himself close, and she couldn't help but be grateful for his proximity, even if he was an arrogant womanizer who was too sexy for anyone's good.

"Rohan," he said suddenly, breaking the tense silence. "I *will* be leaving in the morning with Jordyn."

The taller warrior looked in Jordyn's direction, and said nothing.

Eric's fingers tightened almost imperceptibly around her elbow, and she realized that the morning exit might not be as easy as she'd hoped. Which was fantastic, because the pursuit of Rhiannon wasn't challenging enough on its own, without five overgrown flunkies trying to stop her. She would be so appreciative if they made it even more difficult to find one small woman in the middle of a jungle. Really. Such thoughtful guys.

Men. She could definitely live without them...and yet it appeared she was going to spend the night with six of them.

Because *that* was every woman's dream.

Not.

* * *

By the time Rhiannon had set up camp hours later, Zach had gotten nowhere.

For three hours after the fire, they'd hauled ass through the jungle, and he hadn't figured out a damned thing about how to get his fire back.

He'd tried igniting six different plants, and hadn't so much as given them a steam bath, let alone set them aflame. Nada. Nothing. Zilch. The big zero. None of which were going to be much help when they finally faced down José.

How the hell did he get his fire back? It was bad enough that he'd lost the essence of what defined him, but to know that Thano and Rhiannon were going to pay because he wasn't stepping up was weighing on him even more heavily.

He could practically hear the clock ticking, as Death rubbed his hands together, gleefully counting the hours until he added a couple more souls to his stable, souls that Zach could save with the snap of his fingers if he wasn't dropping the ball so badly.

With frustration mounting and obscuring his ability to think rationally, he'd finally abandoned his questions, sinking back into observation mode so he could figure out the best way to accomplish what he needed given their limitations. So, instead of playing with fire like he needed to be doing, he'd spent the rest of their trek observing Rhiannon and learning from her actions, as she'd led them relentlessly through the thick jungle, barely pausing to check her path. She was clearly at home in the woods, and already, he was learning the secrets of the jungle... but he knew it wouldn't be enough to take on José.

Like him, Rhiannon was edgy and tense, always looking over her shoulder. There was fear in her dark eyes, a grim awareness of the danger hunting them both.

And, to make matters even more complicated, he was discovering that there was a level of physical connection between them that was inopportune, inconvenient, and distracting as hell. He knew it wasn't one-sided, which made his own need even stronger. Several times, he'd moved close to Rhiannon during a particularly treacherous part of the jungle, and he hadn't missed the flashes of desire that crossed her face when his arm brushed against hers.

And that moment when he'd caught her arm when she'd tripped? She'd rewarded him with a tiny smile of vulnerability and appreciation before she'd pulled free. The woman was loaded with emotional baggage, and he found himself wanting to know every damn secret she carried.

He hadn't been able to stop thinking about her statement that the fire god was hunting her, a fact that had jacked up his adrenaline sky-high all day, ready for an attack at any moment. This was all wrong. He should be focused on the offensive, luring José to follow him so he could set a trap, but instead he'd been screwing up with his own fire, and obsessing over how he could protect the woman who was acting as his guide.

He needed to protect Thano, but somehow, someway,

Rhiannon had gotten under his skin and he needed to keep her safe as well. Rhiannon might be a warrior, but she also brought out his protective instincts, which he hadn't experienced in a long time. Last time he'd responded to a woman like that, the situation had been devastating.

Shit. He didn't need to go back there. He needed to focus on Thano, and not another woman again. But as hard as he tried to distance himself from his attraction to her, he'd stayed close behind her all day, ready to react if anything happened.

And now, after almost a full day of trekking through the jungle with her, and breathing in the delicate, feminine scent as it wafted behind her, he'd pretty much used up all his self-control. He wanted answers, he wanted fire, he wanted to focus on the mission, and he wanted his damned hard-on to get a life. At the minimum, he at least needed to get information about José and the jungle, but Rhiannon had been in no mood to talk, refusing to go into detail about José or what was going on.

Now that they were settled for the night at their campsite, however, he was going to get the answers he needed from her. There had to be a solution he'd overlooked. He just had to find it.

When she'd set up camp, Rhiannon had taken the same tactic as Rohan. She'd selected a campsite next to a river and had set up torches on the other three sides. By the time night fell, they were protected by fire and water. Rhiannon, however, was not settled.

She was pacing the perimeter, an arrow nocked in her bow as she searched the trees.

Zach watched her as he roasted the fish that she'd caught for their dinner. He'd been perfectly capable of catching a fish and setting up the perimeter, but he'd sensed that she needed to do it herself. She hadn't wanted his help, and she'd worked tirelessly, almost frenetically, as if she were trying to outrun something that only she could see.

"What's out there?" He tossed the question casually at her, but his body was taut and ready to fight if anything came after them. It was time to get answers, to slowly and carefully pull back the layers she was hiding beneath. "José?"

"Probably not José. He doesn't waste time hunting.

He'll have sent more of his team. Like the one you stopped from attacking me earlier today." She was moving easily, her body lithe and muscular, but there was a weariness to her frame that belied how relentlessly she had been pushing herself all day. "They hunt at night because it gives them an advantage if no one sees them coming." She glanced over at him, fear etched deeply in the lines of her face. "They like to create a sense of terror in the jungle. People fear them because they can't see them. Every morning when people get up, they count their family to see if anyone was taken during the night. No one fights them, because they don't even know what they are." She turned sharply, as if she'd heard something, and then relaxed again. "Most people in the jungle think that they are half-man, half-monsters. Only people like me know what they are—"

She cut herself off, as if realizing she'd said more than she'd intended.

Giving her a moment to think she had space, Zach turned the fish on the spit, studying her even as he kept his senses attuned to the jungle around them. He'd been assessing her all day, laying the plans to get her to talk. Why had she stopped herself from telling him more? Why was she so guarded? He wanted to know about her personally almost as much as he wanted to know about the fire god that could save Thano, and who was hunting her. "What are 'they?' Calydons like the guy hunting you? Or something else?" He thought of the fire he'd seen in the woods the previous night, and a grim sense of focus settled over him.

She didn't answer his question, instead resuming her pacing along the perimeter. "It was unusual for Luther to be out during the day," she mused aloud. "Why was he out there?" She glanced at Zach to see if he was listening. When she saw him watching her, she bit her lip, and fell silent, but it didn't take much for him to connect the things she wasn't willing to say.

"Luther?" he asked, though he was pretty sure he knew who she was referring to. "Who's Luther?"

"The man who tried to take me." She slanted a look at him. "The one you almost killed."

He raised his brows. "Almost? You don't think he was dead?" Yeah, granted, Luther's body hadn't vanished the way dead Calydons did, but the young ones always took a while to disappear. He replayed his strikes again, and shook his head. "It was a killing blow."

"No." She was quiet again. "He'll be hunting us again."

"Again?" He considered that. Though he'd been certain he'd finished Luther off, this was Rhiannon's jungle, and he wasn't going to discount her knowledge of their situation... but hell, if that hit hadn't killed Luther, they were up against some serious opponents. He turned the fish in the campfire, his jaw clenching as adrenaline simmered through him. He would be ready, and he would use tonight to get the information he needed from Rhiannon. "So you think he knew you were there. Or coming, at least. That's what you're wondering, isn't it? If he stumbled across you, or if he was already hunting you?"

She looked over at him, unable to hide the stark terror in her eyes, fear so deep that something primal and fierce roared to life within him. Instinctively, he rose to his feet, the need to protect her raging through him.

He understood her edginess. She didn't think it was a fluke that Luther had found her. She was pretty damn sure that José and his team already knew she was back, and that they were closing in on her. His brands began to burn in his arm. He'd already been highly focused on their surroundings, using his preternatural senses to sift through all the sounds and scents of the forest, but now he went on even higher alert. "Why? Why does he want you?"

She looked over at him, and for a long moment she said nothing. Finally, her lips parted, and he thought she was going to reply. Then she shook her head and turned back to her vigilant stance, but even as she stood there he could see her legs trembling and knew she was exhausted. How long had she been on the run? How long could she keep it up? He knew damn well that a warrior pushed beyond his limits was a warrior who ended up dead.

He strode over to her. "I'll take watch. You do the food and take a load off."

"No," she said, shaking her head. "We can't relax. Luther can get through this. They all can."

"What *can't* they get through?"

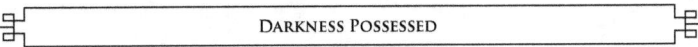

She shook her head. "Nothing—" she cut herself off, whirling around suddenly to stare out into the jungle.

Chapter 13

Zach eased up beside her, peering past her. "What is it?"

"There is one thing that could help," she said softly. Tentatively she let go of her bow with one hand and held her palm out toward the woods. Zach felt a shift in the air pressure immediately, as if it had come alive and was swirling around them. He tensed, readying himself to call out his weapons as the wind began to hammer at them.

Then the wind died as suddenly as it had begun, and she dropped her hand. "I can't do it," she whispered.

"Do what?"

She looked over at him, and he was shocked by the absolute exhaustion in her eyes. No longer did she look like the fierce warrior who had unleashed an arrow at his forehead. She looked like a woman who had been pushed beyond what she could handle. He moved closer to her, angling his body so he was between her and the trees. He reached for her shoulder, and then stopped himself when she jerked back, out of his reach, new fear flashing in her eyes.

Growling, he let his hand drop, anger fermenting inside him at the bastard who had taught her to be afraid of a man's touch. "What are you trying to do? What would stop them?"

She shook her head. "It's not going to work—"

"Tell me," he demanded. He could hear the forest coming alive as the night creatures awoke, and he knew damn well that Rhiannon was not up to another battle right now. He was all for a good fight, but with Thano's life at stake, he wasn't interested in jumping into a war that he didn't know how to win. Now was not the time to fight. Now was the time to go to ground. "What are you trying to do?"

She stared at him. "I can't—"

"Tell me!"

"Fine!" Anger flared in her eyes. "As I told you earlier, I used to be able to communicate with the vegetation in the forest. I was asking it to weave protections around us, but I can't do it! If I'm not focused, I can't do it, and I—" She shook her head, and all the fight seemed to drain out of her. "I can't do it when I'm scared," she admitted softly, shrugging her shoulders in a show of ultimate defeat. "Or tired, but especially scared."

He could feel what it had cost her to admit she was scared. For a warrior to admit fear was almost impossible. To allow fear to become so great that it affected one's ability to fight was the kiss of death, and he could tell that she knew it. Of course she knew it. Whatever else Rhiannon was, she was a warrior as much as he was. Something inside him softened at her vulnerability, and he had a sudden urge to pull her into his arms and promise her that he would take care of her.

He'd made that promise before to someone he'd loved, and he'd failed them. He would never make a promise like that again, no matter how badly he wanted to. Rhiannon should never truly trust him, not with her life. "We'll be okay," he said instead. "I won't sleep. I'll be ready."

She shook her head. "We won't survive the night out here," she said quietly. "Can't you feel the jungle's energy? The animals are carrying messages through the night. It will be only a matter of time before they find us." She turned away, reset the arrow on the bow, and faced the night. "I was such a fool to think I could come back here and win," she muttered.

Zach's eyes narrowed. "Fuck that," he said quietly.

She looked back at him, her eyebrows raised in surprise. "What?"

"If we die tonight, then there's no one left to save Thano. So, I said, fuck that. If you can save us, then you need to do it."

"Weren't you listening? I can't do it—"

"Yes, you can." He strode over to her and jerked the bow out of her hand, ignoring her squawk of protest. "Fear debilitates," he said. "So, you need to drop the fear, *now.*"

She stared at him. "What is wrong with you? It's not that easy to do—"

"You're a coward," he snarled, intentionally pushing her to the limit, trying to stir up enough anger to overshadow the fear. Anger was one of the few emotions powerful enough to trump terror. "You're going to let us die because you're afraid? What the fuck is that?"

She stared at him, and he saw the anger beginning to simmer in her dark eyes, and he knew he was choosing the right tactic for their survival. "I'm not a coward," she bit at him. "It's just that—"

"You're afraid. There's not a damn thing in this circle right now except you and me, nothing to hurt you, and you're sitting there like some fragile flower afraid of being crushed." He felt like shit riding her so hard, but he knew they had no choice. If she could save them, then she needed to do it. Hell, maybe he could get himself angry enough to make his fire come back as well. "What the hell is wrong with you?"

"Hey!" She spun toward him and shoved at his chest, her palm slamming against his shirt. "Shut up! You don't know what you're talking about!" Her fingers tightened around her dagger, and for a split second, he wondered if he had pushed her too far.

The last thing he wanted was another knife in his chest right now.

Then again, if it gave her back her connection with the plants, he'd take the knife. He knew what it felt like to lose a part of what defined you, and the knife would be a small price to pay to help her overcome her trauma.

Hell, he'd take a knife to his balls if it would give him back his fire to save Thano.

Well, maybe not to his balls...but then again, to save Thano's life?

That was a choice he hoped he was never going to have to make, but from the shocked look on her face, and the way her fingers were digging into his chest, he had a bad feeling that the knife in the chest was about to be repeated.

He stiffened, preparing himself to take the blow.

Whatever it took to save her and Thano, he was ready.

* * *

Rhiannon froze the moment she felt Zach's chest under her bare hand. Fear exploded through her, but at the same time, she couldn't make herself pull away. She just froze, one hand on his chest and the other suspended over the hilt of her dagger, overwhelmed by the sensation of touching him.

For a moment, she let herself be consumed by the feel of his body beneath her hand. His chest was warm. His muscles were hard beneath the softness of his shirt. Heat rose from his flesh, caressing her palm with a promise of passion and connection. It felt so intense and amazing that she didn't want to move. Ever. She just wanted to stand there and lose herself in the enormity of his being.

Her fear vanished, and her anger faded, until there was nothing left but the steady thud of his heart beneath her palm, and his marvelous scent wrapping around her. She looked up at him, and saw that he was watching her intently. She flushed at the heat in his gaze, and her throat tightened when she saw him glance at her mouth, as if he were as affected as she was. What if he kissed her? Would she still be afraid? Would she want to run away or stab him? Or would it feel amazing and wonderful, like the kisses she'd dreamed of as a little girl? Would it be that magic that enfolded her in a web of seduction and desire, so beautiful that it chased away all the darkness in her soul?

She wanted him, she realized. Not just for a kiss. She wanted him to slide her shirt over her head, kiss his way over her body, across her breasts, down her belly to her—

She gasped suddenly, stepping back in shock as she realized that her need to touch him felt just as strong as her compulsion to touch José had been when she'd first met him. Dear God, not again! She recoiled in terror, fighting to free herself from his spell. Instinctively, she went for her dagger again, but Zach grabbed her wrist. His fingers were like steel around her arm, and she jerked back, all anger forgotten, obliterated by the sudden crash of fear. "Let go of me—"

"No." He followed her movement as she pulled back, not fighting her retreat, but moving with her instead. He didn't release her wrist, and he didn't give her space. "You're going to deal with this now." His grip was firm, but his voice was gentle. "I'll help you. We'll do this together."

She barely heard his words as panic closed in around her. All she could think about was that she was trapped by him. "Stop it!" Terror began to bleed through her mind, shattering her focus. Suddenly, it wasn't Zach holding her. It was José, leering down at her, knowing that she had no chance to stop him or even refuse him. She lost all ability for rational thought and went into panic mode, striking out blindly with as much strength as she could muster. She heard the grunt as she made contact with flesh, then steel-corded arms closed around her, locking her down. "No!" The scream tore from her throat, an inhuman scream of terror that seemed to rip from her body, tearing all sanity from her. "Not again—"

"It's me." A low, male voice whispered against her ear, a voice that was devoid of the edge that had hurt her so many times. "It's Zach. I'm not going to hurt you, Rhiannon. You don't have to fight."

Zach? *Zach?* His words seemed to hover somewhere on the outside of her terror, but she couldn't process them. All she could think of was the arms around her, trapping her, holding her captive. Terror screamed through her, and she fought harder. She kicked. She punched. She scratched. She twisted. She did everything she knew, and still he held her tight.

"Rhiannon," he said again, his voice still quiet and calm. "I'm not going to hurt you. Let yourself see that. I swore to protect you, even if that means I have to protect you from yourself." Again and again, she heard that voice, a deep-male voice that never deviated from its non-threatening demeanor as he kept talking to her, but she knew she couldn't trust it, knew she couldn't stop fighting and fighting...and fighting...

Until she had nothing left to fight with.

Finally, agonizingly, she sagged in his arms, too drained to fight a second longer, exhausted. She was at his mercy. She squeezed her eyes shut, but a tear still slid out of the corner of her eye, a tear that revealed too much about the weak, vulnerable woman she tried so desperately not to be.

But his arms didn't tighten cruelly around her now that

she couldn't fight back. He just continued to hold her gently, securely enough that she couldn't break free, but not enough to hurt her, not at all. "Rhiannon," he said again, in that same gentle voice. "Look at me."

How many times had José demanded that? *Look at me, Rhiannon! You will see who owns you. Now!* She shuddered and closed her eyes tighter, trying to drown out that voice that haunted her so ruthlessly. Her body was shaking violently, drained of all resources by her useless, frantic battle for freedom. She could barely even stand up, but the fear still pounded at her, augmented by the realization that she didn't have the strength to fight back.

"Rhiannon." Again, Zach spoke. "It's safe now. Open your eyes and see who is holding you. Trust this moment."

Trust. *Trust.* That one word seemed to dive deep into her soul, ripping her away from the terror gripping her so tightly.

That was not a word that José had ever used. He didn't care about trust. He didn't even know what it was. It had been so long since she'd felt safe enough to trust, so long since she'd even registered that the concept existed, it felt like Zach's words had reached into the dark recesses of her being to pry free something that had once been a part of her. Something about the choice of that specific word seemed to crack the grip that the fear had on her. She finally began to grasp that this was different. Zach had made a request for her to face him. It had not been an order. *It was different.*

Slowly, she forced herself to open her eyes, and then instantly recoiled when she saw Zach's grim face inches from hers, in her space.

He didn't move, or release her, forcing her to face him. "It's me," he said softly. "I'm the one who saved you from the bad guy, remember?"

Again, the kindness in his voice touched a chord deep inside her, and the blinding fear began to abate enough for her to actually see *him* and not the monster in her mind. She stared at him, trying to drink in all that he was. His hair was short, but a little disheveled, and his cheekbones were defined, as if his face had been hardened by many battles. His eyes were dark and moody, and heavy whiskers lined his jaw, but there was a kindness about his visage that made her chest tighten. Maybe it was the wrinkles at the corners of his eyes, or the concerned furrow to his brow. She wasn't sure what it was, but there was no doubt that she sensed there was something good and humane about the man who was holding her.

Guilt echoed through her as she began to notice the injuries she'd inflicted upon him. There were several cuts on his brow bone, blood was trickling down his temple, and he even had a black eye. She'd done all that to him, and he'd never struck back. Not once. Not one spot on her body was throbbing or aching, and she knew that somehow he'd absorbed all her blows and contained her without inflicting so much as a bruise upon her.

She swallowed, suddenly wanting to touch his damaged flesh and take away the pain she'd caused him, but her hand fisted at the thought. Never could she bring herself to touch him voluntarily, and why would she? He had to be angry with her for hurting him. The thought sent a ripple of tension through her as she realized a reprisal would be coming, but before she could react, he spoke, but not about what she'd done to him.

"Don't let him win."

His words were simple, so simple, but something about them struck deep into her heart like an arrow honed to a razor sharp edge. *Don't let him win,* as if there was really a chance she could defeat José, not just in the end, but in this moment. As if there was a way to purge him from her mind and her soul and free herself from the damage that she felt she could never escape. God, was there really a chance? Her lungs suddenly expanded in a deep inhale of shaky relief, the air shuddering through her. Her legs went numb, and she sagged to the ground.

Zach eased down with her, crouching beside her as he set her gently on the floor of the jungle. His eyes were riveted to hers, and there was no aggression there. None at all. Just concern. He was still holding her, but for some reason, his arms didn't feel as threatening anymore. She was actually experiencing an almost unrecognizable sense of safety, as if those huge muscles were weapons at her disposal that she could launch at any enemy who tried to get her.

"Can you focus on me for a second?" Zach asked, a low

urgency in his even tone.

Focus on him? All she could *do* was focus on him. He was tremendous in his physical presence, and in the way he took over her personal space. He was invading her senses on all levels...but not creating fear. "Yes, I can focus on you."

She suddenly realized that she had, at some point, wrapped her fingers around his wrist and was holding tightly... not to try to contain him and keep him from hurting her, but because she didn't want him to go away or leave her. She was shocked by the realization that *she* was holding onto *him*, yet, even as she realized it, she tightened her grip on him, her instinct to keep him close triumphing over her instinct not to touch him.

He didn't pull away, or even comment on her tight grip. He just stayed as he was. "You said you can manipulate vegetation," he said. "How would you use it to protect us?"

His question made reality come crashing back, and her gaze skittered past him to the torches burning so brightly. How soon would José and his team arrive? Did they know where they were even now? Her heart began to pound, and she tensed. "I—"

"No." His fingers slipped beneath her chin and gently directed her gaze back to him. "Focus on me. You know I won't hurt you, right?"

For a long moment, she didn't respond. Did she really *know* he wouldn't hurt her? *Really?* Of course she didn't. Trusting a man was like baring your throat to a wild beast. They might appear to be harmless, but the animalistic nature that lurked beneath the surface was never gone. They were constantly treading the edge of control, always ready to turn into the predator they were born to be.

"Rhiannon? Do you understand that I won't hurt you?" His thumb swept across her chin, a simple movement that was so tender that it seemed to eradicate all rational thought, leaving her only with the pounding of her heart and the sensation that she was in the presence of something so beautiful and powerful, something that would gift her only with protection and never with harm. The feeling was so intense and real that, incredibly, she felt herself nodding in affirmation of his statement.

Even as she acknowledged her trust for him, she didn't understand why she was doing it. How could she trust him? She knew better than that. But he'd saved her life. He'd let her attack him. He'd protected her. He'd had every chance to show himself as the predator that she expected him to be, but he simply wasn't. "Yes," she whispered, this time with more conviction. "Yes, I do think that I'm safe with you." Simply saying the words was such a relief, an incredible sensation of finally letting down the steel walls that she'd been surrounding herself with for so long, as if she didn't have to stand alone and fight anymore. She couldn't believe how good it felt.

He smiled then, a smile that seemed to light up his grim face. He looked so much younger, handsome even, that her heart actually skipped a beat. "You know that I kicked Luther's ass, right?"

She almost smiled then. "You stunned him," she clarified.

He shrugged. "I still kicked his ass, which means that if he comes catapulting through these torches right now, I can do it again and give us time to get away." His fingers tightened on her jaw. "So, what that means is right now, in this minute, you're safe. Got it?"

She shook her head, sobered by his lack of understanding of exactly how daunting the enemy hunting them was. "More will come—"

"Are they here yet?" he demanded.

"No, but—"

"Are they here yet?" he repeated.

She narrowed her eyes at him. "No." He was pushy and demanding, but for some reason, his demeanor didn't scare her. It was different from José and his team, aggressive, but not threatening.

"Then, in this exact second, is there anything to be afraid of?" he pressed on relentlessly.

She sighed, her rational mind finally accepting the point he was trying to make, the point that she could have been able to get to on her own if she had been a fraction of the trained warrior she had once been. "No, there isn't."

He nodded. "In that case, there's no reason why you can't focus, do your plant magic, and whip up something that will keep us safe tonight, is there? You focus on that, and I'll unleash my worst and kill anything that tries to cross the border while you're at work. Deal?"

He would protect her. She took a deep breath, and let his words settle into her bones and muscles, allowing his strength to begin to uncoil the tension from her body. As she did so, she instinctively tightened her grip on his wrist, needing to connect with the man who was rebuilding what was left of her broken soul. She could feel the hard bones of his wrist, and the steel cords of muscle beneath her fingers. He was sheer, raw strength, but his skin was soft and warm, like hers, an unassailable reminder that he was a living creature, not a monster.

A monster. The mere word sent a chill down her spine, and the image of José flashed into her mind. Instantly, she tensed again, and fear dug its sharp claws into her heart again.

Zach's eyes narrowed, as if he could sense her sudden apprehension, then he leaned forward until his lips were beside her ear. His breath was warm against her skin, sending shivers down her spine as he whispered to her. "I know you're a warrior, Rhiannon. You have strength that you've forgotten, but I *know* that you can do this. You're not alone, never alone, not anymore. I'm with you, and I know you can do it. I'm counting on you, Thano's counting on you, and *you* are counting on you."

She closed her eyes as his voice seemed to caress her, letting it fill her with a power that seemed to infuse strength into her depleted muscles, and courage into a heart that was long broken. Slowly, needing to touch him and access what he was giving her, she raised her hand and laid it against the side of his neck. She felt him tense as she slid her palm around the back of his neck, pulling him closer to her until their cheeks and foreheads were touching. The intimacy was exhilarating and intoxicating, and heat seemed to burn through her flesh. She became viscerally aware of his arms, realizing that one of his hands was on her hip, and his other arm was locked around her lower back from when he'd gone to the ground with her when she'd collapsed.

Slowly, unable to stop herself from basking in the scent of his being, she turned her head toward his, her lips sliding over the roughness of his whiskers until they reached his mouth. She didn't kiss him, but their lips were touching, burning heat through her soul. Her heart hammered through her, and she knew that if he made one move to kiss her, she would panic. She went still, every part of her soul yearning for him not to betray her and shatter the desire burning through her. Was he going to move? Or was he going to let this moment become something that she'd been craving her whole life?

CHAPTER 14

Zach didn't move. He simply went utterly still, as if they had become two statues made of flesh, entangled in a position of burning desire that would never be satisfied.

She closed her eyes and inhaled his scent. It was a mixture of sweat mingled with the freshness of the jungle and something deeper and more primal. It swirled through her belly, tightening her muscles with desire that sent a ripple of fear through her, but when he remained utterly still and made no move to capitalize on the yearning that she was sure he could sense, she was able to relax. She focused entirely upon him: the heat of his body everywhere they touched, the weight of his hand on her hip, the seductive temptation of his mouth against hers. Her blood surged through her, ignited by the desire he was stirring up, and she allowed it to build inside her, becoming stronger and stronger.

Zach sucked in his breath, and his fingers tightened on her hip, but other than that, he showed no reaction to the heat growing between them, as if he sensed that any response would destroy what was happening.

The need for him grew stronger, pulsing through her, and her heart began to hammer. It felt like an eternity since she had tapped into her power this way, and she was stunned by the pulsing energy beginning to build inside her. Anger was powerful, but raw, sexual desire had a power of its own. It was pure energy that drew its force from the utter capitulation of the mind and soul, and the absence of conscious thought to clutter it.

Her skin began to feel hot, and adrenaline raced through her, excitement at the forces amassing inside her. It had been so long since she'd felt so bold and in touch with who she was. She slid her hand from the back of his neck up through his hair, entangling her fingers in the soft strands until she was gripping him tight, holding him even more securely against her.

He let out a small groan that plunged right into her core, and his hand slid lower on her hip, palming her as his mouth shifted ever so slightly against hers. Not a kiss, just a move that sent sparks exploding through her. Her fear was gone, completely obliterated by the desire building inside her, burning through her very flesh.

The need to kiss him pulsed through her, an almost overwhelming urge to break the tension being held so tightly between them, to unleash the energy vibrating within them both—

"Thano," Zach whispered against her mouth. "Remember Thano needs our help."

His voice was taut with lust so thick that it made her belly clench, but Thano's name was enough to help her regain her tenuous control over the need for him that was crawling over her skin like a temptation that would never be satisfied. Gripping his hair even more tightly, she pried her hand off his wrist and held her palm out toward the jungle. *Help me.* She sent the plea out to the jungle that had once been her home, to the plants that she had played with as a young girl, to the vines that had hung there uselessly, unable to protect her when she'd been caught in José's thrall and unable to bridge her connection to them.

No longer were they a distant memory of a partnership that had once been real.

The sexual tension amassing between her and Zach exploded into the night, plunging into the vegetation surrounding them. The air crackled with energy as the plants rejoiced over her return, and she felt the earth lurch in response. Wind exploded around them, making their clothes flap ruthlessly under the onslaught as the earth churned in response. The night filled with the howls and chirps of the plants as they crawled across the soil toward them, coming alive at her invitation.

Zach lifted his head and started to pull away, leaving behind a cold void where he had been. Instantly, her energy faltered and the wind began to die down. "No!" she cried as she pulled him back. "Don't! I need you!"

His eyes flashed with darkness as he turned back toward her. "I'm running out of willpower," he said, even as he slid his hands back around her. "I'm the good guy, but I'm not made of ice."

She swallowed as she reached for him, needing to pull him close. "Just don't scare me," she whispered, knowing that she was asking almost the impossible from him. What man had the self-control to do what she was asking? To hold her so intimately and yet not make a move on her? Even as she thought it, she began to tense, and the plants began to quiet.

He swore under his breath and hauled her onto his lap. His eyes were blazing fiercely as he palmed the back of her head, forcing her to look at him. "I would *never* betray your trust," he said. "*Never.*" Then, before she could say anything, he bent his head and kissed her throat.

The feel of his lips on her bare flesh sent a shock of sensation catapulting through her. She gasped and shuddered, gripping his shoulders as he trailed gentle, tantalizing kisses over her collarbone. His arms were around her back, supporting her even as he bent her back to give him better access. "Do it," he growled. "Focus on your plants. I swear that I won't so much as breathe on your breasts unless you beg me to do it, and even then, I might refuse, just to piss you off."

Relief rushed through her, and she closed her eyes, surrendering to the incredible sensation of his lips on her flesh. Desire crackled through her, a passion so intense that every muscle in her body tightened. She turned it outward, once again, thrusting it into the night.

The plants roared to life, and the night howled with the fierce energy of the vegetation. She felt the strength of the earth and plants rushing through her, cleansing her body of all the filth that had been fermenting inside her for so long. Adrenaline filled her and she sent out more power into the night. *I need a wall! An impenetrable fortress!* The night filled with the hiss of plants rushing along the earth, climbing over each other, and tangling their leaves as they rushed to do her bidding. Elation filled her as the wind grew even stronger. The ground shifted beneath her, and she relished the power of the earth as it flooded her body.

Now! There was a final burst of energy and a loud snap, as if a tremendous door had been slammed shut, and she knew without even opening her eyes that they were surrounded by a thick wall of vines, a barrier that would hold against any invader, a barrier that would hide their scents and sounds from even the most refined hunter. They were completely hidden, even in the middle of José's territory.

There was one final crash of the last plant slamming into place, and then the crescendo went silent, leaving behind nothing but the sound of her breathing, and the quiet hum of plants at peace. The wind faded into stillness, and all the power that had been rushing through her faded away...leaving her drained, exhausted, and suddenly aware that she was flat on her back with Zach's full body weight on her, his rock-hard erection pressing into her belly as he trailed kisses over her throat. Her hands were on his shoulders, her fingernails digging into him as if she had been trying to pull him closer. Her legs were around his hips, and her feet were locked behind him, as if she'd tried to trap him between her legs.

She froze, shocked by the realization that she was pinned beneath him, completely trapped, horrified that she had been so caught up in her plants that she hadn't even noticed it happening.

But before she could become afraid, a deep, powerful burning desire swept over her, a need for this man that was so intense that nothing else mattered. Her fingers involuntarily dug into his shoulders, and her legs tightened around him, and she realized that he hadn't pinned her to the ground against her will. She'd dragged him down with her, and the only thing that had kept their clothes on was his sheer strength of willpower. He could have violated her in a thousand ways, and she would have let him, but he hadn't.

And that fact made her entire body clench with longing and need so stark and raw she felt like her soul would break if she didn't have him.

Zach suddenly went still, as if he'd sensed the change in her.

Slowly, he raised his head to look at her. The lust burning in his eyes made her suck in her breath, and her heart began to race. After years of being terrified of being touched or kissed by a man, suddenly all she wanted was for Zach to kiss her. Not just a kiss. The kind of kiss meant to sear her soul and rip away all the damage that she'd carried for so long.

Her fingers began to tremble, but she didn't let go of his shoulders. She simply met his intense gaze. "Kiss me, Zach," she whispered, her voice trembling. "Kiss me now."

* * *

Eric liked her.

He sat on a patch of dirt, watching Jordyn as she strolled around the perimeter of Rohan's camp. She was edgy and tense, and had opted for takeout with her stew instead of sitting around the campfire trading stories. She'd finished her dinner on her second circuit, and he'd accepted the bowl from her as she'd passed him by.

The others were all watching her as well, and he knew they were not used to having a woman in the camp. Rohan and his team were uncivilized, raw, and stayed as far away from women as they could, except for the occasional foray into a town for a night to relieve the typical Calydon lust. Having Jordyn strolling around their camp as if she owned it was interfering with their solitary maleness.

Eric, however, was thoroughly enjoying watching her take inventory of the camp. He respected Rohan's crew, but enduring the hard, deprived life wasn't his style. He was damned happy to have a woman around, even one who gave him a lot of shit. In fact, he kind of liked that aspect of her.

Jordyn suddenly stopped at the far end of camp, near the black pit that hid Thano and the other rogue warrior. "What's in here?"

Again, silence. Every question she'd asked had been ignored by Rohan and the crew. "Jesus, guys. Be a little more rude," Eric said aloud. "You did invite her."

Again, no reply.

Bunch of chumps. Nothing much about this crew bothered Eric, but their absolute silence around Jordyn was beginning to grate on him, though he had to admit the others were probably asphyxiating under their hoods, which they usually wore only in battle to hide their true identity. Having Jordyn among them meant they couldn't drop the secret identity thing, which he found sort of amusing. Who the hell cared who they really were? "It's where Rohan keeps the rogues that are waiting to be saved," he offered. "He has them tied up and—"

"Enough!" Rohan was suddenly on his feet. "She doesn't need to know."

"Rogues?" Jordyn suddenly looked wary. "Why aren't they dead?"

"Because they're good warriors," Rohan snapped. "I don't kill rogues unless I have to. That's not my mission."

"No?" She turned back to face him. "What is your mission? Aren't you Order?"

Eric raised his brows. "How the hell did you know that?" Even he hadn't realized they were Order of the Blade until six months into his time with them. All the warriors were Order of the Blade, but they weren't like any of the Order he'd heard about over the years. Not once had they gone after a rogue Calydon, like the traditional Order was supposed to do.

No, they went after other shit. Darker shit. Monsters.

"Because I was the *sheva* of one of the most powerful Calydons in history," she said simply. "I paid attention." She studied Rohan, and then looked around at the others. "What is your deal? Seriously? There's so much melodrama here, I could choke on it, but you guys aren't doing anything but sitting around. I thought Calydons were action guys, not the kind who dwell in introspective silence."

Eric grinned at the rise in tension as she challenged them. "They're afraid of the fire god," he offered.

"I'm not afraid," Rohan snapped, apparently unwilling to hold his silence in the face of an accusation of fear. "I'm a smart warrior, and—"

"Are you?" Eric stood up. "You sent Zach off by himself. Did it ever occur to you that maybe he could use some backup?

He sets the fires, and you do other shit?"

"Zach?" Jordyn walked toward them, clearly pleased she was finally getting some response from Rohan. "Who's Zach?"

"The poor bastard Rohan sent off to try to get the staff from the fire god to save his team. He's holding the guy's best friend hostage until he gets back."

Blue lightening crackled from Rohan's fingers. "I liked you better when you weren't being an ass," he snapped.

Eric blinked, surprised by the normalcy of Rohan's sentence. The warrior was usually formal and proper, never hinting at his emotions, but that one line had been spoken like a man who was alive and cared. Around them, he felt the other warriors shift, as if they, too, were surprised by this change in Rohan.

Jordyn strode across the clearing and stood in front of Rohan. "You sent another man off to save yours? What kind of leader does that? You hide behind a cloak and—"

"Enough!" Rohan snapped, spinning toward her.

"Hey." Eric leapt between Jordyn and Rohan, holding up his hands. "Let's everyone chill. There's no need to kill anyone here." His fingers hummed with magic, and he let it roll through him, willing to intervene if necessary. He doubted he could kill Rohan, but he could do enough harm to let him and Jordyn get away. The damage, however, would be unpredictable, and he had learned to save his strongest magic for a last, very last, resort.

Rohan spun away and stalked across the clearing, standing with his back toward them.

Silence fell over the campsite, and Jordyn looked at Eric with a small shrug. "Sorry," she said. "It just makes me mad when I see people who have the ability to help, but won't do it. I feel like everyone who is in a position to help someone else has an obligation to do so."

Ah...he was beginning to understand. "Which is why you are here to help Rhiannon?"

She nodded. "Her soul mate is a bad man," she said. "A woman bound to a jerk is in a very rough spot. No matter how awful a man is, it's hard to sever the ties with him once an emotional bond is created. I know that, and her ex is..." She grimaced. "Bad news. I need to help her." She sighed, glancing back at Rohan. "It's so sad when someone as powerful as he is refuses to use that power to help."

"I do help." Rohan didn't turn around. "I do what I can, but I'm bound by limitations."

Eric raised his brows at the unusual confession from the stoic leader. "What limitations?"

Rohan didn't answer. Of course he didn't. Jordyn's influence could go only so far to make the man human. But just as Eric was turning away, Rohan whispered softly, so softly that he could barely hear the words. *"They have her."* Rohan's lament was like a whisper on the breeze, so faint it drifted away before the words had even taken shape.

Eric stopped, uncertain that he'd heard right. "Who has her? And who is the woman being held?"

Rohan's shoulders shuddered, and then he turned back to face them, his face still shrouded behind the cloak. "I do what I can," he said quietly. "I do *all* that I can."

Then he turned and strode past them, into the darkness that held the two rogues.

Silence fell upon the campfire, with Rohan's team sitting in silence. Eric looked at the warriors. "Does anyone know what he's talking about? Or *who* he's talking about?"

For a moment, no one spoke, and then Ethan pulled back his hood, not bothering to hide his silver hand from Jordyn. His ragged blond hair tumbled down around his shoulders, and he fastened his blue gaze on her. His jaw was heavy with whiskers, and the fluorescent lime-green of his tee shirt was barely visible above the neckline of his cloak. "You were really Walter's *sheva?*"

Jordyn nodded, not commenting on the sudden revelation of his face. Eric was a little surprised, however. He wondered what it was about Jordyn that Ethan had decided to trust. He wasn't sure he liked it, to be honest. There didn't need to be any bonding between Jordyn and other men. Seriously. There really didn't.

"You killed him?" Ethan asked.

She nodded again, but Eric saw her shoulders stiffen, belying her casual stance. He thought of what she'd said about Rhiannon, how difficult it was for a woman to break free of a man she was bound to. He wondered what she had endured with

Walter.

"Was it hell when he died?" Ethan asked.

She bit her lip, and Eric walked over to her and set his hand on her shoulder. "Of course it was," he said softly, sparing her the need to respond to Ethan's question. "She killed her soul mate. What do you think that was like?" Everyone at that fire knew of the *sheva* destiny, that she would kill herself after she killed her rogue mate, because the anguish of his death was too powerful for her to survive.

Ethan nodded quietly, and his shoulders relaxed, as if he'd decided that he could trust Jordyn. "Back when I first joined the team, Rohan used to talk at night in his sleep," he said. "He spoke of a woman. He never said her name, but he called to her. It's like he's searching for her, and can't ever find her." He looked at Jordyn. "I've been with Rohan for over two hundred years, and you're the first one who has ever gotten to him. What is it about you?"

As he spoke, Eric saw the others take down their hoods. Zane Hart with his shaved head and row of black diamond earrings in his left ear. Maddox Crowley with his gray-flecked crew cut and matching goatee. James Wolfe with his pale blue eyes that seemed to drill straight into the heart of anyone he looked at. Ethan Lagat, with his silver hand that could do shit Eric still didn't believe was possible. And lastly, slowly, as if not convinced that Jordyn was worthy, Axel Knight eased back his cowl, revealing the white blond hair, pale flesh, and stark complexion of a man without a soul.

Eric was shocked at the sight of all of them exposing themselves to someone outside the team for the first time since he'd met them. He glanced at Jordyn, stunned by the response she was evoking in this stoic, hardened team of loners who had never acknowledged even the slightest bond between them.

She looked around at them, her face softening in the flickering firelight as she took the time to really look at each man, honoring him with her attention. Eric watched each warrior sit taller, as if emboldened by her attention. Was it Jordyn herself affecting them like that, or the fact she was the *sheva* of a warrior they had all heard so many heralded stories about?

Personally, with his limited knowledge of Calydon

lore, Eric had never heard of her ex, which meant that his own fascination with her was entirely Jordyn herself...which stumped him. Women didn't impress him. Women didn't interest him. At least, not the way Jordyn did.

"I think," she said softly, as if she'd spent hours contemplating Ethan's question about why Rohan was reacting to her, "that I am the first person he has met who isn't afraid of him. I see him as a man, not as a warrior, and that's different for him." She looked at all of them. "I see all of you the same way."

As she said it, Eric realized that she was right. She didn't look at Rohan like he was some god. She gave him attitude. She stood up to him. But at the same time, she was so compassionate about Rhiannon that her softness made him want to be a better man, for her. Soft and tough. A dynamite combination.

She walked over to the fire and knelt next to the flames, finally stopping her restless pacing. "I was the soul mate of a warrior so powerful he could have destroyed the earth if he'd chosen, and yet, beneath that visage was simply a man. A man who loved me." She held her palms out to the fire, as if absorbing the heat into her body. "After that, every Calydon I met was simply a man." She smiled. "Most of them are complete jerks, I'll be honest. Very few warriors have retained enough humanity to make them admirable, but even those...they are simply men."

Her words fell over the campfire, settling into the grooves of the silence, filling the gaps with something real. Something humane. Something laced with the faintest hint of irreverence surrounding the legend of their kind.

"You're right, you know," Eric said, breaking the silence. "Most Calydons are shits." He grinned as the other warriors glared at him. "But not these guys," he added, after a deliberate pause. "These guys got it going on." He meant it too. He'd never seen a crew so brave and willing to sacrifice for what was right. In the year he'd been with this team, four Calydons had already died fighting the monsters they hunted, and yet the remaining ones never faltered in their commitments. "You can trust them."

Jordyn smiled at him, her face softening. "You're going to miss them, aren't you?"

He cleared his throat. "Shit, no. I got more important stuff to do than mourn for guy time." He winked at her with just enough lustful deliberation to make heat rise to her cheeks. "You know. Got stuff to do."

"Shut up," she said, but her voice was tinged with laughter.

He grinned just as Ethan cleared his throat. Eric and Jordyn looked over at him. The warrior was hunched forward, his muscular arms braced on his thighs, his cloak shoved up around his hips to reveal well-worn jeans and heavy black boots. He stared into the fire, a dark look on his face that made him look more like a venomous raptor than the good guy Eric had just claimed he was. After a moment, Ethan looked up, his gaze going slowly and defiantly around the circle, daring anyone to interrupt what he had to say. "Gloria."

That was it? Gloria? What the hell did that mean?

CHAPTER 15

Eric glanced around the campfire, and saw that everyone was staring at Ethan with the identical stoic expressions, and he knew that not one of them had a clue what Ethan was talking about. "Who's Gloria? An ancient battle or something?"

"No." Ethan met his gaze. "I had a pet rabbit once," he said, daring anyone to defy him. "Her name was Gloria."

All the other warriors stared at him. Eric blinked. "What? Did you just say you had a pet rabbit named Gloria?" Surely he'd heard wrong, or that was some code phrase warning them that he was about to attack or something. Right?

Ethan shrugged. "I've been running around for two hundred years chasing monsters." His blue eyes flicked toward Jordyn. "I haven't sat and talked to a woman since before then. I never sit. I don't want to sit. But..." He ran his thumb absently over his brand, caressing the blade of the sword that had defined his life. "Jordyn reminds me of what life was like before this, so yeah, I admit it. I had a rabbit when I was a kid. She was white. She slept on my pillow, and she had the cutest damn fluffy tail you've ever seen."

"No shit?" Wolfe asked, his blue eyes looking even paler than usual as he stared at Ethan like he'd lost his mind.

Ethan held out his arm. "I got a tattoo of her." He pulled back his cloak to reveal a black drawing on his biceps. "I know it looks like a skull, 'cause you know, I couldn't have a bunny on my arm, but when I bend my arm like this, see? It's Gloria."

"Damn." Wolfe leaned over to inspect it. "I had no idea.

You told me it was the skull of the first guy you killed."

Ethan pulled his sleeve down. "You guys tell anyone, and I'll kill you."

"Word." Wolfe hesitated, and then spoke up. "I actually like the smell of flowers," he muttered. "It's pretty cool."

Eric stared in shock. "Flowers? You said the roses remind you of the blood that spilled across your mother's body when she was murdered by your dad. That's why you always have that rose shoved into your back pocket when we go into battle. Because it provides motivation."

Wolfe shrugged. "Yeah, well, they do, but they still smell good, right? Hyacinths are my favorite. Damn, I like that shit."

Eric sat back, listening in shock as Maddox then spoke up, as if all the warriors were desperate to take advantage of this opportunity to simply be a regular guy, and not the lethal, ruthless warriors they had to be all the time. "I still remember my first kiss," he said. "I was fourteen. She was the baker's daughter. Almost got thrown into the bread oven by her dad when we got caught, but yeah, her lips are still the softest thing I've ever felt in my life."

Ethan nodded. "Women's lips are like that. Soft as hell."

"No shit," Wolfe said. "You know that moment when her lips first touch yours? It's like the world stops, right? Nothing like it."

Jordyn grinned, raising her eyebrows to Eric. "What about you? What makes you human?"

He narrowed his eyes. No chance was he going there. "I already told you. Not human."

She leaned forward, laughter dancing in her eyes. "Really? Then what is it about you that makes you more than a cold, ruthless killing machine? What would make a woman see you as a *man* and not as a monster?"

He was aware that the other warriors had stopped talking, and were riveted by the exchange. Swearing under his breath, he leaned forward, meeting her challenge, until his mouth was almost touching hers. "You really want to know why a woman would fall into my arms and never want to leave them?"

Her eyes widened, and she sucked in her breath ever so slightly. "Tell me."

He let his gaze fall to her mouth. "It's because I'm naturally gorgeous, an incredible kisser, and I never, ever litter."

"Really?" She stared at him, then pulled back with a snort. "Well, that's disappointing. When will guys realize that women want a guy for more than just good sex?"

What? He'd thought that was pretty good. "You didn't think the litter joke was funny?"

"It was a joke?" She gave him a baleful look. "So you *do* litter? Is that what you're saying? Because that's not all that appealing. Let's see, a guy who is so self-absorbed that he lists his hotness as one of his attributes, who makes fun of keeping the environment clean, and then declares to the world that he's a great kisser, as if it's his own opinion of his sexual prowess that makes him good. Wow. Be still my beating heart."

Eric stared blankly at her. "What? That's not what I meant."

"It's what you said."

"Well, shit, I didn't say it like that." He was vaguely aware of the other guys chuckling, and he felt heat prickle down his back. "I was just—"

"Trying to flirt instead of answering the question? Don't you know that women like men who can bare their souls?" She nodded at Ethan. "A pet bunny is completely endearing. Flowers are, well, just awesome. And remembering your first kiss? It's every woman's fantasy to have a guy that romantic."

The other guys grinned wider. Wolfe even leaned back on his elbows and stretched his legs out as if he'd just finished a brilliant lovemaking session and was basking in his accomplishments. Shit. Eric knew they were enjoying the payback for the insect attack. Swearing under his breath, he leaned forward and caught her arm. "Listen, Jordyn, I don't play games. I already told you I don't have fancy words. I'm not romantic. I don't remember my first kiss. But I know that every time you speak, your voice rolls through me like a thundercloud promising rain after a decade of drought. That's all I got, woman. That's it. No bunnies, flowers, or memories. Just thunder."

With a growl of frustration, he released her, leapt to his feet, and strode across the clearing. In the entire year of traveling with the toughest warriors he'd ever met, not once had he felt out of control of the situation. And yet, one conversation with Jordyn had him twisted up and irritated. He didn't like being off balance. Screw this whole thing. He was going to get answers about Tristan from her tonight, and then he was out of there. Let her track down Rhiannon herself. She had Rohan's whole team wrapped up so tight they'd all follow her off a damn cliff if she asked them to. They were damn good at what they did, and she was in good hands with them.

Yeah, decision made. He was going his own way in the morning. Tomorrow, he was going after Tristan.

With the certainty of his decision pulsing through him, he folded his arms over his chest and turned toward the gathering at the campfire. To his surprise, Jordyn was staring at him, and the other warriors were no longer laughing. "What?" he snapped.

"Ten." Ethan said. "Great reversal. Nice work."

"Nine and a half," Zane said, the row of black diamond studs glittering in the firelight along his earlobe.

Wolfe held up five fingers. "He lost points for walking away. So, yeah, only five. You have to stand your ground after a great speech like that."

Eric glowered at them. "What are you talking about?"

Maddox was rubbing his goatee. "Based on the look on Jordyn's face, I give it a ten. Shock factor is always in the guy's favor."

Even Axel, who had kept silent until now, had his pale face turned in Eric's direction. "Seven," he said, his voice raspy, as if he hadn't used it in months, which Eric was pretty sure he hadn't. He was even more silent than Rohan. "Thunder was sort of weak, but the pissed-off attitude gave it good believability. Definite seven."

He had no clue what was going on. All he knew was that Jordyn was still watching him, and there was something in her gaze that made heat rush straight to his cock. He scowled, really not happy that his body was trying to get jacked up right now. "What the fuck are you guys talking about?"

"They're rating it as a pick up line, I think." Jordyn said. "I think you impressed them."

"It wasn't a pick up line," he snapped. "I was just pissed."

"I know," she said softly. "That's why it worked so well."

"That's why it worked..." His words trailed off when he finally realized that what was shining in Jordyn's eyes was a sultry, hooded heat, and she was directing it right at him. He met her gaze, realizing exactly how dangerous she was to him. She was more than a distraction. She was already almost a compulsion, a need so intense that it seemed to seize him by the gut and twist the air right out of him.

He jammed his hands into his pockets and glared at her. "I just want to know about Tristan," he snapped. "No more of this shit. I just have to find my brother."

She nodded. "I know. Me, too."

As the others started lowering their scores of his pickup line based on "too much ongoing attitude," Eric's world seemed to narrow until it was only Jordyn. She nodded once, and he knew they were on the same page. The momentary descent into flirtation had gotten too dangerous, and it was over. They had two missions: Rhiannon and Tristan. Nothing else mattered.

Nodding with satisfaction, he walked back over to the fire and sat down beside her, taking his rightful place by her side. Yeah, maybe they weren't going to start getting naked and nasty, but she was still his, for as long as it took to save his brother.

She looked up at him, then held out her hand to him, palm up.

He slapped his hand over hers and gripped tightly. Not holding hands. Not a handshake. A commitment to a common goal. Nothing else. "You sleep with me tonight," he said, not meaning sex or intimacy. He meant it only one way: that they were in it together, and he wasn't letting her out of his sight until everyone who mattered was safe.

For one split second, she hesitated, and her gaze flashed to their entwined hands, then she nodded once. "We sleep together," she agreed. She met his gaze. "Until Rhiannon," she said.

"Until Tristan," he added.

She bit her lip. "That could be a lot of nights."

"Yeah."

She met his gaze. "You can handle it?"

"I can handle anything." But even as he made the

promise, he couldn't quite make himself forget about those two brief kisses they'd shared, and how damn soft her lips had been. Shit. It was all Maddox's fault for bringing up soft lips.

He was going to have to kill him in the morning, he really was.

* * *

Kiss her? Kiss her?

Zach went utterly still, his entire body shaking with need at Rhiannon's breathless request. He wasn't a saint. He wasn't even close. The need to possess her was so strong that his muscles were actually cramping from the effort of controlling himself.

Still pinned beneath him, Rhiannon was staring up at him, her blue eyes dark with desire so raw that it seemed to thrust right into his gut. She wanted him as badly as he wanted her. But he'd seen her terror. Hell, he was still carrying the marks from her attack when she'd thought he was going to hurt her.

"Zach?" Her hands slid from his shoulders to the back of his neck, her touch a tantalizing caress as she wove her fingers through his hair. "Kiss me," she whispered. "I need you to kiss me."

He swore under his breath, knowing damn well that all she was asking for was a kiss. She wasn't asking for him to rip her clothes off or to make love to her until neither of them could move. He knew that, but could he really kiss her and stop there? He could feel her breasts against his chest. Her legs were wrapped around his hips, pulling him against her. The heat from her body seemed to flood him, a pulsing, relentless need that pushed ruthlessly against his self-control.

No. He couldn't do it. He wouldn't take that chance.

But even as he had the thought and made the resolution not to kiss her, he looked down into the turbulent depths of her eyes and saw the desperation in them. He realized suddenly that the kiss wasn't simply about the raw lust that had been stirred up between them. She *needed* him to kiss her, a need that burned from the very depths of all the pain and trauma she carried with her. She needed him to show her what a kiss was supposed to be like.

Jesus. That was serious pressure. But what was he going to do? Abandon her, when all he wanted to do was sweep her into his arms and gift her with whatever kindness he had left, with whatever beauty hadn't already been stripped from his soul?

No. He knew he wasn't going to say no. He was going to kiss her, and prove to her that some men were worth trusting, and that he was one of those men.

Gritting his teeth against the need to consume her, he slowly bent his head, forcing himself to move with agonizing precision, giving her time to stop him or pull back. But with each inch that he closed between them, her fingers dug more tightly into him and her legs clamped that much harder around his hips.

She wanted him. There was no going back. At all.

Desire flashed in her eyes as she suddenly comprehended that he was about to kiss her, then wariness, and then, before the turbulence of her emotions could stop him, he closed the distance between them and kissed her, delivering the most chaste kiss he could summon.

Her lips were the softest things he'd ever felt in his life. They were like the spun silk, warm with life and passion. Lust exploded through him, a fire so hot it felt as if it were searing his veins as his blood raced through his body.

Swearing under his breath, he started to break the kiss, knowing that he was in over his head, but before he could pull back, she wrapped her arms around his neck and trapped him. Then, she parted her lips beneath his and kissed him. Hard. Passionately. Intensely, but with the tentative skill of a woman who had no idea how the hell to kiss a man, who was simply following her instincts.

And it worked.

He cradled the back of her head in his palm, braced himself on his other forearm, and kissed her back. No longer chaste and protective, he kissed her with all the passion of a warrior who had gone too long without the oxygen needed to sustain him, only to find that the woman in his arms was that missing piece of his survival.

The kiss went from tentative to inferno in a split second. Rhiannon seemed to explode with passion, and he was right there with her. Hot kisses. Flesh. More flesh. His hands were suddenly on her bare belly, her stomach muscles quivering under his touch. Her skin was so smooth, and it made him want more. No, he didn't want more. He *needed* more. He needed more of her skin, more of her kisses, more of everything that she was. He slid his hands up her rib cage and rested his palms over her breasts. She arched beneath him, pressing her body against his as she continued to devour his kisses. This was no shrinking maiden he was kissing. She was a warrior woman who craved him as desperately as he burned for her. There were no apologies, no fragility, and no tentativeness. It was about strength between two equals fighting for that which would make them breathe once again.

He felt her hands on the button of his jeans and lifted his hips just enough for her to fit her hands between their bodies. His body quivered in anticipation as she unbuttoned his fly and unzipped the zipper. Before he could even respond, her hands were on his butt, sliding beneath his boxer briefs. His body began to shake with need and with longing at the sensation of her hands on him. It had been so long since anyone had touched him like this. All the discipline he'd been trying to sustain deserted him.

No longer could he hesitate or pretend to be the good guy. He dragged her shirt over her shoulders, taking her bra with it. Her body was lean, well–muscled perfection. At the same time, coating the hardness of her body was a layer of soft flesh, of a woman who had let her body soften and round into that which made her who she was. She tugged down his jeans, taking his boxer briefs with them in one smooth move. There was no doubt that she wanted all of him, just as he wanted all of her. With a low groan he rolled off her just long enough to kick off his boots and yank his jeans over his feet.

The light from the torches flickered over her body, casting her in warm oranges and reds, flickering with the shadows. Her gaze was riveted to his as she unfastened her own pants and slid them over her hips. He grabbed her boots and unlaced each one with violent speed, ripping them off and setting them to the side, making sure they were within reach in case she needed them in a hurry. By the time he'd turned back, she was naked, gloriously naked.

She was propped up on her elbow, her breasts soft mounds. Her nipples were brown and taut, welcoming him. Along her arms from wrist to shoulder were a myriad of tattoos, intricately woven designs that looked vaguely familiar to him. But his mind couldn't be bothered to process the markings on her skin. He was consumed by the burning desire in her eyes, by the need and hunger simmering so close to the surface.

With a low growl of anticipation he crawled across the ground toward her. Her eyes widened and her tongue flicked across her lower lip as she watched him approach. She didn't pull back, and he caught the scent of her desire in the air. He moved until he was over her. Bracing himself on his arms and legs, he lowered himself until their bodies were a breath apart, but not touching anywhere. His erection was pulsing with heat and desire, his quads burning with the need to launch himself into her.

But he didn't.

The memory of her fear and terror was still so vivid that there was no way that he could take her unless he knew that she was with him completely. For a long moment neither of them moved, and the air between them seemed to sizzle and steam with the heat from their bodies. She didn't reach for him. She simply remained still, leaning back on her elbows, staring at him. Sweat trickled down his temple as he waited for her to make that first move.

They were naked. The desire and lust were so thick in the air he could practically see it and feel it coating his flesh. If she kissed him, if he touched her, there was no question about what would happen, which meant he would not cross that border first. She had to make that choice.

Then she held up her arms to him, inviting him into her embrace. It wasn't a raw, mindless move of lust. It was a gesture of tenderness and trust, inviting him not just into her space, but into her inner circle.

He lowered himself onto her. Her arms encircled him, and she pulled him close as he kissed her. The kiss was different this time. It wasn't chaste, but it wasn't untamed fire. Somehow the mere sight of her holding out her arms to him in an embrace had changed things. This time the kiss, although still laced with lust and desire, was also lit by a tenderness he hadn't felt in so long.

He was so shocked by his feelings that he actually stopped the kiss. He went still. The tension radiating through his body was no longer about sexual anticipation. It ran deeper than that, penetrating scars that had branded his soul long ago and settled into hard, unforgiving barriers of protection. Memories he had long since buried, ones he had managed to forget about, came surging to the forefront of his mind.

Shit. Sex was one thing. Tenderness? Trust? No fucking way. He couldn't do that again, not to her, not to himself.

"No." Swearing, he tensed and started to roll off her… then he made the mistake of looking at her face. She was watching him with such softness on her face that something inside him seemed to shatter. What the hell? No one looked at a Calydon with such tenderness. It made him uncomfortable. It seemed to penetrate through walls he'd spent centuries erecting. "What?" he couldn't keep the gruffness out of his voice. Hell, he couldn't even fucking concentrate. He was being assaulted by memories, tempted by the feel of her body beneath his, and undone by the vulnerability and emotions on her face.

"I'm sorry," she said quietly, reaching up to brush her finger over his forehead. "I'm sorry for whatever it is that haunts you."

He closed his eyes, unable to resist the temptation of her touch. Shit, it felt good. Too damn good. He could not go there again. "I can't do this," he gritted out. He wrenched himself off her and vaulted to his feet, grabbing his jeans as he did so. He yanked them on, almost catching his damn erection in the zipper he was so frantic to get dressed.

Running his hand through his hair, once he had his pants on, he turned to face her, knowing that he owed her an apology. This woman with demons on her tail had trusted him, and he'd pulled this shit on her. But when he turned to face her, he was shocked to see her staring at him with a look of absolute disbelief on her face, but she didn't appear to be hurt. Damned if it didn't look like she was impressed with him.

"You got up," she said, still lying there propped up on

her elbows, naked as hell.

"Yeah." He ran his hand through his hair as he grabbed his shirt. Shit. He didn't even know what to say. He was still caught up in memories he didn't want to revisit.

"Why?"

Swearing, he looked around, trying to find an excuse not to answer her, then he took a second look when he realized what was around them. Woven at least thirty feet high on all sides of them, just beyond the circle of torches, was a wall of vegetation. Flowers danced above their torches, and the plants seemed to undulate gently. Stunned by the sheer magnitude of what she'd created, he walked over to it and placed his hand on the wall. The plants were cool and damp beneath his palm, and he could feel their energy vibrating gently against his flesh. "It's a living wall." He looked up, stunned by the sheer artistry of the tapestry she'd woven. It was pure natural art, and he could even see the outlines of assorted forest animals, as if the plants had mimicked the creatures of the jungle beyond.

He pushed lightly at the wall, and it parted for him, allowing his hand to go through. But when he pulled it back, it quickly closed back up, sealing off the spot that had opened. "Unbelievable."

"It only lets you through because you're on my side," she said. "It's impenetrable from the outside."

He glanced back over at her, and saw that she was dressed now, her neck craned as she looked up at the top of the wall. "I haven't created anything like this in a very long time," she said softly as she walked over next to him.

She laid her hand on the wall beside him, and the plants immediately wove themselves around her hand, like a custom glove holding her in place. She smiled and wiggled her fingers. The plants loosened their grip, and then a pale white flower emerged from the wall, right between her thumb and forefinger. Her face softened into an incredible smile of wonder, and she leaned forward, inhaling the scent of the blossom. "Thank you," she whispered, so quietly that he knew she was speaking to the plants.

He couldn't take his eyes off her. The look of wonderment and rapture on her face gave her a radiance that was riveting. She looked almost innocent, a part of nature so pure that he was in awe. Her hair was still in a bun, but strands of the raven-black tendrils had fallen free, draping over her shoulder.

She turned to him and held out her hand. "I want to show you something."

He knew that he had to walk away. He knew he couldn't go to these kinds of places with her, but in that moment, he didn't care. She was different from any woman he'd ever known, from anyone he'd ever met, and he wanted to be a part of it, as if she could chase away all the rot and filth he carried in his own soul.

Wordlessly, he placed his hand in hers. The electricity that jumped between them made his muscles tighten, and she sucked in a small breath. Then she smiled at him and pressed his hand to the wall, just as he'd done by himself. This time, however, she kept her hand over his, tangling their fingers together.

The plants wove over their joined fingers, like a seductive caress that sent chills racing down his spine. Energy seemed to spark through his flesh all the way to the bones of his hand. It was a vibrating, visceral power that was so strong it actually hurt. But at the same time he could feel it running down his arm like a hot, desert wind whipping through all the blockages in his body. "What is it?"

"It's the earth," she said quietly. "Can you feel it?"

He nodded.

Her fingers tightened around his, and he looked over at her. "You gave that back to me," she said. "I haven't felt that connection with the earth and the plants in a very long time. I forgot what it felt like." She smiled, a tender smile that was so full of peace and serenity that she was like a different person from the one who had recoiled from him in such terror.

He turned toward her, suddenly wanting to know. Yes, granted, he needed to grill her on the fire god and the Calydons hunting them, but the wall gave them time. Right now, he needed to know about the woman who had dropped into his life. "Tell me," he said. "Who hurt you so badly that it stripped away from you the very essence of who you are? Was it Luther?"

Shadows drifted into her eyes, and the leaves that had been tangled around their hands retreated back into the wall.

She met his gaze, and there was such trauma in her eyes that he wanted to sweep her into his arms and fight the world for her. "I don't think you want to know," she said quietly.

She turned away then, and walked back across the clearing to the fire. She sat down and picked up the fish that he'd left in the flames. "Dinner's ready. I hope you like it a little crispy."

"Dinner?" He turned to stare at her. *Dinner.*

Fuck dinner. He didn't want to eat. All he wanted was to find out what haunted Rhiannon so badly that it had stolen the magnificence of her talent from her. All he wanted was to hear her secrets and find a way to take away her pain.

He took one last look at the wall to double check its security. Satisfied, he then turned his attention to his guide. He had an entire night behind the barricade with just her, and he knew exactly what he was going to do with her.

CHAPTER 16

Rhiannon's skin prickled as Zach approached the fire. She didn't look up from the fish as he stopped right beside her, his bare feet only inches from her. Why was he so close? Didn't he realize he could sit on the *other* side of the fire?

Then he eased himself down next to her, and she answered her own question. Of course he knew. The man was far from an idiot. He was doing it intentionally. Why? Maybe he had changed his mind about making love?

The moment she thought it, intense pangs of desire pulsed through her, but this time, she was able to keep a rational thought about it. She didn't make love with men. It was a foolish, dangerous thing to do, even if it was Zach. She was grateful that he'd had the sense to stop before they had taken it too far.

Wordlessly, she scooped up some fish onto a metal dish from her backpack, and handed it to him.

"Thanks," he said.

"Sure." She took some fish for herself, and then they sat there in silence, eating. Rhiannon stared into the fire, watching the flames dance as she ate, viscerally aware of every move that Zach made.

He was so close to her she could feel the heat from his body. She counted his breaths. She watched his biceps flex when he reached to put more wood into the fire. She was riveted by his woodsy, earthy scent that seemed to wrap around her. She noticed the way his jeans encased his muscular thighs as he stretched his legs out. She remembered what he tasted like. She couldn't stop thinking about how it had felt to have his naked body on hers, all that hot flesh touching hers. The memory was so vivid, including the fact that she hadn't been afraid, and the fact that *he had stopped.* She knew how badly he'd wanted her, and yet he'd stopped. The strength of his will was astonishing. Unreal. She would have bet that there wasn't a male alive who would have the discipline and emotional depth to halt on the edge of sex. It was incredible, and it made her want him even more, because it made her feel *safe.*

He was all male, and she was aware of every single part of him. He didn't seem to be unsettled by the rising silence between them, but it seemed to be wrapping around her, sending chills through her body, increasing in intensity with every passing moment.

Finally, she whirled around to face him. "What? What is it? What do you want?"

He paused, a forkful of fish halfway to his mouth, his eyebrows shooting up in surprise. "What are you talking about? I'm just eating."

"You're not just eating! You're sitting too close to me, you're breathing too steadily, and you're just oozing all this temptation right at me, and then not saying anything! What do you want from me? Just stop this!"

He stared at her, and then his massive shoulders gave a slow, lazy shrug. "Sweetheart, I'm just eating—"

"No, you're not! I'm not an idiot, you know. Sometimes the greatest weapon is the slow, stealthy approach, and you're doing that! It's not going to work because I noticed it, so just tell me what you want!"

A slow grin spread across his face, and he shifted to face her. "Well, now, I have to disagree on that one."

"On what one?"

"That it didn't work." He grinned wider. "I wanted you to start talking to me and stop shutting me out. Seems to me it worked."

She stared at him. "You're such a jerk."

He shrugged again. "If that's the worst you think of me, then I'm having a good day. I've been called a lot worse." Pain suddenly flashed across his face, pain so stark that she sucked in her breath, but it was gone a split second later.

Suddenly, her anger fled, and exhaustion set in, because she knew that pain. Maybe Zach wasn't so different from her. Maybe he would understand. With a heavy sigh, she set down her plate and turned to face him. "What do you want to know?"

He finished off his fish with one bite, tossed the plate aside, and then turned to face her. His dark eyes were intense, and his humor was gone. "I want to know a lot of things."

She swallowed. "Like what?"

"I want to know about the fire god. I want to know about the flames I saw in the forest. I want to know every damn thing there is to know about our enemy, and I want to know it before that damn wall comes down around us."

Relief rushed through her at his answer. He just wanted to know about the enemy? That was easy. She picked up her plate again to resume eating, grateful that he wasn't going to pry deeper. But even as she relaxed, she couldn't suppress the sudden surge of disappointment that he hadn't wanted to know more, to know why she was so scared, to know *her*. Which was stupid, of course. She didn't need him or anyone else to hold her hand, or to know the demons that haunted her. It wasn't as if he could take them away—

"I also want to know who hurt you. I want to know why you're so damned scared that you couldn't even run up your veggie wall." He leaned forward, and she caught her breath. "I want to know it because you're my partner in this little venture, but I also want to know it because you're a woman who has gotten under my skin so badly that I can't even think until I get it sorted out."

Heat washed over her, a full-on wave of emotional and physical response to him that made her gut clench. "Stop."

He cocked his brow. "Stop what?"

"That." She waved her hand at his pushy stance. "Being so close to me. Being in my space."

"Why?" He was relentless in his questions, and she started feeling the pressure from his closeness. No longer did he feel like a comfortable cocoon of safety. He felt like a threat.

"Why?" She challenged him by meeting his gaze, refusing to allow herself to be intimidated. "I have a question for you. Why did you stop when we were about to make love?"

Guilt flashed over his face. "Why? Were you offended?"

"No. It was a relief. I just… I've just never been in a position where a man has gotten that close and stopped. I don't understand."

He turned toward her then, giving her his full attention. "It's the fire god, isn't it? He's the one. What did he do to you? Were you his slave? Were you his captive?"

His questions hammered at her, forcing her into memories she didn't want to face. She shook her head vigorously and held up her hand, palm out, denying him access. "Just stop —"

"No. We both need you to be able to function in order for us to still be alive by the end of the day tomorrow. What's going on with you? What are you so afraid of? What did the fire god do to you? What hold does he have over you?" He grasped her upper arms gently, turning her so she was facing him. "I already told you that I failed to keep my sister and her kids alive. That's how I got you to trust me. It's your turn. Tell me what's going on. Tell me everything."

Anger rushed through her. Anger that José could still make her so scared that she couldn't connect with her plants unless Zach was almost making love to her, and anger at Zach for shoving his face in her business. "Fine! You want to know what's going on? I'll tell you. I was born in this jungle, for the sole purpose of protecting the jungle from José and his crew. I'm part of an ancient tribe assigned with the task of keeping this jungle safe. José is just the latest enemy in a centuries-long battle to preserve our home."

Zach's eyes narrowed, and he nodded. "I figured it was something like that," he said. "You're too much of a warrior and too familiar with the jungle for it to be anything but that. So José wants to kill you because you're the last thing standing in the way of his ownership of the jungle?"

"Yes, I'm the last one left of my tribe. I was the chosen one. I was the one that was supposed to have the power to stop him. The seers had projected my coming for centuries." Bitterly she held out her hand and showed him her palm. The only non-tattooed spot on her arm showed a seven-pointed black star on her skin. Nothing had ever stuck to it. Nothing she'd done had ever been able to hide it. The tattoo needles that had covered José's brands had been useless against that black star. "This was my gift, and my burden. The infant born with the seven-pointed star would save the jungle. That was me. I spent my entire childhood learning how to fight and be the best warrior ever. When I turned sixteen, I went out to find him."

God, she remembered that day. She remembered the celebration with all the women in her tribe who had gathered to honor her. They'd come from thousands of miles away, even from other countries, those who had left the jungle had come back to bid her good fortune on her quest. "I thought it was so great," she said softly. "I thought my legacy would give me strength that I didn't have to find on my own. I had my dagger. I had my bow. I had my quiver. On my way there, I actually had the jungle dancing around me. I thought I was unstoppable." She could recall with vivid clarity the strength that had been surging through her body on that day. She had been so excited to fulfill the mission that she'd been born with, the one that her mother and the tribe had been training her for since the moment of her birth.

Zach's grip on her arms softened, and he leaned forward, watching her intently. "I was once like that too," he said. "I thought I was the king of the world. No one could stop me. "

She looked at him then, right into his dark eyes. She saw in them an understanding she hadn't expected. For the last fifteen years, she'd looked back at her sixteen-year-old self, and wondered if it would have turned out differently if she hadn't been so arrogant. She had expected condemnation from Zach, and she hadn't softened the retelling in order to avoid it. Yet, as he watched her, she saw only understanding and compassion.

"What happened? Were you unprepared for his strength?" Zach asked.

"No." She met his gaze, suddenly wanting to tell him, this heroic stranger, about the fatal flaw that had doomed her. The one thing she hadn't been prepared for, the one thing that had swept her off her feet in a whirlwind, until it had become too late to stop. "I was unprepared for the fact that I was his *sheva*."

* * *

His *sheva?*

Zach froze at Rhiannon's confession. The implications of what she'd just revealed were staggering. She was the soul mate of the warrior he needed to kill. Jesus. *She was another man's woman.*

He immediately released her, dark emotions cascading through him. Intense fury and possessiveness roared through him. He was consumed by a need to rip apart her bond with another man, and he felt like he was drowning in an almost insurmountable sense of loss, as if he were plummeting through the air into a yawning canyon that would never end.

And it wasn't just any other man, it was the one he was hunting. Jesus. Was she leading him into a trap? "So you love him?" Shit. That was the question he asked? But even as it hung in the air, he knew it was a stupid question. Of course she did. The *sheva* bond allowed for nothing else. She fucking loved this prick, which meant that he couldn't trust her. Not even for a second. "Why the hell isn't he protecting you from all this crap that's chasing you?"

"Protecting me?" Her eyes widened, and bitter revulsion darkened her face. "You want to know if I love him? *Love him?* How can you ask that? Do you have any idea what it's like to be some man's *sheva?*"

He hesitated at the sudden venom in her voice, at the depths of her anger and bitterness. Her emotions were stark and raw, and he knew they were real. What was going on? How could she sound like that when talking about the man she was meant to be with? "No," he said carefully, now uncertain as to what he was dealing with. "I've never been another man's *sheva.*" He'd seen enough of it though. He knew that the connection was unshakeable…until the rogue took over the male. But when the rogue took over, that only affected the male. The female's bond with him was so strong that after she killed her mate to stop him, she always wound up killing herself because she couldn't live without him.

"Well, then, let me enlighten you," she snapped. "The day José took me, I thought my world would stop if he didn't kiss me, touch me, and take me into his arms forever."

Something hardened in Zach's stomach. Something so hard it hurt. Yeah, he didn't want her, he didn't need her, but every word she spoke about herself with her mate felt like she had taken her dagger and jammed it right into his flesh, twisting it with every syllable that she uttered. "Yeah. I know all about the physical need between a *sheva* and her mate." He couldn't keep the bitterness out of his voice, and he lunged to his feet, needing space between them.

"Do you?" Her hard-edged voice followed him across the clearing. "Do you really know what it's like to be unable to resist a man who you know is so evil that he makes your skin crawl? Do you know what it's like to try to run away from him, only to be stopped by the mere sound of his voice calling you back? Do you have any idea what it's like to hate a man so deeply, recoil from his touch, and be disgusted at the thought of him making love to you, but to be completely unable to make yourself stop him? Your body betrays you. You become the victim of an unstoppable, amoral lust that drives you into the arms of a man who is so despicable that you would have killed him a dozen times over and happily burned in hell, just for the chance to cleanse the earth of his presence. You know he's that awful, and you hate him that much, and yet you can't stop yourself from opening your legs every time he comes near you. Do you know what that's like, Zach? Do you really? Because it's hell."

Zach spun around to face her, stunned by the depths of torment in her voice. She wasn't faking it. She hated her mate... and yet couldn't stop herself from responding physically to him. He stared at her, and he didn't see the warrior anymore. He saw a woman, a vulnerable woman who had been victimized by the man who was supposed to protect her. Her dark hair was tumbling out of her bun, her eyes were burning with pain, and her fingers were clenched around her plate so tightly that her fingers were white. He had a sudden vision of her focusing those dark eyes on him, begging him to stop, but being unable to stop him if he chose not to listen to her. What kind of man would do that to a woman? To his mate? Rhiannon wasn't even *his*, and yet the need to protect her was so strong that he'd give his fucking life to keep her safe.

Suddenly the magnitude of what had happened between them earlier weighed heavily upon him. No wonder she had been shocked when he'd stopped, but even more incredible was the fact she'd surrendered to him. She had no reason to trust a man, and yet she'd completely given herself over to him. She'd trusted him so deeply that it was his touch that had given her the strength to connect to her plants again.

Son of a bitch. What she'd given him was extraordinary.

Slowly, he walked back over to her and crouched in front of her. "I've known many Calydons and their *shevas*," he said gruffly, his voice hoarse with emotions he could barely grasp. "I know there's a draw between them, but I thought it was mutual. That they wanted each other." He needed to understand what was happening, what she lived with.

She shook her head. "It's an uncontrollable kind of desire," she said softly. "Not voluntary. I—" She hesitated, her gaze sliding away from his.

"You what?" He asked the question gently, but something inside him was on fire with the need to know. This was so far beyond his comprehension, what she had endured at the hands of her soul mate.

After a long moment, she looked back at him. "It wasn't just the sex. It was more. It was as if he could control me with his will, as if he could infuse his own desires and wants with mine, so that what was inside me became his soul and not mine. My mind was there, and I knew that I hated what was happening, but I couldn't make my body listen to what I wanted, and I couldn't turn off the desire that he stoked in me." She shrugged, a gesture of complete helplessness. "I couldn't stop it. He liked to watch me have sex with his warriors. He liked the fact that I hated it, but he could make me do it anyway."

A deep, visceral sense of betrayal settled deep in Zach's gut. "That's not how it's supposed to be. A Calydon protects his mate. He insures her well-being. He claims her as his own, and he would never be able to handle watching her with someone else."

Rhiannon shook her head, and he sensed a great sadness from her. "It wasn't like that. He was...depraved." Her face paled. "Not 'was.' 'Is.' He's so powerful, Zach. He's so far beyond an ordinary Calydon."

Zach ground his jaw. Jesus. This bastard was still alive, and hunting Rhiannon. He had to die. There was no other possibility. Instinctively, he set his hand on her hips, needing to encircle her, to use his body to protect her and keep her safe. "How did you get away?"

Her fingers went to the red amulet at her throat. "Do you see this? This saved my life."

Zach studied the red stone more closely. He had noticed it before, but only in passing. He wasn't really the jewelry type, but now that he inspected it, he could see that it was marked with ancient designs that looked vaguely familiar. "What is it?"

"It protects my mind from him. When I have it on, I can think for myself. I still sense my body's need for him, but I can think and I can make my body respond to my own wishes, instead of his." Her fingers tightened around it, as her voice softened with a memory only she could see. "I found it buried in the dirt beside a river. José and his men had just finished with me, and had left me there so I could clean up." She ran her hand over her stomach as if she were trying to wipe away the memories of all that they'd left on her flesh.

Dark anger coiled through him, but he shut it down, staying focused on her. It had been so long since he'd encountered a woman who was so strong and so vulnerable, and she awoke in him things that he hadn't felt in so long. She inspired him to be a better man so that he could protect her. So, instead of getting all pissed off, he simply took her hand, lifting it away from the almost frantic wiping of her belly. She looked at him in surprise as he encased her fingers in his, trying to draw her back from the memories trying to trap her. He pressed a light kiss to the back of her hand, trying to give something good back to her.

She smiled faintly, and didn't pull away. "José was messing with me," she continued, her voice slightly stronger now. "He was calling me back to him, just to prove to everyone that even though my body hurt so much I could barely even crawl, that I would still come back to him for more."

Jesus. What a bastard. He'd thought there was no one lower than Rohan, but he knew now he had not even begun to scrape the surface. Rohan had betrayed Dante, but what

Rhiannon's mate had done to her was beyond comprehension.

She studied their entangled fingers, hiding her face from him. "I was so exhausted and felt so hopeless that when I felt my body respond to his command, I started to cry. I hated it when he made me cry, and when I showed weakness, but I couldn't handle any more. I was so drained and horrified by what I had done." She lifted her eyes to Zach's, and he felt a part of his soul crack from the agony in her eyes. "I was starting to crawl back to him, dragging myself across the dirt that was churned up from what had happened earlier. The earth was soft and loose, and my hands sunk in with each move I made. It felt so good, so healing, the way it was cool against my skin. It reminded me of when I'd had a connection with the earth, you know? When nature had been a part of me."

He nodded. "Your connection with the plants is extraordinary. He took that from you, too?"

She nodded. "I was so broken and scared that I couldn't even feel them, but that day, the earth felt different. It felt like it was alive again, like it was telling me not to give up, that the strength was still in me somewhere."

Zach leaned forward, watching intently, riveted by her story. "What happened? Were you able to use the plants?"

"No." A small smile flickered on her face, a spark of defiance that reminded him of the woman he'd first met, a woman fighting for her life and her freedom. "Better. I found this." She touched the amulet around her neck. "My fingers sank into the earth, and my pinky suddenly felt like a shock exploded through it. I jerked my hand back, and I saw this stone sitting there in the dirt, completely clean and exposed, as if someone had just finished polishing it and then set it down for me to find. A small, red, misshapen piece of glass that changed everything for me. "

She smiled, and this time, it was a beautiful, real smile, that made his heart actually tighten. "What did it do for you?" he asked

She continued to finger it. "I reached for it, and the instant my fingers closed around it, my head cleared, and my body belonged to me again. It's so hard to explain that moment, but literally, it was as if I had been a puppet, and someone cut every single string at the same time. Suddenly, I controlled my body and my thoughts, and the best thing of all was that I didn't want him anymore." She grinned at him, excitement flashing in her eyes at the memory, her expression so vivid that he felt like he was in that moment with her, experiencing freedom for the first time. "Do you know what that felt like? Not to want him? Not to be facing this huge battle in my head against what he wanted and what I felt? It was just gone. It was just me."

"That must have been incredible." He knew what that was like. He had such a clear memory of the moment he'd discovered he had fire, at a most opportune time. Freedom was incredible. Freedom earned by your own strength was the most powerful of all.

"It was. God, it was." She was smiling openly now, but she was still holding his hand. Her fingers were relaxed now, though, idly stroking his as if she wasn't even aware she was doing it. "José called my name, and I tensed, waiting for it to crash through me like it always did, but it didn't. It was simply a sound, an empty, powerless sound." She grinned. "That moment was so amazing. He called me, and instead of turning toward him, my hand instinctively reached for a stick, a stick I wanted to use against him. I still remember sitting there on my knees, staring at this stick in my hand, barely able to even understand what was happening. I didn't even really make a conscious decision to get the stick. It was just instinct, a need to protect myself in a way I hadn't been able to do for so long. I didn't even know what was going on."

"But you did know, didn't you?" Zach asked.

She laughed softly. "Even after all those years of being trapped, I still had the instincts that I was trained with. It took me about thirty seconds to figure out what was going on. I didn't have time to fully process it, but I knew that something critical had happened." She met his gaze. "I knew I had been given the power to resist him, but there were eleven warriors there. Just because I could think for myself didn't mean I could defeat them, you know?"

Zach couldn't believe what she was saying. How could anyone have that kind of self-discipline? "You went to him anyway, didn't you? You made yourself pretend you didn't have it?"

She nodded. "I just grabbed the stone and clenched it in my fist, and then acted like everything was the same."

Zach heard the agony in her voice, and understood what she wasn't saying. Even when she was back in full control of her faculties, she had understood that to fight prematurely would reveal what she had found, and José would have taken it from her. A warrior, which she was, would have held onto that stone until she had the right moment to escape. "How long did it take until you had the right opportunity to escape?"

"Eleven months."

Zach swore under his breath, barely able to imagine what she had endured for so long. And then, to have to fake it, to force her body not to fight for survival... He shook his head in disbelief. "How did you make yourself stay for eleven months when you didn't have to?"

"I did have to. I knew I would have only one chance to get away, so I had to make sure I timed it perfectly." Rhiannon managed a small, half-smile.

"But how did you make yourself not fight back?" He wasn't blind. He could see the torment in her eyes, and hear the pain in her voice. She'd suffered every minute under her soul mate's power, and yet she'd managed to hide that she could think for herself for eleven months. "How did you let him..." Shit. He didn't even want to think about what she'd endured, let alone say it. But if she could survive it, then he could say it. "How did you keep yourself from fighting back when he and the others raped you?" Because that's what it was. It didn't matter whether she chose to submit or was drawn to José on a deeper level. It was rape, clear and simple, an unfathomable act for a Calydon to perpetrate on the mate he was born to protect.

A smile flickered briefly across her face, and he saw it for what it was, an appreciation for how he had phrased it, for the fact he accepted and acknowledged it for what it had been. "The only way to do that was to become numb, and not be present in my body, my heart, or my mind. In some ways, that was even harder than the nine years I spent trying to resist him, because at least then I'd been alive and fighting. Once I had to turn myself off, I felt like I was already dead." She met his gaze. "When I was under his thrall, at least I was trying to fight. During those eleven months..." she shook her head. "A part of me had to die in order to pull it off."

Her pain seemed to plunge right into his gut, and he closed his eyes, knowing exactly how she must have felt. "I'm so sorry," he said quietly. He opened his eyes. "I'm so fucking sorry, Rhiannon." He didn't know what else to say. There were no words to lessen what she'd endured, and a compliment as to how amazingly strong she was seemed to dismiss what she'd faced. "I know what that's like, to die inside. I've been there, and it's hell."

She lifted her head to look at him. "You have?" There was hope in her voice, a tiny hope that maybe she wasn't the only one in the world who had felt the pain of a living death. "Will you please tell me what happened to you? I need to hear it, Zach. I need to know that I'm not the only one."

CHAPTER 17

Rhiannon waited while Zach bowed his head. His shoulders hunched, and exhaustion seemed to shudder through his massive frame. Instantly, she was sorry. No one should have to relive that which had almost killed them. "I'm sorry. I shouldn't have asked—"

"No." He raised his head to look at her, his eyes dark with turbulence. "You were honest with me. I'll be honest with you." He shrugged. "It's not that long of a story. I met a woman—not my *sheva*—and fell in love. Not the Calydon-*sheva* lust. I loved her."

Rhiannon was startled by the depth of emotion in his voice. She'd never been around a man who felt anything. She was born of a tribe of women who protected the jungle, and men had never been a part of her life, until José had taken her. But the edge to Zach's voice told her that he was telling the truth, that he had truly loved this woman.

Riveted, she scooted forward, as if the mere act of discovering that one male on this earth was built from human emotions would suddenly make things feel better and take away what she'd just relived. Strangely, after recalling her life with José, she didn't feel as scared as she usually did. Sharing it with Zach while he was holding her hand had somehow lessened the impact of the memories. She felt better, as if her past had loosened its grip on her a tiny, tiny bit. "Did she love you back?"

A grim smile played across his stoic features, a smile that didn't reach his eyes. "Yeah, she did. I was working for the Order at the time, running around and saving innocents. She didn't want me to do that anymore, so I left." He shook his head, and she felt the bitterness in his voice. "I had made an oath to my sister and her kids that I'd protect the world against other rogues, and yet when I met Jacqueline, nothing else seemed to matter. She won my heart, and I had no choice but to follow."

Rhiannon narrowed her eyes. "Are you sure that wasn't the *sheva* bond? That sounds like what it was like with José."

"No. No *sheva*." He held up his arm. "Runes, remember? I can't do the *sheva* thing. So, yeah, I just loved her. She had a child, and they reminded me of my sister and her two kids. They were alone in the world, and they had no one to help them. They needed me, and they became my family."

Rhiannon's heart softened at his story. Here was this big, strong warrior whose job it was to save the world, and yet he had been won over by a single mom and her child. "What happened?"

Something darkened in Zach's eyes. "She became pregnant. We had a baby girl. Her name was Madeline."

Rhiannon went cold, so cold with terror at his words, at his use of the past tense to describe his daughter. Her heart began to hammer, as her own memories came flooding back to her. "What happened?"

Zach turned his head away, staring at the wall of vegetation surrounding them. "One day, there was a rogue terrorizing a nearby village. The Order wasn't around, so I went to help. I couldn't stand back, you know? I was Order in my blood, even if I'd walked away from my duties, and I needed to go help. Jacqueline didn't want me to go. She was scared. She was afraid of what would happen if there were more rogues around and they found her while I was in the village, but I didn't listen. The screams from the village were so visceral, I could feel them in my bones. *I had to save them.* We fought about it, but I went anyway. How could I possibly ignore that?"

"You couldn't." She knew that he couldn't. Just as she hadn't had the choice of refusing to face José. Her job had been to protect the jungle, and with José and his team destroying it, she had to go. She understood that he'd had to go, but she could hear in his voice that he didn't. "What happened?"

"There was only one rogue, and I took care of him pretty easily. I was on my way back to our house, and I heard more screams. This time coming from my house."

Rhiannon scooted closer to him, instinctively setting her hands over his balled fists. He turned his hands over and wrapped them around hers as he looked at her.

"The father of her first child had been a Calydon. He'd been killed for going rogue after they bonded, freeing her from the *sheva* bond. But he had a brother who blamed her for his brother's death, and he'd been hunting her. When he found that she'd married another man, he felt she'd betrayed his brother's memory, and he came to kill her. The attack in the village had merely been to lure me away from her."

Rhiannon's mouth dropped open. "Oh, no." Zach had been too late.

He shook his head. "When I got there, one of them was attacking my wife. She was covered in blood, but she was somehow still managing to stay alive. Her daughter was behind her, and she was trying to protect her."

"Oh, God." Her hand went over her heart. "Zach—"

"Another Calydon was going after Madeline, my daughter. I saw her running from him on her little legs, screaming for her mommy. Madeline saw me, and she ran right toward me, her arms out, screaming my name, screaming for me to save her." He turned his hand over and opened his palm, as if remembering something. "When I saw my family in danger, I lost my shit and attacked, unleashing more fire than I'd ever done in my life. The fire and the explosion were massive. I went after that bastard with everything I had. All I wanted to do was kill him. His friends jumped out of the trees to help him, and I went after them. Ten against one, and I burned all those Calydons up."

"And Madeline? And your wife and stepdaughter?"

He met her gaze. "After it was done, after the enemy had been vanquished, I turned around. Jacqueline, my stepdaughter, and Madeline were dead. All three of them were dead." His voice was empty now, as if the pain was so great that he couldn't even feel it.

Rhiannon moved between his knees and placed her

hands on either side of his face. "The Calydons killed them?"

"No. They'd killed Jacqueline and her daughter while I was on my rampage, but not Madeline." He looked her in the eyes. "I killed her myself. I lost control of my fire, and I killed her. My own daughter burned to death in my fire. I can still see Madeline running toward me, arms up, screaming for daddy to save her. She believed in me, and I killed her. "

Rhiannon put her hand over her mouth, horrified by what he'd endured. There were no words to bring comfort to him. She could feel the depth of his pain in the shuddering of his shoulders, and the tension in his jaw. "I'm so sorry," she whispered. Such empty, meaningless words, but they were true. She meant them.

Zach placed his hands over hers, and squeezed. "Since that day, I've never been able to summon fire during a battle. And now, I can't even so much as light a match. If the fire god comes after us, I've got nothing." He ran his fingers over her hair, and she closed her eyes, her soul crumbling at the touch of kindness and gentleness. "And now," he whispered, "I've met this incredibly brave woman who has somehow kept her heart alive despite what she's endured. She's up against an enemy who is too strong, and she needs help. She needs *my* help. And I have no flames left to help her. My fire killed my family, and now it can't save you. I've failed in every possible way."

He pressed his lips to her forehead, a kiss so tender and gentle that tears burned in her eyes. Wordlessly, she lifted her face to his. For a moment they simply looked at each other, then she whispered the words she'd kept hidden inside for so long. "Three years after José took me, I had a baby. A daughter. José killed her the moment she was born, because he didn't want a girl. Only a boy would do. He did it in front of me, and I couldn't stop him." Tears bled down her cheeks, tears for the child she had failed to save, just like Zach.

Zach sucked in his breath, and then traced his thumb over the tears streaming down her cheeks. He said nothing, but he didn't need to. She knew that he understood. He understood the guilt, the loss, and the agony. She knew in that moment, that Zach would always protect her. He'd suffered too much loss that he'd failed to prevent. His heart still bled for those who had died.

She knew that he would never let anything happen to her. *Never.*

The tears grew stronger and thicker, and this time, it wasn't for the daughter she'd never known. This time it was for the fact that this man in her arms would never betray her. He'd never let her down. She could trust him. For the first time since she was sixteen and she'd walked out of her tribe's village with nothing but a bow, her arrows, and her dagger, she wasn't fighting the battle alone.

"Rhiannon." Her name whispered reverently on his lips was her only warning before he lowered his head and kissed her.

* * *

His lips were barely a shimmer against her mouth, a butterfly's kiss so light that it made chills cascade through her body. She went still, her eyes closed, as he feathered a kiss across the corner of her mouth. Then another across her jaw. Kisses so light that they were pure seduction, so light that her entire soul strained to feel them, as if she could draw them into her.

Then he trailed a single finger across her throat, barely skimming her flesh. She swallowed, her heart pounding as he traced the faintest circles across her chest, lower, and lower, until his fingertip brushed over the swell of her breasts. His touch was delicate, like a silken caress across her flesh. It was pure temptation, a whisper of seduction that was barely a tease, making her shiver for more, instead of running for cover.

There was none of the heavy palms or ruthless grabbing, just the most incredibly delicious sensation of his fingers trailing so light, so tempting, so wonderful over the surface of her skin.

She closed her eyes, barely breathing as he continued to ignite sensations in her that spiraled through every cell of her body and pooled in her lower belly. She didn't want to move, think, or speak. All she wanted was to stay motionless and absorb what it felt like to have Zach touch her so reverently. She felt like the heavens themselves were dancing across her skin through his touch.

"So beautiful," Zach whispered, his voice so soft it was more of a breeze across her than words spoken aloud.

She opened her eyes to see him watching her intently. His dark eyes were riveted on hers even as his hand continued to trail ever so delicately across her flesh, sliding lower inch by inch across her breasts, closer and closer to her nipples. Every nerve ending in her body seemed to be on fire, and she jumped each time he touched a new area of her skin. She felt like every inch of her was straining to be the next area that his caress slid across.

He smiled, a smile so laden with the grief of the memories they had both unearthed, that she felt her own heart become heavier with emotions she had suppressed for so long. In Zach's arms, it finally felt safe to feel. She felt the pain of her captivity. She felt the grief of not being able to protect her daughter. She felt her longing for the tribe she'd left behind, even though they'd never appeared to rescue her or even contacted her after she'd escaped. And most of all, she felt sadness for her own loss of humanity, and the fact that she'd gone for so long without feeling the connection with another human being that she was feeling with him right now.

His face softened, as if he had heard all the thoughts that had been cascading through her mind. Without a word spoken, not aloud at least, she seemed to understand what he felt and what he wanted. He wanted the connection to her as much as she yearned to be aligned with him. They had suffered similar things, and yet had emerged with him holding such strength and her being a survivor.

She raised her hand, the one that had first touched her amulet on that night by the river, and she rested it on his muscular shoulder. His muscle spasmed beneath her palm as if he had the same reaction to being touched gently that she had. She slid her hand along his shoulder to the back of his neck. His skin was warm and incredibly soft, his hair like the strands on a newborn kitten. Lightly, ever so lightly, she pressed her fingers into him, inviting him closer, asking him for more.

He responded instantly, but with the same deliberate reverence, closing the distance between them for a kiss. His lips feathered over hers ever so gently, just like he'd done before. But this time, he didn't break the kiss. This time the kiss continued, a magical intertwining of his mouth and hers. It was such a tender kiss that it brought tears to her eyes. How was it possible for a man to touch her so gently? How was it possible for one kiss to say so much?

He whispered her name against her mouth, and the mere sound of her name seemed to melt any last resistance from her. His use of her name personalized everything that was happening between them, a way of saying that he knew who she was, all the way down to her soul, and that he acknowledged her and wanted this moment to be with *her.*

"Zach," she whispered his name in response, and his muscles tensed beneath her palms in a reaction that mirrored hers of a moment ago. Two empty souls, somehow being brought back to life by each other.

His fingers drifted to the back of her head, sweeping the loose strands of her hair back from her face, but not trying to tear her bun free. He allowed her the control of her own hair, but his touch was so soft and seductive that a part of her wanted to unpin her hair and let him slide his fingers through it.

But she knew she couldn't. José had trapped her by her hair too many times, and never would she allow a man to do the same again. But still… what Zach was giving her felt amazing. A tender, non-aggressive caress, that made her want to sigh like the girl she had once been, and surrender to his touch.

His mouth was still on hers, gently working kisses that seemed to cascade through her like a butterfly in a summer dawn. It was so tender and gentle, but at the same time, desire began to pulse in her belly. It started with the faintest tremor of excitement, and then it began to build, swirling through her with increasing intensity. It wasn't the blind lust of earlier, mingled with the power of her magic. This time, it was pure connection and desire, a yearning for something that would uplift her.

Instinctively, she tightened her fingers against his shoulders, trying to draw him closer. He responded easily, locking his arm around her lower back as he shifted, so that their bodies were against each other. There was so much heat between them, and it was so incredible to feel her breasts crushed against his powerful chest. He slid his hand beneath her shirt, and she almost cried out at the sensation of his bare palm on her side, tracing her ribs one by one, as if he had all the time in the world to investigate every curve of her body.

His kiss deepened ever so slightly, sweeping her into a devastating seduction of magic as his tongue swept across hers, dancing and entangling with hers. The desire pulsing through her body escalated, and when his hand slid beneath her bra and cupped her breast, she gasped in response. "That feels so incredible," she whispered, unable to stop herself from arching her back and pressing her breast into his hand. She had no fear that he would hurt her, just an awed response to his caress. The way his palm encompassed her breast, as if he was shielding her body against the world with just his hand, was so intoxicating that she shuddered. Every part of her breast fit perfectly into his hand, as he encased it in the warm, sensual strength of his touch.

"Good," he whispered back. "I want you to feel incredible." He began a teasing trail of kisses over her chest, toward her breasts. She swallowed, her fingers sliding through the soft strands of his hair as she tipped her head back, unwilling to do anything to stop him. Her body tingled in anticipation as his mouth grew nearer and nearer to her nipples, as his lips trailed over the swell of her breasts. He pulled back ever so slightly, but before she could cry out in dismay at the separation between them, he tugged her shirt up, exposing her breasts to him. For a split second, she froze as the fresh air hit her bare flesh, flesh that had never been willingly exposed to a man, until tonight.

There was no time for fear, because he lowered his mouth to her nipple in the most incredibly tender kiss of reverence and adoration. Desire leapt through her as his teeth grazed ever so lightly over her hardened nipple.

A small cry of pleasure escaped her lips, and she felt her cheeks heat up with embarrassment. She quickly bit her lower lip, fighting to keep her emotions hidden. Just as she had held back her cries of pain and fear, she was afraid to show what she was feeling. Vulnerability was dangerous, and it resulted only in pain and betrayal.

Zach lifted his head from her breasts as his hand supported her shoulder blades with easy strength. His dark eyes searched hers, and he thumbed her lower lip gently. "It's okay," he said softly. "It's okay to just let it go. You're safe with me. Every sound, every response, and everything you feel is okay. I loved someone once, and I haven't wanted to hear a whisper of pleasure from a woman since then. Until you." His well-muscled arms tightened around her lower back. "I want to know that you feel good. I want to know how you respond. It matters to me. It really does."

More tears burned in her eyes, for the words that were so gentle and caring. "You're a stranger," she said. "How can you possibly make me feel so safe? You're a Calydon and—"

"No. Don't see me that way. Just see me with your heart." He pressed his mouth to hers, cutting off her protest.

Tears were trickling down her cheeks now, too much for her to withhold. She closed her eyes, letting the fullness of Zach's kiss fill her. She reached inside herself for answers, the kind of answers she had refused to be open to for so long, the kind of answers she could reach only if she broke through the brittle, unyielding walls around her heart and soul. She took a deep breath, giving her trembling body permission to relax and to experience the depths of sensations he was stirring up inside her.

"That's my girl," he whispered against her mouth as his hand slid lower, again tracing her ribs, and then over her belly, dipping lower and lower, each gentle sweep of his hand bringing his fingers closer to the top of her cargo pants. He swept his hand over her hip, and across her butt, and then back to her bare stomach, leaving behind a burning trail of heat everywhere he touched.

And God, it felt so good. As wonderful as his kisses were, she couldn't concentrate on them, not with his hand stirring up such incredible sensations. The tips of his fingers slipped beneath the waistband of her pants, and she sucked in her breath. Her entire body was trembling now, not in fear, but in anticipation.

He deepened the kiss, his tongue asking for more. Not demanding. Asking. Teasing. Seducing. And she wanted to give it to him. Delight leapt through her as she realized how desperately she wanted to kiss him back. She *wanted* him to touch her and kiss her, but even more, she wanted to touch him herself.

With rising excitement, she tightened her fingers around the back of his head. Instinctively, they both deepened the kiss, and it suddenly went from a teasing seduction to a new level. It became hot. It became intense. It became about two people wanting everything the other could give them.

Desire escalated through her, and she was so aware of every touch between them. Of her breasts pressed against his chest, of his hand sweeping lower and lower beneath the waistband of her pants, of the taste of his mouth.

"Touch me," he whispered. "If you want to, touch me."

His suggestion sent an embarrassing surge of lust through her body, and her thighs clenched in reaction. Touch him? It was one thing to let him touch her, but for her to be the aggressor was so different. It would mean that she took ownership of her need for him.

Her heart began to pound, and all she could think about were the times José had forced her to touch him. It had been such an insult to make her reach for him, as if she were betraying her soul that was screaming inside in protest. It had been the worst when she'd had to touch him. When he'd assaulted her, she could lie there and pretend it wasn't him, and take pride in the fact that she was not the aggressor. But when José had realized that, he'd changed the rules and forced her to be the one to initiate. That had been the ultimate humiliation, the final proof to her that she had lost.

"Hey," Zach said softly. "You don't need to touch me. It's okay." He pressed his lips to her cheek, and she felt him kiss away the salty dampness from her tears.

She nodded, and lightly clasped his face in her hands. She searched his dark eyes, and saw only kindness and desire. His hand had stilled on her belly, and his other arm had loosened around her lower back, backing off and giving her space. "No," she said. "Please don't stop. Please." She didn't know how to put into words how much she needed this from him. She wasn't even sure she understood it herself. All she knew was that Zach's kisses and his touch were wiping away memories that had haunted her for so long.

For a moment, he searched her face, looking for the truth behind her words. As she watched him taking the time to make sure that she truly meant her words, one of the little pieces of the hard shell around her heart cracked the tiniest bit for the man who would not touch her unless he truly knew it was okay with her. "How do you exist? How is it that you are who you are?" She traced her fingertips along his jaw, noticing that as she trailed her fingers downward, his skin was decadently smooth, but as she ran her fingers in the other direction, the pads of her skin caught on the whiskers, as if they were trying to trap her and not let her go. "I never noticed it before."

"Noticed what?" His hand resumed its slow, circular path on her lower belly again.

"That in one direction, a man's whiskers are smooth. I thought it was always rough." She moved her fingers back and forth along his jaw, marveling at the difference of how it felt in the two different directions. The shadowy whiskers along his jaw were so dark, a tempting seduction of raw masculinity that should scare her, but didn't. "But it's not always rough. I mean, your whiskers are so thick, but they're like silk in this one direction." She met his gaze. "It's as if your whiskers reflect the man who is both a warrior, and the man who can kiss so tenderly that my heart flutters in response." She leaned forward and lightly pressed her lips to his jaw, trailing them along in the soft direction of his whiskers. "A warrior who is part silk," she whispered. "Beautiful."

He slid two fingers under her jaw and lifted her face to his. "I won't lie to you, Rhiannon. I'm as far from silk as it's possible to be," he said. "But I will never hurt you or take away your choices." Then he kissed her, a deep, intoxicating kiss that felt like fire unleashed inside her body.

A soft noise of desire slipped from her as she wrapped her arms around his neck, pulling him as close as she could. His tongue tasted like seduction and primal need, and excitement leapt through her. Suddenly, she didn't want soft anymore. She wanted a kiss so deep that it plunged into her very soul. Embarrassed to admit it aloud, she told him in the only way she could, with her response.

He let out a low growl, and eased her onto her back as his hand slid lower beneath her pants. His fingertip brushed over the swollen nub of her desire, and her entire body lurched in response. "Oh, wow," she gasped, startled by the shock to her system at the intimate touch. "How does that feel so good?"

He chuckled against her mouth, a deep rumbling that seemed to reverberate from the depths of his chest. "Oh, sweetheart, you have no idea what it can be like when it's right."

He pulled his hand out of her pants, and with one swift move he had unbuttoned them and unzipped them, even as he continued his relentless, incredible assault on her mouth. He spread his hand wide, and swept it across her belly in a touch that was so tempting and yet so unsatisfying because it was no more than a tease for where she really wanted him to touch her. His fingers went over her hipbone, across the top of her pubic bone, to her other hip. Then he cupped her between the legs, as if he were protecting her from all the world, except for his touch, his hand, and his attention.

She writhed beneath him, wanting more, asking for more with each shift of her hips. But he didn't give her what she wanted. He kept his hand cupped there, agonizingly still, as he broke the kiss and bent his head to her belly. A kiss on her belly button. Then along her ribs. And then up her sternum. Oh God. He was going to kiss her nipples again. Her entire body clenched in anticipation as his mouth drifted nearer to her breasts. A light kiss on the underside of her breasts, and then his hot, damp mouth closed around her nipple. He bit gently, and she nearly came off the ground as her body lurched in response.

At that same instant, he pressed his palm against her clitoris, and she gasped at the shock that bolted through her. She arched her back, helpless against the sensations ricocheting through her as he moved his hand again and slipped inside her. She gasped at the feel of the invasion, so tempting and liberating. Another light bite to her nipple, his fingers teasing the folds between her legs, sensations catapulting through her on so many levels. Suddenly, she needed more. She needed to feel him against her, not just the heat through his clothes. She needed to feel his skin. *Now.*

With a low cry of desperation, she tugged his shirt out of his jeans. He shifted slightly to help her, and then his shirt was off. He grasped her, and pulled both her shirt and her bra over her head. Another moment, and they were both naked, deliciously, tantalizingly *naked.*

He moved back over her, and lowered himself on top of her, even as he caught her mouth up in another kiss. Intense now. No longer a gentle seduction. It was more desperate and ragged, as if he were struggling for breath as he kissed her. She threw her arms around his neck and kissed him back just as fiercely, her entire body shaking with need as he pressed his hips between her legs.

For the second time in less than an hour, they were skin to skin, but this time was different. This time she was so present in the moment. It wasn't about the high of her power. It was about him and her, and how he made her feel. It was about wiping away the memories of the past with something beautiful, something that was about pleasure, not pain and fear.

He broke the kiss and lifted his head, his dark eyes boring into hers as his erection pressed against her entrance. "Rhiannon?" he asked, his breathing ragged.

It was the hesitation in his eyes that took away the last of her doubts. She nodded, unable to keep the smile of anticipation off her face. "Make love to me, Zach. Show me what it's supposed to be like."

His face darkened with fierce resolution that made her body clench in anticipation. "I will *never* hurt you," he vowed, and then he buried himself inside her.

CHAPTER 18

Rhiannon gasped as Zach sheathed himself inside her in one easy move. She flinched, preparing for the pain, but there was none. Just the most incredible sensation of connection, electricity, and bliss. Bliss? From being with a man? Oh, *yes*.

Her body welcomed him, and she was consumed by intense, searing pleasure cascading through her, as if fireworks were igniting every cell as they ricocheted through her.

She grinned at Zach, and he smiled back, his fingers playing in her hair. "It feels good," she said.

"Of course it feels good. It's me." His genuinely pleased smile belied the arrogance of his words, and she actually giggled as he pulled back and then buried himself even deeper.

"Oh, *wow*." She arched her back, drinking in the sensations he was evoking in her. Every nerve in her body felt as if it were on fire, and all of her senses were attuned to his every move, his every touch, and even his every breath. She grasped his shoulders, her attention riveted to his face as he began to build up a rhythm inside her. She had never felt so liberated or free, and yet at the same time, she felt so grounded and connected.

For the first time in a very long time, she wanted to be fully present in her body, absorbing every single nuance of what was happening to her. All the damage that had clung to her for so long seemed to be splintering away, disappearing into the atmosphere. She felt as though she were standing on the top of the highest cliff in the world with the wind whipping around her, stripping away all the baggage and darkness that had held her captive for so long.

Their lovemaking grew more frantic, both of them becoming more consumed by the passion building between them. She couldn't touch him enough, her hands all over his back, his butt, and his shoulders. He was gripping her hips, locking her beneath him as she writhed and bucked, consumed by the desire coiling in her belly. Tighter and tighter the coils twisted, and then it took her, exploding through her. She screamed, basking in the feel of her body twisting out of control, held together only by Zach's weight and strength.

"Rhiannon," he gasped, and then he bucked against her, taken by the same orgasm that was streaking through her body. Together they clung to each other, fighting to hold on in the face of the sensations ripping through them.

She couldn't believe how right it felt to be in his arms, to be held so tightly against him, to be cherished so completely on a physical, emotional, and spiritual level. Her entire soul seemed to be singing, glorying in what it felt like to finally be nurtured, elevated, and ignited.

Happiness.

A moment of pure happiness.

With a deep sigh of contentment, she pressed a kiss to the top of his head, smiling at how his face was buried in the crook of her neck, as if all he wanted was to breathe in her very essence. "That was perfection," she whispered.

"Yeah, it was." His voice was muffled against her skin, his warm breath inciting little sparks of response in her.

God, you're fucking hot.

She grinned, almost laughing at the crass words Zach had used, amused that she'd taken him to the point that he'd forgotten to be nurturing. His voice was deeper and raspier than it had been, as if he'd barely survived their lovemaking "Thanks."

Zach collapsed on top of her, his muscles limp as the aftershocks of the orgasm continued to rock them both. "No, thank you. That was amazing."

I forgot how you fucking scream when you get off. You've been holding back on me, you bitch.

"What?" Rhiannon froze, her heart suddenly hammering. "What did you just say?" He'd called her a bitch?

He'd never call her a bitch, would he? What was he doing?

Zach didn't move. "I didn't say anything. I'm too busy trying to catch my breath. Give me a sec, and I'll wow you with sweet nothings."

You fucking whore. You'll scream like that for me again, I swear it.

Realization tore through her, along with a deep terror. It wasn't Zach's voice she was hearing. It was José's voice, in her head. "Oh, my God!" She hit Zach's shoulders frantically. "Get up! Get up! Get up! He's here! Oh, my God, he's here!"

Zach was off her in an instant. He leapt to his feet and, with a crack and a flash of black light, called out his weapons. He was dressed and armed within a split second, almost moving faster than she could see. His sai slammed into his palms as he spun around, his weight light on the balls of his feet, and every muscle in his body taut with readiness. "Where?"

Grabbing her clothes, Rhiannon stumbled to her feet and lunged for her dagger. As her fingers closed around the handle, she spun around, frantically searching their campsite. Around them rose the walls of vegetation that she'd spun, and within the enclosure, the light from the torches flickered, making orange shadows dance across them. There was no one in there except for her and Zach.

Zach shot a look in her direction. "Where?" he demanded. "I don't see him."

Rhiannon shook her head as she searched. "I don't either."

Zach didn't lower his weapons, and he circled the enclosure carefully, his gaze scanning their surroundings with ruthless intelligence. "He's outside the walls, isn't he?"

Rhiannon's hands were shaking, and she fought to focus as she quickly pulled her clothes on. The thought of being naked in front of José was terrifying. She needed to be dressed and armed, to have a shield to hide behind. "I don't know. I heard him in my head. He heard us making love. He has to be nearby." A shadow passed over the campfire, and she suddenly looked up.

To her horror, she saw the stars in the night sky above her head. She sucked in her breath, and her fingers went numb around the hilt of her dagger. "I forgot the roof," she whispered.

"Oh, my God. I forgot to put on the roof."

Zach looked up. "Can they fly?"

"No," she whispered, "but they can climb."

She raced over to the wall, and pressed her hand to the plants. The moment she touched it, she felt heavy vibrations as the wall took impact. Fear clenched in her belly, and she looked at Zach, who was watching her. "They're already climbing it. They'll be over the top within seconds."

* * *

"They'll be over in seconds?" Zach swore as he looked up. His skin still hurt from the fire that had burned him before. He wasn't going to stick around and let José finish the job, not when he didn't have a damn thing to use against him. "If they're going up, we're going low. Open us a doorway, Rhiannon!" His sai felt heavy and awkward in his hand as he continued to look upward. A warrior needed his weapons to be an extension of himself, so intertwined with his soul that he could will them to act simply with his mind. As a Calydon, that was supposed to be his relationship with his sai, but they had never felt as comfortable as fire.

Right now, facing an enemy more powerful than he was, with the lives of Thano and Rhiannon at stake, the lack of his weapon of choice was a glaring, grim, vulnerability for him. He wanted fire. Jesus, he wanted fire. One well-placed fireball would incinerate them before they could even get over the top.

"A doorway? What are you talking about?" She spun around, searching the wall that was keeping them alive. "They're on all sides—"

"In the ground! Go through the ground!" He grabbed one of the torches she'd lit and shoved his hand directly into the flame. The pain burned through him, but he didn't pull it out. He just focused on the heat of the fire and tried to draw it into his body like he used to do. He steeled his jaw as he kept his gaze on the top edge, waiting for the enemy to crest it. He felt a flash of heat in his palm, and elation ripped through him. Was it working? Was he absorbing the fire? "Now, Rhiannon. Now! "

She dropped to her knees and shoved her hands into the dirt. He heard her whispering frantic chants as she asked the plants to clear a path for them.

His hand was on fucking fire, and he finally tore it out of the flame just as the first warrior crested the top. With a roar, he balled his hand, but no fireball appeared on his palm.

"Shit!" He hurled his sai straight up. It slammed into the warrior and knocked him back over the edge. He called his weapon back, and it was streaking though the air toward him as another warrior topped the wall. Zach threw his second weapon, and it smashed into the warrior, but another Calydon was already climbing the south ridge before Zach had even gotten his first sai back. "Now!" he shouted to Rhiannon. "We need to get out of here!"

"I can't!" she screamed. "I can't concentrate!"

"Come on!" Zach sprinted across the campsite to where Rhiannon was on her hands and knees, her fingers digging into the dirt. He hurled his sai again, and took out two more warriors cresting the top, but there were already three others coming over the edge. He stood right next to her, pressing his calf against her hip, trying to connect them the way they'd done before. "Come on, babe, you can do this!" Electricity burned through him at the contact, and he pressed more tightly against her, hurling his sai and calling them back in rapid succession.

The night was alive with metal blades streaking through the darkness as he fought, but he couldn't keep up the pace. There were simply too many of them. They were going to defeat them with sheer force of numbers, he realized. Not a single one of them had thrown a weapon at him, and he realized it was because he was so close to Rhiannon. Clearly, they had orders not to kill her. That gave them time, an extra three or four seconds at least. "Rhee?"

There was a sudden burst of wind, and he looked down. The earth was splitting beneath their feet, and green vines were streaking through the opening. It was working, but not fast enough. Swearing, he grabbed another torch and hurled it upward. It crashed into one of the Calydons, and Zach felt a rush as the flames erupted, as if he'd done it himself. Instinctively, he palmed his hand to call another fireball...and nothing happened.

They were halfway down the sides now, at least twenty of them. Jesus. How many had José sent for her? "Rhee?"

"Come on!" She grabbed his arm, and he looked down. A dark tunnel lined with vines had opened up beneath them.

Without hesitation, they leapt into it. They dropped about ten feet, and landed hard on the dirt. As they landed, the earth closed over their heads, plunging them into pitch darkness. It took a moment for Zach's eyes to adjust, and then his preternatural vision took over just enough for him to see that the tunnel opened up to the west. Rhiannon grabbed his hand, and they ran down the tunnel...about twenty feet, and then they hit the wall. The vines were still sweeping around them, and dirt was churning, but that was as far as they'd gotten.

The earth above their heads trembled as the warriors landed on the ground, and he felt the vibrations as they began hammering at the earth, tearing up the dirt as they fought to open the tunnel.

Zach lunged forward and swung his sai through the dirt, moving at top speed as he helped the vines dig through it. Rhiannon stood right behind him, her hands pressed against his back as she commanded the vines. Electricity seemed to hum through him from her touch, galvanizing him. His sai whipped through the earth, ruthlessly clawing a tunnel, working side by side with the massive tropical vines. The dirt sprayed through the air past them, and he had to close his eyes against it. He felt Rhiannon bury her face against his back, and she coughed, no doubt sucking in the dirt contaminating their air.

He kept his mouth shut and fought not to breathe as he cleared the earth. Faster, and faster, desperation rising as the noise behind them grew louder. Each chunk of dirt they cleared went behind them, refilling the tunnel as fast as they dug it, leaving the two of them in a very small, mobile crater beneath the earth. They'd made it twenty yards now. Thirty. Forty.

"I think we're past the river," Rhiannon said, then gagged from the dirt.

"We have to go up," he told her, tucking his head to try to get enough clear air to talk. The air was so thick with damp soil that it was almost impossible to breathe, or even talk. "Tell your vines to go up. José's warriors are almost breaking through in back. We need to be able to run."

Energy hummed through him, and the vines changed

trajectories instantly, tearing ruthlessly through the earth as they headed up. Zach fought beside them, his head turned as the dirt poured down upon their heads. The dirt was in his mouth, caking his eyes, filling his nose, lining his throat. Rhiannon was tucked up behind him, pulling at his shirt, and he hoped she was using the cotton as a filter to enable her to breathe.

The air was so thick now, thick with wet, damp dirt, almost up to their hips. Despite his efforts not to breathe, it felt like the dirt was filling his lungs, suffocating him. The vines were spewing it behind them, filling the tunnel they had just been through, but it wasn't fast enough to combat the tons of dirt falling down upon them.

Rhiannon suddenly let go of his shirt and collapsed.

He spun around. She was on the ground, not moving. Not breathing. Fear tore through him as he scooped her up, digging her out of the earth. Jesus. She was suffocating! He used his shoulders to try to block the falling dirt, frantically trying to clear the dirt from her mouth and nose, but it was falling faster than he could clear it—

And then he realized that the vines had gone still. They were laying in quiet lines around them, no longer commanded by her. Without Rhiannon to direct them, they had simply become plants again. The dirt was cascading down around them, their tunnel collapsing.

Jesus. She was going to die. Right then. Right there. In his arms. "No!" The anguish ripped through him, a grief more virulent than anything he'd felt since the day he'd held his dead wife in his arms. Something seemed to break inside him, a dam that had held him in check for so long. Heat exploded through him, a violent, wild fire beyond his control, just like the one that had killed his daughter.

He couldn't hold it back. He had a split second of horrified realization that he was going to turn into a ball of fire and incinerate Rhiannon just like he'd killed his child, and then he dropped her between his feet, and thrust his palms upward toward the sky. His skin ignited, and he thrust all the fire upward, slamming it into the dirt coffin above their heads. With a furious boom, the earth exploded upward, showering thousands of tons of dirt into the night. The fireball tore up into the night, an inferno of flame a hundred meters wide streaking though the sky, ripping every last bit of flame from Zach's body.

Flaming dirt showered down upon them, pouring from the sky.

He fell to his knees, his body shaking violently as sweat poured off him and nausea churned in his belly. Beneath him, Rhiannon lay still, her face streaked with dirt, her eyes closed. "Rhiannon," he rasped, scooping her up in his arms. He had to get her out of there. He had to get her to clean air. He had to get her away from the others.

He stumbled to his feet and looked around, trying to see through the flaming embers cascading around him. They were in the bottom of a massive crater at least a hundred yards wide. Swearing, he started to run, but the loose, scorched earth slid under his feet, robbing him of traction. He fell to his knees, and then lurched back to his feet.

He could hear shouts in the distance, and he knew they were coming. He had to get out. He had to go. He fought across the slippery dirt, going down on his knees repeatedly and struggling back up. The solid earth was fifty yards away now. Thirty. He was almost there.

The shouts were louder now.

Rhiannon still wasn't breathing. She was limp in his arms, flaming embers sizzling on her skin as they landed on her.

Swearing, he pulled her tighter against his chest, trying to shield her from the carnage as he fought toward the edge. His body was screaming with the agony of the fiery explosion, and his muscles were trembling. It hurt to breathe. His eyes felt like they'd been stabbed with a red-hot knife, and the pain of keeping them open was almost unbearable. His skin was charred and half-melted, severely damaged by his own fire. And still he fought, keeping his attention focused on the firm ground at the edge of the crater.

Once he got there, he could run. He could get away. He could stand without falling.

Ten yards away.

Then five.

Shadows loomed behind him, and he smelled the dark, rancid odor of sweat. The warriors were close.

With a last effort, he threw Rhiannon over the rim of the crater. She rolled out of sight, and then he clawed his way up the last of the loose, burning dirt, his hands sinking into the blackened earth as he fought for purchase.

His hands finally closed around the top edge, around solid ground, and he grabbed hold, hauling himself over the rim. He landed on his shoulder, and rolled away from the edge to drag his legs out of the pit.

Rhiannon lay on the ground before him, inert.

Zach lunged to his feet, risking a glance over his shoulder as he picked her up. Swarming around the rim of the crater were more than three dozen huge warriors, each moving with the grace and speed of predators in their prime. *Jesus.*

A new burst of adrenaline galvanized him, and he spun toward them, holding out his palm to summon a fireball...but nothing came. Jesus. His body was completely drained internally. The fireball had taken it all. Shit!

He spun around and broke for freedom, forcing his beleaguered body to run, willing his muscles to work as they'd never worked before. Rhiannon bounced against his chest, but he held her tight, ducking his head against the branches lashing at him. He knew he couldn't keep it up, not for long, not with the state of his body. Desperately, he scanned their surroundings, searching for something, for *anything*, he could use to save them or escape.

But there was nothing but jungle. Plants that Rhiannon could use to destroy everything sat useless while she lay unconscious in his arms. He tried again to summon a fireball, but there was nothing, *nothing*, inside him. Where the fuck had it gone? Why hadn't that explosion changed things? *Where the fuck was his fire?*

Ahead of him, he heard the quiet lap of water. Another river. Water wasn't what he needed right now. He needed heat. He needed fire. He needed—

Something moved above his head, a black shape sweeping past him. Even as he ducked, he called out his sai with a crack and a flash of black light. The gleaming steel appeared in his hand as he shifted Rhiannon to free his right arm. He looked up as he ran. Something was circling above his head. Something large and black. What the hell was it?

Too late, his instincts screamed a warning. He jerked his gaze back to the ground just as a massive warrior stepped out of the jungle less than twenty feet in front of him...a warrior who appeared to be entirely made of flames.

Zach hurled his sai at the exact moment that the other male flung a fireball. His weapon hit the fire and melted instantly, and then a second fireball exploded at his feet.

The earth opened up beneath him. He tried to stop, but he was too close, and he fell, catapulting into the crater that had just been created. He cradled Rhiannon in his arms, using his body to protect her as he tried to right himself to get his feet beneath him. He almost managed it, landing on his hip and tumbling sideways as they hit the dirt.

With Rhiannon still anchored in his arms, he leapt to his feet as he called out his other sai with a crack and a flash of black light. He spun toward the direction where José had been, just as the flaming warrior walked to the edge of the pit. He was tall and broad-shouldered, wearing only black pants and boots. His bare chest was emblazoned with ancient symbols that Zach recognized as fire and fury. His dark hair was long and loose, whipping about his face in the wind. His eyes were black and his face triumphant as he gazed down at Zach and Rhiannon.

Zach stiffened as he stared up at the man who had brutalized Rhiannon. Anger and hatred burned through him, along with a merciless need to destroy him. "You're not a god," he snarled. "You're just another Calydon who knows how to play with fire."

José smiled, his dark lips stretching across gleaming white teeth. "I am a god," he said. "Feel free to underestimate me. I enjoy it." His voice was like pure evil, rolling across Zach's skin like the sharp teeth of a shark, a thousand rows of pain and torture at his command.

Zach gripped his sai, and then tensed when the rim of the pit darkened as all the other warriors that had been pursuing him rimmed the edge of the pit. Shoulder to shoulder they stood, a vertical wall of Calydons, headed by their leader.

There wasn't even an inch of clear space around the rim. Son of a bitch. They were trapped.

* * *

Zach whirled around, fisting his sai as he frantically searched for an opening. Forty-to-one usually wouldn't be a problem if he had fire, but without it? They weren't the best odds even against regular Calydons, but these warriors were different. They were bigger. More muscular. Stronger. And their eyes were flecked with glowing red light...the red of a rogue's eyes. Not full rogue, but enough. Jesus.

Forty rogues? And a fire Calydon?

Son of a bitch. There weren't many situations where he'd been in trouble, but right now, if he had a mayday button back to his team, he'd be punching that sucker until the damn thing shattered.

But he had no mayday button.

He just had himself, and Rhiannon and Thano's lives depended on his ability to get them out of this situation.

José walked to the very edge of the rim and looked down at them. His eyes were not red at all. In his hand was a twelve-foot wrought iron staff with a dragon's head on the top. Was that the staff that would save Thano's life?

Live fire was coming out of the dragon's mouth, and smoke was drifting up into the air, forming the image of a winged dragon above their heads. Zach realized that the smoke dragon was what had distracted him right before José had appeared. Son of a bitch. It had been a decoy that had worked on him. He'd been taken by a decoy? God, his team would laugh their asses off at him for being such a fool.

In José's right hand was a sword with a gleaming blade. "Give her to me."

Zach tightened his arms around Rhiannon, a thousand ideas whirling frantically through his mind as he tried to figure out how the hell to get them out of there. "Never."

"She's dying." José bit out the words. "I'm her soul mate. I can bring her into my healing sleep and save her. If you keep her, she will *die*. You are useless to save her."

Zach looked down at Rhiannon, and his heart seemed to stop when he saw that her skin was turning gray, and her lips had become a ghostly shade of blue. "Shit!" He dropped to his knees and frantically wiped the dirt from her face, trying to clear her nose and mouth. "Come on, babe—"

"She's dying!" José shouted. "I can save her!"

"No!" Son of a bitch. He couldn't turn her over to him. That would be the ultimate betrayal. He bent low over her and pressed his mouth to hers, trying to breathe air into her lungs, but it was blocked. There was too much dirt in her throat and lungs. He pressed his fingers to her pulse...and felt nothing. Anguish tore through him, and then he felt one tiny, faint heartbeat. Jesus. She was still alive, but barely. Did she have one minute left? Two? Could he really make that choice for her, to let her die when she could be saved?

He pulled back to look at her and brushed the stray wisps of her hair back from her face. He knew she would choose death over being subjected to José again...but he couldn't let her die. He bent low over her, whispering into her ear a promise that only she could hear. "I will come for you," he whispered vehemently. "You stay alive, and I will come for you." He brushed his finger over her amulet that was hidden beneath her shirt, and tears suddenly burned in his throat. "I swear to God, Rhiannon, I will not let you become his victim again. *I will do whatever it takes to free you. Just do not die.*"

She didn't move.

Tears burned in his eyes as he set her gently on the ground and then stood up. He took two steps back, and sheathed his sai. "Save her," he said grimly.

At the flick of José's fingers, two warriors leapt down into the pit. One put his sword to Zach's throat while the other picked up Rhiannon. Every muscle in his body tensed as he watched the warrior cradle Rhiannon against his body, but he didn't move. He had made the choice to give her a chance to live, and he would not stand in her way.

He watched grimly, his attention riveted on her limp body as the warrior leapt back to the rim. Fierce, dark anger burned through him as he watched the warrior transfer her to José. When the fire Calydon's arms closed around Rhiannon, Zach felt like he heard her soul scream in anguish and terror. *I swear I won't let him hurt you again, Rhiannon. Stay alive for me. I will not fail you.*

Not like he'd failed his wife and his daughter. He would not fail again.

His brands burned with helpless anger as he watched José trail his fingers along Rhiannon's slack jaw, as if he were basking in the triumph of having reclaimed his woman. "Save her," he shouted. "Fucking save her now!"

José's hand closed around the cord that held Rhiannon's amulet, and then he ripped it from her neck. Zach felt like he'd been sucker-punched when he saw José hurl it into the dark jungle, stripping Rhiannon of her only way to defend herself against him. When she awoke, she would be utterly trapped by José's will once again, as she had been for a decade. *Sweet Jesus. What had he done?*

Then José waved his hand at his team. "Kill him," he snapped. "He fucked my woman and has to die." Then he whirled around, and vanished into the night in a swirl of black smoke and fire.

Zach had only a split second to call out his sai before they attacked.

CHAPTER 19

Jordyn leapt up as the earth shook violently and a resounding boom shook the night. The flames in the campfire fluttered, and two of their torches fell over. "What was that?"

"I have no idea, but I'm thinking that it's not good." Eric was already on his feet, swords out as he leapt in front of her. With a crack and a flash of black light, the rest of the team was armed and on the perimeter of the campfire, ready as they searched the night, trying to figure out what had just happened.

Rohan sprinted into the circle from the dark part of the woods, his swords exploding into his hands in a crack and a flash of black light. "What is it?" he directed his question at Eric, as if he were Rohan's second in command.

"I don't know." Eric was circling the campfire, staring out into the jungle that surrounded them.

Movement behind him caught Jordyn's eye. "The sky looks lighter over to the north," she said, trying to shade her eyes from the glow from their torches.

Eric looked where she was pointing. "It looks like dawn over there. What the hell?"

Together, they sprinted past the torches and into the dark jungle. Without the glare of the torches, Jordyn could see that the entire sky was lit in bright orange. "Oh, my God," she whispered. "The night is on *fire*." It looked like a billion flashes of light were cascading through the night sky, floating down over the jungle about ten miles to the west.

"The fire god," Eric said grimly. "The Calydon that

Rohan sent Zach to hunt."

"Holy shit." Ethan sprinted up beside him, his shaggy blond hair reflecting the orange in the sky. "That'll melt the hair off a guy's chest in a heartbeat."

A cold fear began to creep through Jordyn as she gaped at the sky. "Rhiannon's ex is a Calydon. Powerful." Not the same one, right? Not a fire god? Not a creature who had lit up the entire sky and shook the earth? But she didn't need to ask it. She knew. She just *knew*.

"The fire god is the one who controls this jungle," Eric said, moving closer to her as the other warriors joined them. Rohan stopped by Eric's other shoulder, his swords crackling with blue electricity. "I've never seen anything like that. Rohan?"

Rohan shook his head. "Never." His fingers tightened around his swords, and Jordyn could feel the tension emanating off him. "He lost control."

Jordyn knew what could make a Calydon lose control: his woman. His *sheva*. His mate. "Rhiannon," she whispered in horror, grabbed Eric's arm. "It's Rhiannon's ex. She's there. We have to go."

He looked at her sharply. "*That's* her ex? Hell."

"We have to help her! Now!" She whirled around to sprint back to the campsite to grab her bag, when Rohan grabbed her arm and stopped her. "No," he said.

"No?" She tried to tear out of his grasp. "What do you mean, 'no?' You can't stop me! My friend is in danger!"

"We can't interfere! It must be Zach!"

"Zach?" She suddenly realized he was talking about the warrior who he'd sent after the fire god. Was that who had set the night on fire? Not José? She looked suddenly toward the sky again, hope leaping through her heart. Maybe Rhiannon had an ally. Maybe she had enough help to stay alive until Jordyn could get there. "Well, I hope he's good. Come on, Eric!" But when she turned to him, he was gone. Where was he?

Rohan's grip tightened on her arm. "We must let Zach do it. He's the only one who can. The prophecy decrees—"

"Prophecy?" She stared at him. "Are you kidding? Screw prophecies! That's my friend out there!"

There was a sudden burst of white light and a black

cloud exploded around them. Jordyn gagged on the toxic fumes, stumbling backward as it burned her eyes. The other Calydons all shouted and leapt to the side, gagging and coughing. The cloud dissipated suddenly, and she saw that Rohan was gone. In his place was a patch of raw, ragged earth, scorched and burned. "What—"

"I buried him alive in the ground," Eric said from behind her.

She whirled around to see that he was on his knees just behind where Rohan had been standing. His hands were covered with black soot, and his face was drained of color. "It won't last for more than a few minutes against him since he's so powerful. Let's go!" He grabbed her hand and sprinted past her into the campsite.

"What did you do?" Jordyn raced over to her backpack and grabbed her gun. Did she have enough demon bile to take down a Calydon strong enough to burn up the entire sky? God, she hoped so.

"It's an ancient, spiritual magic," Eric said as he grabbed his duffel and slung it over his shoulder. "I appear to have a special talent for it, but I never know exactly how it's going to work. That worked, so we get to live another day. Always a bonus." He swept her backpack out of her hand and threw it over his other shoulder. "Run!"

She didn't bother to argue with his manly offer to carry her backpack. She knew she wouldn't be able to run fast with it. "Thanks." She spun around and bolted back out of the circle of torches. She saw the rest of Rohan's crew up ahead, blocking her path, and she hesitated. "Can you bury them, too?"

"No need. They won't stop us. Go!"

She grimaced at the sight of all the swords, but had no time to question Eric. The glow over the trees was already fading, and once it was gone, it would be almost impossible to track where it had been. So, she just gripped her gun more tightly and ran right toward the warriors.

To her surprise, they stepped aside, opening a gap as she neared. She burst through, Eric right behind her. They'd gone only a few yards, when she heard footsteps behind her. She glanced over her shoulder, and was shocked to see all the warriors behind them, racing single file, weapons out. "They're coming?"

"Their teammate's gone rogue and about to die at the hands of that webbing. They're not going to sit around if there's a chance to save him, just because Rohan thinks they shouldn't interfere." He grinned at her as he fell in beside her, his long legs keeping up with her easily, despite the fact he was carrying two heavy bags. "Rohan's their leader, but they don't have the same faith in his visions that he does. We fight for what we believe in and what we can see. It's what we do. Never leave a man behind, if we can help it."

She noticed that Eric said "we fight," not "they fight," and she knew that the stoic warrior who decried this tight band of warriors was more connected to them than he had been willing to admit. Not a Calydon in real life, but in his heart, maybe. The idea should have unsettled her, but it didn't. It made him seemed more grounded in normalcy. She didn't know anything about his spiritual magic or his "I'm not a man" background, but she understood Calydons. His bond with the other Calydons made him seem more approachable...and more dangerous.

He looked up at the sky. "I don't know what we're walking into," he said grimly, "but I sure as hell hope we're in time."

Jordyn thought of Rhiannon's scared face when she'd said that she was going to go back and face her ex, and she felt her throat tighten. She'd seen what Calydons could do to their mates. She'd lived the aftermath of having to kill her soul mate. She'd seen carnage and destruction that would haunt her forever. And even worse, she'd already lost one best friend to an abusive man, and she couldn't bear to lose another. "Me, too," she whispered, as she pushed herself to run even faster, giving it every last ounce that she had to offer.

* * *

Zach unleashed a battle cry as the first of his attackers landed in the bottom of the pit. He swung fast and swung hard, taking down the first three that attacked. The sai that José had melted had not regained form yet, but he kept trying to call it out, knowing that he was toast if he didn't get it back. And even then—

A blow hit him between the shoulders, and he staggered under the force of the hit, even as he swung around and took out the warrior behind him. But as he laid him out, he got pummeled in his right shoulder, tearing a gaping wound that cut right through the muscle, leaving his arm useless.

Grimly, he whirled around, spinning in a circle, faster and faster, using himself as a hub and his sai as a deadly spoke, moving so fast that none of the attackers had time to dodge his blows and attack. Even as he gained speed, he felt the fatigue screaming through his body. He'd been at the last of his resources before the attack, and he knew he had only minutes left to continue to move at this speed before he couldn't sustain it.

He thought of Rhiannon, clasped in José's arms somewhere, and fresh energy surged through him. *I'm coming, Rhiannon.* He sent the thought out into the night, even though he knew she wouldn't hear him. The earth was hot beneath his feet, burning through the soles of his boots, and he knew that José's fire still smoldered in the ground from when he'd created the pit that had trapped him.

Zach shut his eyes, and opened his preternatural senses. He became viscerally aware of the location of each of his attackers. He could smell their sweat. He could hear the beat of their hearts. He could feel their bloodlust to kill him. He knew exactly where each of them stood, and how they were balanced on their feet, ready to take advantage of the slightest falter by Zach.

Then, he reached deeper inside him, for the part of him that had been dead for so long, the part of him that had once been so volatile that he couldn't control it, the part of him that he'd shut down the day he'd killed his daughter. He reached past the memories of his daughter's charred body. He surged past the guilt and grief of her death. He tried to cut loose the iron grip of fear of who he was. Deep inside him, he felt something stir, that same something that had exploded so violently when he and Rhiannon had been trapped beneath the earth.

It rumbled deep in his core, a shifting of a great weight that slid roughly through him. Elation rushed through him, and he opened himself to it, sending his focus into the embers in the earth beneath his feet, trying to open the connection to the fire. The connection was almost there. He could feel it at the edges of his consciousness, straining to get free, but he couldn't access it. He couldn't break through the wall that surrounded it so tightly and kept it trapped inside him.

"Come on!" he shouted. "Now!" But even as he shouted it, his mind flashed to the image of his daughter's face, her rosy cheeks, and her blue eyes, staring up at him with such adoration, worshipping the man who would soon kill her. Guilt and terror tore through him, and the heat simmering inside him slipped out of his grasp, receding into the chasm it had been in. "No!"

He screamed his frustration, and then something hit him in the chest. He looked down and saw a battle axe embedded in him. He had a fraction of a second to register it, and then he felt his heart stutter, and blood rushed into his lungs. He stumbled, and there was a cry of victory as his attackers closed in for the final kill.

* * *

The acrid scent of smoke was the first thing Rhiannon registered. It burned her nose, jerking her awake. Gasping for air, she rolled onto her side, coughing the searing smoke into her lungs. She dug her hands into the dirt, her body aching and sore as she tried to regain her breath. Her chest felt like it was on fire, and her throat was raw and sore. Even her eyes stung. As she sucked in air, she wiped her hand across her mouth. Grit scraped her lips, and she realized her hands were covered in dirt.

She suddenly remembered being trapped in the tunnel with Zach, and she instantly bolted upright. "Zach? Zach!" She scrambled to her feet as she scanned the jungle around her, searching for him...but there was no one there. "Zach!" She swung around, frantic, trying to get her bearings. What had happened? Where was he?

Movement caught her eye, and she searched the dark woods. "Zach?"

No one answered, but she felt something watching her. The hair on the back of her neck stood up, and her mouth went pasty dry. "No," she whispered, as she took a step back. It couldn't be. Not like this.

But as she watched, a man stepped out of the shadows into the moonlight, a tall, muscular man who made fear lodge in her throat. Instinctively, her hand went to her hip, but there was no dagger. Her bow and quiver were gone. She had nothing, and he was here.

Fighting the urge to run, she stood taller as he walked toward her. José was just as she remembered. His dark hair flowed over his shoulders, and his heavily muscled chest was bare. Flame tattoos cascaded down his arms and wrapped around his torso. Across his stomach was a scar, the scar from when she'd tried to kill him, a scar he, apparently, had chosen not to heal entirely. A reminder of what she'd done to him.

His eyes were a dark, bottomless black, and around his neck was a beaded necklace. Black leather pants were slung low over his hips, and the top button was undone, revealing a V of dark hair disappearing into his pants.

Against her will, her eyes followed that V to the bulge in his pants. Nausea churned in her belly, but she couldn't take her eyes off it. God, what was wrong with her? Why was she responding to him like that? She didn't want him. She wanted Zach...*Zach.* Where was he? How had José separated them?

Fear gripped her belly, an icy cold terror for the man who had made such incredible love to her, who had made her feel safe and free for the first time in so long. "Where's Zach?"

"The bastard who fucked you?" José's voice was hard and bitter. "He's dead."

"Dead?" Her voice broke, and her legs went numb. She couldn't breathe. The world suddenly seemed to spin, and she lost her balance. Zach gone? A bottomless abyss of grief swelled up inside her, sucking her down as tears fell from her heart. *Zach? Are you gone?* Desperately, she reached out with her soul, trying to find him, but there was nothing.

José caught her arm in an iron grip just as she started to fall. "You whore," he snapped. "You're my woman. How could you fuck someone else?"

The agony of his fingers digging into her flesh jerked her from her grief about Zach. Anger rolled through her. This was the man who had killed Zach? Fierce strength rushed through her, and she ripped her arm out of his grasp. "You're supposed to protect your *sheva*," she snapped. "How could you do what you've done to me?"

A smile stretched thinly across his face. "It's how it works, bitch."

"No, it's not!" She'd always hated what he'd done to her and how he'd treated her, but until she'd met Zach, she hadn't truly grasped how it should have been. She knew now what it was supposed to be like between a man and a woman. Zach had taught her what it felt like to be cherished, and he'd done it simply out of love and humanity, not because he was bound to her by some supernatural bond.

Her upper lip curled in disdain as she looked at the man who had trapped her for so long. She didn't see his handsomeness. She didn't crave his touch. She just saw a creature who was depraved and twisted, who had contaminated the *sheva* bond into something horrific and evil. "You don't get to have me again," she said. "It's over."

"No," he whispered. "It's just beginning." As he spoke, a sudden wave of desire rushed through her. Heat pooled in her belly, and longing throbbed between her legs.

"What?" Horror congealed through her, and she grabbed for her throat...and then went ice cold. The amulet was *gone.*

José laughed, that deep, booming laugh that she hated so much. "I figured it out, bitch. That rock is gone, and you will never get it back. You're *mine*, and this time, you're going to love it."

Bile churned in her belly, even as desire coursed through her. She felt filthy responding to him, disgusted with herself. "I will never love it," she snapped.

"Oh, but you *will.*" He pulled her close so that her breasts slammed into his chest. She winced and then wanted to cry when she felt her nipples tighten. How could she be so weak? She couldn't believe it was happening again.

His lust flooded her, and he slammed his mouth down over hers. Just like she'd done before, the moment his mouth clamped down over hers, she hardened herself to his influence, and tried to distance herself. The moment she did so, Zach's face appeared in her mind. She saw his smile. The twinkle in his eyes.

She heard his laugh, and the affectionate tenor of his voice. She saw the way he'd looked at her with such admiration when they'd first met, how he'd called her a warrior. She thought of how his touch had helped her focus her energy and call the plants to life. As all those memories tumbled through her head, a strange sense of fierce determination began to course through her, beneath the lust that was boiling through her.

Why did she have to be weak? Why did she have to be his victim? Jordyn had killed her soul mate, right? Why couldn't she do it, too? She squeezed her eyes shut and envisioned calling out his weapon. A *sheva* could call out her mate's weapon whenever danger threatened. She'd done it once, when one of his crew had attacked her. That had been the final stage to seal their bond, and it wasn't until much later that she finally realized that he'd commanded the rogue to attack her, to force her to call his weapon and complete the bond, trapping her forever.

Since that one time, she'd never been able to call it, no matter what he'd done to her.

But now, with his mouth on hers, and Zach's voice in her mind, she felt different. She felt like she had a chance. She felt like she could do it! She focused all her energy on the brands on her arm, urging them to come to her, to save her, to allow her to defend herself against José. She could feel their energy humming in his arms, but she couldn't reach them. Frustrated, she tried harder, and they began to recede from her, refusing to respond to her call. Why wouldn't they let her call them against her own mate? Was destiny so stupid that she didn't even realize that a woman's greatest threat could come from her own soul mate? Apparently. Tears burned in her eyes, as she realized it was the same as before, *the exact same.*

José suddenly broke the kiss, his eyes dark with rage. "I can taste him on you." He flung her backwards, and she stumbled, but stayed on her feet. "You will bathe in the river," he snapped. "Clean his touch and the filth from you. And then you will come crawling to me, and you will beg me to take you again, and again, and again. And I will, until you never, ever think of another man again. Now, go!" He pointed behind her, and she felt his mental push in her mind, commanding her acquiescence.

She didn't try to fight it. A bath gave her time to try

to figure out how to stop him. She whirled around and raced toward the river, her skin prickling at his gloating laugh. Even as she reached the riverbed, and plunged into it, not daring to take off her clothes, she felt his lust settling in her belly. Desire rushed through her, and she had a sudden image of him standing over her in his naked glory. *"No!"* She forced her mind to picture Zach, shoving José's image out of her head. The lust poured over her even more thickly, but this time, it felt empowering, because it was her own desire for Zach. Excitement pulsed through her as she ducked her face in the river and scrubbed off the dirt. If she could use José's lust to call up her response to Zach, then maybe she could use Zach to summon her relationship with plants, even though he wasn't with her.

Was he really dead? The thought made her falter, and she immediately dismissed it. Zach would never die on her. He'd promised to keep her safe, and he would. *He would not die.*

She whirled around and faced the shore, which was lined with heavy jungle plants. She let the lust fill her, and her belly clenched at the thought of Zach. She opened herself to the desire, and let it flood her, focusing on a vine at the edge of the riverbank. Energy pulsed through her, the energy of her life, and one of the leaves on the plant rippled. Elation leapt through her. *Yes. Yes!* Another leaf began to move, swaying purposefully in rhythm with the first one. And then another, and then another, and then—

Stop! José's fury exploded through her, and she lost her contact with the plants.

"No, no, no!" She scrambled up the riverbank, and dropped to her knees in front of the plants, laying her hands on the leaves. "Come on, come on," she begged. She tried to think of Zach again, but José was all over the place in her mind and emotions. She could hear his voice. See his eyes. Feel his cold, dark will entangled with hers.

You don't get space from me, anymore. You are mine, Rhiannon. All mine.

Tears burned in her eyes as she enfolded one of the leaves between her palms, struggling to free herself from José's cold grasp on her mind. She focused on Zach, imagining his kiss. Recalling the sensation of feeling his skin against hers. That magical moment when he'd made love to her—

I do admit, I think it's hot as hell that you were able to best me. I knew you were worthy of being my mate. A rumble of satisfaction rippled through her, jerking her focus away from Zach. *You have proved yourself worthy, Rhiannon. It is time for us to create a son, and my new legacy.*

A son? She froze, horrified by his words. He'd killed her daughter, and now he wanted her to bear him a child for him to twist into his depraved world? Never. She couldn't let that happen! Frantic, she renewed her efforts with the plant, but then, as she watched, the leaf turned brown and crumbled through her fingers.

What? She'd killed it?

José's poisonous spirit pulsed through her. *That will happen every time from now on. You will slowly kill your precious jungle each time you try to connect with it. Finish your cleansing and return to my side. I am waiting.* He pushed at her to get back in the river, and this time she fought it.

She dug her fingers into the earth and bent her head, straining with every last bit of her strength to resist. She thought of Zach. She thought of her daughter. She thought of the son she would doom to a life of hell if she were unable to resist José. She even thought of Jordyn, who possessed the emotional strength to kill her own soul mate. She pictured the banners of her tribe drifting in the trees. She tried everything she could to ground herself in her own identity, but all she could think about was getting in that river.

"No!" She bent her head, fighting as hard as she could, but it was no use. She lurched to her feet, swaying as she fought it. She felt José push again, and she turned obediently toward the water and walked toward it.

When she reached the shore, she found herself reaching for her shirt to take it off. Dammit, no! She was not going to get naked!

And, just like it had for ten years, her mental resistance failed. Within moments, her clothes were in a pile on the shore, and she was walking naked into the river to rid herself of every last remnant of her time with Zach.

CHAPTER 20

The attack by José's Calydons was fast, brutal, and unstoppable. They surged upon him from all sides, attacking with merciless efficiency as Zach stumbled. But as he went down to his knees and felt their blades slice his flesh, all he could think about was the fate that he delivered Rhiannon to. If he died, there would be no one to save her.

Fuck. That.

"No!" He lurched to his feet but fell again, barely even feeling the pain as his attackers blades cut him. Fine. Who needed to stand? He swung with violent, ruthless efficiency from his knees, refusing to die, refusing to give up. One assailant fell after another, but each time, another Calydon took his place, fresh and ready, opening yet another wound in Zach's body. The ground was soon damp, saturated with the blood of his assailants, as well his own blood, which he really needed in his body and not spewed out over the earth.

Weakness pervaded his body, until he couldn't even think. All he could do was fight on instinct, willing the strength for one more strike, and another, but he knew he was losing.

He always hated losing, but this time it was unacceptable. "Rhiannon!" He surged to his feet, then gasped in pain as a blade sunk into the back of his leg. This time, as he fell, he knew that there was no respite. He rolled onto his back, using his feet as weapons as he swung with his sai, reduced to fighting defensively and trying to protect his throat. It was hard as hell to kill him as an Order member, but taking off his head would do it. If they decapitated him, it was over.

Someone hit hard, and his sai flew out of his hand. Swearing, he called it back. It streaked toward him just as two of the warriors brought down their swords, slicing through the air toward his neck.

He tried to roll to the side, but it was too late. The blades hit simultaneously and—

The warriors both screamed and flew backwards. Their swords clattered to the ground as they fell. Within moments, all his assailants were shouting and scrambling away from him. Trying to suck in his breath, Zach rolled onto his side as his sai flew back into his hand. He lurched to his feet, staggering for balance as he took in the scene.

Rohan's team was surging down the sides of the pit, their swords flashing as they took on José's warriors. Blue electricity crackled through the air, and the rogues lit up like lightning with each strike of Rohan's team. The six warriors were evenly matched against the forty attacking Zach, and it was a stalemate of vicious violence, with no one paying any attention to him.

He was so out of there. "Rhiannon! I'm coming!" Zach didn't hesitate. He bolted for the rim of the pit and scrambled up the side of it. He didn't even feel the pain from all his gashes, and fresh energy galvanized him. He hauled himself over the edge, then a blade crashed into his skull.

He went numb and started to slide back into the pit, when there was a loud boom. His assailant flew backwards, careening into the pit, as a woman in jeans and a hot pink tank top came out of the bushes carrying a bazooka.

What the hell? He must have been hit harder than he thought. Hallucinations were not a good sign. With a fierce grunt, he hauled himself back over the edge and rolled onto his knees, struggling to stand up.

"You're Zach?" The woman, who was apparently real, hurried over and helped him to his feet, which he found seriously damaging to his ego. "The one who everyone thinks can stop José?"

"Yeah." He rubbed his head, trying to stop the jungle from spinning. Behind him, in the pit, raged the sounds of battle, but he didn't bother to turn around. He needed to go after her...but then he stumbled and went down to his knees. Swearing, he tried to stand and fell again. Of all the times for his body to give in to a few battle wounds, this was not it. "Come on!" He fought to stand, and wound up on his hands and knees, gasping for breath as fluid began to fill his lungs.

"I'm Jordyn, Rhiannon's' friend. Do you know where she is?" The woman knelt beside him, her face frantic.

"You know Rhiannon?" His vision was blurring, but he tried to focus on her.

Jordyn grabbed his shoulders. "You've met her! Where is she?"

"José got her." Zach lunged to his feet again, and this time managed to stay vertical. "I gotta go. He took her and threw away her amulet." He had just taken another step, when there was a sizzling display of blue electricity ahead and then Rohan burst out of the jungle. Because that was what he needed right now, right? Another battle with a pig-headed seer who had betrayed his leader? "Get out of my way."

Rohan glanced toward the scrum in the pit, then turned his head toward Zach, as if inspecting him. "You need to heal."

Oh, yeah, that was just precious. "Heal? Really? You think I should lie down and take a little nap while some piece of shit has my woman and Thano gets eaten alive by that black webbing? I don't think so."

Rohan strode over to him, and set his hands on his shoulders. "Merge with me, Zachary."

"No way." He didn't trust Rohan. He flipped the man's hands off his shoulders. "Get off me—"

"Wait!" Jordyn rushed over to them. "Let him help you. Rhiannon needs you!"

Grinding his jaw, Zach shook his head. "If I merge with him, he can control me. I don't trust him."

"Well, then, trust me." Jordyn hoisted the bazooka onto her shoulders again and aimed it at Rohan. "If he messes with you, I'll take him down. Rhiannon needs you."

Zach stared at her. "Are you insane?"

"No, but you're the guy who can help her." She smiled, a cheerful grin that was completely out of place in the blood-soaked jungle they were in. "It was in your eyes when you said

José had her. She matters to you, and that's enough for me. You're the guy she needs, so I'm on your side. If Rohan thinks you can kick José's ass, then you probably can, because I've already figured out that Rohan's a bit of an arrogant jerk, but he's a smart warrior. So, since you can save Rhiannon, and you want to, I'm all over this thing between you guys." She pointed the gun at Zach. "So, if you don't let him help you, I'll shoot you just because I'm pissed." She then swung the gun toward Rohan. "And if you mess with Zach and keep him from saving my friend, I'll shoot you, but that will be to free Zach. Plus, I'll be pissed. So, you guys in or what? Because I need to shoot someone soon."

Zach looked back and forth between the gun-toting chick and the moody seer who had betrayed his leader. Trust them? Not a chance.

But even as he thought it, his legs gave out. He sank to his belly in the dirt, not even able to support himself. He turned his head to get his face out of the dirt, not amused by the smug grin on Jordyn's face. So, yeah, okay, maybe he needed to examine his options in a different light, given how limited his alternatives were and the fact that Thano and Rhiannon were counting on him. Maybe he should categorize his choices a different way: so, the question was actually, should he go it alone on legs that weren't actually capable of holding his weight, or try giving his trust to a woman who could blow a Calydon to hell and a warrior who was the most powerful seer Zach had ever met? Yeah, okay, when he put it that way... "Okay." He wasted no time. He simply dropped his mental shields and opened himself to the one man on the earth that he would never have thought he'd trust again.

Then again, he'd never thought the life of a woman he loved would hang in the balance either. Oh...had he really just thought that? A woman he *loved*? He had no time to recant his thoughts before Rohan's energy surged into his brain and took over his mind.

Zach gripped his head against the pain that shot through his skull. His skin sparked with blue electricity, leaping from his fingertips to the ground. He bent over, unable to hold himself still under the onslaught of energy. It wasn't simply healing energy. It was as if an entire millennium's worth of life force had been thrust into him so violently it felt like it would rip his flesh from his bones. He gritted his jaw, fighting back the howl of agony, fighting desperately to hold onto his corporeal form and not be shredded by the onslaught.

"What are you doing to him?" Jordyn shouted. "Don't kill him!"

"If he dies, then that's what he has earned," snapped Rohan.

Zach's eyes rolled back in his head, and his mind began to blacken. Still the onslaught continued, plunging all the way into his organs, ripping through the damage, ruthlessly attacking the injuries with energy so strong that it hurt as much as it healed.

"Let him go or I'll shoot you!" Jordyn yelled. "Stop it—Oomph!"

"He has to do it that way," Eric shouted as he grabbed Jordyn's gun and wrenched it out of her hands, ignoring her screech of protest. "Zach's too badly hurt! Let Rohan heal him!"

Healing? Was that what this shit was? Because it felt like death by electrocution.

Zach raised his head and looked at Rohan, then sucked in his breath at what he saw. For the first time in his life, he could see Rohan's face. Beneath the hood, his face shone with blue light, showing high, skeletal cheekbones, haunted black eyes, and a brutal scar that seemed to bisect the right side of his head. A heavy beard covered his jaw, and a gold skull hung from his right ear. He was creepy as hell, but at the same time, he was clearly a man, a man who could be hurt badly enough to scar.

His eyes met Zach's, and suddenly Zach was flooded with a feeling of anguish and loss so deep that it stripped all hope from him. He realized he was caught in Rohan's emotions, a suffocating mire of grief and despair, an echoing emptiness that never ended, that stripped all that was good and living from Zach. His lungs constricted, and he couldn't breathe, gasping for breath under the weight of the doom flooding from Rohan.

Then, just as suddenly, it cut off. Rohan withdrew his energy, and with that, took back the emotional weight he carried. Sudden strength flooded Zach's body, and he knew without looking that his wounds were healed. Yet, for a moment, he didn't move. He simply stared into the face of the man he'd never looked upon in the flesh even though they'd known each other for hundreds of years. The weight of Rohan's suffering was so great that he could still feel it crushing his soul. "What the hell happened to you, Rohan? How do you live with that?"

A faint smile curved the warrior's lips, an expression so human that Zach almost couldn't believe it. "We all do what we must, Zachary." Then the blue light faded, and Rohan's face descended into impenetrable darkness again.

But Zach would never forget that glimpse of the man he'd hated and distrusted for so long. There was more to Rohan than what he knew. Something deeper to his suffering. Something that he had hidden from everyone all this time, a burden that he carried silently on his own.

"Wow." Jordyn's voice jerked him back to the present. "That was super impressive."

Zach leapt to his feet, his senses clear and vivid, as powerful as they'd ever been. He could hear every sound of the forest, even the whisper of insect wings and the slither of a snake in the distance. Jordyn had apparently wrested the bazooka back from Eric and was now aiming it at Rohan. Eric was standing between the gun and his leader, using his body as a shield to protect him. Eric was not wearing his cloak, and Zach was pretty sure that his brands were in a slightly different place than the last time he'd seen him. What the hell?

Not that he cared. All that mattered was finding Rhiannon—

Rohan caught his arms. "Retrieve the staff, Zach. Not the girl. The staff."

Zach pulled his arm free. "I know—"

"No, you don't." Rohan's fingers tightened around Zach's arm. "José is the only one who can power the staff. If you kill him, the power of the staff dies. Thano will die. You cannot kill him."

Zach stared at him in disbelief. "*What?*" He was no fool. He'd seen José. There was no way he could be allowed to live if Rhiannon was going to escape, and he also knew that there was no way he was going to get José to run through the jungle zapping rogue Calydons with his staff upon request.

"Yeah, *what?*" Jordyn appeared at his elbow. "You can't keep José alive. He'll kill Rhiannon. Don't you understand?"

Rohan met his gaze. "My teammate must live."

"So must my friend," Jordyn snapped, in an imitation of Rohan's overly proper speech that would have been funny if the pile of shit they were in wasn't so deep.

"Not today." Before she could react, Rohan reached out and touched her gun. Blue electricity sparked through it. She yelped and dropped it. It crashed to the ground, and shattered into a thousand pieces, fragmented by Rohan's power.

"Oh my God," she whispered, falling to her knees. "How could you do that? That was the only way to stop him! Don't you understand how powerful he is?" She lurched to her feet, her fists balled. "You're such a bastard! All you care about is your stupid prize. You honored me because I killed Walter, but he would never have honored you." Her voice dripped with disgust. "Men suck," she snapped.

Eric walked quietly up behind her, and touched her shoulder. She whirled on him, and then her body relaxed when she saw it was Eric. As Eric's fingers tightened on Jordyn's shoulder, he looked over at Zach. He gave one silent nod, and that was all Zach needed to know. No matter what Rohan decreed, Eric had his back, and he knew he was going to need it.

With a low growl, he shoved past Rohan, and then broke into a run. He sprinted past the rim of the pit, where Rhiannon had last been. The battle was still raging below, but he shut out the noise and the carnage, focusing his enhanced senses on Rhiannon.

For ten minutes, he ran blindly, leaping through the jungle. He couldn't sense her at all, but he was going on instinct, following the path that his gut told him to follow. But still, he couldn't pick up any trace of her. What if he was going the wrong way? Swearing, he finally stopped. He went down on one knee and thrust his hands into the earth. His fingers closed around a vine clinging to the dirt, and he gently pulsed energy into it. "Tell me where she is," he whispered. "Tell me."

There was no response from the vegetation. He couldn't channel her connection to the plants. He ran his hand through his hair, wiping away sweat. "Rhiannon," he bellowed. "Where are you?"

The only response was the pulsating sounds of the jungle.

He looked down at his arms, at the runes etched into his flesh that blocked the *sheva* connection. He remembered when Dante had carved his own, similar wards from his body so he could bond with his *sheva.* Zach hesitated. What if Rhiannon was his *sheva*? The moment the thought went through his head, he knew she was. The connection between them was too intense, his need for her too overwhelming.

She was destined to be his.

Intense rightness surged over him, and possessiveness raged. *Rhiannon was his woman.* He knew it in every fiber of his being. It didn't matter that she was José's *sheva,* because she was also his, and his connection with her would triumph because it was mutual. He studied the runes, adrenaline racing through him as his mind subconsciously tracked each passing minute that Rhiannon was under José's control. What if he could connect with her by taking down his safeguards? They'd made love, which would satisfy one of the stages of the *sheva* bond. They'd shared their darkest secrets, which would satisfy another. They'd done enough that the bond would have begun. He might be able to reach her telepathically!

The runes would have to go. For a thousand years he'd been protected from the *sheva* curse that had made his father murder his mother, teaching him all he needed to know about the dangers of it. For a thousand years, he'd lived life knowing that he would never become the rogue that would murder those he loved. And now, for Rhiannon, he would enter that realm. He called out his sai with a crack and a flash of black light, but paused with it poised over his arm. What if she wasn't his *sheva*? What if he took off those protections, and then found himself linked to another woman, against his will, just as she was linked to José? Or what if she was indeed his *sheva,* and he bound her to him against her will, just as José had done? He thought of Rhiannon, and the depth of her fear of being controlled, and he shook his head. If he bound Rhiannon to him, it would betray her trust of him forever. He could not do it.

Even if Rhiannon was his *sheva*, he would never trap her like that. Never would he call upon a supernatural bond and bind her to him. Never would he ask her to trade bondage with José for bondage with him.

There had to be another way. *There had to be.* But what?

Behind him, he heard the clang of weapons, and suddenly, it brought back a memory of his daughter, of sparring with her when she was five. She'd been too small to hold his sai, so he'd made her a miniature one. He remembered the day she'd played hide and seek, and gotten lost. He remembered how he'd called upon his fire to find her. His body stiffened at the memory. Hell, he'd forgotten about that. All he ever remembered was that his fire had killed her. He'd completely forgotten that it had saved her once as well.

He bent his head and went still, softening his mind to the memories as he pulled them back from where they'd been locked up for so long. He recalled that moment of desperate fear when night had fallen and he hadn't been able to find her. The woods had been too vast to track, and the rain had been coming down all day, wiping away all traces of her trail. So, he'd called upon the essence of what defined him, and he'd become the smoke that could infiltrate an entire land in one windy afternoon.

Zach thought back to that moment, to the desperation that he'd tapped into. That same paralyzing fear was in his heart now, that same need to find someone who mattered to him more than his own life. He took a deep breath, allowing his fear for Rhiannon's safety to fill him as he pictured that moment from so many centuries ago when he had transcended the boundaries of his human frame and become that which burned inside him so fiercely.

He inhaled again, sucking air into his lungs. He held it inside his body, letting it settle in his lungs and mingle with his cells. He let it permeate his body, winding itself through him. Then he pursed his lips and blew it out into the jungle, a billion droplets of his soul drifting into the night, the ashes of his spirit riding the wind and smoke as it dissipated through the air.

The breeze caught the particles, and they cascaded away from him. He closed his eyes, and focused on the droplets, keeping the connection. He felt every breeze that rippled through the jungle, and he felt the vibrations of energy as they fluttered past living creatures. It was working! Tracking the smoke particles as they flew through the woods, he opened his mind and his heart, searching the forest not for a scent or a sound, but for the rhythm of Rhiannon's soul, for the signature of her emotions: a combination of fear, courage, softness, and vulnerability. He searched for that flicker of warmth that had somehow remained a part of her, despite all she'd endured. He called for the essence of her being that made her who she was.

For an agonizingly long moment, he felt nothing but the wildness of the jungle...and then he sensed her emotions as they came tumbling over him. Fear. Desperation. Determination. A spirit warring with hope and defeat at the same time. "Rhiannon!" He honed in on her location and then leapt to his feet, breaking into a dead sprint as he tore through the jungle toward her. Toward José. Toward a fire god that no one could stop.

This time, he had to win, or everyone who mattered to him would be dead. Again.

* * *

Rhiannon knelt before José, her wet hair dangling loose over her shoulders. On all sides of her were his warriors, standing in silence with their weapons clenched in their fists. Before her, José sat on his throne of branches and vines, the one she'd made for him when they'd first met.

Flames burned all around them, enclosing them in a ring of orange and purple fire that stretched from the earth to the heavens. The heat from the flames seared her flesh, but no marks appeared.

"You covered my brands." Obviously, he'd noticed that she'd covered his brand with tattoos while she'd been away from the jungle. Her arms were covered with beautiful vines and flowers that hid the ugliness of the marks that their bond had burned into her flesh.

She closed her eyes as his voice rolled through her like a silken caress that made her thighs clench. His control over her was so complete that her desire for him didn't even make her nauseous anymore. Her body craved his touch even more than it ever had, but like before, her thoughts were her own. He never seemed to bother with her thoughts. He didn't care about them. To him, total physical submission, along with knowing that he stoked intense desire and lust in her, was all that mattered. To him, he had won.

He was wrong. Her mind mattered. He hadn't won, and he wouldn't win this time either.

"Yes," she said. "I did cover them."

She couldn't call out his weapon and kill him with his own blade. She couldn't call the vegetation that surrounded them so thickly. But one thing that he wasn't strong enough to defeat was the destiny of the *sheva* bond. For ten years, he'd stayed sane and not gone rogue, despite their destiny. But fate decreed that once their bond was complete, the Calydon would go rogue, and the only one who could stop him was his soul mate, who would kill him, and then kill herself.

It was time to finish their fate.

The *sheva* destiny commanded that after the bond was complete, the Calydon would lose his woman somehow, and that was what would make him go rogue. Her escaping him hadn't sent him over the edge, but maybe that was because he hadn't really believed he'd lost her. He'd remained confident that he would track her down, and he had.

So, how could she make him lose her for real? And if she did make him go rogue, then what? Could she really kill him?

She watched him through slitted eyes. Did she hate him enough to kill him, and accept that she would then have to die? Was that better than living under his rule again? Or did she hate him enough that she could kill him, but not need to kill herself? But even as she asked it, she knew it was impossible. The *sheva* destiny was too strong. She wouldn't be able to break it. If she killed him, she would kill herself. And she was okay with that. If Zach was already dead, what was her life worth? It was worth saving the jungle she was born to protect. Something had to be preserved from his poisonous touch.

José's gaze drifted to her breasts, which were barely covered by the silken gown he'd told her to wear when she'd gotten out of the river. Her breasts strained at the thin fabric, and her nipples puckered under his heated gaze. "You can make my body respond," she said quietly, "but you will never get my heart."

His eyes narrowed. "I have all of you."

"No, you don't." She looked right at him. "I love Zach." She'd intended the words simply to torment José, to draw him out of his controlled state, and to make him go rogue, but the moment she said it, she realized it was true. Her heart stuttered for a moment, and a great weeping sadness swept over her for the man who she had barely had time to know before she'd lost him. Fierce determination swept through her. José would hurt no one else. As his *sheva*, she was the only one with the power to destroy him. "I don't care if he's dead. He's the one I love. The *sheva* bond means nothing to me. Nothing."

The words hung in the air, and she held her breath as José's face darkened. He'd been able to share her body with his men, but what about her heart? Could he share that too? Or would she finally trigger the soul mate instincts to covet his woman? "*I love another man.*"

José suddenly exploded off his throne. He leapt at her, howling with rage. He was so angry that he forgot to hold onto her mind, and she leapt sideways, dodging his blow. He lunged for her again, but this time, she knew what she had to do. With courage she didn't know she had, she forced herself not to flee, but to let him catch her.

His hand closed around her throat, and he jerked her off her feet, squeezing until she couldn't breathe. He was going to kill her. She'd triggered the final stage. He was going to destroy her, and now was her time to kill him, as fate decreed. It was time for his weapon to come to her to save her.

But when she called it, *it didn't come.*

With sudden terror, she realized that his eyes weren't red. He wasn't rogue. Until he went rogue, the destiny wouldn't be triggered. How was he not rogue? His *sheva* loved another man. How could that not turn him?

But it hadn't. Anger and bitterness were seething in his eyes, and his lips were snarled with disgust, yet his eyes remained black, fixed ruthlessly on her face as he strangled her. Gripping his wrist, she fought desperately, trying to pry his fingers off her throat. Her vision was starting to blacken. Damn it! Why wasn't this working? Tears bled from her eyes as she fought to stay conscious. She kicked desperately, trying to find purchase, and her foot slammed into his throne, knocking his staff to the earth.

The staff. In shock, she stared at the staff, understanding dawning too late. The staff that brought back his team from the state of rogue somehow kept him from crossing that line in the first place. No wonder he could hand her off to others without it affecting him. No wonder he could hear her love another man and not lose it. Dear God, as long as he had the staff, there was no way to drive him over the edge and trigger their destiny.

No way to kill him.

No way to break his hold on her.

She jerked her gaze back to him. Triumph gleamed in his eyes. "You are mine," he said. Then he jerked her over to him and slammed his mouth onto hers just as she felt the lack of oxygen triumph. She slithered into oblivion, knowing all too well what he and his team would do to her while she was unconscious... and knowing there was nothing she could do to stop it.

CHAPTER 21

Another ring of fire.

Swearing, Zach sprinted up to the wall of flames, but the heat was so fierce, he had to stop several yards away. His shirt began to burn, and he ripped it off, stepping backwards. He focused his mind and tried to summon up heat from within. But just like before, nothing happened. Swearing, he backed up a step, then sprinted toward the fire. He leapt right into it, and it flung him straight up toward the sky, the flames melting his flesh. He screamed in agony and threw himself backwards, out of the fire.

He landed hard on the ground, groaning as he struggled to his feet. The band of fire had to be yards wide. He couldn't even leap through it. Beyond it, he could sense Rhiannon's life force, fading and in pain. *Rhiannon! I'm coming!* Galvanized with a renewed sense of urgency, he sprinted around the fire, knowing as he did it that there would be no weak link, but checking anyway. He kept himself close enough to the fire for the heat to make his jeans smoke, but everywhere he passed, it was equally as hot and powerful. There was no opening. By the time he got back to his original spot, Eric and Jordyn were there, both of them panting.

Rhiannon was inside that ring. He could feel her presence, but it had faded just as he'd reached the circle. If he didn't already have her location targeted, he would never have been able to track her. She wasn't dead, but close.

Urgency hammering at him, he backed up, studying the

top of the ring of fire desperately. It was several hundred yards high, too far for him to jump. He immediately called out his sai and plunged it into the dirt. He dragged the dirt aside, intending to go beneath the fire, like how they'd gotten out of the campsite before. But the earth spewed out fire through the hole he'd dug. José hadn't just ignited the sky. He'd ignited the very earth they were standing upon. They weren't merely in a ring of fire, they were in a cylinder of fire that went as far into the earth as it did upward.

The only way inside was through the flames.

"Where is she?" Jordyn asked as she hurried up.

"Inside." Zach went still, studying the wall of fire. Every instinct inside him shouted to attack, to just run straight through it, but yeah, tried that already. If he'd kept going, he'd be dead. If he died, no one would be there to protect Rhiannon or save Thano, but the longer he stood there, the more he betrayed her.

"Well, go get her." Jordyn shoved at his back. "You have no idea how fast a man can hurt a woman. You have to get her right now."

Zach ground his jaw, his brands burning in his arms. "I know exactly how fast a Calydon can hurt a woman." And children. He knew. But standing there, outside the ring of fire, he had never felt so powerless in his life.

Eric was standing beside Jordyn, but he wasn't watching the fire. He was watching Zach. His dark eyes were thoughtful. "You don't have fire, do you? Rohan's wrong."

Zach shook his head. "I used to."

"What?" Jordyn turned toward him. "If you once had fire, you still have it. Just call it and go get her!"

"Don't you think I would?" Zach snapped, nearly insane with worry. "I can't fucking do it anymore! I'm not that guy anymore!" Sweat was pouring down his face, and he spun toward the fire. He was going through again. This time he could make it. Fire wouldn't kill him, would it?

He backed up a step, then ground his jaw, his body tensing as he prepared to run—

"Don't be a fool." Eric stepped in front of him, the flames flickering violently behind him. "You'll die. Dying won't save anyone. Turn on your damned fire before you go in there."

"Shut the hell up, and get out of my way. My fire fucked me before, and it's fucked me again. I'm on my own—"

"Wait." Jordyn ran up beside Eric. "How did it fuck you before? What happened?"

"Get out of my way!"

"No!" she shouted. "Don't you understand? I am an expert in domestic trauma, and this screams of it! Do you know how many devastated, scarred souls I've helped? Shut up and listen to me!"

He shut his mouth, staring at her. What the hell was this woman on? "I have to save Rhiannon," he growled. "Get out of my way."

"No." She set her hands on her hips. "Who did you fail with your fire before? Don't you realize that you're emotionally scarred from your fire? You have to let go of your baggage and accept who you are! Accept your true self!"

Zach gaped at her, unable to grasp the fact that this woman was screaming therapy at him. "You're insane! Get the hell out of my way, or you're going into the fire too!"

"Accept what happened before," she said, walking *toward* him instead of getting out of his way.

"Accept it? Hell, woman, I killed my daughter! You want me to accept that? I killed my daughter and my family, and now Rhiannon and Thano are going to die!" He bellowed the words at her.

"Yes!" she screamed at him. "Let it go! You're a precious and beautiful soul, you big ass! Accept your inner beauty and allow peace and harmony to flow through you! You're worthy of a beautiful life!"

"You're fucking insane!" Zach shouted at her. Behind Jordyn, Eric was grinning like some crazy lunatic. What the hell was wrong with these two?

"I know I am! But I'm also right!" She screamed the last words right in his face. "I killed the man I loved," she yelled at him. "I know about murdering someone you love, but don't let someone else die simply because you're afraid of who you are."

"Afraid?" He glowered at her. "I'm not afraid—"

"Dude." Eric walked up behind her. "I think you might be. You've got this sort of glazed look in your eyes. Kinda looks like fear. Listen to the woman. She's kind of impressive on a lot of levels."

Jordyn beamed at Eric. "Thanks. That was nice of you to say."

"I know it was. I'm that kind of guy." Eric looked at Zach, ignoring his stunned expression. "Get with it, dude. You're scared of the monster inside. Seriously."

Holy shit. He was going to lose his mind. Therapy in the middle of a war zone? "I'm not scared of my fire! I'm losing my shit because I can't get to Rhiannon—"

"No." Jordyn touched his arm, a light, delicate touch that reminded him of the innocent touch of his daughter. "You're afraid of who you are, Zach, but you're not all bad. You have good in you, and you have to let it go. Your fire is part of who you are, and until you accept it, you will never be complete."

Tears burned at his eyes, and he looked past Jordyn at the fire that kept him from Rhiannon. He saw a violent, angry inferno, the kind that could destroy life. As he looked at it, the face of his daughter appeared in the flames. He felt his heart shudder with guilt and grief as she smiled at him, waggling her little fingers the way she used to do every time he rode off.

He went down on his knees, overwhelmed by the sight of her. She looked so real, so vibrant, and so alive. It was as if he had never killed her, except, of course, for the fact that her face was in the middle of fire. The same kind of fire that had killed her. Her daddy's fire.

Suddenly, he felt weak. Exhausted. He had failed too many people. His wife, who had been killed when he'd been off doing a job for the Order, instead of staying home to protect them when danger was near. His daughter, who he had killed with his own flames. His stepdaughter, who had also died in the fiasco. His sister and her kids, who he had been too late to save because he'd been too weak, pathetic, and out of control with his fire to save them from the rogue.

He stared at his little girl, riveted by the sight of her in the flames, smiling and waving, her eyes so full of love, an innocent face that had no idea what her father was going to do to her.

"Is that your daughter?" Jordyn walked up beside him.

He could only nod, too overwhelmed to speak.

"She doesn't seem to hate you." Eric was on his other side. "She looks like she still thinks you kick ass. You might want to take that into consideration, you know, when you're doing all that self-hate shit that's keeping you from saving Rhiannon and Thano."

For a moment, Zach didn't move, then their comments registered. He looked over at Eric. "You can see her?"

"I'm not blind, so yeah," Eric said. "But then again, I've got this thing about spirits. They like to talk to me. I'm kind of simpatico with them."

"You, too?" Jordyn sounded surprised. "I'm the same way."

"Really? We should have sex and compare notes."

Jordyn smacked him. "Shut up."

Stunned, Zach looked back at his daughter. He had thought that he'd been imagining her. But if Jordyn and Eric could see her…was she real? Had she come back to see him? Stunned, he lurched to his feet, his heart pounding. "Madeline?" His voice was harsh and rough.

She nodded, and put her little hand over her heart, their little symbol that they'd always used to show their love for each other.

Numbly, he put his own hand over his heart in response. "I love you, too, Madeline." She nodded, and then faded away, vanishing into the fire that raged behind her, taking with her centuries of guilt and fear. "She's okay," he whispered, as a thousand pounds of weight seemed to drop from his soul. "She's okay, wherever she is." *She was okay.*

"But Rhiannon and Thano aren't," Eric said, conversationally. "Time to light up, sparky."

"Yeah, I think it is." Energized by a force he hadn't felt in years, Zach leapt to his feet. This time, when he reached inside his soul, he was met with the fierce, raging power that had once been his. Gone were the ironclad trappings of fear and guilt that had locked down his power for so long. Determination leapt through him, and a sense of calm and control settled around him. With intense precision, he held his hands out to his sides, palms up toward the sky as he let the heat begin to sizzle and burn within him.

Centuries of shutting down his fire had given him control that he hadn't had before. As he manipulated it exactly where he wanted it, he realized that he'd spent so many centuries controlling it that it no longer controlled him. He felt like he was connected to every flicker inside his body. Staring up at the wall of fire in front of him, he called to the inferno that burned within. Flames began to lick at his heart and travel through his stomach. It was burning hot, and yet it didn't hurt. His skin began to glow, a bright orange and blue that could barely contain the fire radiating within him.

"Holy shit. Now that's impressive." Eric took Jordyn's arm and pulled her back. "I think he's going to blow."

His chest began to burn. Orange and blue flames danced on his flesh. They raced up his chest and over his shoulders. They sped down his arms to his palms. He held his hands wide, and towering tornadoes of fire stretched high from his palms. He raised his hands, lifting the whirling dervishes higher. Then he slammed his hands together. The funnel of fire exploded around him, trapping him in a sphere of flames. Encased in his protective cocoon of flames, Zach sprinted toward the wall of fire.

He leapt into the fire, and was instantly engulfed in flames. But this time, they could not touch him. They couldn't break through the protective shield he had erected around himself. Fighting fire with fire, he ran through the barrier, and burst through into a clearing on the other side.

Rhiannon was on her back in the center, motionless and limp, wearing some flimsy gown that barely covered her curves. José was standing above her, unfastening his jeans. Around him were twenty warriors, all of them staring at Rhiannon, waiting for the show to begin.

"Get the hell away from her!" Fury tore through Zach, and he hurled a fireball right at José. The fire god looked up, and unleashed a matching fireball a split second before Zach's hit him. The two flames exploded in the air above Rhiannon, hitting so hard that the ground shook from the explosion. José's warriors whirled around, and the night was filled with cracks and flashes of black light as they called out their weapons.

But this time, unlike at the crater, they had no chance.

This time, the real Zach was in the house. Not even breaking stride, he unleashed flaming spears in all directions. The orange weapons streaked through the air, sliding right through their steel weapons and plunging straight into their hearts. Their screams of anguish filled the air as their blackened hearts shriveled, and they fell, clutching their chests.

José unleashed a battle cry and hurled a fireball at Zach. Zach swatted it aside, and leapt through the air, sailing over Rhiannon, his arm coiled as he spun another fireball in his palm. "No!" He bellowed his outrage as he threw the flaming orb at José.

The Calydon ducked, but Zach followed up with another strike, so fast that it hit José before he could react. The fire god screamed with outrage and spun toward him, nothing but a faint burn on his stomach.

Zach swore as José attacked, not at all slowed down by Zach's fire. They crashed into each other, flames erupting in all directions as they battled. Zach could feel José's heat burning his flesh, but his shields were strong...but so were José's. For every blow he rained down on the fire god, José seemed to grow more powerful, absorbing Zach's fire as his own...

Shit. He realized José was taking Zach's fire into his own body and using it to strengthen his own power. Each time Zach hit him with a fireball, it was making José stronger.

Swearing, Zach broke free and retreated several yards, catching his breath as José circled him. Between them lay Rhiannon, her body deathly still. *Rhiannon. Wake up. You have to get out of here.*

Yeah, they didn't have the *sheva* bond, but he felt like he should be able to connect with her telepathically. They were too connected not to be able to find each other. *Rhiannon! Get up!*

But she didn't move, and he felt no energy in her mind. Was she dead? Fear hammered at him, and for a split second, he was tempted to burn the wards off his arms and try to connect with her. If she was his *sheva*—

"She's not yours!" José screamed his outrage, and leapt at him again, raining flaming arrows down on Zach.

Zach flung up his own shield of fire, but the assault was so violent and so penetrating that he couldn't fend them all off. The arrows plunged into his flesh, burning his skin even as he dissolved them. He kept retreating, drawing José away from Rhiannon and toward the edge of the circle, even as the arrows kept hammering at him. He couldn't fight back, because it would just make José stronger. Frantic, he assessed his options, sweeping though his choices.

José suddenly unleashed a bloodthirsty scream and hurled a massive fireball right at Zach. He swore and slammed his fists together. The impact ignited a tremendous explosion that blew up the fireball before it hit him. The explosion threw him backwards through the ring of fire. He landed on his back at Jordyn's feet, and then skidded across the ground, shooting past her.

"Get up!" she shouted at him. "Rhiannon needs— Oh... that must be José. God, I wish I had my gun."

Zach leapt to his feet as José charged toward him. The ring of fire was gone, and Zach felt the immensity of power rolling through José. He was twice as powerful as he had been, and Zach realized he'd been splitting his power to maintain that ring of fire, and now he was channeling it all into the attack. He hammered at Zach, a relentless assault of flaming weapons, coming in such rapid succession that Zach could barely block them. He had no chance to attack him. No chance to regroup, no chance to do anything but try to keep his shields strong enough to stay alive.

Out of the corner of his eye, he saw Jordyn run to Rhiannon, and kneel beside her. She shook Rhiannon, but got no response. Jordyn then looked up, tears streaming down her face as she shook her head at Eric. *What?* Denial roared through Zach, a deep-seated fury at what Jordyn was trying to tell Eric.

Rhiannon had to be okay. She had to be. *She had to be!*

With a roar of fury, he suddenly went on the offensive, attacking José as fiercely as he was being attacked. He hurled fireball after fireball, moving forward toward his enemy, hammering relentlessly. José grinned and moved forward as well, both of them surging with power as they advanced on each other, José was still feeding off Zach's assault, getting stronger with each blow.

Well, fuck that. If José could absorb Zach's fire, then

why couldn't Zach do the same thing? Zach dropped his shields and let the arrows hit him. The first one struck right in his chest, and he staggered. The second one hit his gut, and he went down on his knees. But he still didn't shield them. He just accepted them into his body, drinking in the fire that was trying to kill him. *Bring it on,* he gasped, as his body shook with agony. *I want it.* He closed his eyes as he lost his balance and fell onto his stomach, unable to hold himself up. Again and again he was hit, and he just lay there, opening himself to the fire. He felt as if his internal organs were burning up, incinerated by José's assault.

"Get up!" Jordyn screamed at him. "Get up, Zach!"

He didn't move.

He cracked open his eyes, and saw Eric with two swords, charging at José from behind. Jesus. The stupid bastard. He'd never take him down. "Get her out of here," Eric yelled at Jordyn, just as José flung him backward with a burst of flame. Eric was catapulted into the air, and he disappeared into the darkness of the jungle, still shouting commands at Jordyn to get to safety as he sailed out of sight. There was a crash and a thud, and then silence from Eric. Shit! No more were allowed to die for him!

Zach's gaze shot to the women, and he saw Jordyn trying to drag Rhiannon's inert body away from the fire, but flames were raging all around them, ignited by the fire raging between the two warriors. The women were trapped. They were going to be burned.

Horror welled inside him, numb, terrifying horror. Rhiannon was going to burn to death in his flames! "No!" As he screamed in rage, he felt something shift inside him. José's flames stopped attacking him, and they merged with his, becoming a part of who he was. Strength and power exploded through him, and he lunged to his feet, insane with terror for Rhiannon. He slammed a fireball at José, throwing him backward a hundred yards as he raced toward the last spot he'd seen the women before the fire had cut them off from him. The flames were torrential now, destroying everything in their path. He charged though the fire, searching desperately for his woman. "Rhiannon," he bellowed. "Where are you?"

"Zach!"

Jordyn's scream came from his left, and he spun around. He burst through the flames and saw Rhiannon and Jordyn huddled in a tight ball, trapped by the fire that was only inches away on all sides. He leapt over the flames and landed with his feet on either side of them. He had no time to get them out. He had only one chance, and this time, it was going to work.

He called out his own fire, the one that had killed his daughter, and he swept it around the three of them, erecting a flaming shield. The sphere took shape instantly as he crouched over them, encircling both women with his arms. As he did it, he pushed the heat of his fire to the exterior of his sphere, knowing that the heat alone could kill them.

Flames and heat hammered at him from all sides, but he fought to keep his shield around them, and to keep the heat at bay. Jordyn's arms were still around Rhiannon, and she looked up at him, her face flushed and red from the flames. "See what happens when you stop fighting who you are? I'm good, aren't I?"

He was not in the mood for therapy right now. "Rhiannon," he said. "Wake up!" He gave a gentle mental push at her. She was so close that he should be able to feel her, but still he couldn't. Fear began to lick through him, and he shoved harder at the heat, trying to protect her. "Rhiannon!"

Again, no response.

He was almost overwhelmed with the need to pull her into his arms, but he couldn't break the circle of protection. He knew his touch had helped her before. "Come on, Rhee." He shifted his weight enough so he could move his leg against hers. "Pull up her dress, Jordyn. I need skin to skin contact with her."

Jordyn leaned over to Rhiannon and slid her dress up enough to expose her leg.

"My jeans," he ordered.

"I don't undress men anymore, just so you know," Jordyn grumbled as she yanked up his jeans and shoved his sock down. "Men need clothes."

He moved his leg against Rhiannon, and this time, he felt the warmth of her skin against his. His heart seemed to skip for a second, and then electricity poured through him. He could feel her life force weakening. He could hear the slow thudding of her heart. He could sense the enormity of her soul, all of it weaving through him with such beauty that it was almost overwhelming.

Using the connection between them, he pushed all his life force at Rhiannon, pouring all his healing energy into her. He didn't even care that he couldn't call upon the *sheva* bond to connect them. He didn't need to. Her soul was such a part of his that healing her was like breathing life into his own heart. *Come back to me, my love. I'm here for you.*

She coughed suddenly, her body shuddering as air surged back into her lungs. She opened her eyes, and her gaze met his. "Zach?" she whispered, her brow furrowing in confusion. "I thought you were dead."

He grinned, elation flooding him. How was it possible that one woman's voice could change his entire world? "Never. I had to rescue my woman."

She smiled, a smile so filled with affection that he was filled with a sudden urge to do a Tarzan chest-pounding thing and claim her as his own. "You were almost too late," she pointed out.

"I know. Sorry about that. "

Jordyn wrapped her arms around Rhiannon's shoulder. "No sex while I'm here. That would just gross me out."

Rhiannon turned, her eyes widening in surprise. "Jordyn? What are you doing here?"

"I'm on vacation. It was a total surprise to find you unconscious, about to be raped by your ex, while Zach here set the jungle on fire trying to save you." Jordyn looked up at Zach. "What now, big guy?"

Forcing himself to tear his gaze off Rhiannon, Zach looked around. The flames were raging around them, becoming even fiercer, and he knew José was feeding them. "I think—"

Rhiannon suddenly sucked in her breath and stood up. "He's calling me," she whispered.

"What?" Zach rose with her, changing the shape of his protective dome to accommodate her new position. "You can't go there—"

"I can't help it." Agony coursed through her eyes. "I can't stop myself." She started to walk, and Zach swore, moving with her to keep her protected.

"Rhiannon!" Jordyn grabbed her arm. "Stop it!"

"Get off!" Rhiannon flung Jordyn away, and the woman fell backward, tumbling into the fire.

Swearing, Zach widened the sphere of protection, just barely getting it wide enough to keep Jordyn from burning up. "Get up," he snapped at her "Get back over here!"

Jordyn scrambled up, racing over as Rhiannon broke into a run. Swearing, Zach kept pace with her, and so did Jordyn, who was frantically shouting words of empowerment at Rhiannon, words that were making as much difference as using a squirt gun on a forest fire.

He couldn't grab her to stop her, or he'd lose control of the sphere keeping her from being burned. Fucking José didn't even care if she burned up. He just wanted to exert his control over her. "Rhiannon," he said. "Look at me."

She didn't even turn her head, but waves of anguish poured off her.

"Dammit, Rhiannon! I love you! Can't you feel it?"

She still didn't look at him, and started running faster, away from him, into the fire, toward José, but tears were pouring down her cheeks.

Zach ran with her, and Jordyn kept pace, her athletic build having no trouble keeping up with them. Shit. How could he reach her?

"You have to kill José," Jordyn shouted at him. "Or she does. One of you does! It's the only way to free her. The *sheva* bond is too strong."

Rhiannon was running in a dead sprint toward José, and it was all Zach could do to keep the sphere moving along with her, keeping it big enough to protect both women. "There has to be another way," he yelled back. "He needs to stay alive until I can save my teammate!"

"You have to make a choice," Jordyn yelled. "You can't save them both!"

"I have to!" Suddenly, they reached the end of the fire, and burst out into the jungle. The flames stopped, as if contained by an invisible wall, and they were surrounded by lush, green vegetation. Rhiannon's realm. That was how to do it. This was her world. Her power zone. He dropped the flaming shield, freeing them all. José stood between two massive trees, his hands on his hips, a smug look on his face to see his *sheva* racing toward him.

Well, fuck that. This was her world now. Zach touched her arm, and sparks leapt through them. "Rhiannon—"

She whirled toward him suddenly, and for a moment, elation swept through him. She had come back to him. Then there was an explosion and a crack of black light, and then in her hand was José's sword. It was then that he saw the anguish in her eyes, and he knew that something was terribly wrong. "Rhiannon—"

"I love you, Zach. I'm so sorry," she managed, tears streaming down her cheeks, just before she plunged José's sword right into Zach's heart.

CHAPTER 22

Rhiannon screamed in horror as she watched herself plunge José's sword into the heart of the man she loved. She staggered back, the scream still reverberating in her head as she watched Zach clasp his chest and go down to his knees. How could she have done that? How could she be so weak as to have let José force her to hurt him?

Zach grabbed the handle of the sword, his gaze fixed on hers. "I love you, Rhiannon. *I love you.*"

His words burned through her, and she whispered the words back, the words that were so loud in her mind. "I love you, Zach—"

But even as she spoke them, she felt José push at her mind. *Turn around, bitch. Show your lover who you really belong to.*

Her body turned against her will, and she faced him. He was standing there in the bold, aggressive stance of a war god. Feet apart. Arms folded across his chest. Shoulders back. Powerful. Arrogant. Utterly male. He smiled at her, an empty, lascivious leer that bisected his angular face. "Come over here and fuck me while your lover dies."

His words plunged straight into her mind, and she felt the familiar call of resistance warring with the compulsion. Somewhere inside, her soul screamed in agony and protest, but her feet began to move toward him. *Stop it, Rhiannon! Just stop it!* But her body didn't belong to her. It belonged to the man whose brands marked her body.

The *sheva* bond. So romantic. So horrific. Slavery of the worst kind.

"Stop it!" Jordyn screamed, as she ran up to Rhiannon. "Don't do this, Rhiannon! You're too powerful for this! Stop it—"

José flicked his hand, and a burst of hot air flung Jordyn back. Rhiannon's body tensed with the need to grab her friend, but she couldn't break José's spell. She watched helplessly as Jordyn landed beside Zach, who was down on his knees, trying to get José's sword out of his chest. Jordyn groaned and rolled onto her side, alive, but hurt.

The blade of José's sword was on fire, and Zach's skin was glowing orange as José's fire burned him from the inside out.

What had she done? How pathetic was she? She was the chosen one the prophecy had selected to save her jungle, and yet her tribe had been exterminated, the man she loved was dying by her hand, and her only friend was being tossed around like a tumbleweed. And what was she doing? Ignoring them all to get fucked by her soul mate. Yeah, because she was a warrior, right? No, it couldn't end like this. She could not let it end like this. Being a *sheva* didn't control her. She had to be strong. *She had to fight.*

Her soul screamed in agony as she tried to erect mental shields between her and José, but their blood bond gave him easy access. Every shield she erected, he tore down, his laughter echoing in her head. Tears of frustration and anguish streamed down her cheeks as she continued to walk right toward the man who owned her.

Zach jerked the sword out, gasping in pain. He looked up at her, his eyes glowing so fiercely she could see flames dancing in them. "Rhiannon," he growled. "You're stronger than that."

Adrenaline rushed through her, followed by a stab of hope. Was she really stronger than the destiny that had controlled the fates of every Calydon and their *shevas* since the beginning of time?

"Look at me, not him," José snarled, snapping her out of her thoughts.

Involuntarily, Rhiannon dragged her gaze off Zach and focused on José. His thought pulsed at her, his unyielding push.

You are mine. His words echoed through her, twisting until they were her own. This man, this brutal man, was her soul mate. She was his *sheva*. Bound to be a part of him until one of them died. She was his—

No! Those weren't her thoughts! She realized suddenly that he was trying to direct her thoughts now. Always before, he had never bothered. He'd just wanted her body and her lust. But now, she could feel the tendrils of his power crawling through her brain, trying to take over her thoughts.

Fresh resolve surged through her, a sudden influx of self-preservation. If he took her mind, she had *nothing*. Frantic, she willed her mind to focus, to think, to own itself. Her jaw clenched, she focused on the staff in his right hand, concentrating all her energy onto it, so he would feel her attention on him and maybe relinquish his efforts, not realizing that she was controlling her own thoughts, not him. She stared at that damned torch, examining every engraving on the staff. Dozens of flowers, like the ones that should be a part of her. The faces of demons. Assorted Calydon weapons. She saw a sword. A battle-axe. A dagger. A spear. There was a man having sex with his *sheva,* doggie style, yanking her head back by her hair. Not loving and romantic. It was domination and ownership, and she hated it. Was that what the *shevas* were originally created for? It wasn't about love and protection. It was about creating female slaves who could never say no to their masters.

Disgust flared through her, and she tore her attention off the staff, dragging her gaze upward. Vines were engraved on the staff, winding their way up to the top, where flames were flickering out of the end of it. Vines and fire woven together. It was as if the staff represented them both, twisted into one, depraved unit until the end of time.

She stared at that staff, fighting to keep control of her thoughts. It had to be destroyed, or José would never go rogue, and she would never be able to kill him.

Even as she thought of killing him, she felt something inside her wail with anguish at the idea of losing the man she was bound with. This man, this horrible, despicable creature who had tormented her for so long and destroyed her village was connected to her by the very blood that ran through their veins, entwined in her soul through the blood bond that was supposed to force him to keep her safe...and that forced her to protect him at all costs.

And yet the man she actually loved, the one who had given his life trying to save her, lay dying behind her, because of her failure. She had killed the wrong man. *The wrong man.* Anger and betrayal burned through her, and her heart bled with the tears that her eyes were forbidden to shed. With her tribe decimated, Zach had become her only salvation, the only thing left in her life to hold onto, and José had made her kill him. Because of José, she had lost everything that mattered to her. Her tribe. Her home. Her freedom. Her only friend. And the man she loved. *She had lost everything that mattered—*

She sucked in her breath as her words flew through her mind again. *She had lost everything that mattered most to her.* Shocked, she stared at him. The first stage of the decimated *sheva* destiny was that they both had to lose all that mattered to them. She had lost it all. Her heart began to pound. Was it not too late? Was it possible? Was there a way? All that was left was for José to lose everything that mattered to him as well.

You will bow to me. At José's silent command, she fell to her knees in front of him, staring up at him as her mind raced frantically to put the pieces together.

What did he value? What was most important to him? His power? His staff? The jungle? Her? Control? Frantically, she raced over what she knew of him, trying to figure out what mattered most to him. What could he lose? Her? By rights, it should be her, right? As his mate? "I love Zach," she whispered, forcing herself to picture the man she loved, until Zach's presence seemed to fill her whole mind and body. "Zach," she said, louder. "I love him. You might control my body, but I love him."

He smiled. "You don't know what love is." He reached down and grabbed the front of her dress, jerking her to her feet until her breasts were smashed against his chest. "You love me, *sheva.* Your heart beats for me. Your body craves me. You dream of me. You cannot turn me down, no matter what I want. *That* is love."

Revulsion churned through her, but her body would not fight him. "You piece of shit," she whispered.

His eyes widened. "What?"

She went still, shocked by what had just come out of her mouth. How had she spoken to him like that? Where had that power come from? She searched through her mind, but she felt the same, lost and lustful, captured by his spell. But still, the words came again. "You will never own me, you bastard."

He smiled wider. "I love a woman with spunk. Fight me, Rhiannon. *Fight me.*" Lust gleamed in his eyes, and her heart twisted in agony at the realization that her resistance was a turn-on for him. Dear God. What could she do to stop this? What could she take away from him that would make him snap?

"Rhiannon." Zach's voice drifted across the clearing, sounding harsh and raw. He called to her in a way that José never had, infusing her with a power that seemed to pulse through her. Was it his love that had given her the power to speak up to José? Together, could they do it?

She turned her head to look at Zach, and her heart seemed to break when she saw him on his hands and knees, barely holding himself up. José's sword was in his hand, and his blackened body was glowing like faded embers after a fire had burned itself out.

Relief flooded her so fiercely that her legs started to tremble. He was in trouble, but not dead. Not yet. No. She hadn't lost him. Good, because he was alive. Bad, because if he was still alive, then she hadn't lost all that mattered to her, which meant the *sheva* destiny wasn't being triggered and she wouldn't be able to kill José.

"Walk toward me," Zach said. "Walk away from him."

She stared at him as José's fingers tightened around her arm. "What?"

Zach looked at José. "She loves me, and love is stronger than the *sheva* bond. She's not yours, José. She's..." His gaze met hers, and she tensed. Was he going to claim her, too? Was he going to say she was *his?* Even though she loved him, the thought of him staking an ownership claim made fear shiver through her. Not again. Not with him. Was this going to be a battle of dominance?

Zach met her gaze. "She belongs to herself."

To herself? Not to him? Oh, wow. He hadn't claimed her.

He'd given her his love, but not asked for her freedom. It wasn't the Calydon way, not at all, but it was beautiful. Somewhere deep inside her, a warm feeling spread through her, enveloping her in a sensation of safety and love. The tightly coiled tension inside released ever so slightly, and she felt like she could breathe for the first time in years.

And he wasn't finished. "Test her," he said to José. "See whether your will or hers triumphs."

Rhiannon's feeling of happy warmth vanished. She'd spent a decade testing José's will against hers, and she knew which was stronger. She looked at Zach, but he just nodded, his face calm and confident.

Slowly, her fear eased. For the ten years she'd failed to resist José, she'd been alone. This time, it was different. This time, she had Zach. This time, she had the man she loved giving her strength. She nodded once. Together, they could do it. Together, they could defeat him.

José's grip was brutally tight on her arm. "I don't need to prove it. I know I own her."

Zach dragged himself to his feet. "You're afraid. You're afraid that she'll walk away." His voice held a challenge that no warrior could resist. "You spend your life bullying weaker people, and you keep Rhiannon trapped because you know that she despises you. You know that you are a failure as a man, because even your own *sheva* recoils from your touch."

Oh...that was good. Brilliant, even, to attack José's manhood. She knew he'd never be able to back down from that challenge. She took a deep breath, already beginning to steel herself against José's influence, waiting for him to agree to the challenge. She knew that she and Zach would break his spell. It was time.

"I fear no one, but I would love to watch you suffer before you die. You will be the one to lose her, not me." José dropped her arm and stepped back. "Go between us, *sheva*." He pushed at her mind, and she had no choice but to walk...heading right for Zach.

With each step closer to him, her body began to vibrate with energy and longing. This was the man she wanted. She didn't want any man, not ever, and yet somehow, someway, Zach had opened her heart and taught her that it was safe to love and to trust.

José loosened his grip on her mind slightly, and she felt a bright ray of hope flood her. Quickly, as fast as she could, she wove protections in her mind, trying to shield herself even as she walked closer to Zach, forcing herself to walk slowly and not alert José as to what she was doing. Zach was watching her intently, his dark eyes focused and intense. He had a plan, she realized. What kind of plan?

She tried to read his expression, but it gave away nothing. Jordyn was standing beside him, her blue eyes blazing with determination. Rhiannon looked back and forth between them. What were they planning?

"Stop." José's voice halted her muscles, but she didn't try to fight it, keeping her resources focused on shielding him from her mind.

She realized she was exactly halfway between the two men. She slid one foot to the right, so that she was closer to Zach by several inches.

He nodded.

"Now," José said. "Walk to me. Show this piece of shit that you are mine." And then, a mental push at her mind, so hard and fierce that she gasped in pain. She stumbled and gripped her head, tears streaming down her cheeks at the force of his mental invasion. It was a thousand times worse than anything he'd ever done to her. It felt like a thousand daggers stabbing her brain, slicing it to pieces, a million voices reverberating in her mind, hammering at her to go to José. Her muscles convulsed, and raw, depraved lust flooded her. *No! No! No!* She fought him with every resource she could summon. She threw every fiber of her being into fighting him...and she couldn't stop him.

A pawn in his complete control, she whirled toward José, her entire existence merged with his. He was her man. He was the one she wanted. Always José—

"Rhiannon! Come to me. I love you."

She heard Zach's voice somewhere on the outreaches of her mind, but it was so distant that she couldn't register it. She barely even noticed it, a voice passing in the distance. She was already walking toward José. Then running. He held out his arms to her, victory brimming on his face. "You're mine," he said. "I knew you would—"

There was a ferocious boom, and José suddenly exploded into a violent fireball. Rhiannon screamed and threw herself to the side, barely avoiding the flames. She hadn't even hit the ground, when Zach's arms were around her, catching her before she crashed to the earth.

She screamed, trying to get out of his arms to go to José, who was twisting and bellowing, his body engulfed in flames.

"Rhiannon!" Zach's arms were gentle but strong, holding her back. "Come on, sweetheart. Come back to me."

"You distracted him on purpose," she screamed, her soul crying for José. "You used me to distract him so you could attack him!"

Zach's face was twisted with pain at her words. "He's not dead, Rhiannon. I'm just holding him so we can take him back to Thano. He's not dead."

She stared at him, catching her breath as his words sank into her mind. "He's not dead?" Relief seemed to pour through her, relief so great she felt like she couldn't breathe. "José's not dead?" She turned in his arms, and saw her soul mate sprawled on the earth, his body twisted and contorted as dozens of flaming cords wrapped around him, covering every inch of his body except his face. His hands were locked behind him, encased in flaming manacles. He was locked in a straitjacket of fire, just like the one Zach had used to shield them. He was trapped, immobilized, and stripped of his power. His eyes went to hers, and she saw in them such suffering and pain that she realized he was dying.

"José?" She tried to get out of Zach's arms to crawl over to him, but Zach tightened his grip on her.

"Rhiannon," he said. "Look at me. This isn't you. You don't love him."

"Get off me!" she screamed, fighting to get out of Zach's arms. "He's dying! You're keeping him alive just long enough to serve your own purposes! You bastard!"

Anguish flared in Zach's eyes, but still he didn't release her. "Rhiannon," he said softly. "I love you. Feel how much I love you."

Jordyn knelt beside Zach, her hands on Rhiannon's arm. "Come on, babe. Come back to us. It's just the *sheva* bond making you crazy. You don't love him."

"Let me go!" Their words rang falsely in her ears, and she knew they were lying. "Get away from me!" she screamed. "I need to help him!" Anger and desperation tore through her, and she felt power surge inside her. *Yes!* She looked up, and saw the jungle on all sides of her. Branches waved gently over her head, and underbrush was everywhere. *Help me!* More power surged through her, and she felt Zach tense as the wind began to whip around them.

"Oh, man," Jordyn said. "I've seen this before. We need to knock her out."

"No." Zach grabbed her shoulders, and forced her to face him. His eyes bore into hers, and his blackened skin glowed with the fire he was barely containing. "Rhiannon. Look at me. I believe in you. Look inside you. Find yourself. You're brave. You're strong. José's thoughts are not yours. The *sheva* bond doesn't control you."

"I love him," she said, her voice strangely distant as the wind got even stronger. "You tried to kill him. I can save him. You're the enemy."

"Zach, seriously!" Jordyn shouted. "You need to knock her out! She's going to kill us!"

"Rhiannon!" He gripped her arms more fiercely. "You're stronger than this bond! Don't let it control you!"

"Let me go!" Her scream tore from her throat. "José is mine!" Trees erupted from the earth, and a massive trunk slammed into Zach. It flung him backward, but he didn't let go of her. She screamed as she flew through the air with him, quickly calling upon the plants to catch them. They landed on a bed of thick leaves, and she called out vines. "Trap him!" she commanded the plants. They surged over Zach, sliding over his flesh, but he yanked her tighter against him, pulling her so tightly against his chest that the plants could not get between them. His legs clamped around hers, his muscles bulging as he trapped her against him. Everywhere along the length of their bodies, they were locked together, their bodies so tight against each other that even the vines could not break them apart.

"Get him," she screamed again. The vines jabbed at him, trying to squeeze between them to trap him, but there wasn't even the slightest crevice to fit through. He even had her face crushed against his neck, so the vines could not clamp over his throat.

Outrage tore through her, and she called forth more power. The earth shook, and she heard Jordyn scream. Wind howled around them, and her hair whipped violently against her cheeks, but Zach's grip on her did not falter.

Rhiannon. José's voice drifted through her mind. *You must kill him. It's the only way to break these manacles. Kill him now.*

Yes. She closed her eyes and dove deep inside herself, summoning forces that she'd never been able to access before. Her mate was dying. She had to save him. There was no more fear. No more hesitation. Just the untamed, raw need to save the man she lived for. The wind increased, and trees were torn out by their roots. They slammed into her and Zach, hammering at his arms where they were locked around her back.

She gasped at the pain, and felt a rib crack from the impact of the tree. The pain broke her concentration for a split second—

"I love you." Zach's words breathed in her ear, and then she felt his lips press against her temple. "I will love you until the end of time, Rhiannon."

She went utterly still, every part of her body strung tight, utterly focused on the feel of his mouth against her flesh. It was as if time was suddenly suspended, put on hold until all that remained was this moment, this anticipation, this touch of his lips. Her body was shaking with the need to kill him and save José, but she couldn't move, not while Zach's lips were on her skin.

He feathered another kiss along her neck, and then another. "You're more than my *sheva*," he said. "You are the woman that my heart lives for. I'm not bound to you by a pre-created bond that defines us. I'm bound to you out of love. Out of respect. Out of admiration. I'm bound to you because you are the woman who has brought my soul back to life."

Tears brimmed in her eyes as his deep voice reverberated

through her. She felt as if he was caressing her heart with his love, soothing the cuts that had made it bleed for so many years. She became aware of his body wrapped around hers. She noticed the strength of his muscles. She breathed in his scent, a scent so raw and masculine that it made her body shiver with awareness...not lust. Something more. Something deeper. Something beautiful.

"Zach?" She whispered his name, almost afraid to say it.

"I'm here, sweetheart." His grip on her didn't loosen.

Tears filled her eyes, and she pressed her face against his neck. His whiskers prickled against her skin, a familiar roughness that felt so right. Her heart was thudding against his chest, her breasts flattened against him.

José's voice screamed through her mind. *Rhiannon. Help me. Now. You must kill him.*

She scrunched her eyes shut and buried her face tighter against Zach's neck. "He's making me want to kill you," she whispered.

"I know." He kissed her again, his lips brushing over her hair.

"I want to kiss you," she whispered against his neck. "I need more of you to hold him off."

"I agree, but if you lift your head, those vines are going to wrap about my neck. I think you could actually sever my neck with those things, and that's just not the way to end the day."

She managed a strangled giggle as the vines continued to dig at them, trying to slide between their bodies. "We have to destroy the staff," she whispered. "I think that will weaken him enough to kill him."

There was silence for a moment, and she remembered that he needed the staff to save his friend. Tears burned in her eyes as the vines slammed into them. José's mental pressure hammered at her, screaming at her to save him, and she could feel her shields starting to crumble, despite the protection of Zach's embrace. The wind picked up again, and she felt José urging her to start uprooting trees again. She knew that if she hit Zach enough times, the trees would break his arms and make him unable to hold her so tightly. A fraction of an inch was all the vines needed to rip him off her.

She burrowed deeper against him, her body shaking

with the effort of fighting off José's command to kill him. She had minutes, maybe seconds, until she caved. "What do we do, Zach?"

CHAPTER 23

Zach could feel Rhiannon trembling violently against him. Her skin was cold and clammy, and her heart was thundering. The air was so thick with the weight of José's energy that Zach was actually feeling a little lustful toward José as well, which was pretty damned impressive. How the hell was Rhiannon resisting as much as she was? Because he knew she was. He could feel the love pouring out of her, fighting back at José, while she pressed herself more tightly against him, using their bodies to protect her.

But José's energy was growing more virulent, rising in a dangerous crescendo of desperation fueled by his need to survive. Zach knew they had only seconds left before they were both consumed by José's power. Swearing, he glanced toward the staff that was still tight in José's grip. That staff was Thano's only chance, and it wouldn't work without José, leaving them in an impossible situation. "What is it about that staff?" There had to be another answer. Another way.

"He burns them with it," she said. "When they go rogue, he burns them. It brands them."

"With his brand?"

"No. It's a double crossed sword with a circle."

Zach went still. "That's the symbol of the Order of the Blade. I saw it on Dante's arm." Son of a bitch. "The staff isn't his. It's an Order staff. *It's not his.*" Would it work for someone else?

"No one else can use it." The pressure grew thicker, and

she let out a yelp. He felt a sharp stab of pain in his own mind, and threw up his mental shields. He reached out with his power, trying to protect them both with a protective shield, but his ability to connect with her mentally was limited without a blood bond or the *sheva* bond. "They've tried! The flame dies when it's not in his hand!" A tree uprooted behind them. "Watch out!"

"The flame dies? So it's about the flame?" He rolled them sideways, and the tree slammed down where they'd been, hitting the ground so hard that the earth shook. "You did that?"

"Yes, sorry."

He whistled softly. "Damn, woman, remind me never to piss you off in an argument."

"Never piss me off in an argument. There. I reminded you. You're welcome." Another tree tore out of the earth. "Incoming!"

He log-rolled them again—

"Watch out!" A second tree was streaking toward them like a bark-clad missile.

"Shit!" Too late for them to move, he turned his hand toward it and threw up a wall of white-hot fire. The tree ignited as it hit the flame. For an instant, it looked like a blazing staff of fire, then it disintegrated into millions of burning embers.

"A burning staff," Rhiannon said, echoing what was in his mind. "Maybe *you* can control the staff. Maybe it's fire that controls it, not José—" Then she shouted another warning, and he looked up to see five massive trees hurtling toward them. Son of a bitch. There was nowhere to go.

"Call them off!" he shouted at her.

"It's not that easy! He's forcing me to try to kill you!" Power rolled off Rhiannon, so hot that electricity sparked between them, but José's energy increased exponentially at the same time. She screamed with fury, and the trees skidded to a stop, hovering less than a yard from them, thousands of pounds of force suspended above them by the tenuous thread of control she had on her mind.

Her body was shaking violently, and her fingers were digging into Zach's shoulders. "I love you," she whispered. "I really do."

"I know. I'm pretty hot. It's understandable."

"He's too strong."

"Not for both of us."

She tensed. "If we kill him, then the staff won't work on Thano."

"I'll use the staff, you'll be free, we'll save Thano, and then we'll toast our greatness with champagne. It's all good." He didn't know if he could do it. José's fire was different from his, and he was a fucked up bastard when it came to things that burned. He might set himself on fire, he might be a useless pit of nothing, or maybe he could power the staff. He had no idea if he could work that staff to save Thano... No. Fuck it. He was going to find a way, because there was no other alternative. *I swear I won't let you down, Thano.* He gritted his teeth "On three, sweetheart. We're going to kill him."

"Kill him? I can't do it—"

"Yes, you can. Kiss me."

She wound her arms more securely around his neck. "If I move away from you, the vines will go around your throat. Do you really think now is the time to be decapitated? Because that's what José is telling me to tell them to do. I like you the way you are."

"We need to connect more tightly. You know physical connection gets it going for us." The trees above them dropped several feet and he swore, instinctively rolling over so Rhiannon was under him. She stopped them inches from his back, so close that the branches dug into his skin.

Her face was still buried against him, and his cheek was tight against hers, leaving no space between their throats for the vines to slip between them and rip them apart. "On three," he said again. "We kiss, a major, soul-searing kiss. We use that physical connection to strengthen us both. I use my cords of fire, and you use the trees, and we turn them both on José. We do it together."

Her fingers dug into his shoulders. "And if it doesn't work? And if I kill you?"

"I'll still love you until the end of time. Killing me won't change that. I'm a little deeper of a guy than that. You should know by now that I'm not some shallow guy who requires a woman who won't kill him. Seriously, Rhiannon."

She let out a strangled laugh, and he felt the branches dig in deeper. "I love you, too."

"I know. On three." Shit, he hoped this worked.

"One," she whispered, tightening her grip on him.

"Two," he said, gritting his teeth as the weight of the trees pressed harder on him.

"Three!"

He lifted his head from her neck and kissed her. As his mouth caught hers, the vines snaked around his neck and locked down in a vicious noose. He held his breath, trapping oxygen in his lungs as he deepened the kiss. Rhiannon responded instantly, her mouth hot and decadent as she kissed him. Her lips parted, and his tongue slid against hers. Desire flooded him, a lust that was a hell of a lot stronger and better than the one José had tried to thrust on him.

As before, electricity seemed to leap between them. His power magnified a thousand-fold, and he poured it back into Rhiannon. Her breasts were crushed against his chest, and her mouth tasted so good. As they kissed, the vines cut deeper into his neck. He felt the trickle of blood along his skin, and he knew that Rhiannon hadn't broken José's hold yet.

He ran his hand through her hair, sweeping the tangled locks aside to caress the back of her neck. The vines wrapped around his arms, and jerked them back away from her. She locked her arms around his neck, gripping tightly as she kissed him more frantically.

The kiss grew carnal and desperate, two souls screaming for each other in the howl of battle and threat of death. The trees dropped further, pinning him more tightly on top of her. His cock was straining against his jeans, pinned against her stomach as the trees crushed him on top of her. Swearing, he deepened the kiss, pouring his soul into their connection. "Come—" He coughed, unable to talk over the vine crushing his throat. *Come on, Rhiannon. Come back to me.* He called out his sai in a crack and a flash of black light and sliced through the vine choking him. He gasped, sucking in air as he kissed her again, knowing he had only seconds until she sent another one. "I love you," he said. "I fucking *love* you."

"No!" José's voice tore through the night. "Kill him, you

bitch! Kill him!"

The moment José shouted that, Zach felt Rhiannon stiffen beneath him. He pulled back to look at her, and he saw tears brimming in her eyes. "No," he whispered, sliding his finger gently along her jaw. "All you have to do is follow your heart, babe. That's all. Just look inside—"

She gripped his hair, her fingers clenching tightly as she kissed him back. Power surged between them, and he felt her kiss change—

He was suddenly ripped off her, dragged across the forest floor by the vines. Swearing, he severed the vine with his sai, but another one grabbed him around the throat before he'd even finished severing the first one. They attacked from all directions. His sai was ripped from his hand, and he called it back. It tore free and hurtled back to him, but the moment it hit his hand, it was ripped free again.

The vines wrapped around his throat, tighter and tighter, cutting off his air, slicing his flesh.

Rhiannon rolled onto her stomach, her palms flattened on the dirt as she gasped, fighting for air. Her body was lean and taut, her hair ragged and wild around her shoulders. She was no longer the contained, controlled woman he'd first met. She was raw, untamed power, and the earth around her undulated.

She looked right at him, and he saw a tree hurtling toward him, its broken branch aiming right for his heart. Beyond her, he saw José roll onto his side. The fiery bonds holding him were flaring now with unnatural strength, indicating that José was merging with Zach's fire. It would be only moments until José would be able to harness it. It was now or never.

Zach had no time to take down the tree she was sending toward his heart. He looked right at her. "I believe in you." Then he stopped defending himself against her, and flung all his energy at José, leaving himself completely open to her attack.

* * *

Zach wasn't going to protect himself from her.

Rhiannon gasped in horror when she saw Zach turn his attention to José when her trees were almost upon him. *I believe in you.* His words vibrated through her, deep in her soul, and she struggled to her knees. *I believe in you.* She slammed her hands into the dirt, thrusting her fingers through the earth to the roots below. She closed her eyes, reaching for the energy that had once defined her, the good, life-giving purity of nature.

Kill him, now, bitch. You are mine.

Bitch. The word grated through her mind. The degrading, horrible word that the man who purported to be her protector used on her. A word that she'd had to live with for so long. A word that had become a part of her soul. Until now. Until Zach had flooded her with kindness and warmth. Until Zach had looked at her like she was worth everything the world had to offer. Resistance flooded her, battling against the consuming power of José stripping her will.

José suddenly screamed, and she raised her head to look at him. Zach's flaming bonds had turned purple, and smoke from José's body filled the air. He fought against them, and black flames tangled with Zach's, fighting for supremacy. *Save me, Rhiannon. Now! I command you.*

"I love you, Rhiannon." Zach's words were accentuated by a gasp as her tree slammed into his chest, piercing his ribs and impaling his heart.

Her hands still buried in the dirt, she looked at Zach. She looked at José. Both men on the verge of death. Her hand would be the final blow in one of their deaths. José, with his brutal voice pounding in her head, hammering at her, compelling her. Zach, with his calm intensity, his utter faith, and his absolute conviction that she could choose her own path despite the brands pulsing on her arms, owning her.

The wind howled around them, whipping the flames into a frenzy. Slowly, fighting for every inch, she raised her palm toward Zach. She wrapped her mind around the tree that was buried in his chest. She felt José's command to drive it home, and her muscles shook as his power flooded her.

Zach didn't even look at her. He was entirely focused on holding José with his bonds of fire. His eyes were pitch black, and his face was pale as blood dripped down his neck, minutes away from being strangled or decapitated. But his hands were out, and flames were pouring from his palms, streaking at José, hitting him again and again and again. He wasn't trying to save himself. He was letting himself die, using every last vestige of his strength to try to kill José so she would be free.

Not to save his friend, because killing José risked killing Thano.

Not to save his friend, because if Zach died, he would not be able to wield José's staff.

Not to save himself, because he wasn't even bothering to address the tree lodged in his chest and vines about to rip off his head.

No, in the face of everything he was enduring, his only focus was to kill José for one reason: to free *her*.

He wasn't sacrificing everything that mattered to him because of a *sheva* bond, but simply because he loved her. Just love. Unconditional love, even though she was trying to kill him.

That was love.

That was worth dying for.

That was worth living for.

With a roar of power, she whirled toward José. "It's over," she shouted. "It's over!" She leapt to her feet and flung her hands out to the sides, palms raised toward the sky. "Come on," she shouted. "Help me!" The jungle surged to life in a chorus of music more beautiful than she had ever heard it sound before. The tree impaled in Zach's chest turned into a white flower that spread healing life through his body. The vines slithered away from him, and streaked across the ground toward José.

I command you to save me! Kill Zach! You are mine! José's power thrust into her mind, and she didn't care. She didn't feel it. It was a sound that hammered at her from a distance, like a hurricane banging on the outside of a secure building protecting her: loud, dangerous, but unable to penetrate.

"No!" She called forth trees, vines, plants, and even the earth itself, the wind whipping around them as the jungle attacked. They converged upon him, ripping at his defenses, plunging through the fire he was trying to burn them with. Zach moved up beside her, and took her hand, the white flower still resting in the middle of his chest.

Electricity surged between them, and the fire erupted from Zach's palms, like the sun itself had exploded from him. At the same moment, a massive, twelve-inch coil of vine shot out of the ground and wrapped itself around José's neck. He screamed and tried to burn it off him, but Zach hit him too hard with fireball after fireball, holding him trapped as the vine tightened and tightened and then—

"No—" José let out a high-pitched shriek of terror, and then the vine finished its job, severing his head from his burning body. His head bounced on the ground, then rolled to a stop at their feet, already consumed by flames so it was nothing more than a raging fireball.

Rhiannon waved her hands, and the vines shot past his head, opening a crevice in the earth like the one that they'd escaped through before. José's head toppled into the pit, and then the vines dragged what was left of his burning body into the earth. The dirt closed over him instantly, cutting him off from her jungle forever.

The moment he was gone, a huge weight seemed to vanish from her mind. Her legs collapsed, and she fell to her knees, gasping in relief as a decade of pressure on her dissipated.

Zach knelt beside her, and she fell into his arms. He locked her in his embrace, his own body trembling against hers as they clung to each other. She couldn't seem to get her breath, and Zach was breathing just as heavily, but it felt so amazing. She felt so free, as if she could leap to her feet and skip all the way to the moon and back. There was no anguish or torment streaming through her because her soul mate was dead. Just relief. She knew it was because she had severed the bond with him while he was still alive, so that his death could not affect her. With Zach's help, she had freed herself.

"I knew you could do it." Zach pressed a kiss to her temple, and she pulled back to look at him.

Although he was covered in soot, burning embers, and his own blood, he was grinning, showcasing dimples she didn't even know he had. "Dimples," she touched his cheek. "The man can bring down an entire jungle with fire, and he has dimples." It felt completely ridiculous to be talking about dimples after all they had just been through, but after all the weight she'd been enduring over so many years, dimples were such a silly, nonsensical thing to think about, that it felt perfect to have the luxury to focus on something so minute. The thought of dimples on Zach made her want to laugh. She hadn't wanted to laugh in a really long time, so dimples were perfect.

His smile widened. "I don't have dimples. They're fire pits of hell that I use to channel my destructive tendencies upon deserving enemies."

She laughed, and touched his left cheek. "They're dimples." Her smile faded. "You killed him for me, even though you were supposed to keep him alive for Thano."

"Yeah, I did." His face became serious. "That *sheva* destiny can't hold a candle to love that's built upon real emotion. I will give my life to protect you, Rhiannon. A thousand times if I have to, and this time, I won't screw it up."

Her heart tightened. "How could you screw it up?"

"Last time—"

"No." She put her finger over his lips. "You are a good man, Zach. Your wife, stepdaughter, and Madeline were lucky to have you, just as I am so fortunate to have you, too. You saved my life, Zach. You called your fire for me. You're amazing."

His eyes glistened, and he pulled her close, burying his face in her hair. There were no words, but she felt the depth of his emotion in the desperation of his embrace, and she knew that the failures of his past would always be a part of him. She, like him, had once failed the people she loved. Sent into the jungle to destroy José, she'd bonded with him instead, and freed him to eradicate her tribe.

But he's dead now. Zach's voice caressed her mind, and she looked at him sharply, startled by the feel of him in her head. *You finally saved your jungle, Rhiannon. You fulfilled your destiny. You did it.*

Rhiannon stiffened. "How come I can hear you in my mind?" Suddenly, scared, she looked down at her arms, half-expecting to see his marks on her flesh, but all she saw were the vines and plants she'd had tattooed there after she'd left the jungle.

I still have my wards. He held out his arm to her, showing her the marks on his flesh. *It's just because we're connected in our souls, sweetheart. That's all it is.* He pulled her close, and kissed her. *Try it. I'm here. I'll hear you.*

She shook her head. "No." Although a part of her longed

for that kind of connection with Zach, she knew she would never cross that line. Never would she let a man that far into her mind again, not even Zach. It had been such a horrific nightmare not to be able to shut out José, and now that he was gone, she didn't want to go back there, not ever again. In some ways, talking to Zach in her mind was even more of an emotional hurdle than making love had been. Her mind was all she'd had, and in the end, José had almost taken that as well. "I can't."

Zach nodded. "I understand." He brushed her hair back from her face, his eyes gentle. "It's okay, sweetheart. It really is." He kissed her again, and tears burned in her eyes.

How could she not trust this man? How could she not give him everything she had after what he'd done for her? "I want to, but—"

The night suddenly shook, and they both looked up as a dark cloud formed above their heads. It wasn't smoke. It looked more like a thick net descending over the jungle. "What's that?"

Zach went still beside her. "Holy shit. That's the webbing that Rohan called out to trap Thano. It's coming for him. We gotta go!" Zach leapt to his feet. "We need to get back!" He spun around, then swore. "Where's the staff?"

Rhiannon leapt to her feet, urgency coursing through her. "What do you mean?" Even as she asked the question, she saw that the staff was no longer on the ground beside where José had been lying.

Oh, God. No, she couldn't let this happen, not after Zach had risked everything to save her. She fell to her knees, frantically feeling through the leaves for the hard, metal staff, but it wasn't there. "It's gone!"

CHAPTER 24

Desperation rushed through Zach as the night grew thicker, and an unearthly scream filled the air, resonating from the cloud of webbing taking shape above their heads. Son of a bitch. He couldn't let Thano down now. They were so close. "Where the hell is it?"

He scanned the jungle, searching for the staff, but it was nowhere. Frantic, he tried to remember if José had been holding it when Rhiannon's vines had yanked him into the dirt, but he didn't remember seeing it. But where else would it be? Or maybe José had simply reclaimed it? Calydon weapons vanished when not being touched by their owners. What if the staff was like that? What if it had returned to José? Or what if José had taken it with him?

He spun to Rhiannon. "Send your vines after him," he commanded. "Drag his body back up. He must still have it with him!"

She instantly called out her vines, and the wind began to howl again, but it wasn't loud enough to drown out the increasing crescendo of shrieks coming from the webbing that was getting thicker and thicker above their heads. The vines plunged into the earth, and her eyes widened. "I can sense it! It's not with José." She spun around, holding out her hands as she sent the vines in another direction, away from where José had been.

They had no time for her to be wrong. They had one shot at it. He put his hands on her shoulders, his body taut. "Come on, Rhiannon. Find it for me."

The earth seemed to erupt beneath their feet, and the vines suddenly plunged straight down into the earth, ten yards away. Rhiannon went down on her knees, her eyes closed as she thrust her energy into the earth. The air hummed with her power, but she shook her head. 'I need your help,' she shouted. "I need fire and plants. The staff is fueled by both, so we need both!"

"I'm on it." Instantly, he crouched behind her, wrapping his arms around her waist and drawing her into the shield of his body. He rested his chin on her shoulder, offering her his strength.

She took it, and he was suddenly swept into her mind. He could feel the power of the plants, and the damp warmth of the earth. He could hear the sounds of leaves breathing. He could smell the beauty of each plant around them. He realized he was not only in Rhiannon's mind, but he was merged with her completely, his spirit and energy entangled with hers.

She was completely vulnerable to him, drawing him into the very depths of who she was, not protecting herself against him at all. His throat tightened with the magnitude of the trust she was giving him, and he wrapped his arms more tightly around her. He opened his fire to her, and it slid through her body, becoming a part of her instead of harming her. She swept it up, until their worlds became a tangle of orange flames and the pulsating vibrancy of the plants. His fire rode her vines, sending the burning vegetation through the earth.

Then he felt it. A distant pulse deep below the earth's surface, thick with the vibrations of Calydon energy...not just Calydon. The Order. *The staff.*

I know, she said. *Stay with me.* Together, they sent their merged energies deep beneath the ground, hurtling along the path the staff had taken. Closer, and closer, until suddenly the vines made contact. The jolt of energy was electric, and Rhiannon jumped in his arms. But he held tight, fueling her vines with his flames as the plants wrapped around the staff—

But then they slid right through it, as if it wasn't really there. "It's fading," Rhiannon shouted. "You have to give it fire!"

His flames surged into the staff, and he ignited it. For a split second, it didn't hold, and then he took what was left of

José's fire that he'd absorbed into his body, and he merged it with his own. This time, the flame caught, and power surged through the staff, turning it corporeal again.

"Now!" Rhiannon shouted, and the vines recoiled with stunning swiftness, dragging the staff back toward them, faster and faster. It erupted from the earth in a cascade of dirt. Zach snatched it out of the air. The metal was hot and solid beneath his hand, but he could feel that it was fighting him, trying to fade, as Calydon weapons did when their masters died. Her vines were twisted around it, and he saw that her leaves were aligned perfectly with the etchings of vines on the staff, and his own flames matched the carvings of fire. Plants and fire. That was how it was done. "No wonder he needed you."

But even as he spoke, he felt it shudder in his hand, and he realized that they were barely holding it together, even with their combined efforts. "It was José's fire fueling it," he said. "I can't hold it corporeal for long. We gotta go!"

Together, they leapt to their feet, and began to race back toward the campsite. They tore through the jungle, the woods parting for them as they ran.

"Hey!" Eric suddenly appeared beside them, his body charred and blackened. "Where's Jordyn?" he shouted.

Shit. Jordyn!

"She's back there!" Rhiannon didn't even slow down as she pointed behind her. "Go get her!" she shouted.

Eric whirled around and vanished into the woods, calling for Jordyn as he ran.

The shrieking of the webbing grew louder, and the air became even thicker. Swearing, Zach grabbed her hand. He knew there was only one way they were going to get there in time, and it wasn't running. He was going to have to bring her into his fire.

She looked over at him, as if she'd heard his thoughts, and nodded. "You won't kill me," she said. "Do it!"

He gritted his teeth against the sudden flash of fear that he might hurt her if he used his fire on her, but he shoved it aside, focusing instead on the absolute trust emanating from Rhiannon, her belief in him. He nodded, double-checked to make sure they were still merged, and then he called his fire.

The flames erupted through him, a seething mass of destruction. He kept his connection with Rhiannon secure as he twisted the flames tighter and tighter around them both, amping up the power level with each twist, until they were a coiled bomb, ready to explode.

He tightened his grip on her hand, and then he unleashed it. The fireball exploded with a deafening roar, thrusting them forward. He caught the flames beneath his feet, and rode the wall of fire, surfing through the jungle with Rhiannon by his side, both of them encased in the flaming sphere.

The heat was intense, even for him, and he focused hard on keeping a wall of protection around Rhiannon. Faster and faster they went, hurtling through the jungle. Her hair was on fire, locks of flames streaming behind her. Fear hammered at him. "You okay?" He shouted the question, but his words were swept away by the roar of the fire. Frustrated, he resorted to the only other method of communication that would work. *You okay? Just nod. You don't need to answer.*

She looked over at him, and smiled, and suddenly her voice filled his mind. *Every girl's dream is to surf fireballs, didn't you know? Life is good, Zach.*

Relief rushed through him, intense relief that shook him to his core. *You spoke to me.*

She smiled. *It feels right, doesn't it? I never spoke to José. It's really special.*

Yeah, it is.

She squeezed his hand. *We can do this, Zach. Together, we can save him.*

I know. He tightened his grip on her and the staff as they neared the camp, turning his focus onto the staff in his hand. Ahead of them, the sky was pitch black, and a funnel cloud was forming just above the spot where Thano and Trevor were. The tip was heading straight down into the clump of trees, and the screaming was so loud he felt like his eardrums were going to burst.

Zach directed the fireball straight into Thano's prison. The flames tore through the blackness, and dumped them out into the clearing. Apollo was pacing restlessly, stomping his feet and swishing his tail, gnashing his teeth at the black cloud descending toward them. Thano and Trevor were hanging by their wrists, encased entirely in the black webbing, except for their mouths. Both warriors were twisting and fighting, and he realized it was *their* horrific screams he'd been hearing. He could see Thano's red eyes glowing even through the webbing. He was fully rogue and inches from death. Rohan was standing beside them, a sword in each hand. Blue electricity was crackling all around him, lighting up the clearing. He spun around as Zach approached. "Now, Zachary, now!"

Zach landed just as the tip of the funnel cloud reached Thano's head. "No!" He lunged forward and jammed the staff into Thano's chest, thrusting all the fire he had into the staff. Thano screamed again, and his body convulsed as smoke rose from the end of the staff, as it burned into his flesh, right through the webbing. Thano's howl ripped through his soul, and he gasped, driving the brand even deeper into his flesh as the funnel cloud touched Thano's head—

Then the red glow of Thano's eyes disappeared.

"He's back," Rhiannon yelled. "Stop it!"

Rohan slashed through the webbing instantly, ripping Thano from the cocoon. Thano's limp body fell out of it, shriveled and pale as he collapsed across Apollo, who had dropped to his knees just in time to cushion his master.

"Trevor!" Rohan shouted. "Do Trevor!"

Zach wrenched the staff from Thano's body and jammed it into Trevor just as a second funnel cloud descended toward him. The warrior screamed and convulsed, his eyes glowing vicious red through the webbing. "Come on!" Zach called upon every last bit of flame remaining from his battle with José, and thrust it into the warrior.

His eyes still glowed red. "Rhiannon!"

She grabbed the staff, and vines shot along it and plunged into Trevor's chest with Zach's fire. The tremendous force of the impact tore the staff from their hands and flung them backwards. The staff shattered into a thousand fragments as Zach caught Rhiannon and cushioned their landing. But as they fell, there was a roar of triumph from Rohan and he sliced through Trevor's webbing.

The warrior fell out of the cocoon into Rohan's arms,

sagging against him, clearly unconscious.

Zach leapt to his feet and raced over to Thano, who was sprawled across his horse's back, his body limp. "Thano?" He crouched in front of him as Apollo turned his head, twisting around to nudge his nose against Thano's head.

Thano didn't move.

Rhiannon knelt beside him, and put her hand on Thano's shoulder. A white flower appeared beneath her palm, the same kind that she'd put in his chest after impaling him on the tree. It glowed bright white, and then sank into his body, disappearing from sight. She set another one on him, and then another, and still they kept disappearing.

"What are you doing?"

"The Junto flower has healing properties," she said. "I asked the blossom to share them with Thano, and it agreed he is worthy. There is much damage, which is why they keep disappearing." But even as she spoke, one finally remained on his shoulder, not sinking into his body. "That's all they can do. The rest is up to him."

Zach bent forward, putting his head beside Thano's. "Come on, Thano," he urged. "We need you in this world."

Again, no response, and he felt his throat tighten. "Fuck!" He bent his head, sudden grief overwhelming him. "I was too late."

"Are you gonna cry? I think you should cry." That familiar, cocky voice broke through his grief, and he jerked his head up.

Thano's green eyes were open, and he was grinning. Apollo whinnied, and Rhiannon let out a cheer.

"Thano!" Zach dragged him off the horse, but Thano's legs collapsed, dragging them both back to the ground. Zach had a split second of anguish as he realized that Thano was still paralyzed, despite that brief moment of movement, but then decided he didn't give a shit. Thano was alive and sane, not dead. That was what mattered. He immediately wrapped him up in a massive hug that was so not appropriate for manly, badass warriors. But he didn't give a shit.

And when he felt Thano grip him back, he knew that his friend had been through enough hell not to care either.

* * *

He was happy.

Six hours later, as Zach leaned against a stump with Rhiannon in his arms, watching the flames of the campfire for their last night in the jungle, he was happy for the first time since he'd lost his family. Not just happy. At peace. He rested his chin on Rhiannon's shoulder while she chatted with Thano, basking in the feel of her body nestled against him. *You saved me,* he said.

She squeezed his hand. *Mutual saving. I love you.*

I love you, too.

"Stop with the lovey dovey," Thano said. "Have some mercy on us single guys, you know?"

Zach raised his eyebrows. "You don't want to be single?"

Thano met his gaze, his cheeks still gaunt and pale. "Dude, when you've danced in hell long enough, it gives you some perspective." His focus settled on Rhiannon. "You got a good one, and I have to say, I like that she's not a *sheva*. It's good shit between you two. I can feel it." His gaze darted across the clearing to where Jordyn and Eric were in a hot debate about something. "Unlike those two, who are probably going to kill each other before they find his brother."

Zach grinned. "Yeah, she didn't seem all that impressed with his offer to put lotion on her back to soothe her burns."

"I like her. She's got spunk." Thano watched her. "Eric's kind of an ass who needs a woman who will shut him up. I think it's good. Maybe I'll offer to go with them. Might be fun. I heard them mention vampires, and I'm sort of curious to see what they turn up. I've heard some bad shit about those things. I'd like to see Jordyn go head-to-head with one of them. She'd win, you know."

Zach threw a rock at Thano's shoulder. "Dude, don't go getting hung up on a woman. Take a break from that. The last one sent you rogue, and we lost the staff, so stay solo for a while, will you?"

Thano looked over at him, and the amusement went out of his eyes. "I asked Rohan to put the *sheva* wards on me," he said. "I'm not going through that again. It's not worth the risk. It's fucking hell to lose your mind like that. Trust me."

Zach nodded. "It's too bad the staff is gone."

"Yeah, it would have made the Order's job a lot easier." Thano glanced again at Eric and Jordyn, and Zach sensed a restlessness in him.

He frowned, watching Thano more closely. "You're really thinking of going with them to Louisiana? What about the Order?"

Thano looked at him. "When I was rogue, I knew what I was doing. I knew what was happening. I felt like I was so close to being able to reclaim my mind, but I couldn't do it. I didn't want to die. I wanted to beat that curse. If I go back to the Order, every time I kill a rogue, I'm going to know what's going on in his mind. He's not a monster. He's me. How can I kill them, knowing that they're sane inside their heads? I don't want to do that shit anymore."

Zach went silent for a moment, then finally said, "They can't do it without you. You're the glue. You're the one who holds them together. Now that Dante's gone, there's no one else who can keep them balanced."

"I know." Thano looked away again. He reached down and grabbed his foot, shifting his leg to a new position. Clearly, his time in the cocoon hadn't gotten his legs working. One of the best warriors alive, and the only way he could walk was on the back of his horse. "I can't return to the Order and their mission. Not right now." *And you know exactly what I'm talking about because you're not going back either, are you?* He didn't look at Zach as he said it, but the words were clear.

And Thano was right. He did know exactly what Thano was feeling. He took a deep breath. *Rhiannon.*

Her love flooded him. *Yes.*

Have you changed your mind?

She turned in his arms to face him. Her eyes were dark with emotion, and full of love. "I can't, Zach. This is my jungle. I'm the only one left to protect it. I have to rebuild my tribe. It's what I was created to do. I can't go back to Oregon with you. I have to stay here."

He nodded. "I know." He ground his jaw, and saw Thano watching them. *I can't walk away from the Order, Thano.*

Thano shrugged. *Of course you can. The mission of the*

Order is to protect innocents from rogue Calydons. You just saved an entire jungle from rogues. You will still fulfill your mission. You'll just transfer to a more exotic locale.

Zach went still, sudden hope beating through him. *I hadn't thought of it that way.* He thought of Dante, and how they had once traveled far and wide in search of rogues. Settling in the Pacific Northwest had come later, when they realized that there was a very high concentration of rogues in that area. He looked across the clearing at Rohan, who was sitting beside Trevor, talking to him in low tones.

Rohan was the only one with his hood up. All the others were in jeans and tee shirts, regular warriors, not the hidden, mysterious commandos that Rohan led. They looked so normal, like the guys he had teamed up with for so many centuries.

He thought of his team. Could he really walk away from the teammates he'd been with for so long? He thought of Gideon and Quinn. Elijah. Ryland. Kane. Gabe. Ian. Even Drew, the young kid. He'd been a part of a team for so long, he didn't know how to be alone.

Except that the only time in his life that he'd been truly happy was when he'd walked away from Dante and the Order and set up shop with his wife. And he had that chance again?

He tightened his arms around Rhiannon, inhaling the delicate scent that was so her. What was the right choice?

Rohan suddenly stood up and walked over to them. Apollo shifted restlessly, moving his sleek, black body between the warrior and Thano. Zach stood up, pulling Rhiannon with him. "Rohan," he said.

"It is time."

Zach frowned "Time for what?"

"For you to fulfill your destiny."

Zach narrowed his eyes as he held Rhiannon's hand. "And what destiny would that be?"

"My apprentice. You will join us."

"Whoa." Zach held up his hand. "What are you talking about?"

Rohan cocked his head. "Did Dante never tell you?"

"No...what?"

"He pledged you as my apprentice. I thought you were

dead, but you're not, so it begins now. We leave in five minutes." He turned away and began to stride back across the clearing, message delivered.

Go with them? If he went with Rohan, he would not be returning to his Order, or staying with Rhiannon...and the moment he realized it, there was only one thing that mattered: Rhiannon. Leaving the Order didn't feel wrong. Leaving Rhiannon was untenable. He knew then what his future would hold. He knew what his choice would be. Elation swept through him, and he put his arm around Rhiannon's shoulders, pulling her up against him. "Sorry, but I can't help you."

Rohan looked back at him. "What?"

"I'm not going with you." Zach grinned at Rhiannon. "I'm staying here, with Rhiannon. We have a jungle to protect."

She made a small noise of surprise. "What?"

He turned to face her, and took her hands into his. "If you will have me, I will stay with you. Let's do this together. Marry me. I swear I will never try to control you or own you, but I want to go to bed every night with you in my arms. I want another chance to be a father again. You make me believe I'm worthy of a family again, and I want it with you. We're good together. Let's rebuild your tribe together."

She stared at him. "Our tribe has always been all women. They just have visits to nearby villages with choice males. We raised all the children, and then the males would leave the village when they became old enough, and the girls would stay. It's no men."

He raised his eyebrows at her. "And you think that's a good idea?"

For a moment, she stared at him, and then a slow smile spread over her face. "I have to admit, it took both of us to defeat José. And I do like you."

"Like me? That's it?"

Her smile widened, and she wrapped her arms around his neck, "Okay, I love you, and it totally melts my soul that you want to stay here with me. If you mean it, I would love it."

"I mean it." He bent his head and kissed her. *So, that's a yes, you'll marry me? I'm too old and conservative to live in sin with a woman. I need the ring. I need the forever.*

She giggled, and her joy surged through him. *Yes, I will marry you, as long as you never take those wards off. It is just love, Zach.*

He pulled back and framed her face with his hands. "No, it's not *just* love. It is love, more powerful and more beautiful than any *sheva* bond could ever be. Of course I'll keep the runes on my arms. I wouldn't want you any other way."

She grinned. "I love you—"

"Dante and I made a pact," Rohan interrupted.

"Oh, for heaven's sake," Jordyn shouted from across the clearing. "You need to lighten up, Rohan. That was such a sweet moment. Can't you get sentimental at least once every century?"

Rohan ignored her. "Dante and I made a blood pact," he said. "He offered me one of his team as an apprentice. It's time. I need you now."

"A blood pact?" Zach tensed, his arms going tighter around Rhiannon. Blood pacts held a power of their own. If Dante had really bound him by a blood pact, it was a big deal. "I'm not going—"

"I'll go." Thano spoke from his seated position. "I'll take his place."

Rohan and Zach looked down at Thano. The warrior was leaning back against his horse's front leg, his legs crossed casually at the ankles. Thano shrugged. "You guys don't hunt rogue Calydons, do you?"

Rohan shook his head. "No."

"Then I'm in. I need a vacation."

Ethan snorted from across the campsite. "Dude, this is no vacation. Don't offer yourself up for this."

Thano grinned at him. "It's all relative, Ethan. It'll be fun."

Rohan shook his head. "No."

James Wolfe grinned. "We could use some lightness, boss. Thano's more fun than you are. Let him come."

Maddox rubbed his goatee. "Besides, he's got a kickass horse. We'll look really cool with that horse on our side."

"See?" Thano grinned. "They all like me. I like you guys. It's a perfect match. We'll make s'mores, drink good beer, and chase whatever bad guys you like to hunt."

Rohan walked over to Thano and crouched in front of him. He held his hand out to Thano, who grasped it. Blue electricity leapt between them, and Rohan nodded. "Dante's power runs strong in you." He tilted his head. "You are more than you seem, aren't you?"

Thano grinned and raised one eyebrow. "You'll have to earn the right to that information, my friend."

Rohan rose to his feet, and turned to Zach. "I accept the substitution. I release you from your duty." He nodded at Thano. "We leave in three minutes."

As he strode back across the campsite, Zach crouched beside Thano. "What are you doing?"

His teammate's green gaze was steady. "I can't go back," he said. "I need something else. This is my path. These overly intense testosterone-junkies need me. What can I say?"

Zach ground his jaw as he sat beside him. "You're sure?"

"I'm not doing it for you. I have full faith you would have figured out how to get out of it without my intervention." Apollo bent his head and blew softly in Thano's ear. Thano grinned and rubbed his horse's nose. "I'm doing this for me. Tagging along to Louisiana with Eric and Jordyn doesn't sound like nearly as much fun as goading Rohan into taking that ridiculous hood off." He looked over at Zach, and his face was more serious than Zach had ever seen it. "Take care of this jungle and your woman, Z. You've got it good."

"I know." He hesitated. "What did Rohan mean when he said Dante's power runs strong in you?" Thano had become a part of the team only fifteen years ago, a complete neophyte at age twenty. Dante had never said where he'd found Thano, and neither warrior had ever 'fessed up. "And what did he mean that you're more than you seem?"

Thano grinned. "Melodrama from a seer who has to make stuff up to be impressive. Nothing more than bells and whistles, dude."

Zach studied him. "I don't think I believe you."

Thano winked. "Then you, my friend, are right." He snapped his fingers, and Apollo dropped to his knees beside him. Thano grabbed his mane and swung onto his horse's sleek back. Apollo surged to his feet, and Thano looked down at Zach.

"Thanks for saving me, my friend. I'll never forget it."

Zach grasped his hand in a firm handshake. "See you around, big guy."

"Yeah, you will, for sure." Thano gripped his hand fiercely. "Make lots of babies, have great sex, and save a few jungles." Apollo snorted, and Zach stepped back as Rohan's team congregated near the fire, preparing to dematerialize. "If you see the guys, tell them I'm in the middle of a mid-life crisis, and I stripped the Orders' assets to buy a Lamborghini, a couple South Pacific islands, and a harem of women to make love to me twenty-four hours a day. I'm sure they'll understand. Money, sex, and a great suntan are the basics of life, right?"

"Nothing else matters," Zach agreed with a grin as Thano saluted him and then rode off to join the rest of the group. As he watched Thano greet his new teammates, Rhiannon slipped up beside him, tucking herself under his arm. She wrapped her arms around his waist as the group shimmered briefly and then disappeared. The last thing he saw was Thano's big grin and his green eyes as he gave Zach a thumbs up.

"I think he's going to cause some serious trouble with them," Eric said from the other side of the campfire. "Rohan's pretty uptight, but the others are just looking for a reason to shake things up. Thano's going to be like a stick of dynamite in that crew."

Zach pressed his lips to Rhiannon's head, and then turned back toward Jordyn and Eric. "Thano likes to blow things up. It'll be perfect for him." He grinned at Rhiannon. "Kind of like how protecting a jungle and spawning an entire tribe with the woman I love is going to be perfect for me."

Jordyn sighed, clasping her hands over her heart. "You guys are too cute. I have to say, that I'm really impressed that my advice got you two through all your baggage the way it did. I'm really good, aren't I?"

Rhiannon laughed, a sound that made his own heart seem to dance. "You are one crazy woman, trekking down here to help me, but thanks. I haven't had a friend like you in a long time."

Jordyn smiled. "How about, after we find Eric's brother, I come back, and we go out for drinks. Girls' night out in the jungle?"

"Hey." Eric frowned. "What about the guys? What are Zach and I supposed to do while you guys are out? I think we should all go out together."

Jordyn raised her eyebrows. "You? What makes you think you'll be coming back here? Once we find Tristan, you're on your own."

Challenge flared in Eric's eyes. "Once we have sex—"

"Oh, enough already with the sex." Jordyn rolled her eyes. "Rhiannon, you are so lucky you found a good guy." A flicker of sadness tinged her eyes for a split second. "Love like that is really beautiful."

Zach's chest tightened as Rhiannon looked up at him, and smiled. "I know," she said. "It really is." And then she smiled. *I think it's time for us to be alone, Zach.* She let him feel her desire, and it went straight south, jerking his lower body to attention.

I think you're right. He scooped her up in his arms and nodded at Jordyn and Eric. "We gotta go. Good luck with Tristan." Then, with his woman giggling in his arms, he headed off into the jungle, to explore his new home with the woman he loved.

SNEAK PEEK: NOT QUITE DEAD

NightHunter
Available October 2014

With a sigh, Jordyn spun her chair toward the dining tables, propped her elbows on the counter of the bar, and leaned back against the battered wood. Slowly, she examined every person in the room, going through the same process she'd used at every other bar she'd visited in the last three hours to see if the man she was looking for was present.

Even as she did it, she was aware of the low odds of success. Did she really think she'd find Tristan this way? No, but he'd lived here for at least six months, and he had to have had an impact, right? Somewhere in this town, he'd left a clue before he'd disappeared. According to Eric, this was the last place he'd been seen.

Her gaze wandered over to the Gaston brothers, and then the door to the bar swung open, drawing her attention. The screen door slammed against the wall, and a dark shadow filled the doorway. The man who stepped inside was tall and broad-shouldered, with dark hair. His presence was so powerful that the energy in the room actually shifted, rippling as it tried to accommodate the sheer force of his being. She sucked in her breath and sat up, chills racing down her spine.

Eric.

He was there.

She stared at him, her fingers clenching the seat of her stool. He was so much bigger than she remembered. Taller, wider shoulders, a more dominating presence. He seemed to loom over the entire bar, an unstoppable force of power. He scanned the room slowly, starting with the Gaston brothers.

A part of her wanted to leap up, race over to him, and throw herself into his arms. She was riveted by the raw strength of his body, and she knew exactly how much power radiated from him. He'd been wild and untamed in the jungle, but here, it was as if he were part predator, a feral beast constrained by no one and nothing, stalking through civilization in search of the prey that he would conquer. She recalled his claim that he wasn't a man, and she suddenly believed him. Yes, a man, but there was something else as well. Something more visceral and dangerous. Something so graceful and lethal, physicality far beyond that of an ordinary man.

His hair was longer now, disheveled and ragged as it hung over his forehead. His eyes were blazing and dark, his jaw taut, his muscles flexed. The man standing in the doorway was nothing like the flirtatious, irreverent man she'd met a month ago. This man was moody, dark, and pulsing with an energy so intense that it slid down her spine and settled right in her lower belly. This man was a warrior, and he was pure, unfettered male.

Her heart started to hammer, thundering against her ribs, as she watched his gaze slide over the patrons, moving inexorably toward her. She knew then why she was still wearing her business suit. It hadn't been to prove herself to the town that had once been her home. It had been for Eric.

The only time she'd met him, they'd been deep in the Brazilian jungle, and she'd been wearing boots, jeans, and a ponytail. He'd overpowered her with the sheer force of his person, and she'd wanted to reinforce her shields this time by putting on her work persona, the one that was about the power and strength of a woman.

It wasn't working.

She felt sucked into the vortex of his power, every cell in her body tightening with each passing second as she waited for him to notice her. In the jungle, she'd been so worried about finding her friend that she'd had no emotional space to really let Eric affect her, but now it was different.

Now, she was so deeply aware of him that she couldn't stop thinking about how it had felt during that brief moment when he'd kissed her in the jungle. Fast. Passionate. Intense.

His gaze penetrated the darkest corner of the bar, his brown eyes alert and vibrant. He'd looked rugged and athletic before, but now, he looked rougher, like he'd been spawned by the earth itself. His jeans sat low on his hips, dripping wet, as if he'd been submerged in the bayou for hours. His boots were thick with mud, and there was dirt streaked across his face. His dark hair was damp and tangled, shoved ruthlessly aside so it was spiked and messy. Droplets slid in a wet sheen across his forehead, the sweat of a man who'd been working hard at something, even though it was the middle of the night. Whiskers were heavy on his jaw, and she had a sudden ridiculous urge to run her fingers over them.

So much for thinking that four weeks in Boston was going to make her immune to the effect he had on her. It had gotten worse, exponentially more intense, since they'd parted ways.

She wasn't ready for this.

She wasn't ready for him.

She wasn't ready for any of it.

Jordyn swallowed, her heart almost leaping out of her chest as he turned his head toward her. His eyes met hers, and she knew instantly that, unlike the town that had known her for the first sixteen years of her life, he didn't have any trouble recognizing her. The flash of awareness was instant, and she felt like her skin was on fire. She swallowed, her mouth suddenly dry, and her fingers tightened around her stool, as if she could keep herself from tumbling off it and into his arms.

Instantly, he shoved away from the doorway and headed straight toward her. His jaw was tense, and his stride was long and purposeful, rippling with languid strength. His gaze was fixed on hers so intently that she wanted to look away...except she couldn't take her eyes off him.

She tensed as he neared, sitting up straighter and trying to get a cool expression on her face. "Where have you been—?"

He gave her no time to finish her sentence. He just swung his arm behind her lower back, hauled her up against him, and kissed her.

Sneak Peek: DARKNESS SURRENDERED

The Order of the Blade
Available Now

Ana felt Elijah tense beneath her. He was awake.

His body hadn't so much as twitched, his breathing hadn't changed, and his heart rate hadn't sped up. But there was a vibrating tension about him, a readiness.... A warrior in battle, not giving away anything.

She lifted her head to look at him, trying to move slowly so as not to trigger him into another manic episode. His scarred brown eyes were glazed, unseeing, but they were focused on her face, as if he could see her through some deeper force than his vision.

Her heart started to race and she hesitated, not sure what to do. Was he about to freak out again? Or was he sane? "Um..." She licked her lips nervously. "I'm Ana Matthews... but I guess you already know that."

Elijah blinked several times, the movement awkward and jerky, as if his eyelids were rasping painfully over his damaged eyes. Her heart ached at the sight of all those raw scars on his face, as if he'd tried to claw out his own eyes rather than see the hell he'd been facing. Was she responsible for that? Had it been her illusions that he'd tried to defend against by blinding himself?

Tears filled her eyes, tears of guilt, regret and empathy, and she instinctively laid her hand on his cheek. "Oh, Elijah," she whispered, forgetting to fear him, ignoring all Gideon's warnings about how Elijah might be so violent and insane when he finally awoke from his coma. "I'm so sorry."

He blinked again, wincing at the agonizing movement as he tried to see her.

"No, no," she whispered. "Don't torment yourself. Here." She clasped his wrist and placed his palm against her cheek. "See me this way."

He closed his eyes and let his hand drift across her face.

He moved his fingers over her skin, over her cheekbone, her eyelashes, the bridge of her nose, his callused fingers so light against her skin.

Elijah touched her mouth, tracing the outline of her lips. Heat began to swirl inside Ana as he gave a small nod. "Good." The word came out as a grinding noise, and her heart tightened at the grimace of pain on his face.

But God, to hear his voice again, his real voice, not the whisper in her mind. It burned right to her soul, like the forbidden heat of a sensual danger designed to strip her defenses and possess her completely. She swallowed, suddenly nervous, no longer feeling like a woman trying to protect a man. Instead, she felt like a female being drawn ruthlessly into the spell of the male destined to consume her. "Elijah—"

His arm snaked around her, trapping her he pulled her down against him. He buried his face in the curve of her neck with a deep groan of contentment that made desire pulse through her relentlessly.

Ana froze as he inhaled deeply, and she knew he was examining her scent, memorizing every detail about her body. "It's me," she whispered. "You know me."

He blew out, his lips feathering her neck with heat.

Her skin felt like it was on fire. She became aware of his scent, the raw, fierce pulse of danger and death, mixed with something softer. Vulnerability. Fear. Desperation. Dear God, his suffering was so intense, filling her with the agony of his despair, of his confusion. Had she done that to him? Was all of that her fault? How much worse would she make it if she stayed with him, if he realized who she was? "This really isn't a good idea." She set her hands on his shoulders and gently tried to push him away. "It's the *sheva* bond making you want me. You actually hate—" She stumbled over the words, regret thick and bitter. "You hate me, Elijah. As soon as your mind settles again, you'll remember."

His hands snapped to her hips, trapping her against him. "Mine," he growled. His eyes were still closed, unable to defeat the pain of the scar tissue, but his hands were burning over her, as if he were stripping her clothes off and branding her with every touch.

"Oh, God," she whispered. "Don't pull me into this. I don't have many defenses left." Her heart had bled for this man so many times, and now he held her like she was his salvation, his anchor, the only thing he had to hold onto.

She'd already seen the way he looked at her, with pure revulsion for who she was and what she'd done to him. She knew it would come again the moment he regained his senses. She couldn't let herself fall into his touch, into his need, and then survive it when he took it away from her. He wouldn't survive it either, being sucked into her nightmare. "We can't lie to each other," she whispered as she grabbed his wrist, trying to stop him. "This isn't real. Please, don't do this to me. To us."

"Real," he whispered, sliding his hands beneath her shirt, flattening one palm over her belly. "You're not real?" His voice cracked, and he gripped her sides with sudden intensity. "You have to be real—"

"I am, I am," she soothed quickly. "You're not having illusions. I'm right here." She knew he'd been tormented by illusions. He'd been thrust mercilessly into the world of uncertainty, unable to know what nightmares were real, and which were fake. Men had died from the insanity the illusions caused, from the inability to know truth from delusion, and she knew Elijah's greatest tool right now was reality. She couldn't take that away from him. "I'm not your imagination," she said.

Elijah opened his eyes again, straining to see her, but there was no recognition in those scarred eyes. "I can't see you," he croaked. "You're not real—"

"I am!" Ana grabbed his hands and squeezed. "Feel my touch," she ordered. "Hear my voice. I'm here, dammit! You're not being messed with anymore!"

"You're real?" His voice softened with awe and disbelief. "This is you?" He ran his hands over her stomach, her ribs, and desire leapt through her.

Ana leaned her head back and closed her eyes, her body trembling at the sensation of his hands on her body. God, how long had it been since a man's hands had touched her with kindness? Not just kindness. Reverence. Adoration. Callused hands that would never hurt her, no matter what she did. Hands that would wrap around her at night and keep her safe.

Strong, masculine hands that would seduce her until she was his, forever...

Oh, God. What was she thinking? She couldn't do this, not to him, not to herself. Her only job was to help him regain his sanity, to bring him back so he could fulfill the mission he was meant to do. She had to stop him from weaving this web around them, from drawing them both into the dangerous attraction between them, the one that was only about their *sheva* bond, not reality, not the truth about how much damage there was between them.

"Elijah! We don't have time for this. Your team needs you upstairs. You have to save the damn world." She winced at how she sounded a little too breathless and sensual. Desperate and panicked, yes, but also... intimate. She cleared her throat and leaned back, away from his face still nuzzling her throat. "If you were in your right mind, you'd never touch me like this. You despise me and I—"

"No," he growled. His hands slid up her back beneath her shirt, and he pressed against her bare shoulder blades, pulling her toward him. Toward his mouth.

Anticipation hummed through Ana even as she stiffened, fighting the urges racing through her. God, how she wanted to lose herself in him. "Dammit, Elijah. Stop!"

Her body was trembling with desire, with nervousness, and the need to leap off his lap and bolt. But she knew he'd snap if she broke physical contact with him, and she didn't know if she'd be able to bring him back from his delusions and insanity again. She owed him, and she knew that her soul was already too black to survive causing Elijah's death for a second time. "Elijah—" Her palms went to his bare chest to try to block him from pulling her any closer, and the heated spark was almost instant.

They both froze, and she could feel his heart pounding beneath her palms.

Mine. His possessive growl echoed in her mind, sending spirals of fire and heat racing through her.

Yours. The word popped into Ana's mind before she could stop it.

The moment the word formed in her head, Elijah jerked

upright and yanked her against him. His hand roughly palmed the back of her head to bring her down at the right angle, not giving her a chance to resist or to stop him. He sank his mouth onto hers, and her lips parted instantly for him... and then she felt the beast consume him. His need pulsed at her, shredding all her resistance in a heartbeat.

She barely stifled a scream as Elijah shifted and rolled her beneath him, covering her with his body. His kisses were frantic, his mouth almost violent in its assault on her. His hands were all over her, her stomach, her breasts, his fingers bruising and desperate. She could feel his desperation for her, and she knew he might hurt her.

And she didn't care.

Hot desire rose hard and fast inside her, and she threw her arms around his neck, holding him tightly as her own need met his. God, she'd needed this for so long. Not just any touch. His touch. She knew it in every fiber of her being that he had been inside her soul since they'd met. We will destroy each other. The thought was like a cold hit to her gut and she tried to break the kiss. "I can't—"

He tugged her shirt up and caught her breast in his mouth, a decadent, raging kiss of desperate desire that eviscerated her resistance to him. His fervent passion for her was tearing at her soul with every kiss.

Darkness slithered along the edges of her mind, a danger so vivid and poisonous that her soul recoiled and she tried to pull back. Elijah growled and deepened his kiss, and she realized that the hell she'd sensed was in Elijah's mind, a demonic darkness trying to overtake his sanity. She knew Elijah was trying to outrun it by sinking himself into her body and her mind, seeking solace in their touch, in the kisses.

She was the oasis, the sanity, the beauty that could bring him back from his insanity, from the demons in his mind. A sense of absolute rightness filled Ana with heat and warmth at the realization that she could help him. The hell she would face later didn't matter anymore. Elijah needed her, and as his soul mate, she could help him. I'm here for you.

His energy reached for her through the nightmare that beat at him. His soul wrapped itself around her as he fought for his sanity and control. His relentless need for her consumed both his mind and hers...

Yes, Elijah. Take me. Whatever you need from me, it's yours. She wrapped her arms around his neck, gasping as he kissed her breasts. A growl ripped from this throat, an untamed sound of possession and domination as he lowered his hips between her thighs. His hips began to pump, his erection slamming into her through her jeans.

Desire raged through her, sweeping her up and away from all the anguish she'd been carrying for so long. In his arms, there was nothing left of the woman who'd hurt so many people. Gone was the debilitating guilt and grim awareness of the monster she was. The aching loneliness, the constant fear, the incessant terrors...all gone, cradled in the strong palms of this courageous warrior. Instead, there was simply beauty and passion, a sense of being loved and desired, of being treasured. Yes, she whispered, her heart too full of emotion to dare stop him. She wanted more of this moment, even though she knew she didn't deserve it, even though she knew it would all be torn apart the moment he recovered enough to remember who she was.

His body was rigid under her touch, and she felt every cut, every wound under her hands. There was nowhere to hold him without hurting him more. He shouted and thrust harder, and suddenly she couldn't think anymore, his need for her calling out an answering yearning in her. His body was so hot, his skin serrated and broken, his muscles rock hard beneath her touch, sliding under his skin.

Ana arched her back, her body reaching for him, for his touch, for the heat in his hands and the fire in his kisses until it wasn't just about his desperation, but hers as well. His hand went to her jeans and he fumbled with them, trying to get them undone as his thrusts grew more frantic, more forceful, his erection slamming through the denim into her most sensitive spot.

Utter rightness swelled inside her, consuming her, until the fire began to lick down her limbs, igniting every inch of her until the sensations exploded, overwhelming her soul and her body. She screamed Elijah's name and his deep roar mixed with hers, his body convulsing against her as he drove again and again, his hands braced on the floor by her head, his attempt to get her pants off lost in the blazing inferno consuming them both. He went rigid above her, and then he collapsed, his body sinking onto hers, his chest flush against the bare skin of her breasts, his hips stilled between hers, his breathing raw and harsh on her neck.

She locked her arms around his shredded back and entwined her feet along his thighs, holding him as tightly as she could as the final tremors faded.

Elijah shuddered against her and then his body finally went quiet.

Neither of them moved or spoke, though she was certain he was awake. They just lay together, intertwined, on the steel floor, recovering.

After a moment, she rested her elbow on his shoulder and pressed her hand to her eyes. Dear God. What had she done?

Elijah shifted suddenly. He rose swiftly to his hands and knees, his body going rigid. He straddled her, his palms braced on either side of her head, his legs outside hers. It was the position of a male defending his woman with his body. He stopped breathing, going utterly still, a predator waiting for the enemy to attack.

Ana froze, her heart pounding. What had he seen? Had his mind snapped? *Elijah? What's wrong?*

They're coming. His head was up and he was staring blindly past her with the intensity of an assassin who had targeted his mark.

Who? Demons? Some figment of his ravaged mind? Ana carefully twisted her head to look where he was looking. Relief rushed through her when she saw Quinn and Gideon standing inside the door. Elijah wasn't imagining things. He was all right! "I'm fine," she quickly told them, her cheeks heating with embarrassment at being caught in such an intimate position. Her pants were still on, but it was obvious what they'd been doing.

Neither warrior moved, and Elijah lowered himself slightly, his chest resting protectively against hers. She noticed then that Gideon and Quinn had their weapons out, and they were pointing them at Elijah. Oh, crap! No wonder Elijah was on the defensive. "Put your weapons away," she said quickly. "He's—"

Elijah's hand went to her mouth, silencing her.

Gideon swore and didn't sheathe his weapon. "We're going to grab you and pull you out from under him."

Oh, Dear God, that would make Elijah snap if they went after her! "No! Don't touch me! Don't take me away from him!"

Elijah tensed at her sharp tone, and he immediately shifted his weight to free his right arm. "No, Elijah." She fought to keep her voice calm. "They're your friends—"

He called out his throwing star with a crack that reverberated against the steel wall, and she knew they were a split second away from a full battle, a battle which she knew would end only in death.

SNEAK PEEK: GHOST

ALASKA HEAT
AVAILABLE NOW

"What are you running from?"

Ben Forsett froze at the unexpected question, his hand clenching around the amber beer bottle. For a long second, he didn't move. Instead, his gaze shot stealthily to the three exits he'd already located before he'd even walked into this local pub known as O'Dell's in Where-the-Hell-Are-We, Alaska. He rapidly calculated which exit had the clearest path. A couple of bush pilots were by the kitchen door. They were large, rough men who would shove themselves directly into the path of someone they thought should be stopped. His access to the front door was obstructed by two jean-clad young women walking into the foyer, shaking snowflakes out of their perfectly coiffed hair. The emergency exit was alarmed, but no one was in front of it. That was his best choice—

"Chill, kid," the man continued. "I'm not hunting you. I've been where you are. So have most of the men in this place."

Slowly, Ben pulled his gaze off his escape route and looked at the grizzled Alaskan old-timer sitting next to him. Lines of outdoor hardship creased his face, and wisps of straggly white hair hung below his faded, black baseball hat. His skin hung loose, too tired to hold on anymore, but in the old man's pale blue eyes burned a sharp, gritty intelligence born of a tough life. His shoulders were encased in a heavy, dark green jacket that was so bulky it almost hid the hunch to his back and the thinness of his shoulders.

The man nodded once. "Name's Haas. Haas Carter." He extended a gnarled hand toward Ben.

Ben didn't respond, but Haas didn't retract his hand.

For a long moment, neither man moved, then, finally, Ben peeled his fingers off his beer and shook Haas's hand. "John Sullivan," he said, the fake name sliding off his tongue far more easily than it had three months ago, the first time he'd used it.

"John Sullivan?" Haas laughed softly. "You picked the most common name you could think of, eh? Lots of John Sullivans in just about every town you've been to, I should imagine. It'd be hard for people to keep track of one more."

Ben stiffened. "My father was John Sullivan, Sr.," he lied. "I honor the name."

Haas's bushy gray brows went up. "Do you now?"

The truth was, Ben's father was a lying bastard who had left when he was two years old. Or he'd been shot. Or he'd been put in prison. No one knew what had happened to him, and no one really cared, including Ben. "I'm not here to make friends," Ben said quietly.

"No, I can see that." Haas regarded him for a moment, his silver-blue eyes surveying Ben's heavy whiskers and the shaggy hair that had once been perfectly groomed. Ben shook his head so his hair hung down over his forehead, shielding his eyes as he watched the older man, waiting for a sign that this situation was going south.

He would be pissed if Haas turned on him. He needed to be here. He was so sure this was finally the break he'd been waiting for. He let his gaze slither off Haas to the back wall of the bar where an enormous stuffed moose head was displayed. Its rack had to be at least six feet wide, its glazed dead eyes a bitter reminder of what happened to life when you stopped paying attention for a split second.

Beside the moose rack was the battered wooden clock he'd been watching all evening. Adrenaline raced through Ben as he watched the minute hand clunk to the twelve. *It was seven o'clock.*

"What happens at seven?"

Ben jerked his gaze back to Haas, startled to realize the older man had been watching him closely enough to notice his focus on the clock. "I turn into a fairy princess."

Haas guffawed and slammed his hand down on Ben's shoulder. "You're all right, John Sullivan. Mind if I call you Sully? Most Sullivans go by Sully. It'll make it seem more like it's your real name."

Ben's fingers tightened around the frosty bottle at Haas's persistence. "It is my real name."

Haas dropped the smile and leaned forward, lowering his voice as his gaze locked onto Ben's. "I'll tell you this, young man, I've seen a lot of shit in my life. I've seen men who look like princes, but turn out to be scum you wouldn't even want to waste a bullet on. I've seen pieces of shit who would actually give their life for you. You look like shit, but whatever the hell you're running from, you got my vote. Don't let the bastards catch you until you can serve it up right in their damn faces. Got it?"

Ben stared at Haas, too stunned by the words to respond. No one believed in him, no one except for the man who had helped him escape. He'd known Mack Connor since he was a kid, and Mack understood what loyalty meant. But even Mack knew damn well who Ben really was and what he was truly capable of. Mack's allegiance was unwavering, but he did it with his eyes open and ready to react if Ben went over the line.

He had a sudden urge to tell Haas exactly what shit was going down for him, and see if the old man still wanted to stand by him.

But he wasn't that stupid. He couldn't afford for anyone to know why he was here. "I don't know what you're talking about," he finally said.

Haas raised his beer in a toast. "Yeah, me neither, Sully. Me neither." As Haas took a drink, another weather-beaten Alaskan sat down on Haas's other side. This guy's face was so creased it looked like his razor would get lost if he tried to shave, and the size of his beard said the guy hadn't been willing to take the risk. Haas nodded at him. "Donnie, this here boy is Sully. New in town. Needs a job. His wife left him six months ago, and the poor bastard lost everything. He's been wandering aimless for too damn long."

Ben almost choked on his beer at Haas's story, but Donnie just nodded. "Women can sure break a man." He leveled his dark brown gaze at Ben. "She ain't worth it, young man. There are lots of doe around for a guy to pick up with."

Ben managed a nod. "Yeah, well, I'm not ready yet."

"We gotta get him back on the horse," Haas said. "Got any ideas?" With a wink at Ben, he and Donnie launched into a discussion about the assorted available women in town and which ones might be worthy of Ben.

As the two old-timers talked, Ben felt some of the tension ease from his shoulders. In this small town in the middle of Alaska, he had an ally, at least until Haas found out the truth. Shit, it felt good to have someone at his back. It had been too damn long—

The door to the kitchen swung open, and a cheerful female voice echoed through the swinging door. Her voice was like a soft caress of something...damn. He realized he didn't even know what to compare it to. His mind was too tired to conjure up words that would do justice to the sudden heat sliding over his skin. But a seductive, tempting warmth washed over him, through him, like someone had just slipped hot whisky into his veins, burning and cleansing as it went.

Ben went rigid, adrenaline flooding his body. It was seven o'clock. Based on what he'd pieced together about her schedule and her life, she would be coming on duty now, walking out of the kitchen *now*. Was it her? *Was it her?* Her hand was on the kitchen door, holding it open as she finished her muffled conversation. She was wearing a black leather cord with a silver disk around her wrist. On her index finger was a silver ring with a rough-cut turquoise stone and a wide band with carvings on it. Her fingernails were bare and natural, a woman who didn't bother with enamel and lacquer to go to work. Her arm was exposed, the smooth expanse of flesh sliding up to a capped black sleeve that just covered the curve of her shoulder. She wasn't tall, maybe a little over five feet.

Son of a bitch. It might actually be her. *Come into the bar,* he urged silently. *Let me see your face.* He'd never heard her talk before. He'd never seen her in person. All he had was that one newspaper picture of her, and the headshot he'd snagged from her family's store website before it had been taken down. But her trail had led to O'Dell's, and he was hoping he was right. He had to be right.

The door opened wider, and Ben ducked his head, letting his hair shield his eyes again, but he didn't take his gaze off her, watching intently as the woman moved into the restaurant. Her back was toward him as she continued her conversation, and he could see her hair. Thick, luscious waves of dark brown.

Brown. *Brown.* The woman he'd been searching for was

blond.

The disappointment and frustration that knifed through his gut was like the sharp stab of death itself. He bowed his head, resting his forehead in his palms as the image flooded his mind again, the same memory that had haunted him for so long. His sister, her clothes stained with that vibrant red of fresh blood, sprawled across her living room, her hand stretching toward Ben in the final entreaty of death. Son of a bitch. He couldn't let Holly down. He couldn't let her down again.

"Are you okay?"

He went still at the question, at the sound of the woman's voice so close. She still had the same effect on him, a flood of heat that seemed to touch every part of his body. He schooled his features into the same uninviting expression he'd perfected, and he looked up to find himself staring into the face he'd been hunting for the last three months.

He'd never mistake those eyes. The dark rich brown framed by eyelashes so thick he'd thought they had to be fake, until now. Until he could see her for real. Until he could feel the weight of her sorrow so thickly that it seemed to wrap around him and steal the oxygen from his lungs. Until he looked into that face, that face that had once been so innocent, and now carried burdens too heavy for her small frame.

Until he'd found her.

Because he had.

It was her. Yeah, maybe she'd ditched the blond and let herself go back to her natural color, which looked good as hell on her, but there was no doubt in his mind.

He'd found her.

Son of a bitch.

He'd found her.

SNEAK PEEK: DARKNESS UNLEASHED

THE ORDER OF THE BLADE
AVAILABLE NOW

Ryland spun around, engaging all his preternatural senses as he searched the graveyard for Catherine. He knew she had to be close. He'd touched her backpack just before she'd vanished right in front of him.

"Catherine!" he shouted again. He'd been so close. Where the hell was she? All he could sense were the deaths of all the people in the graveyard. Women, children, old men, young men, good people, scum who had taken their demented values to the grave with them. The spirits were thick and heavy in the graveyard, souls that had not moved on to their place of rest.

They circled him, trying to penetrate his barriers, seeking asylum in the creature that would be their doom. "No," he said to them. "I'm not your savior." Not by a long shot. He was about as far from their savior as it was possible to be.

Dismissing them, Ryland focused more directly on Catherine, opening his senses to the night, but as much as he tried to concentrate, he couldn't keep the vision of her out of his head. He'd finally seen her up close. She'd been mere inches away, the angel who had filled his thoughts for so long. Her hair was gold. *Gold.* It must have been tucked up under a hat when he'd seen her before, but now? It was unlike anything he'd ever seen before. He'd been riveted by the sight of it streaming behind her as she ran, the golden highlights glistening in the dark as if she'd been lit from within.

Her gait had been smooth and agile, but he'd sensed the sheer effort she'd had to expend during the run. Another few feet, and he would have caught up to her easily, but she'd sensed him while he'd still been a quarter mile away, giving her a head start that had gotten her to the graveyard first.

Shit. He had to focus and find her. Summoning his rigid control to focus on his task, Ryland crouched down and placed his hand on the dirt path where he'd last seen her. The ground was humming with the energy of death, but again, he couldn't untangle her trail from all the others. He realized that she'd mingled her own scent of death with those of all the other spirits, making it impossible for him to track her. He grinned as he rested his forearm on his quad and surveyed the small cemetery. "I'm impressed," he said aloud. "You're good."

There was no response, but he had the distinct sensation that she was watching him.

Slowly, he rose to his feet. "My name is Ryland Samuels," he said. "I'm a member of the Order of the Blade, the group of warriors that you protect. I'm here to offer you my protection and bring you into our safekeeping."

Again, there was no answer, but suddenly threaded through the tendrils of death was the cold filament of fear. Not just a superficial apprehension, but the kind of deep, penetrating fear that would bring a person to their knees and render them powerless. Fear of him? Or of the fact he said he wanted to take her with him? Swearing, Ryland turned in a slow circle, searching for where she might be. "There's no need to be afraid of me. I would never hurt an angel."

The fear thickened, like the thorns of a dying rose pricking his skin.

Ryland moved slowly toward the far corner, and smiled when he felt the terror grow stronger. She might be able to hide death, but there was no cover for the terror that was hers alone. He was clearly getting closer to her. "Look into my eyes," he said softly. "I don't hurt angels."

There was a whisper of a sound behind him, and he felt the cold drift of fingers across his back. She was touching him. He froze, not daring to turn around, even though his heartbeat had suddenly accelerated a thousand-fold. Her touch was so faint, almost as if it were her spirit that was examining him, not her own flesh. Was she merely invisible right now, or had she abandoned her physical existence completely and traveled to some spiritual plane? He had no idea what she was capable of. All he knew was that he felt like he never wanted to move away from this spot, not as long as she was touching him. He wanted to stay right where he was and never break the connection.

He closed his eyes, breathing in the sensation of her

touch as her fingers traced down his arm, over his jacket. What was she looking for? Was she reading his aura? Searching for the truth of his claim that he would not hurt her? She would get nowhere trying to get a read on him. He never allowed anyone to see who he truly was, not even an angel of death.

But even as he thought it, he made no move to resist, his pulse quickening in anticipation as her touch trailed toward his bare hand. Would she brush her fingers over his skin? Would he feel the touch of an angel for the first time in a thousand years? He felt his soul begin to strain, reaching for this gift only she could give him.

He tracked every inch of movement as her hand moved lower toward his bare skin. Past his elbow. To the cuff of his sleeve. Then he felt it. Her fingers on the back of his hand. His flesh seemed to ignite under her touch. A wave of angelic serenity and beauty cascaded through his soul, like a breath of great relief easing a thousand years of tension from his lungs.

At the same time, there was a dangerous undercurrent beneath the beauty, a darkness that he recognized as death. A thousand souls seemed to dance through his mind, spirits lodged in the depths of her existence. Her emotions flooded him. Fear. Regret. Determination. Love. A sense of being trapped.

Trapped? He understood that one well. Far too well. Instinctively, he flipped his hand over, wrapping his fingers around hers, not to trap her, but to offer her his protection from a hell that still drove every choice he made.

He heard her suck in her breath, and she went still, not pulling away from him. Her hand was cold. Her fingers were small and delicate, like fragile blossoms that would snap under a stiff breeze. A hand that needed support and help.

Ryland snapped his eyes open but there was no one standing in front of him. He looked down and could see only his own hand, folded around air. He couldn't see her, but she was there, her hand in his, not pulling away. "Show yourself to me," he said. "I won't hurt you."

Her hand jerked back, and a sense of loss assailed him as he lost his grip on her. "No!" He reached for her, but his hands just drifted through air. "Catherine," he urged, as he strained to get a sense of her. "I—"

SELECT LIST OF OTHER BOOKS BY STEPHANIE ROWE

(FOR A COMPLETE BOOK LIST, PLEASE VISIT WWW.STEPHANIEROWE.COM)

PARANORMAL ROMANCE

THE NIGHTHUNTER SERIES

Not Quite Dead
Available October, 2014

THE ORDER OF THE BLADE SERIES

Darkness Awakened
Darkness Seduced
Darkness Surrendered
Forever in Darkness (Novella)
Darkness Reborn
Darkness Arisen
Darkness Unleashed
Inferno of Darkness (Novella)
Darkness Possessed
Hunt the Darkness
Release Date TBD

THE SOULFIRE SERIES

Kiss at Your Own Risk
Touch if You Dare
Hold Me if You Can

THE IMMORTALLY SEXY SERIES

Date Me Baby, One More Time
Must Love Dragons
He Loves Me, He Loves Me Hot
Sex & the Immortal Bad Boy

ROMANTIC SUSPENSE

THE ALASKA HEAT SERIES

Ice
Chill
Ghost

CONTEMPORARY ROMANCE

EVER AFTER SERIES

No Knight Needed
Fairytale Not Required
Prince Charming Can Wait

STAND ALONE NOVELS

Jingle This!

NONFICTION

The Feel Good Life

FOR TEENS

A GIRLFRIEND'S GUIDE TO BOYS SERIES

Putting Boys on the Ledge
Studying Boys
Who Needs Boys?
Smart Boys & Fast Girls

STAND ALONE NOVELS

The Fake Boyfriend Experiment

FOR PRE-TEENS

THE FORGOTTEN SERIES

Penelope Moonswoggle, The Girl Who Could Not Ride a Dragon
(Book One)
Penelope Moonswoggle & the Accidental Doppelganger (Book Two)
Release Date TBD

STEPHANIE ROWE BIO

Four-time RITA® Award nominee and Golden Heart® Award winner Stephanie Rowe is a nationally bestselling author, and has more than twenty-five contracted titles with major New York publishers such as Grand Central, HarperCollins, Dorchester and Harlequin, and more than fifteen indie books. She believes in writing stories where characters survive against all odds, fighting their way through to personal triumph, while discovering true love and sensual, hot passion along the way.

Stephanie is an award-winning and bestselling author of adult paranormal romance, and has charmed reviewers, receiving coveted starred reviews from Booklist for several of her paranormal romances. Publishers Weekly has also praised her work, calling her work "[a] genre-twister that will make readers...rabid for more."

In addition to her vibrant paranormal romance career, Stephanie also writes a thrilling romantic suspense series set in Alaska. Publisher's Weekly praised the series debut, ICE, as a "thrilling entry into romantic suspense," and Fresh Fiction called ICE an "edgy, sexy and gripping thriller." Equally as intense and sexy are Stephanie's contemporary romance novels, set in the fictional town of Birch Crossing, Maine

Stephanie is a full-time author who has been an avid reader since she was a kid (she even won the blue ribbon at her town library for reading the most books over the summer). She wrote her first book when she was ten, but abandoned that fledgling career when people started asking to read it. Fortunately, she now delights in people reading her work, and loves to hear from readers. With more than fifty completed novels to her name, Stephanie is well on her way to fulfilling the dream that started so long ago. Some of her favorite authors are Lisa Kleypas, Dick Francis, and Julie Garwood, but the list goes on and on

In her spare time, Stephanie loves to play tennis, take her rescue dog for walks in the woods, and to make up stories about the people she sees on the street with her daughter. Yes, the author's imagination is always at work.

Want to learn more? Visit Stephanie online at one of the following hot spots

WWW.STEPHANIEROWE.COM
HTTP://TWITTER.COM/STEPHANIEROWE2
HTTP://WWW.PINTEREST.COM/STEPHANIEROWE2/
HTTPS://WWW.FACEBOOK.COM/STEPHANIEROWEAUTHOR